P9-AFM-183

ANYA'S GHOST

VERA BROSGOL

First Second

NEW YORK & LONDON

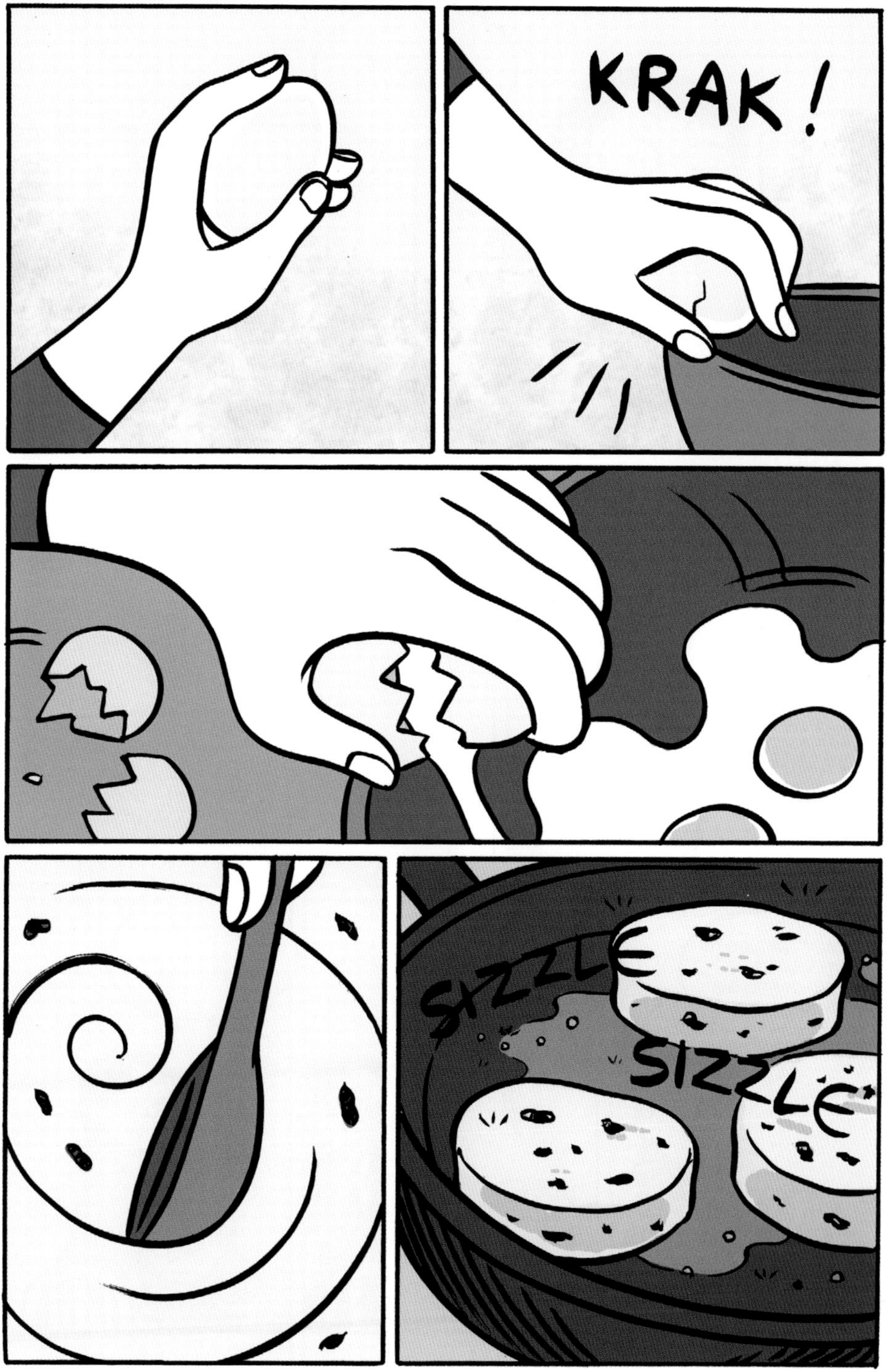
KRAK!
SIZZLE
SIZZLE

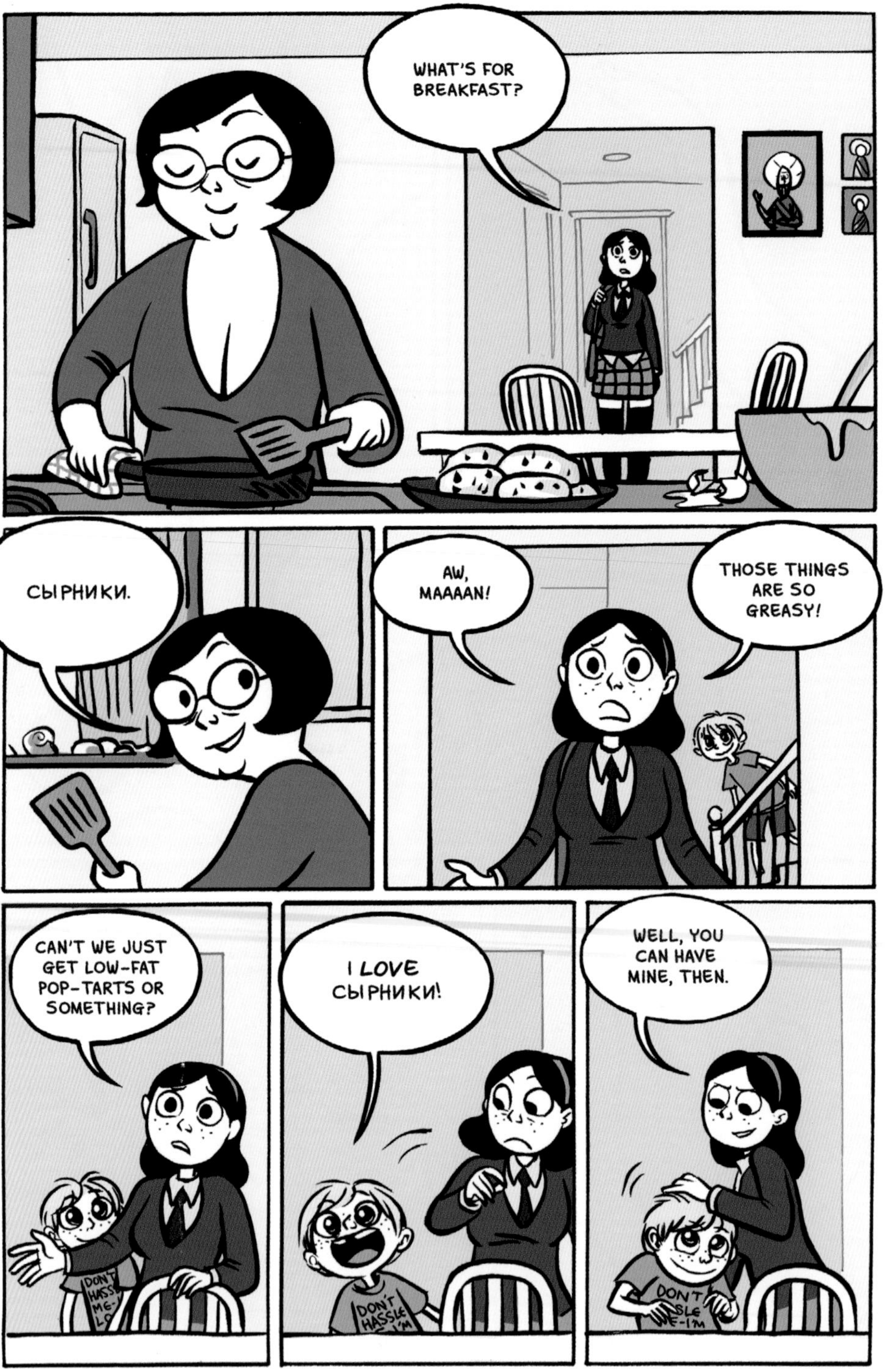
WHAT'S FOR BREAKFAST?
СЫРНИКИ.
AW, MAAAAN!
THOSE THINGS ARE SO GREASY!
CAN'T WE JUST GET LOW-FAT POP-TARTS OR SOMETHING?
I *LOVE* СЫРНИКИ!
WELL, YOU CAN HAVE MINE, THEN.

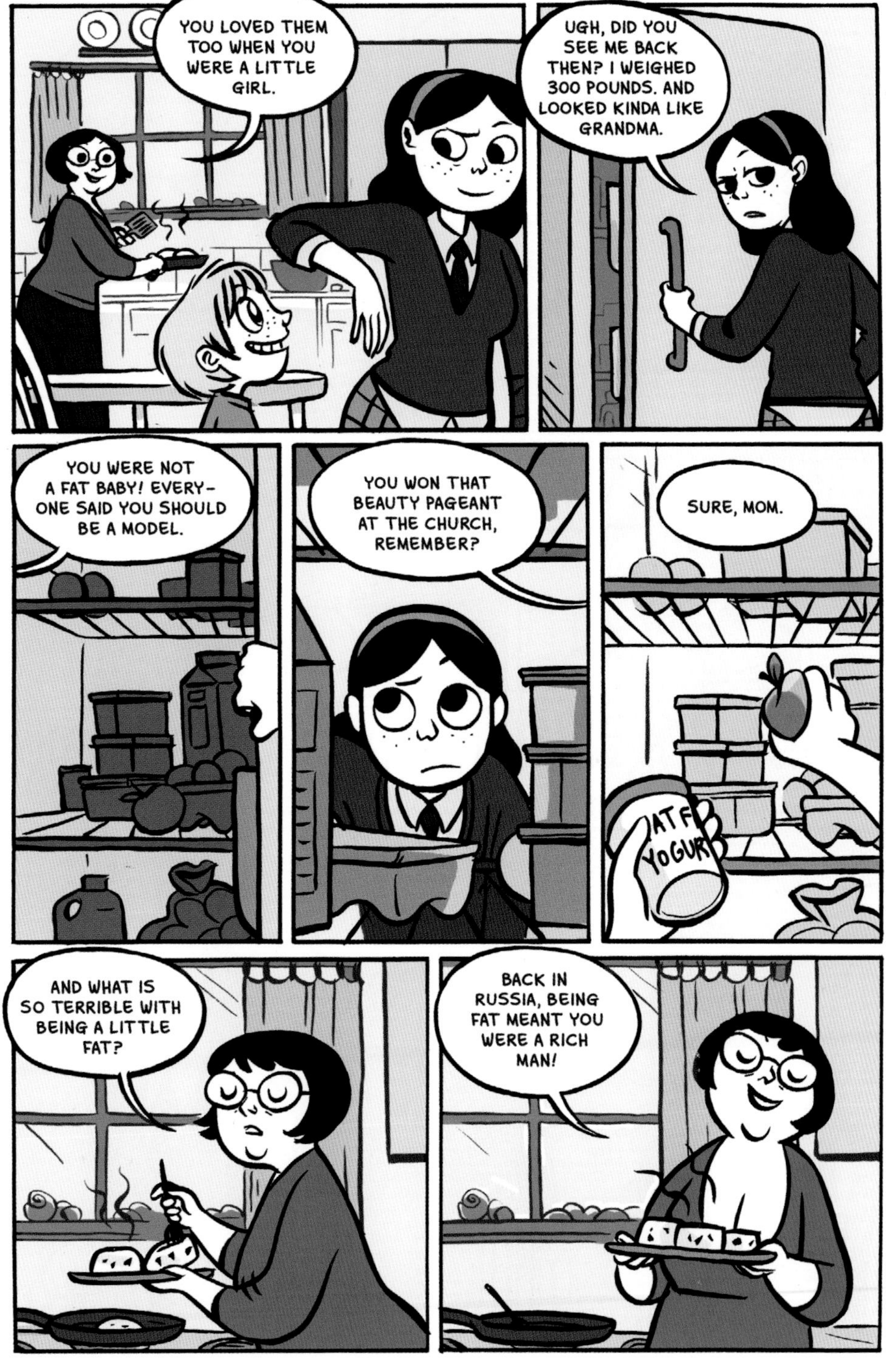
YOU LOVED THEM TOO WHEN YOU WERE A LITTLE GIRL.
UGH, DID YOU SEE ME BACK THEN? I WEIGHED 300 POUNDS. AND LOOKED KINDA LIKE GRANDMA.
YOU WERE NOT A FAT BABY! EVERY-ONE SAID YOU SHOULD BE A MODEL.
YOU WON THAT BEAUTY PAGEANT AT THE CHURCH, REMEMBER?
SURE, MOM.
AND WHAT IS SO TERRIBLE WITH BEING A LITTLE FAT?
BACK IN RUSSIA, BEING FAT MEANT YOU WERE A RICH MAN!

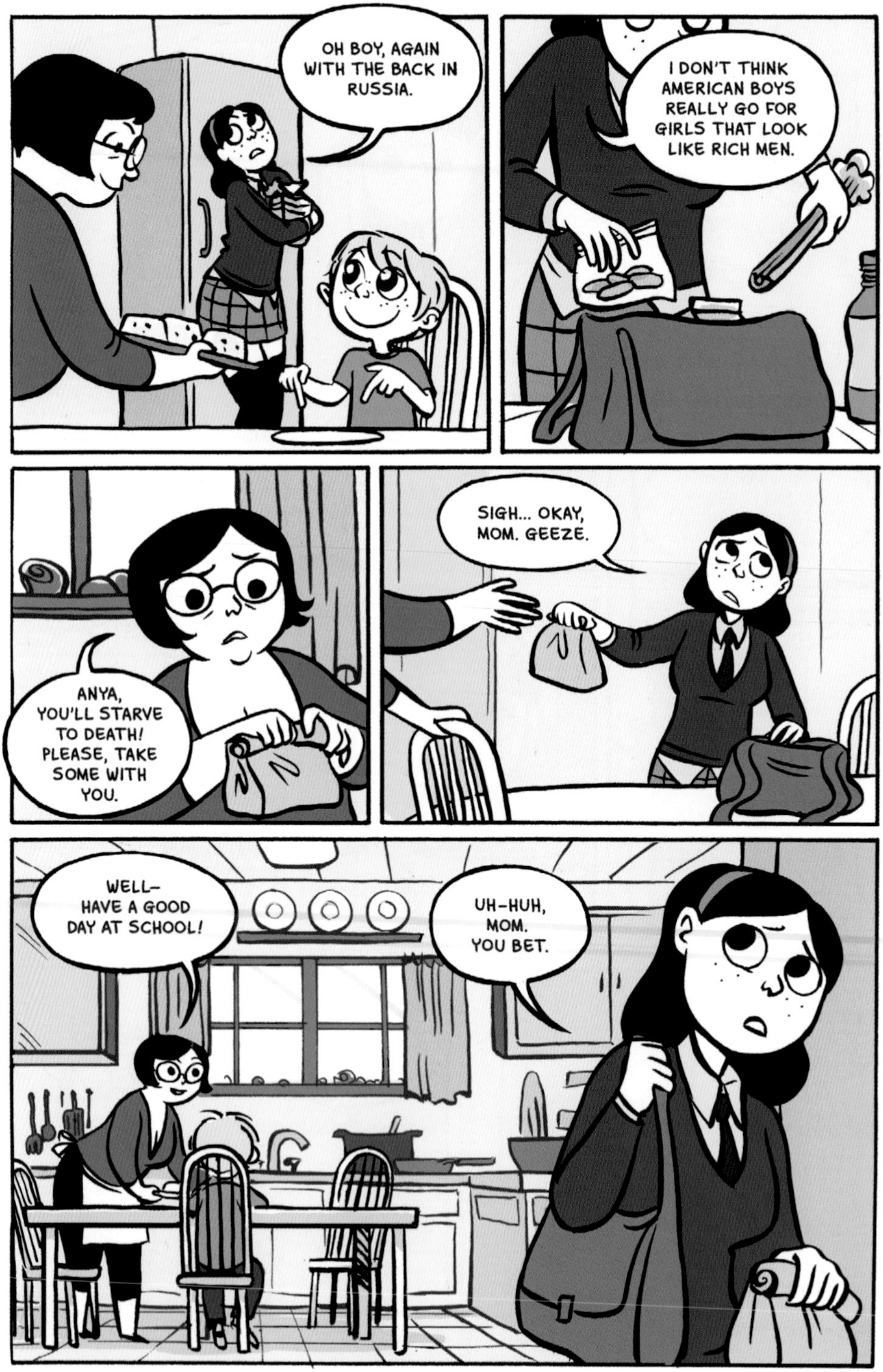
OH BOY, AGAIN WITH THE BACK IN RUSSIA.
I DON'T THINK AMERICAN BOYS REALLY GO FOR GIRLS THAT LOOK LIKE RICH MEN.
ANYA, YOU'LL STARVE TO DEATH! PLEASE, TAKE SOME WITH YOU.
SIGH... OKAY, MOM. GEEZE.
WELL– HAVE A GOOD DAY AT SCHOOL!
UH-HUH, MOM. YOU BET.

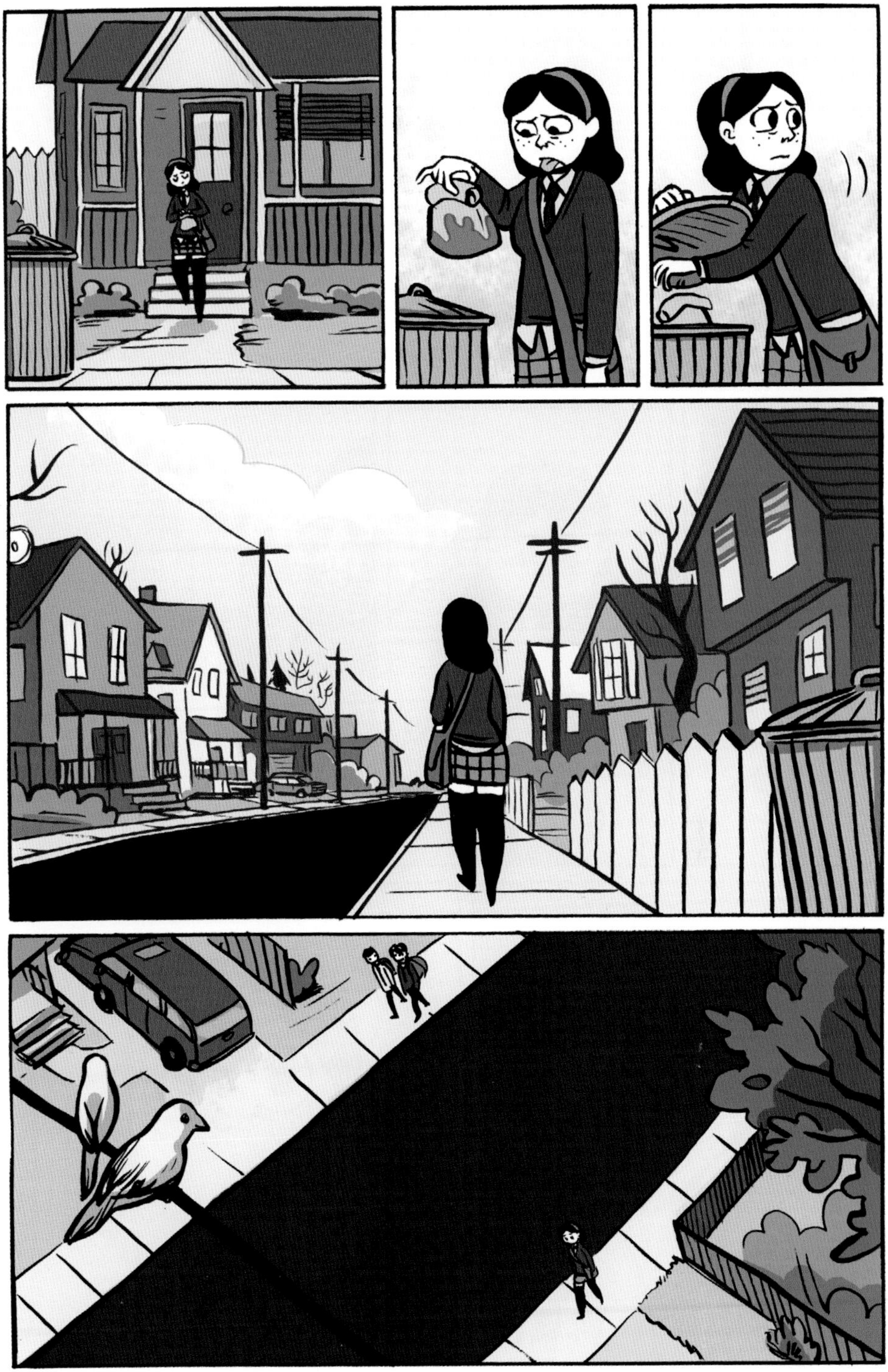

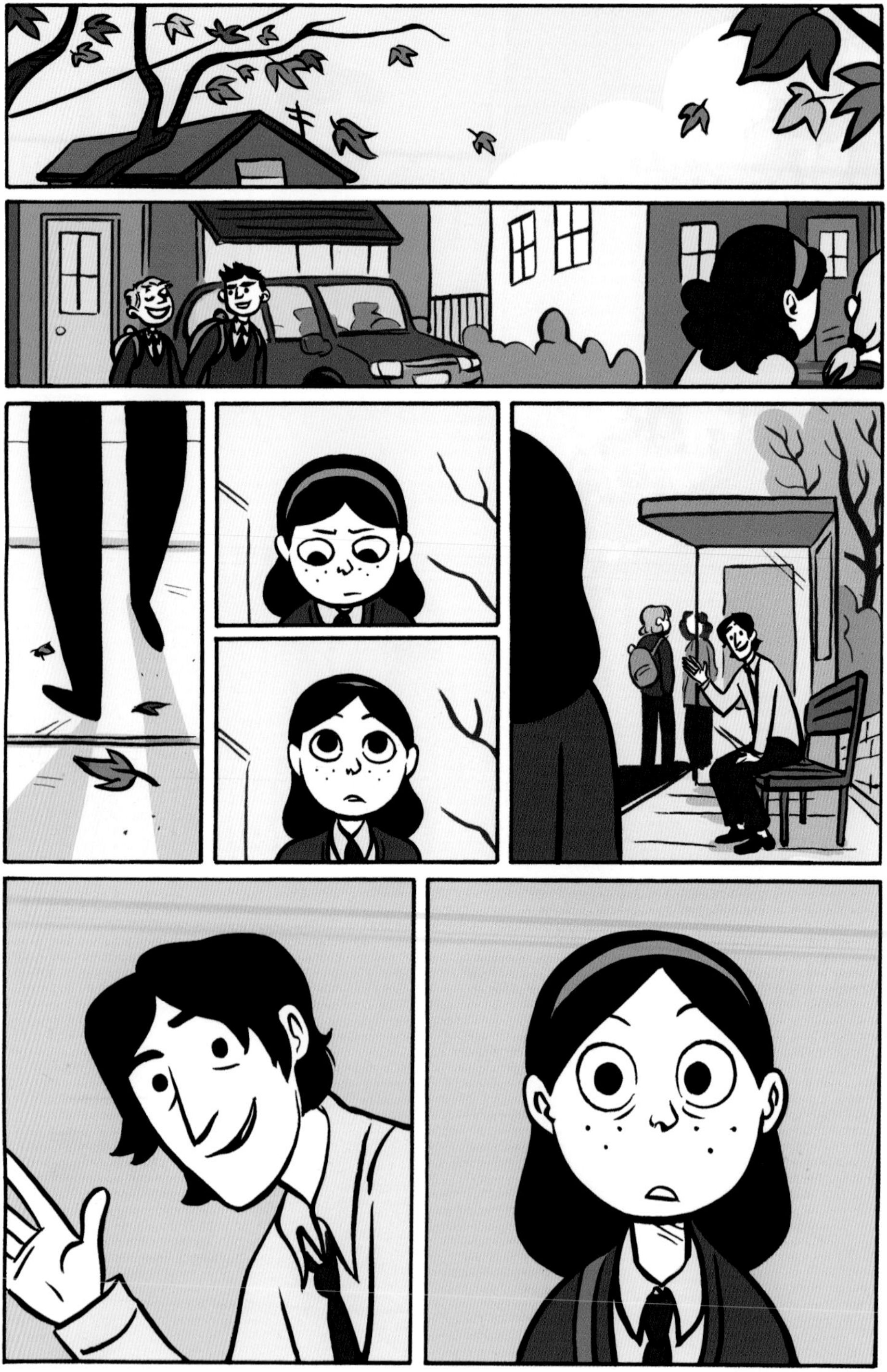

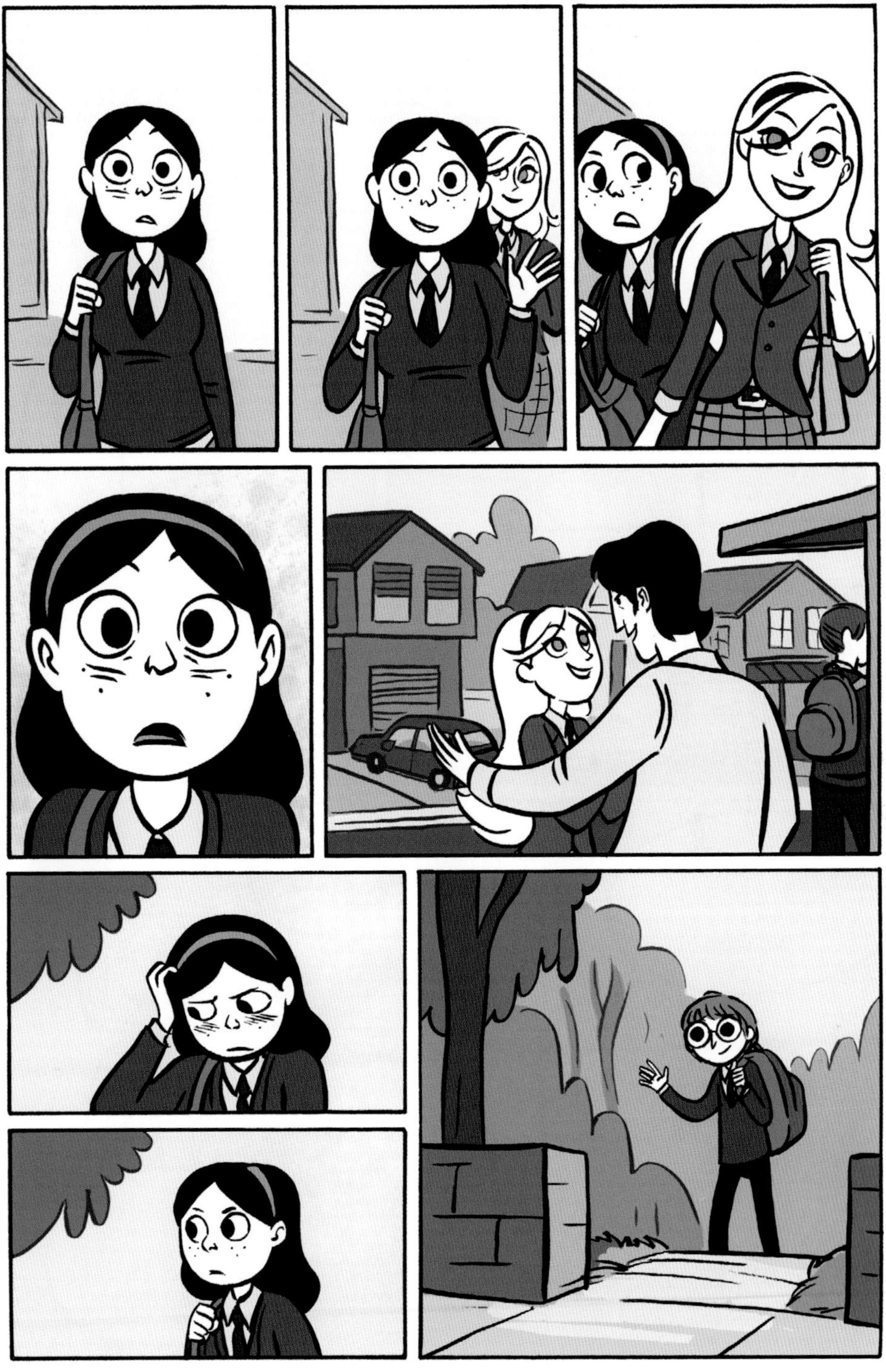

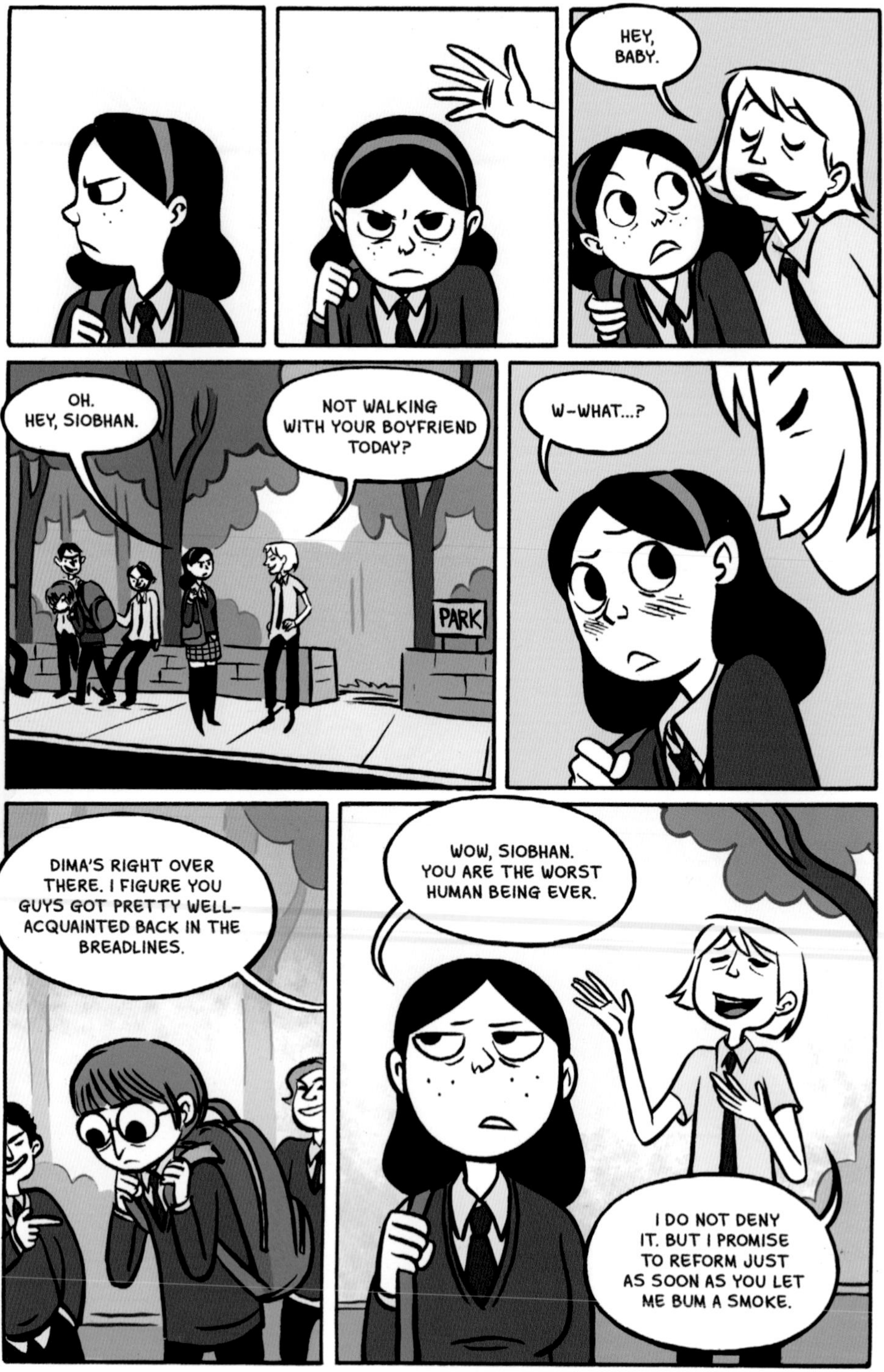
HEY, BABY.
OH. HEY, SIOBHAN.
NOT WALKING WITH YOUR BOYFRIEND TODAY?
PARK
W-WHAT...?
DIMA'S RIGHT OVER THERE. I FIGURE YOU GUYS GOT PRETTY WELL-ACQUAINTED BACK IN THE BREADLINES.
WOW, SIOBHAN. YOU ARE THE WORST HUMAN BEING EVER.
I DO NOT DENY IT. BUT I PROMISE TO REFORM JUST AS SOON AS YOU LET ME BUM A SMOKE.

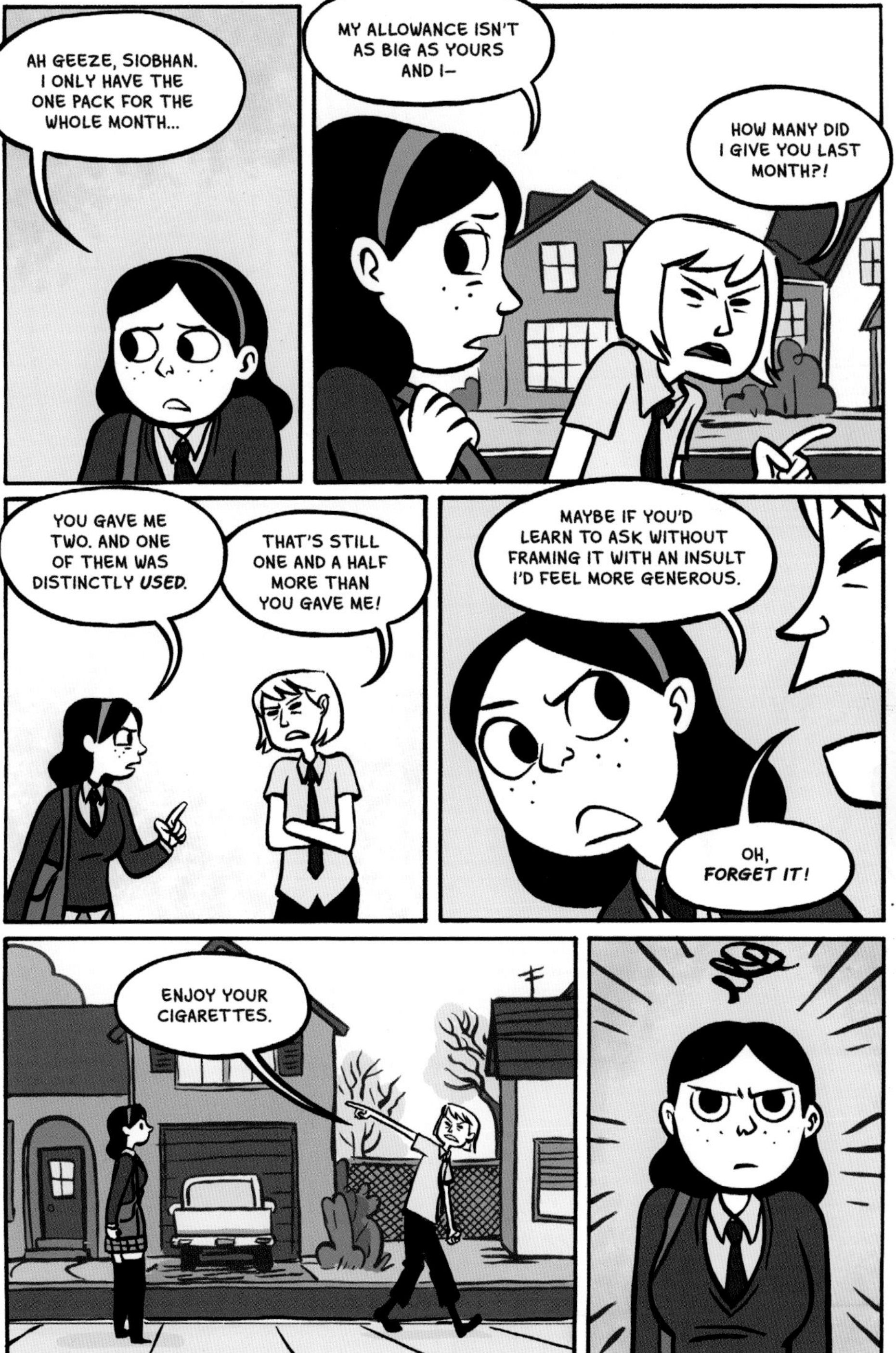
AH GEEZE, SIOBHAN. I ONLY HAVE THE ONE PACK FOR THE WHOLE MONTH...
MY ALLOWANCE ISN'T AS BIG AS YOURS AND I–
HOW MANY DID I GIVE YOU LAST MONTH?!
YOU GAVE ME TWO. AND ONE OF THEM WAS DISTINCTLY *USED*.
THAT'S STILL ONE AND A HALF MORE THAN YOU GAVE ME!
MAYBE IF YOU'D LEARN TO ASK WITHOUT FRAMING IT WITH AN INSULT I'D FEEL MORE GENEROUS.
OH, **FORGET IT!**
ENJOY YOUR CIGARETTES.

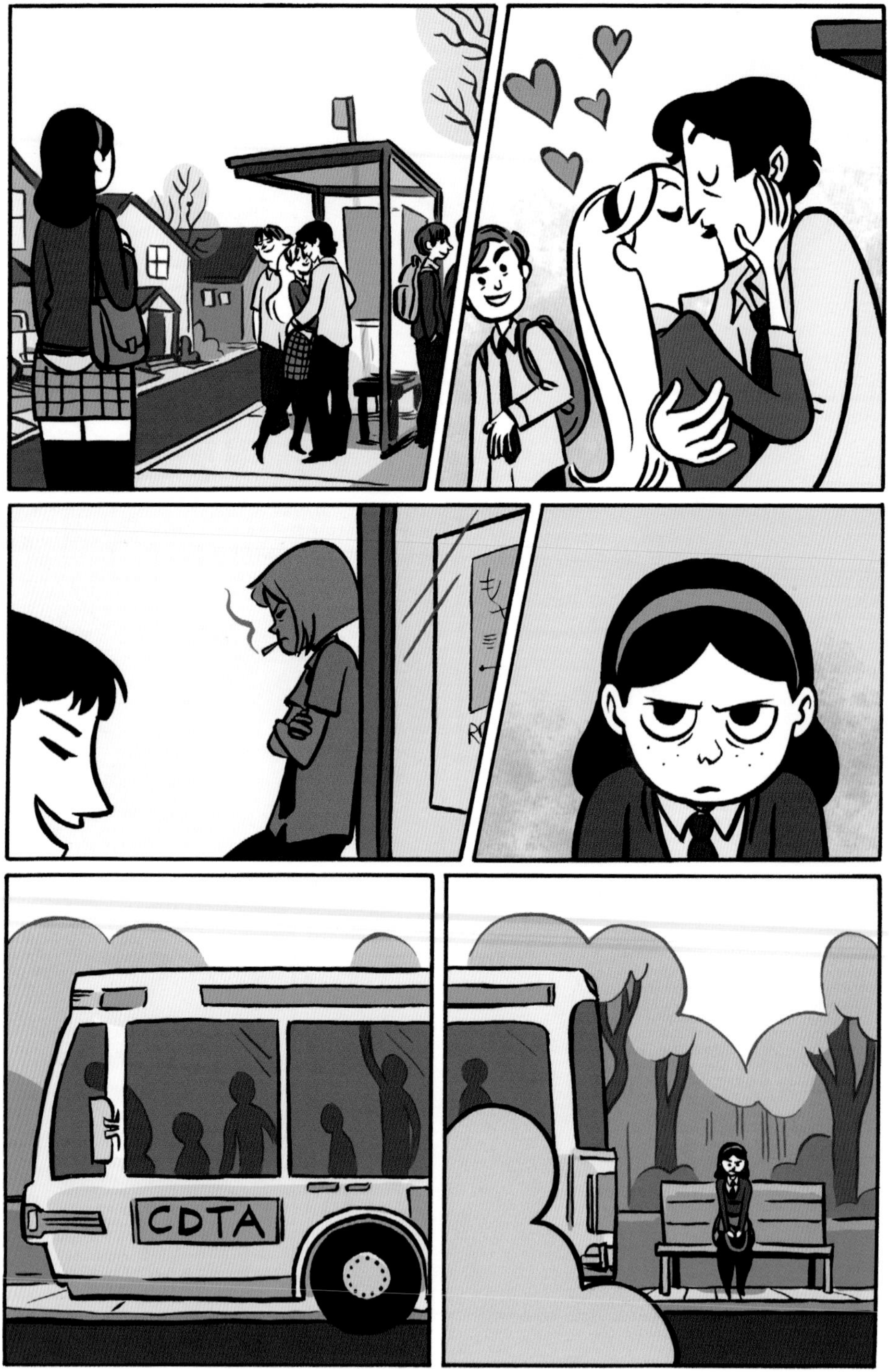
CDTA

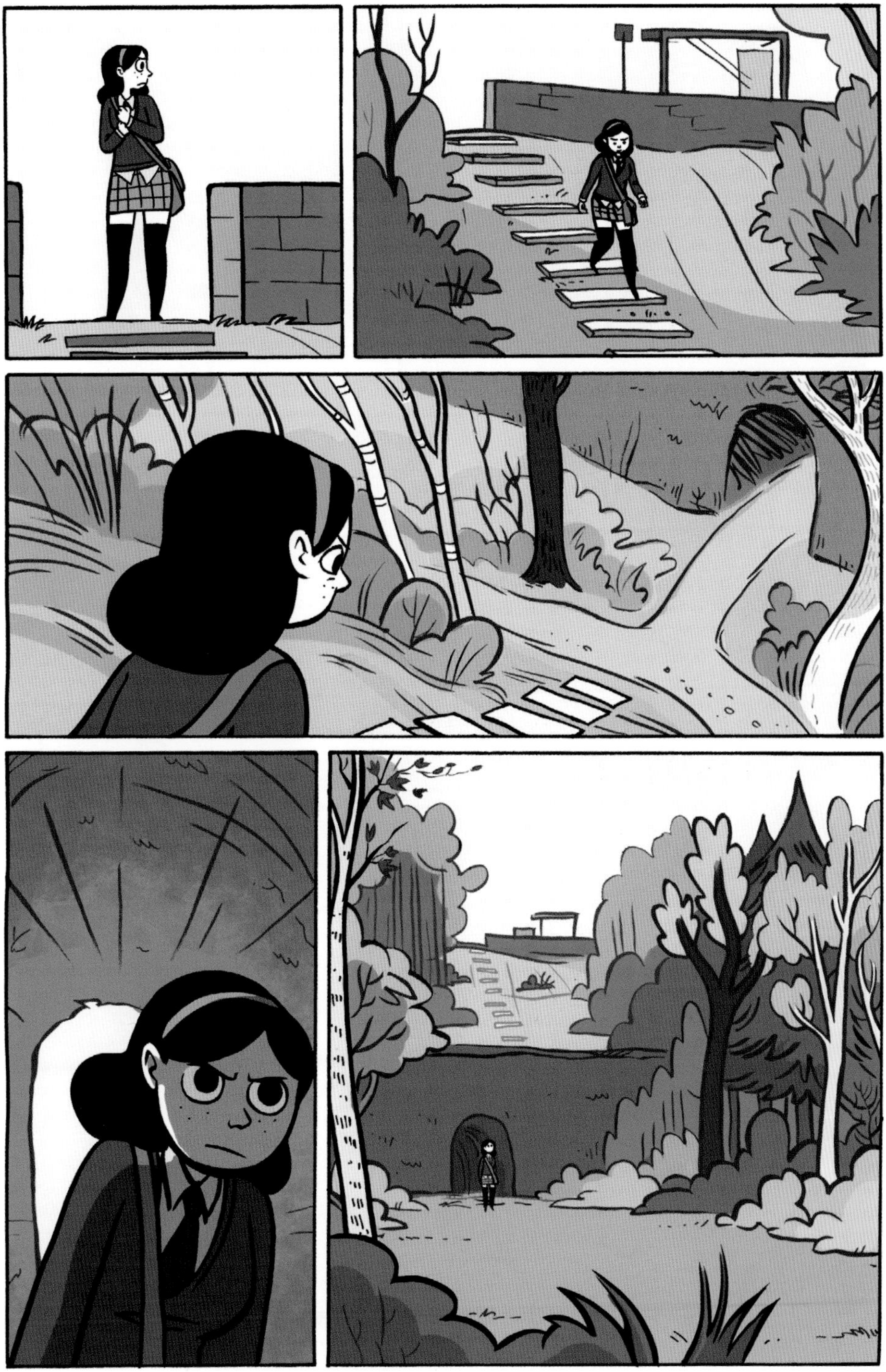

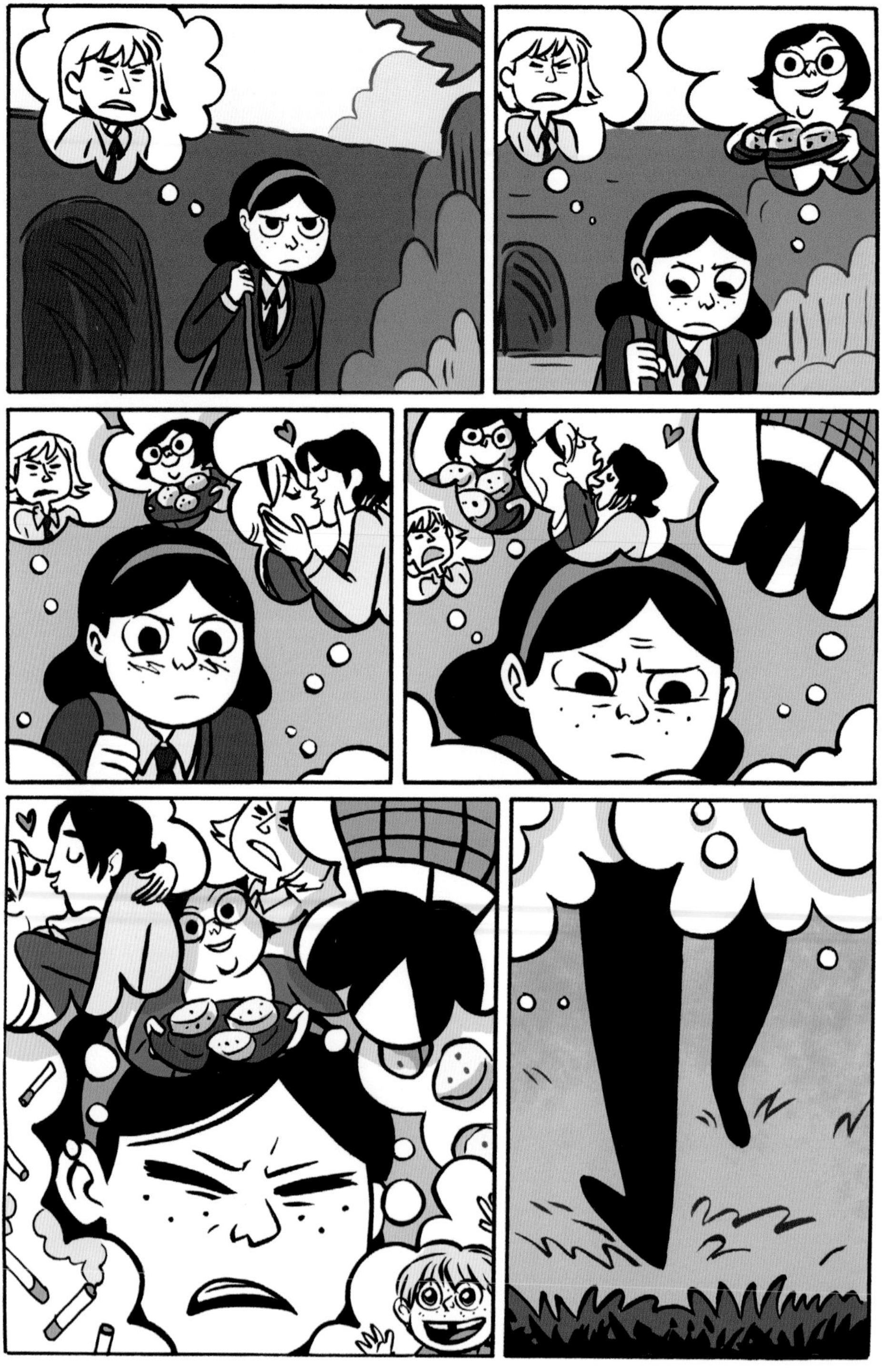

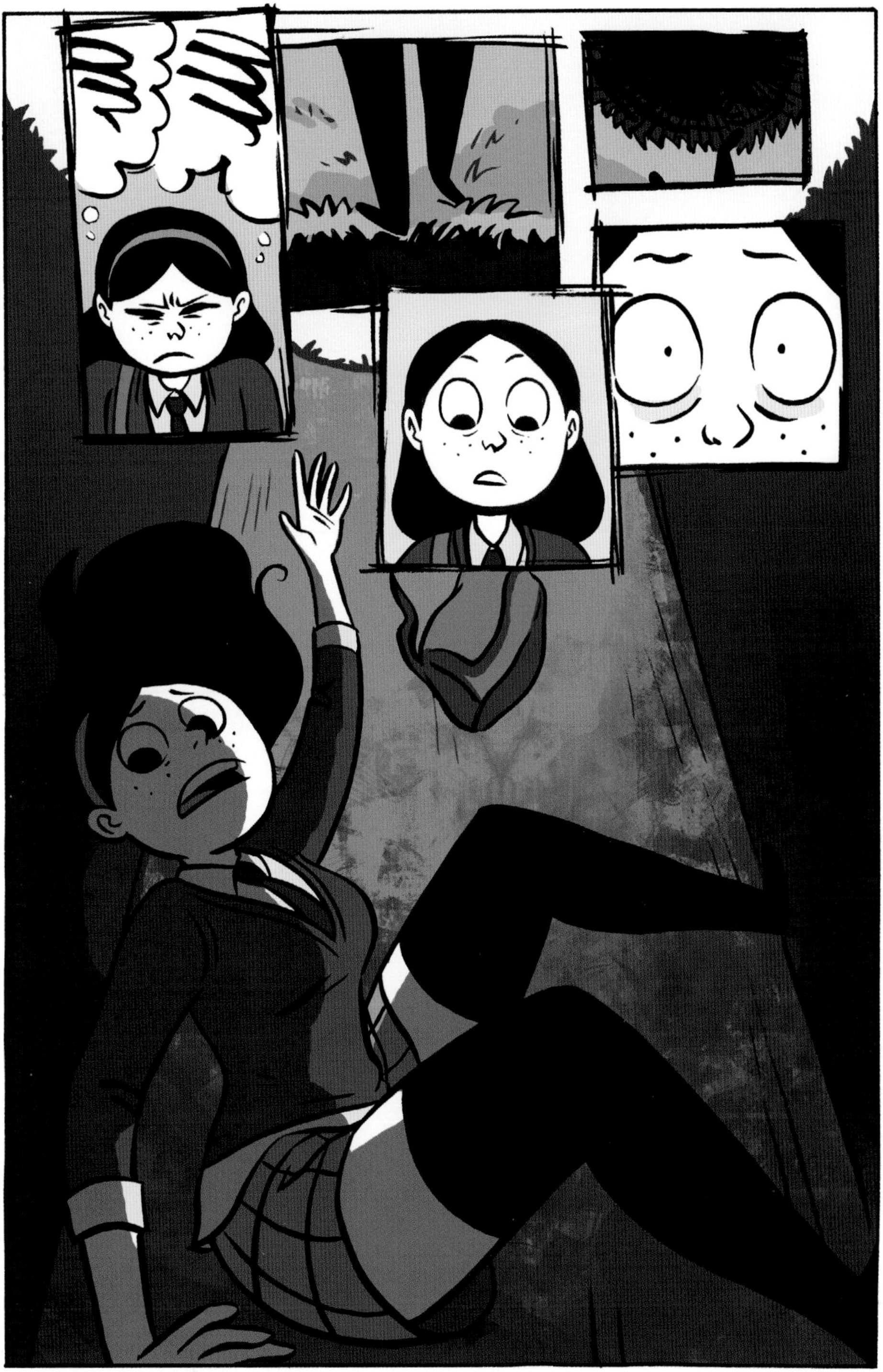

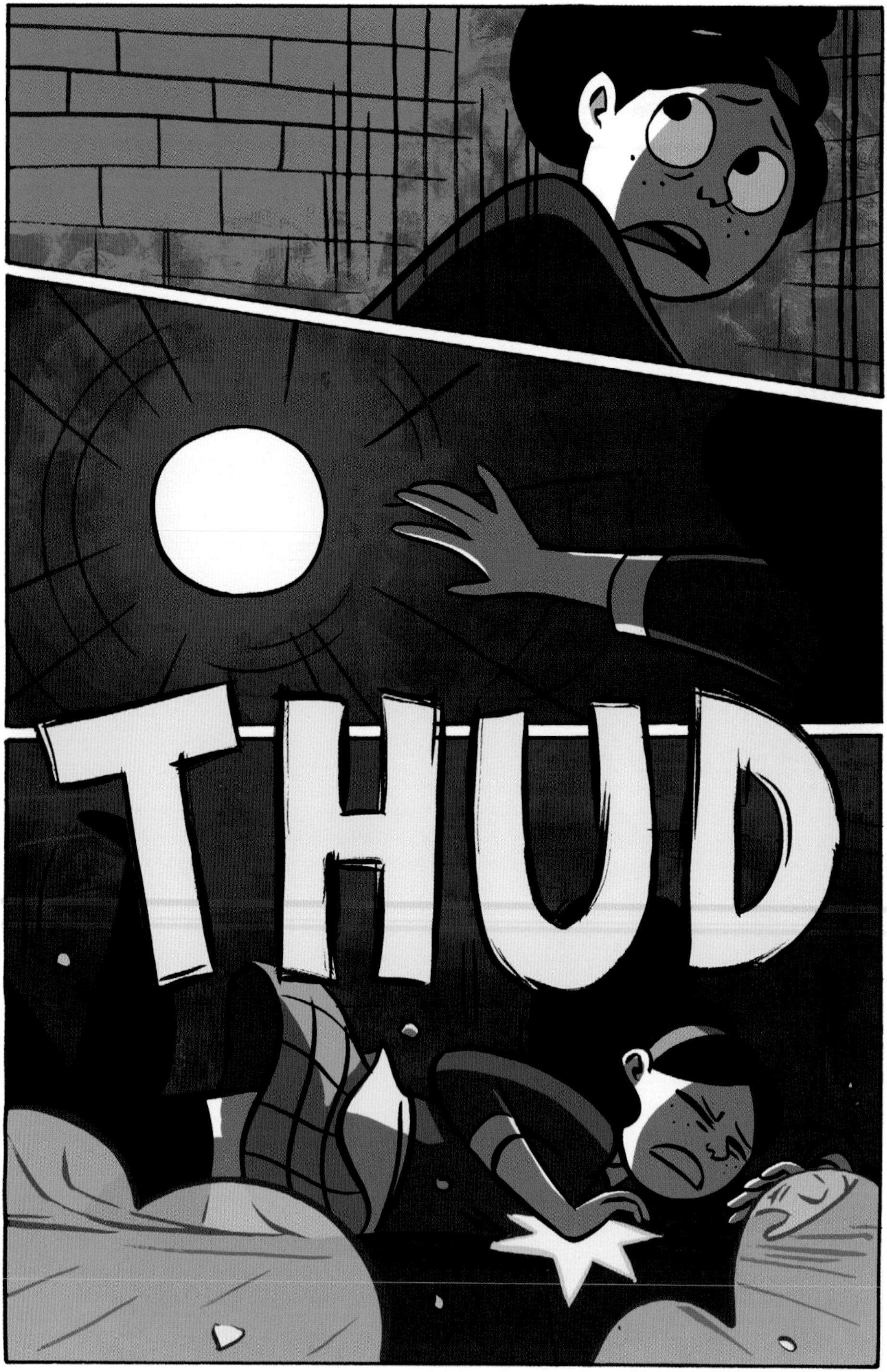
THUD

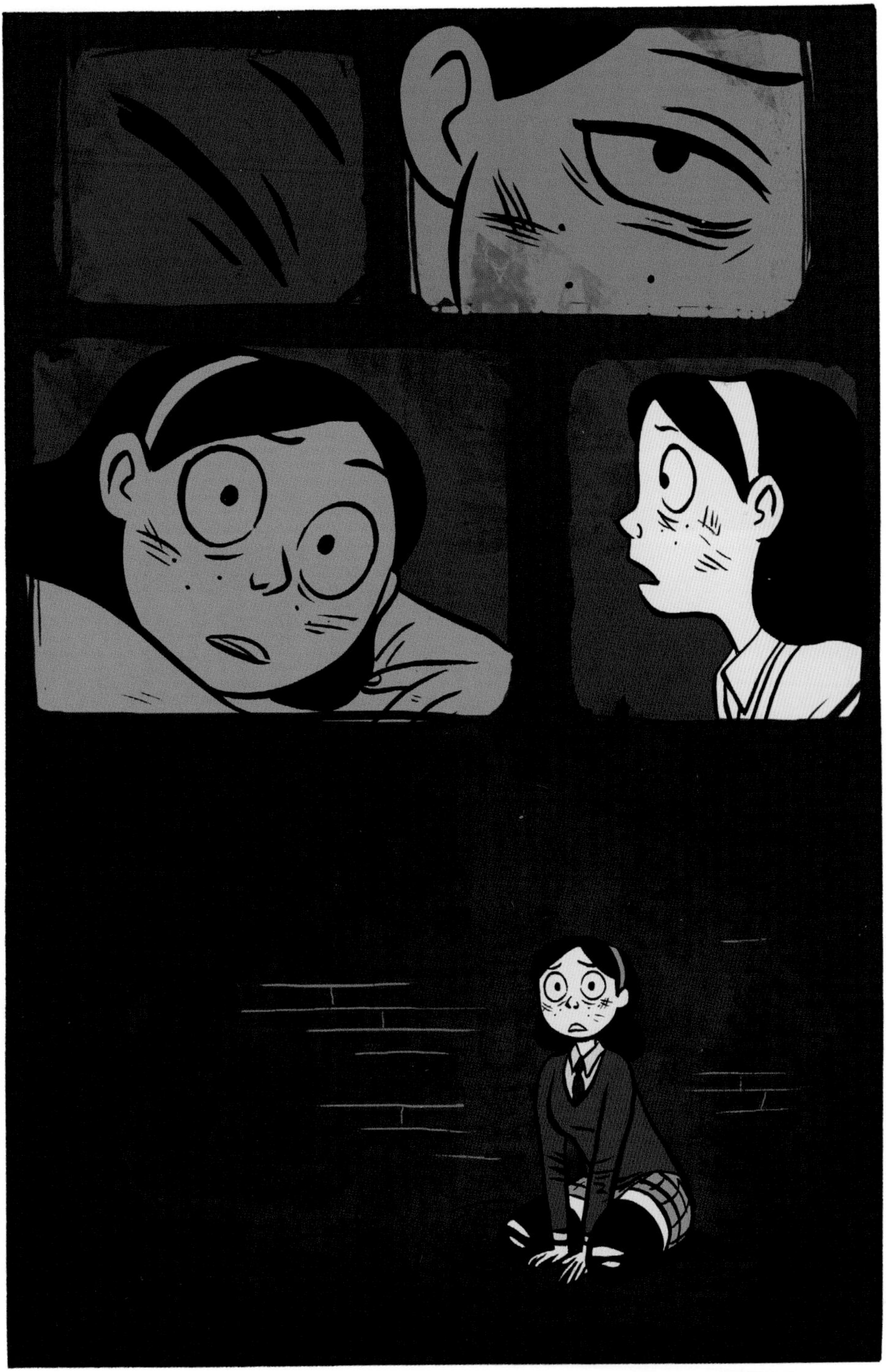

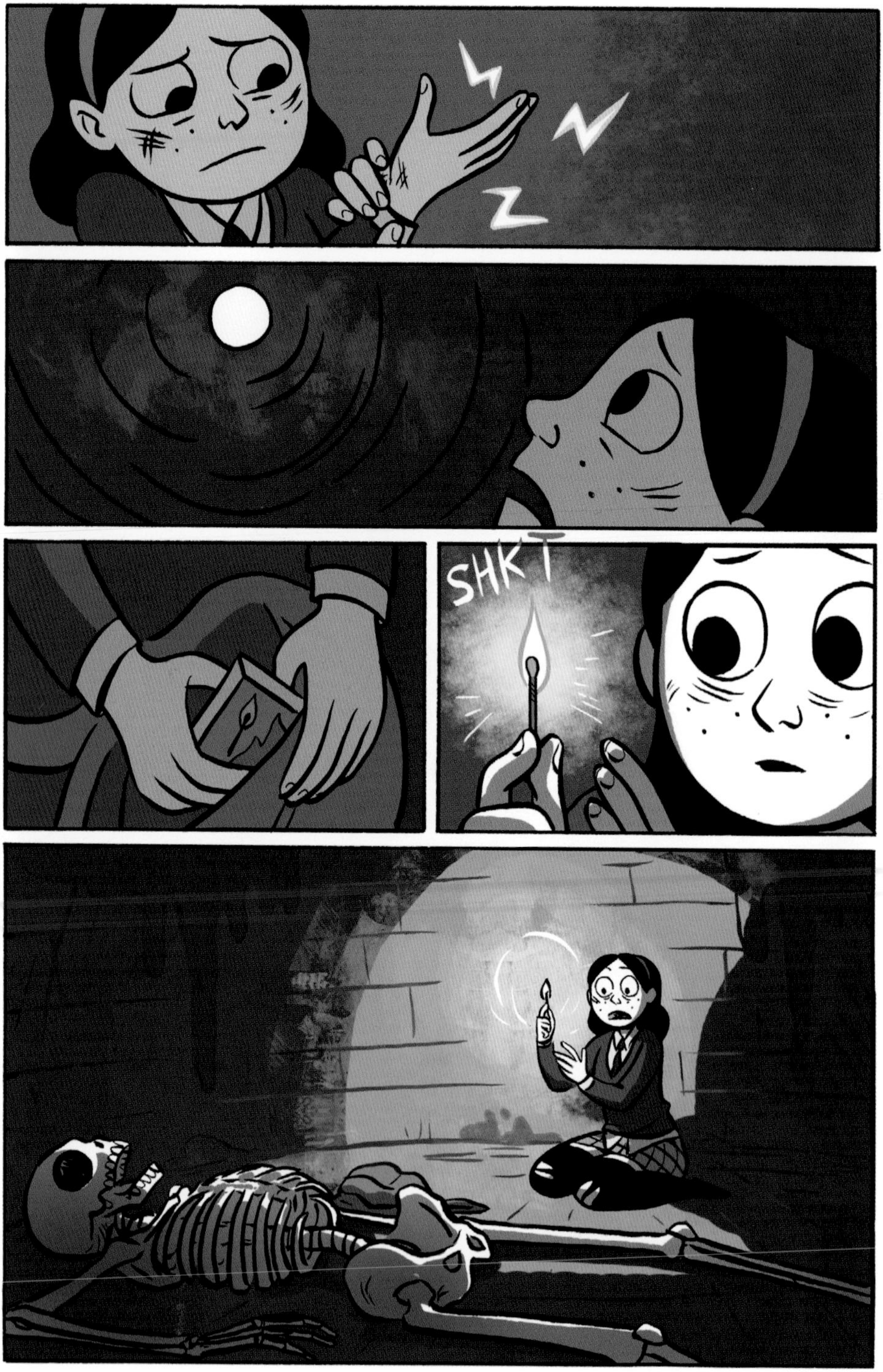
SHKT

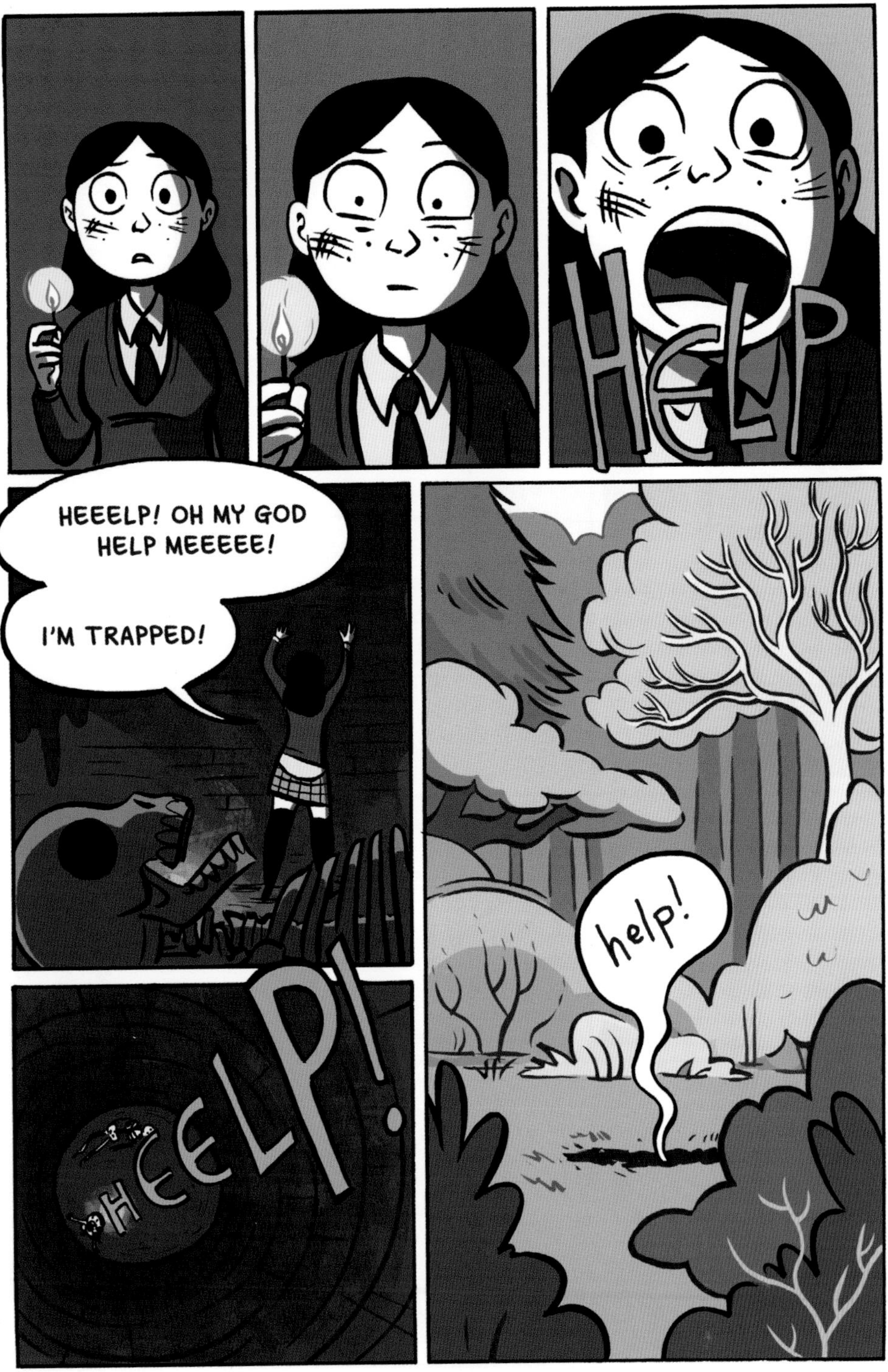
HELP
HEEELP! OH MY GOD HELP MEEEEE!
I'M TRAPPED!
help!
HEELP!

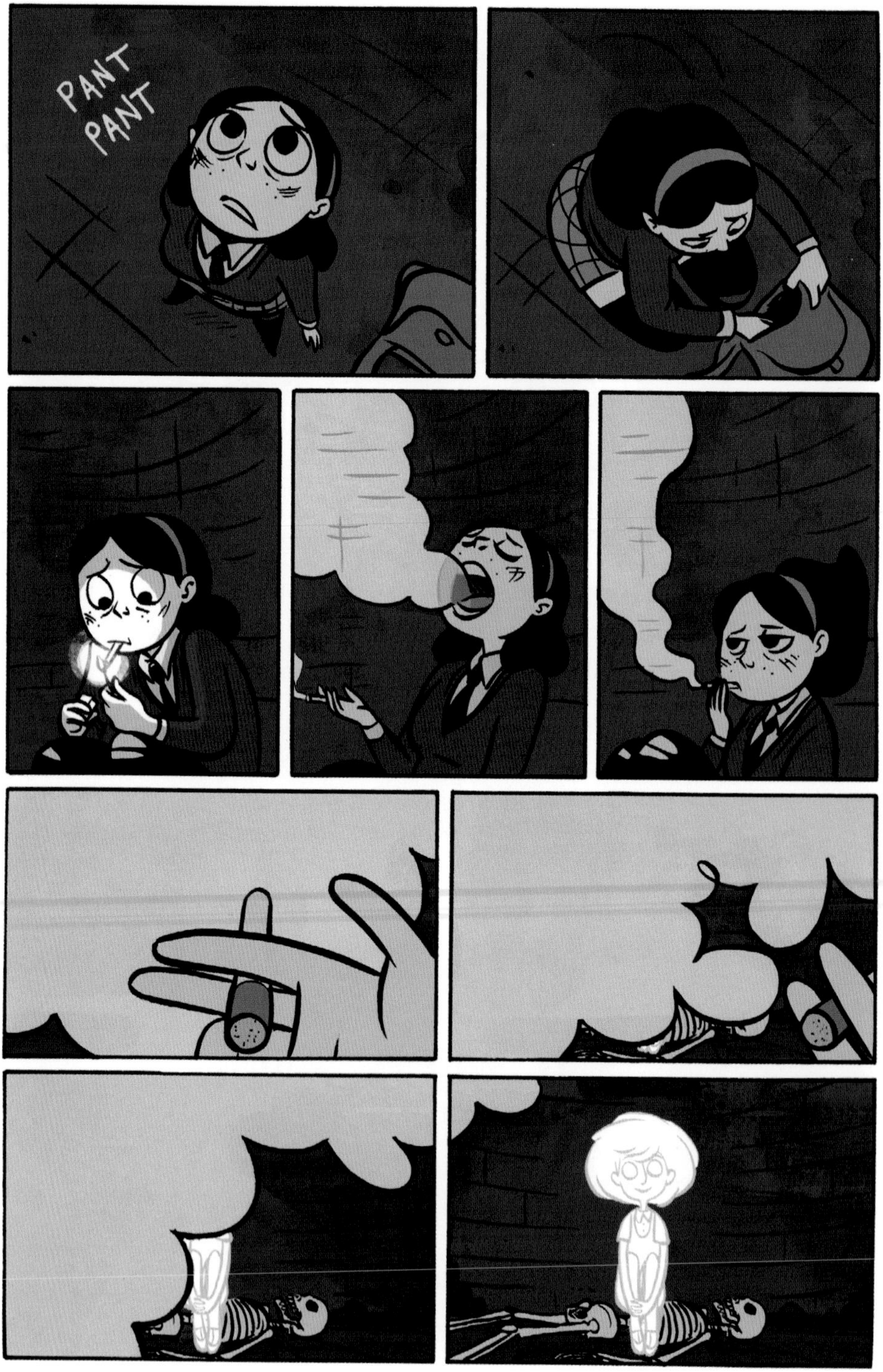
PANT
PANT

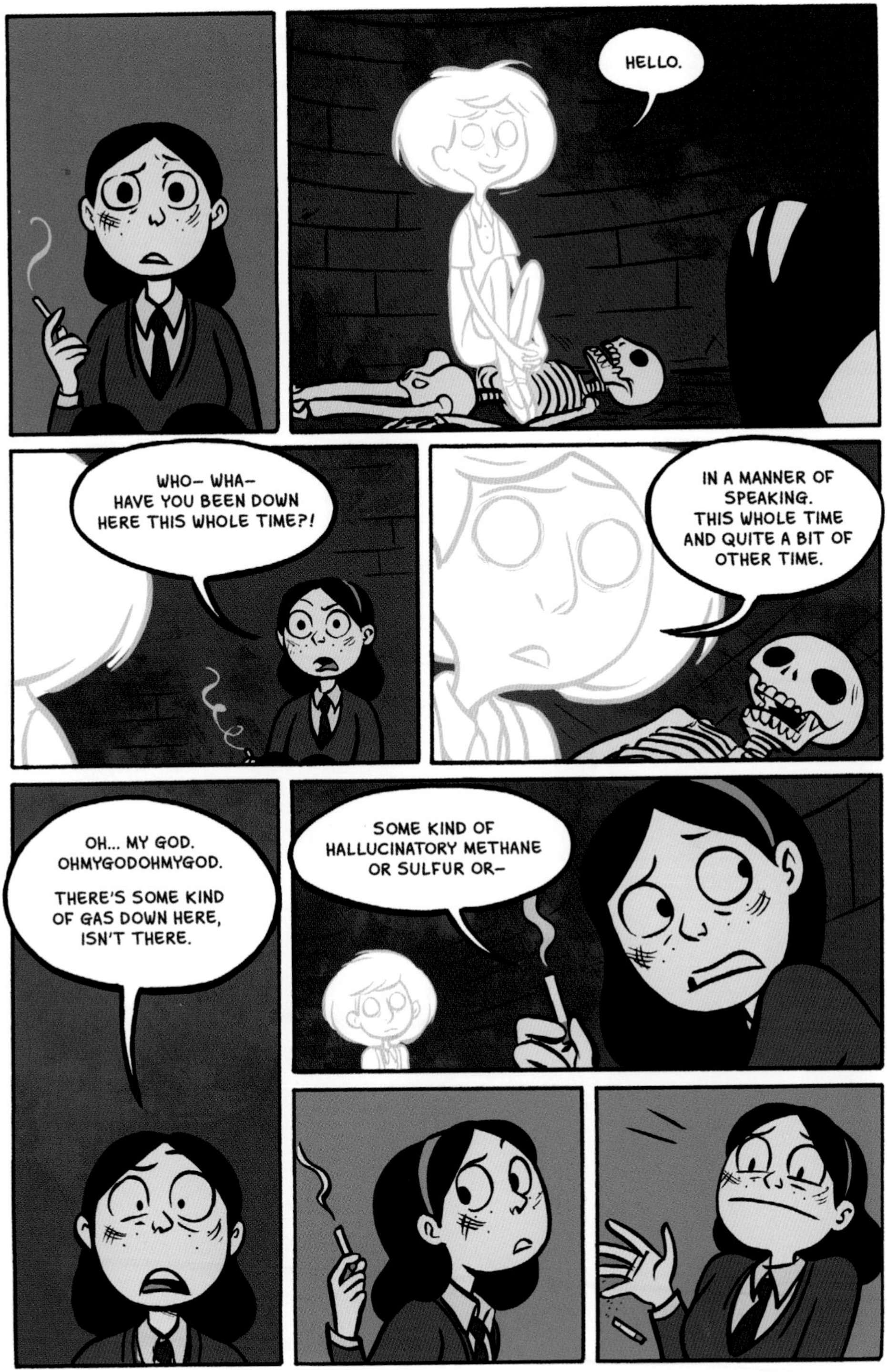
HELLO.
WHO– WHA– HAVE YOU BEEN DOWN HERE THIS WHOLE TIME?!
IN A MANNER OF SPEAKING. THIS WHOLE TIME AND QUITE A BIT OF OTHER TIME.
OH... MY GOD. OHMYGODOHMYGOD.
THERE'S SOME KIND OF GAS DOWN HERE, ISN'T THERE.
SOME KIND OF HALLUCINATORY METHANE OR SULFUR OR–

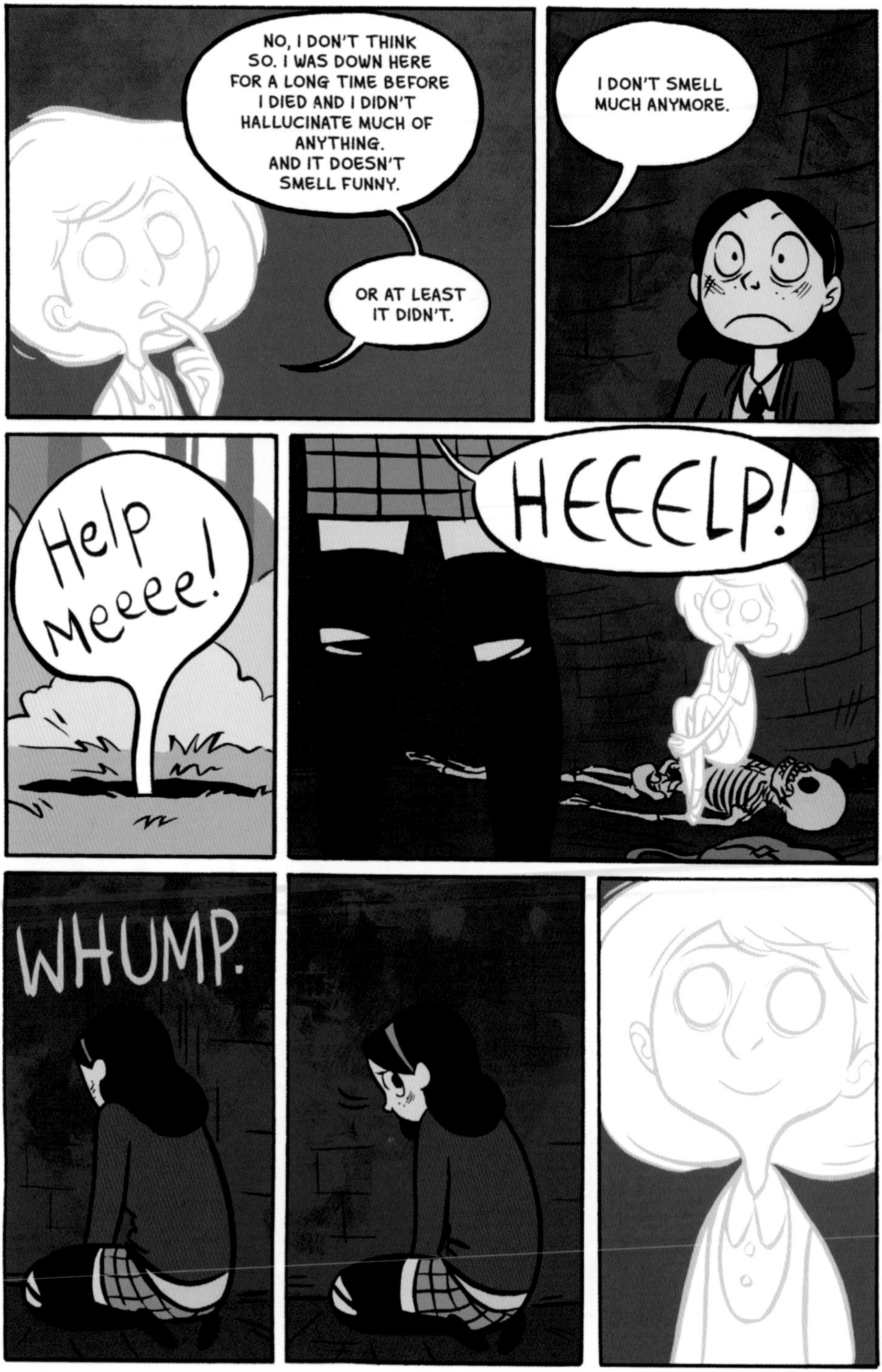
NO, I DON'T THINK SO. I WAS DOWN HERE FOR A LONG TIME BEFORE I DIED AND I DIDN'T HALLUCINATE MUCH OF ANYTHING. AND IT DOESN'T SMELL FUNNY.
OR AT LEAST IT DIDN'T.
I DON'T SMELL MUCH ANYMORE.
Help Meeee!
HEEELP!
WHUMP.

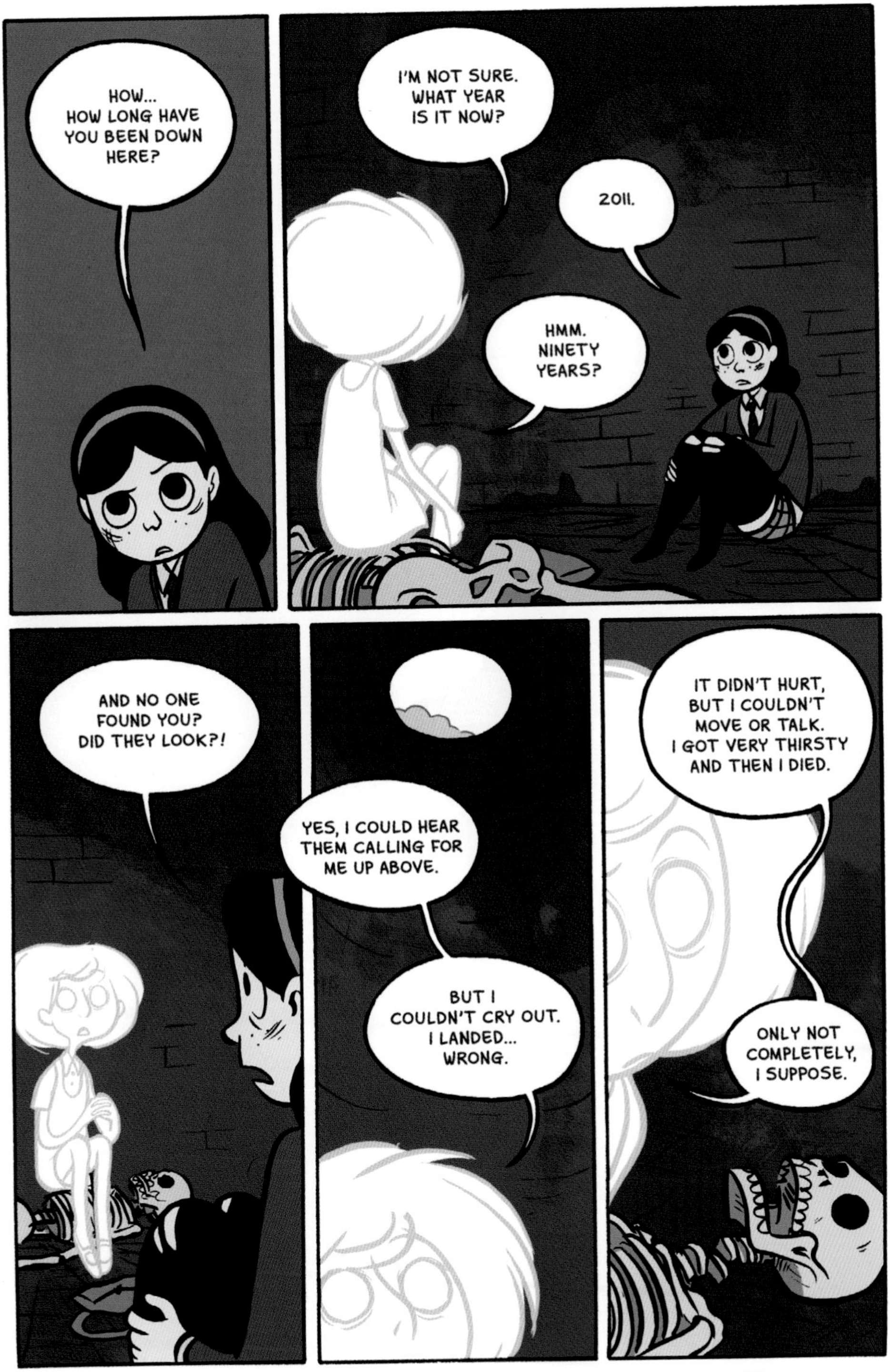
HOW... HOW LONG HAVE YOU BEEN DOWN HERE?
I'M NOT SURE. WHAT YEAR IS IT NOW?
2011.
HMM. NINETY YEARS?
AND NO ONE FOUND YOU? DID THEY LOOK?!
YES, I COULD HEAR THEM CALLING FOR ME UP ABOVE.
BUT I COULDN'T CRY OUT. I LANDED... WRONG.
IT DIDN'T HURT, BUT I COULDN'T MOVE OR TALK. I GOT VERY THIRSTY AND THEN I DIED.
ONLY NOT COMPLETELY, I SUPPOSE.

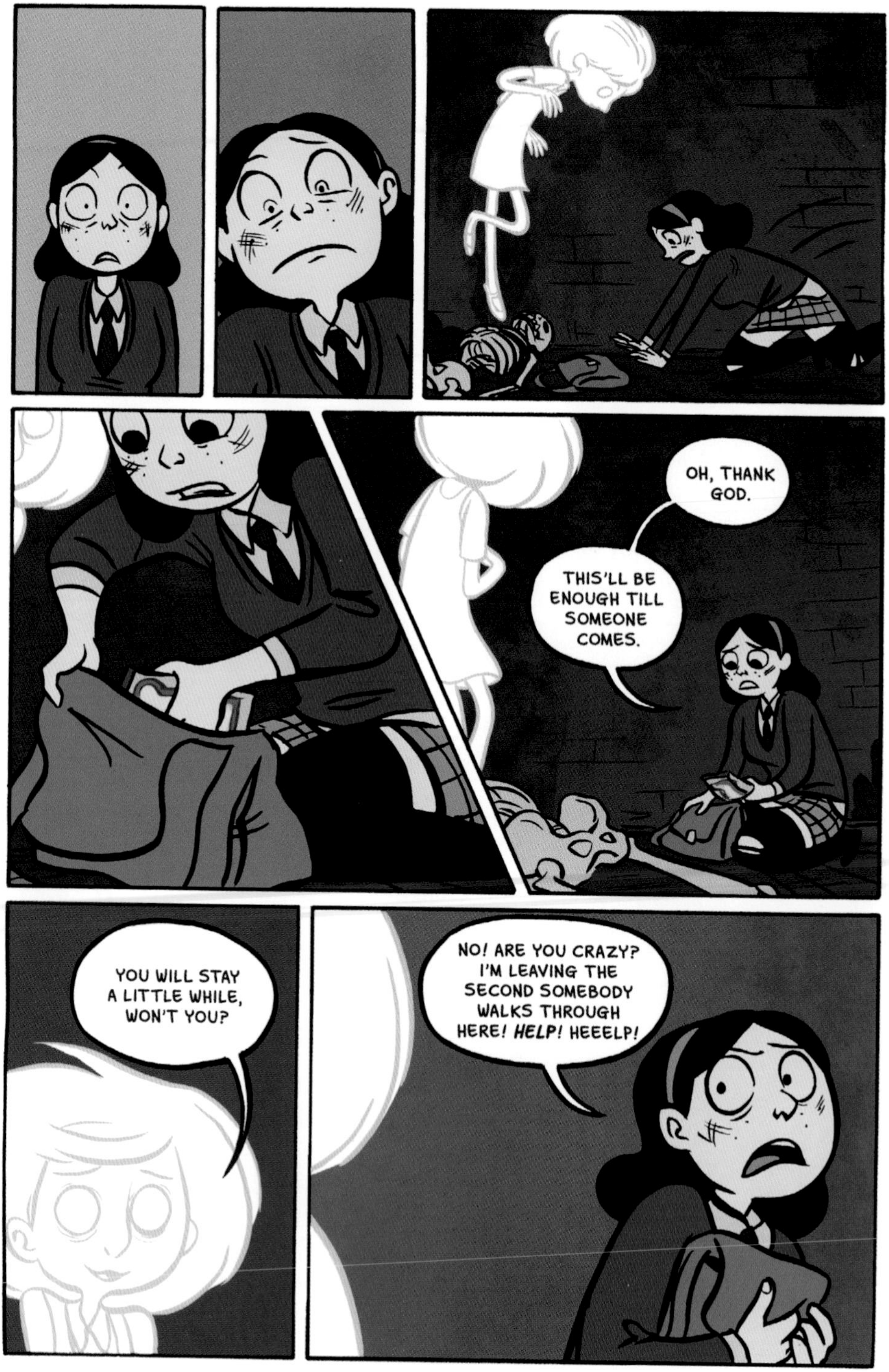
OH, THANK GOD.
THIS'LL BE ENOUGH TILL SOMEONE COMES.
YOU WILL STAY A LITTLE WHILE, WON'T YOU?
NO! ARE YOU CRAZY? I'M LEAVING THE SECOND SOMEBODY WALKS THROUGH HERE! *HELP*! HEEELP!

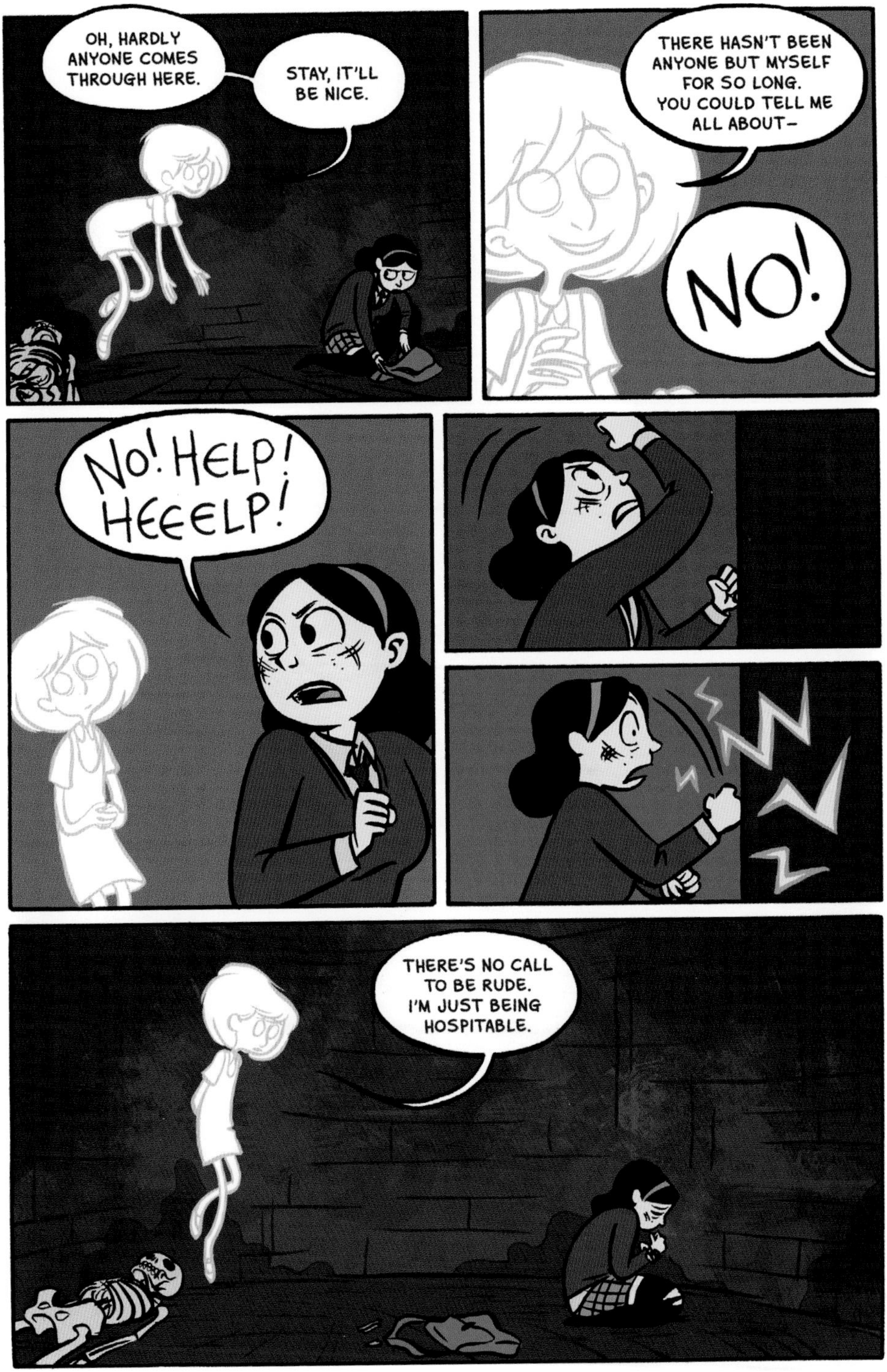
OH, HARDLY ANYONE COMES THROUGH HERE.
STAY, IT'LL BE NICE.
THERE HASN'T BEEN ANYONE BUT MYSELF FOR SO LONG. YOU COULD TELL ME ALL ABOUT–
NO!
NO! HELP! HEEELP!
THERE'S NO CALL TO BE RUDE. I'M JUST BEING HOSPITABLE.

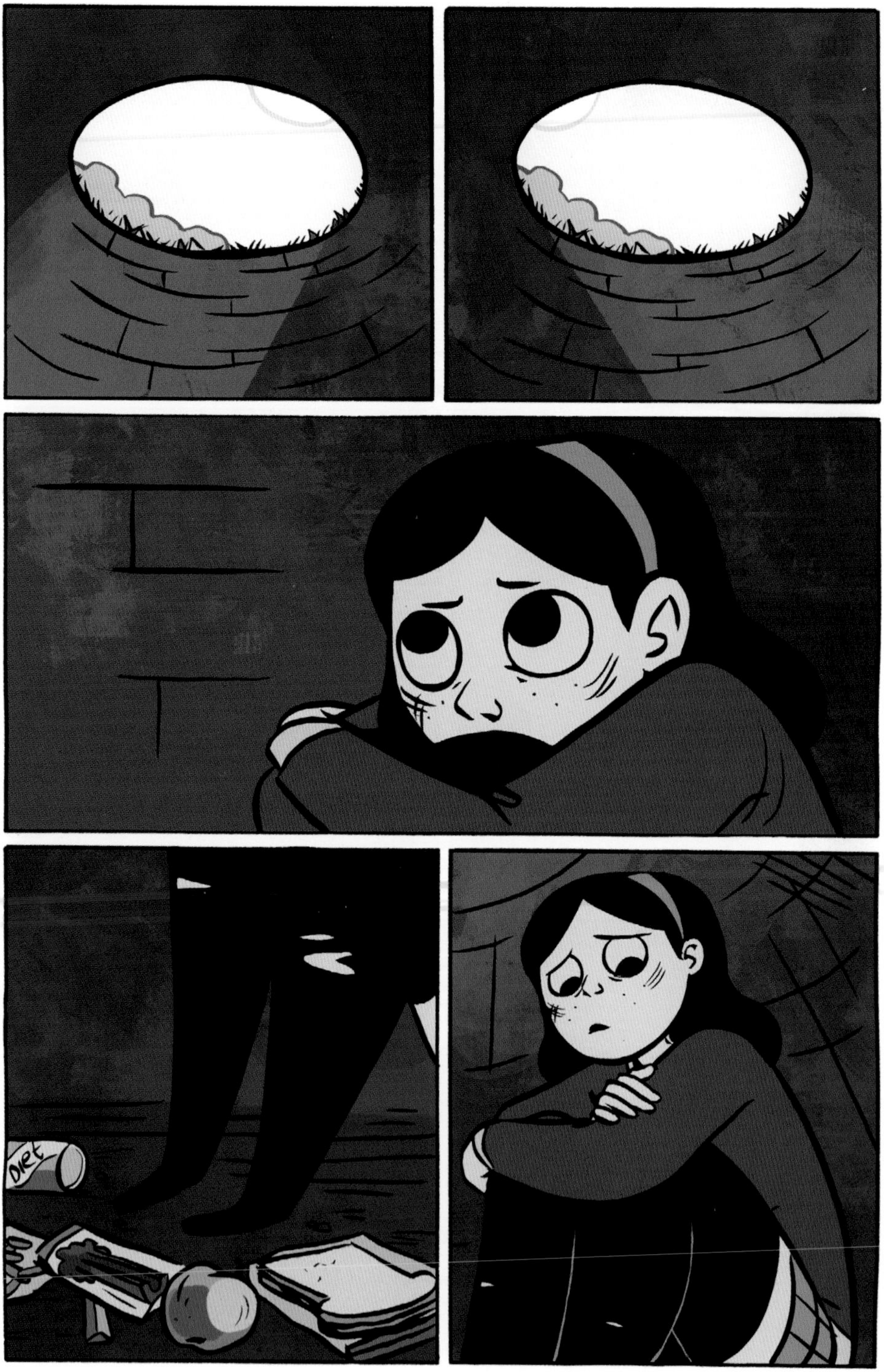
DIET

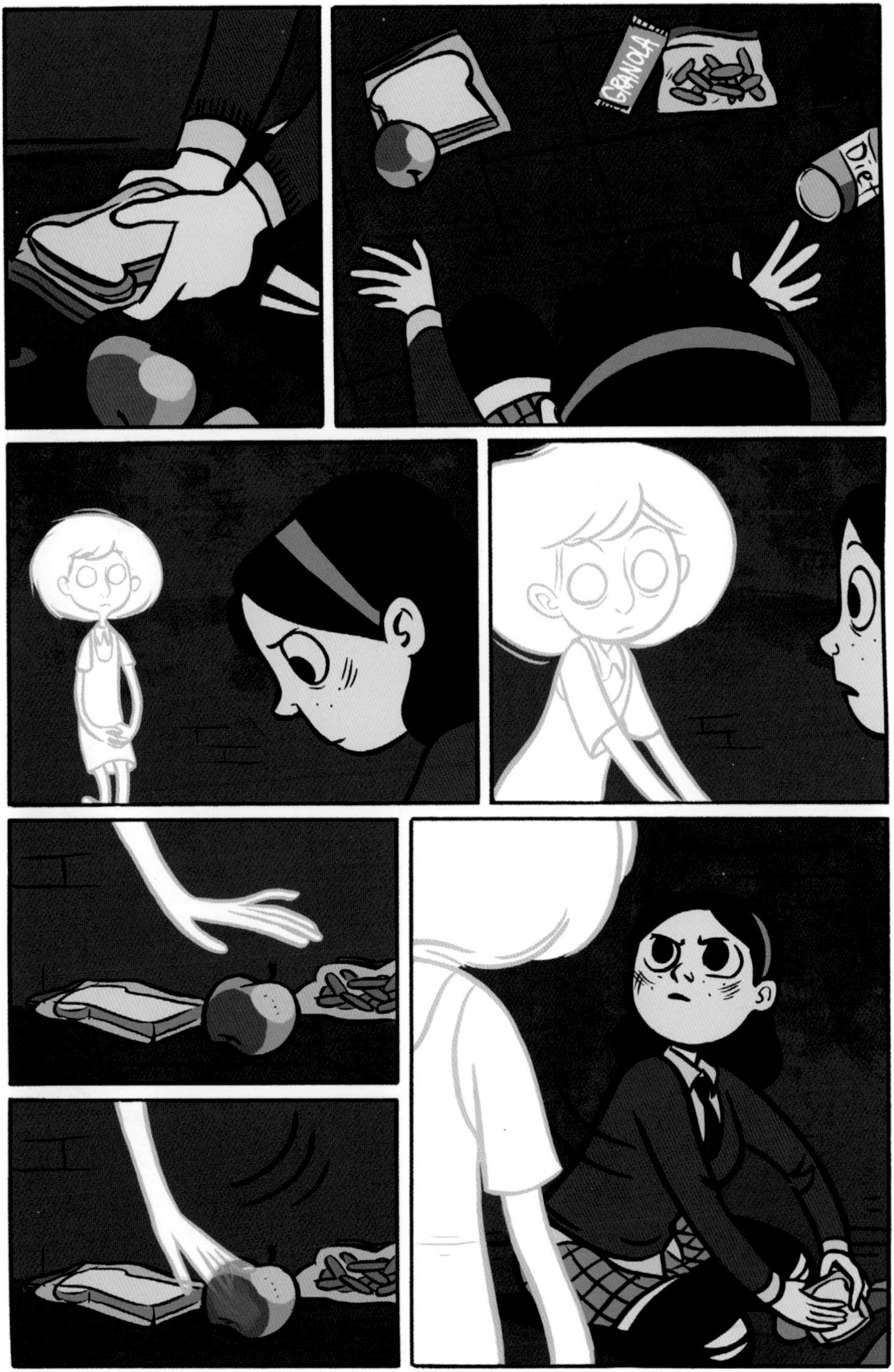
GRANOLA
Die

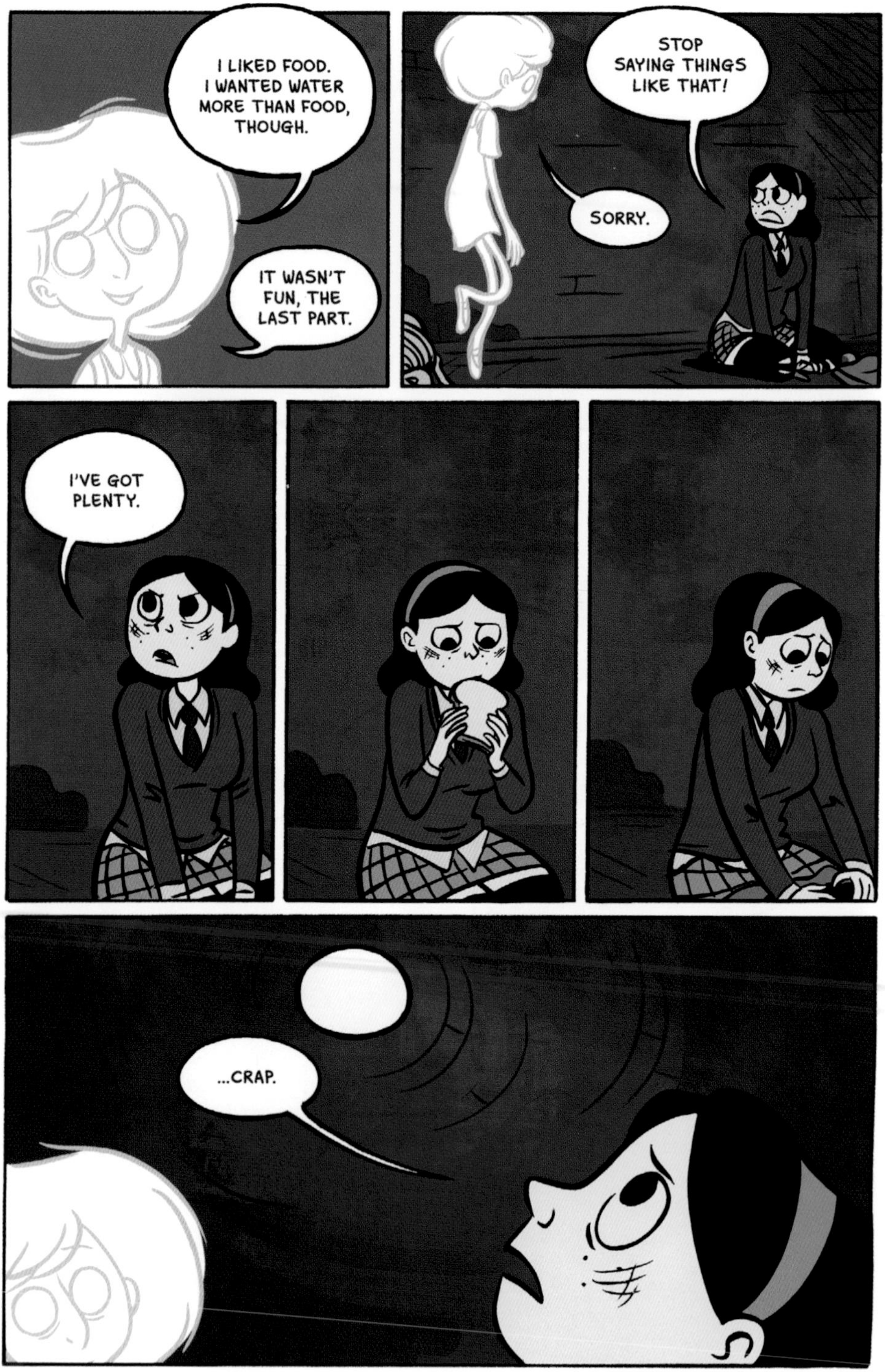
I LIKED FOOD. I WANTED WATER MORE THAN FOOD, THOUGH.
IT WASN'T FUN, THE LAST PART.
STOP SAYING THINGS LIKE THAT!
SORRY.
I'VE GOT PLENTY.
...CRAP.

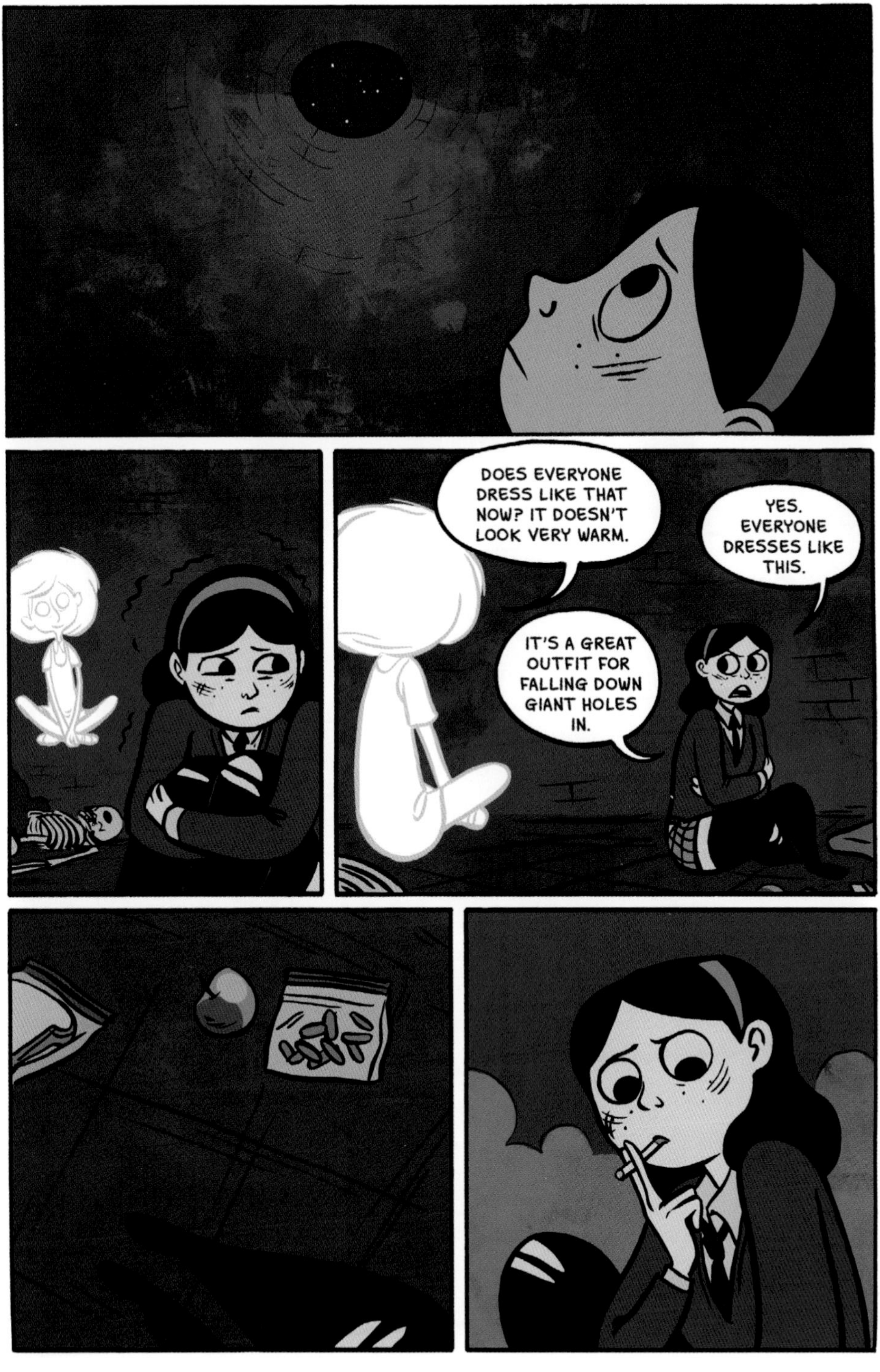
DOES EVERYONE DRESS LIKE THAT NOW? IT DOESN'T LOOK VERY WARM.
YES. EVERYONE DRESSES LIKE THIS.
IT'S A GREAT OUTFIT FOR FALLING DOWN GIANT HOLES IN.

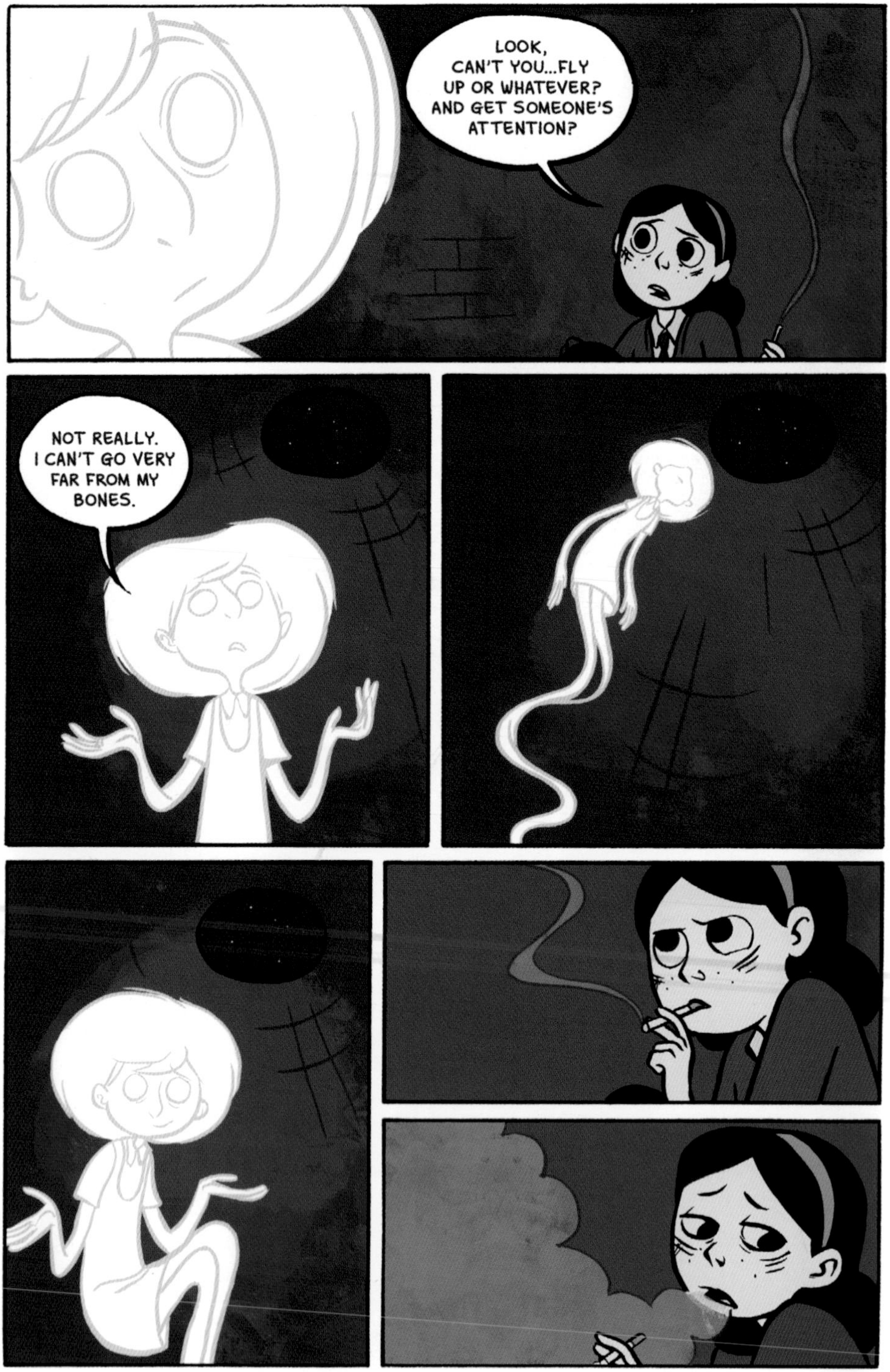
LOOK, CAN'T YOU...FLY UP OR WHATEVER? AND GET SOMEONE'S ATTENTION?
NOT REALLY. I CAN'T GO VERY FAR FROM MY BONES.

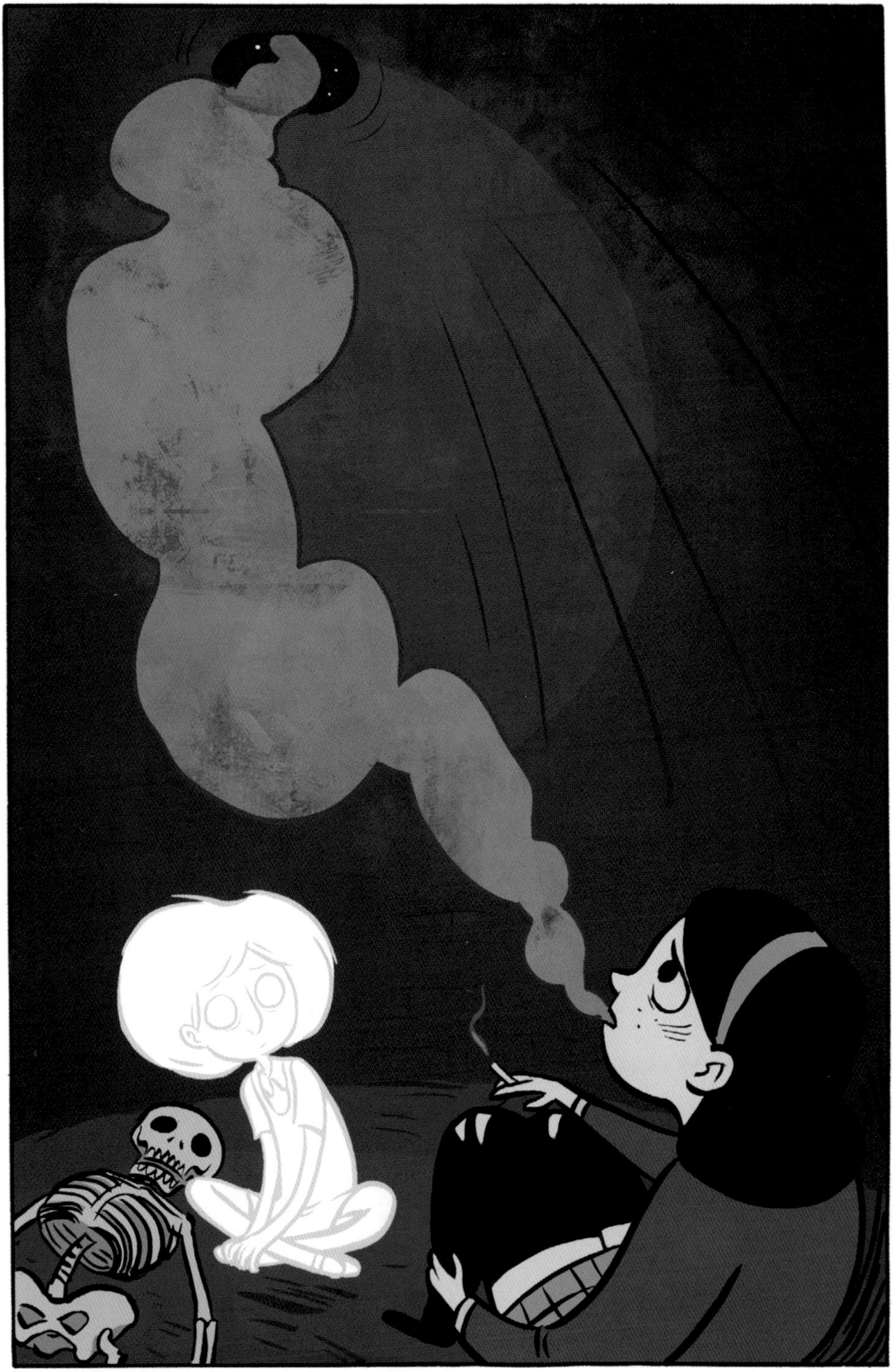

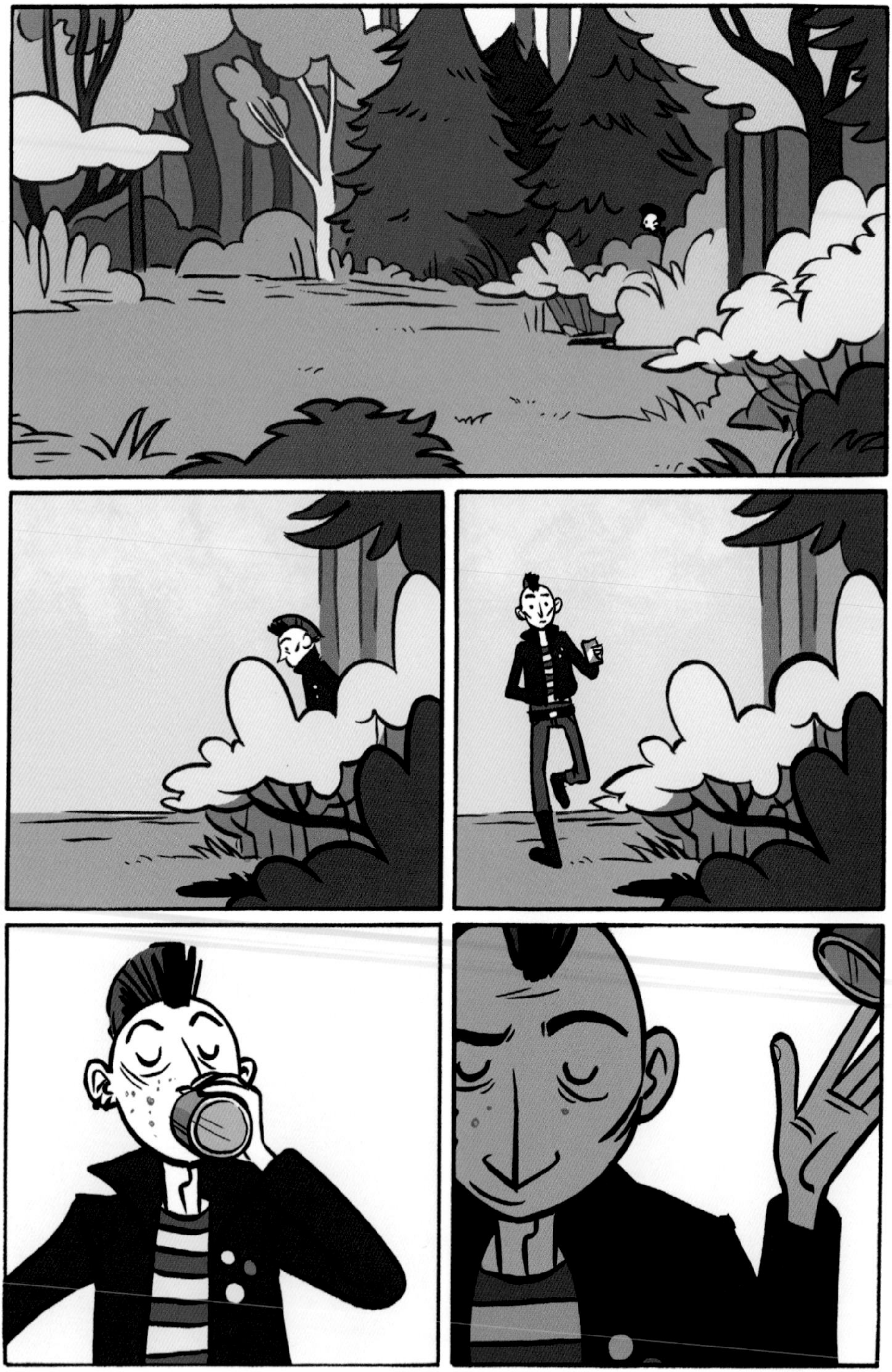

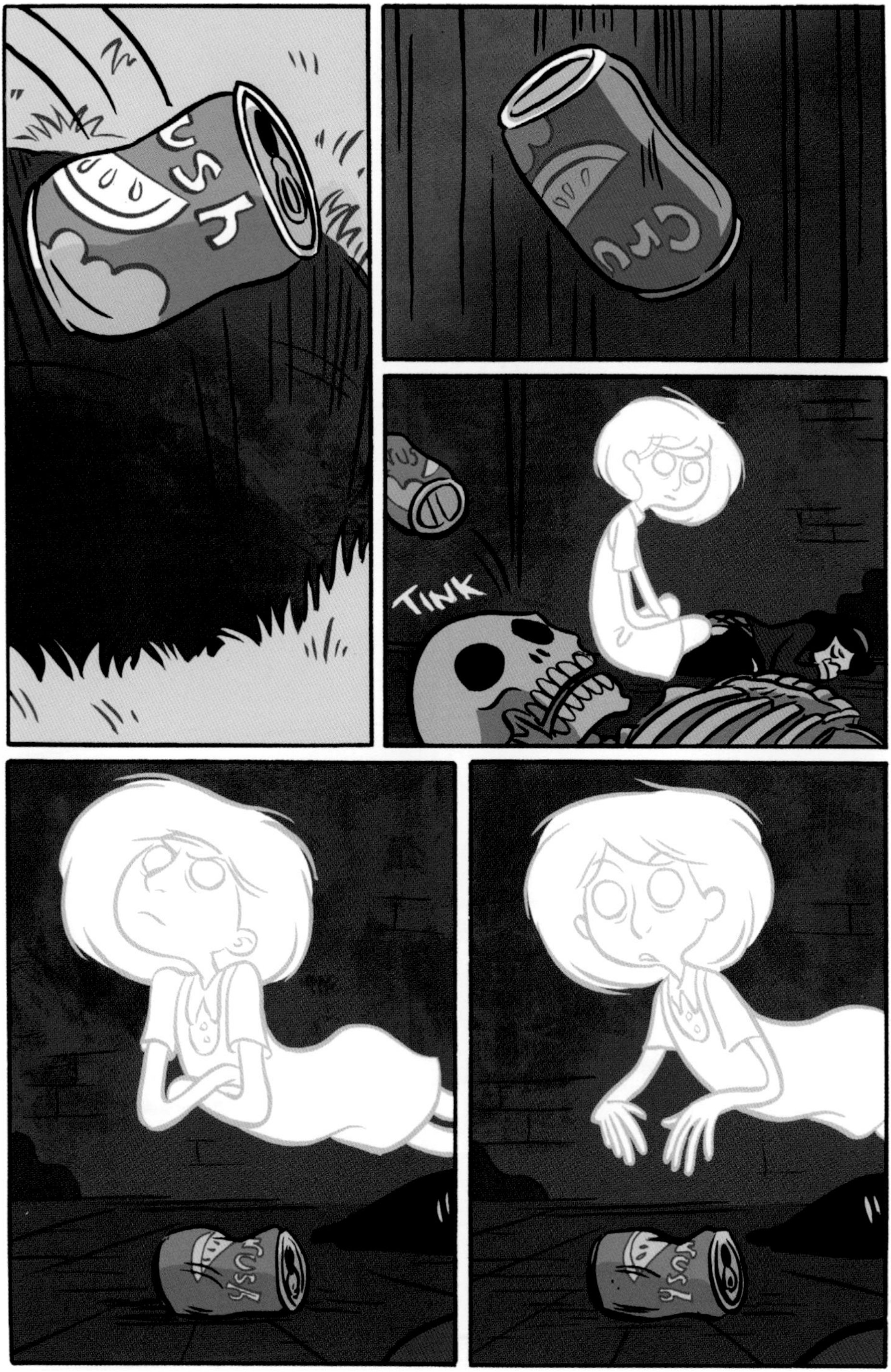
TINK

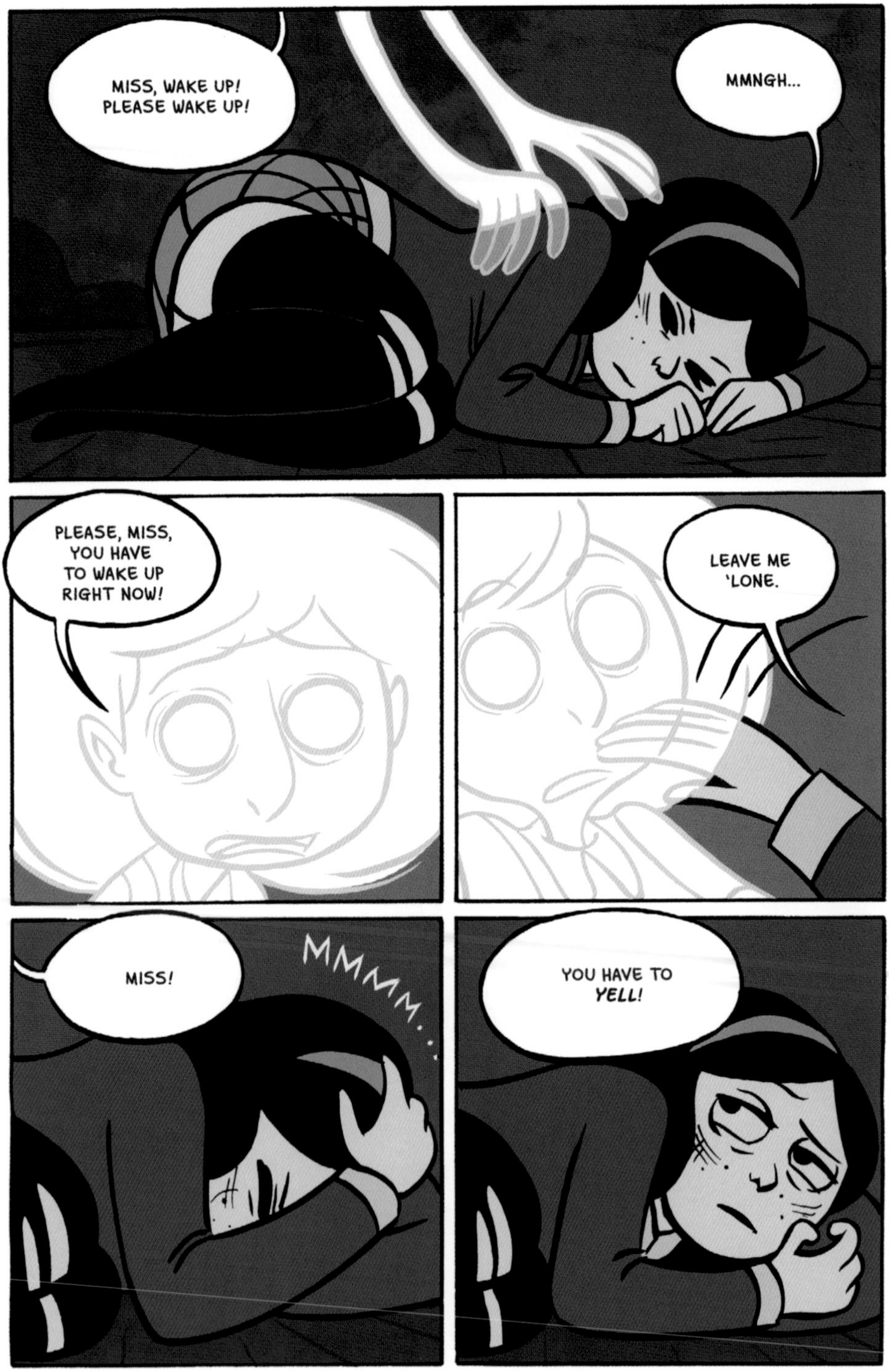
MISS, WAKE UP! PLEASE WAKE UP!
MMNGH...
PLEASE, MISS, YOU HAVE TO WAKE UP RIGHT NOW!
LEAVE ME 'LONE.
MISS!
MMMM...
YOU HAVE TO *YELL!*

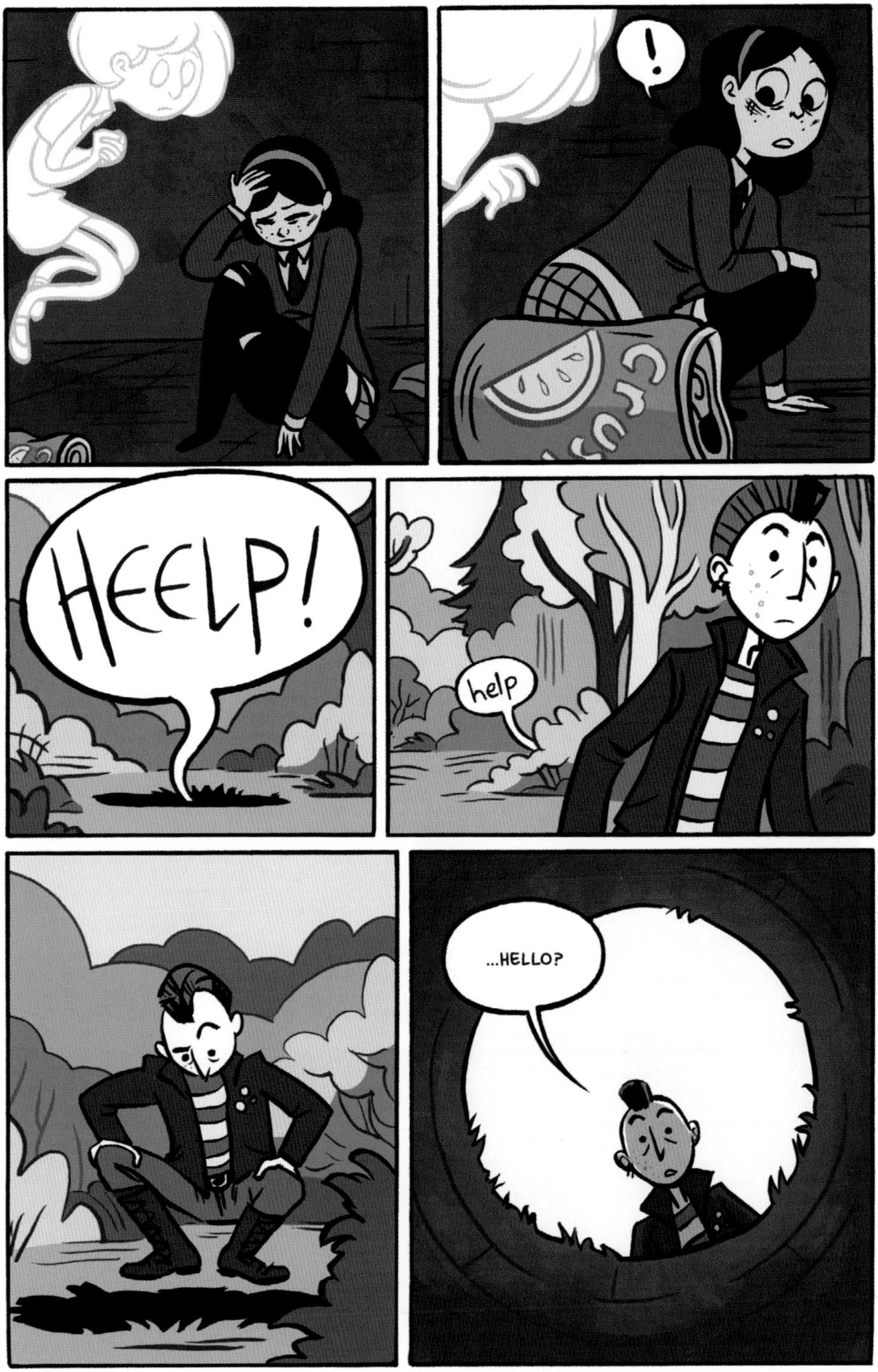
!
CRUSH
HEELP!
help
...HELLO?

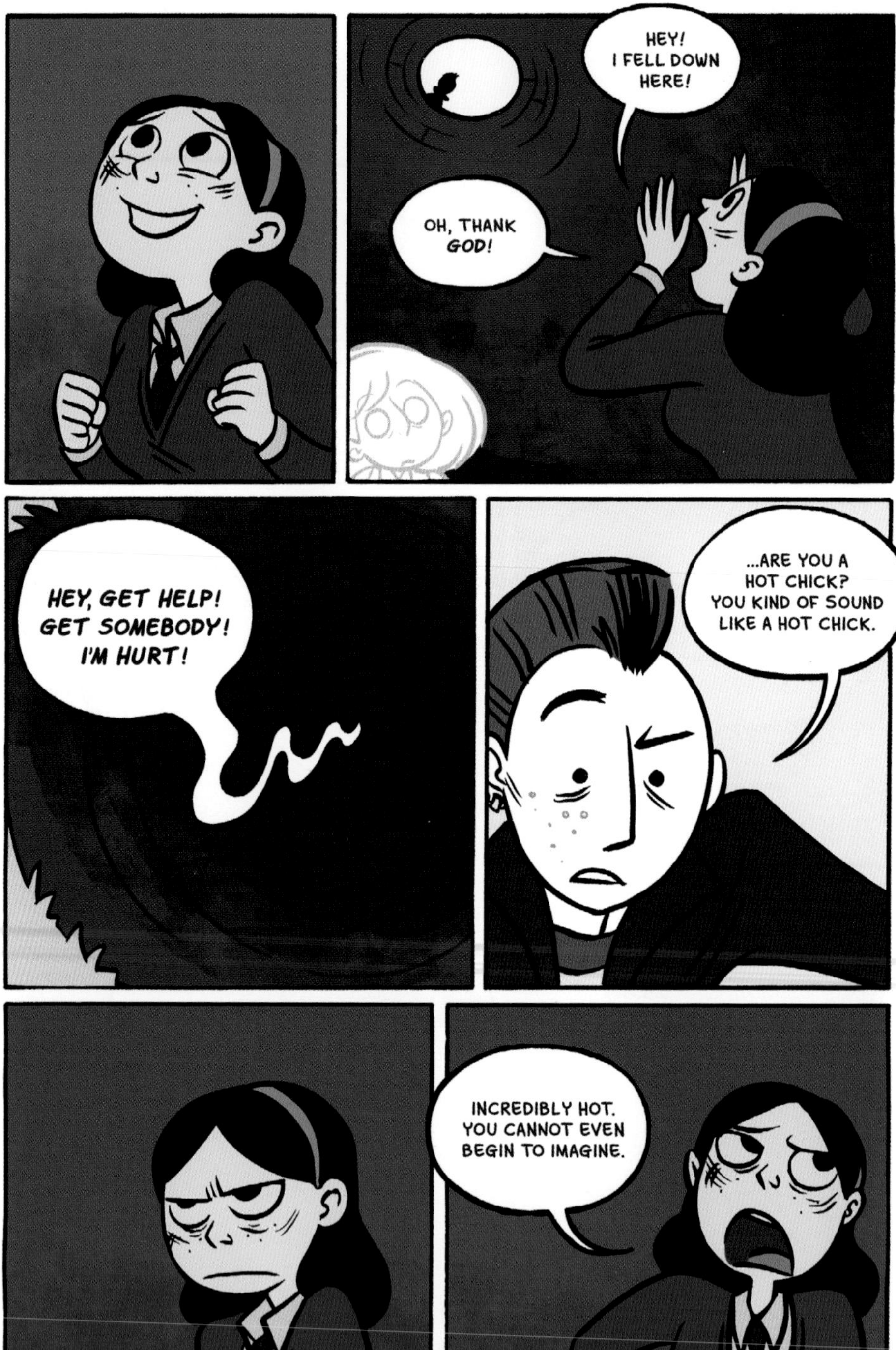
HEY! I FELL DOWN HERE!
OH, THANK GOD!
HEY, GET HELP! GET SOMEBODY! I'M HURT!
...ARE YOU A HOT CHICK? YOU KIND OF SOUND LIKE A HOT CHICK.
INCREDIBLY HOT. YOU CANNOT EVEN BEGIN TO IMAGINE.

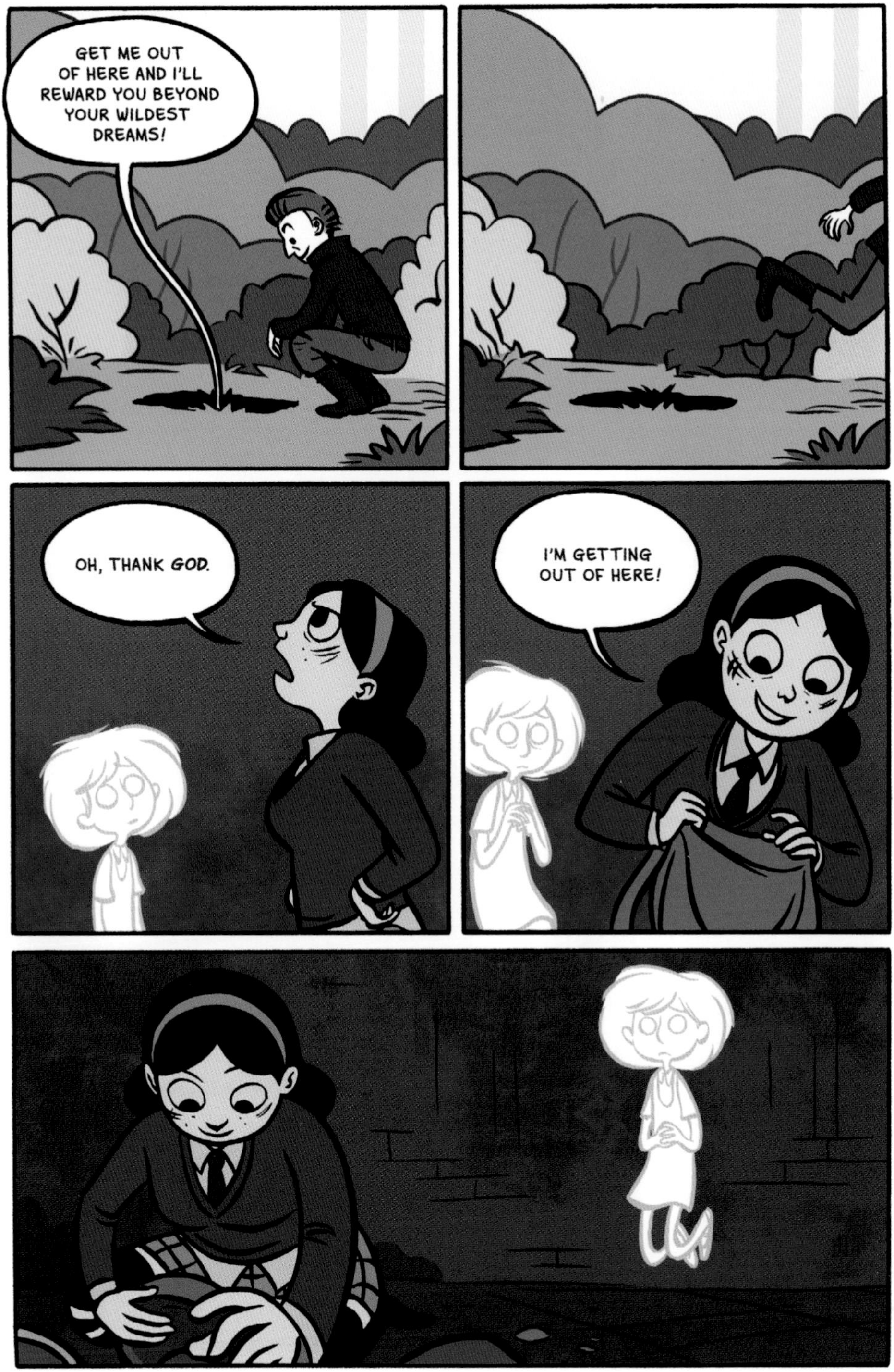
GET ME OUT OF HERE AND I'LL REWARD YOU BEYOND YOUR WILDEST DREAMS!
OH, THANK GOD.
I'M GETTING OUT OF HERE!

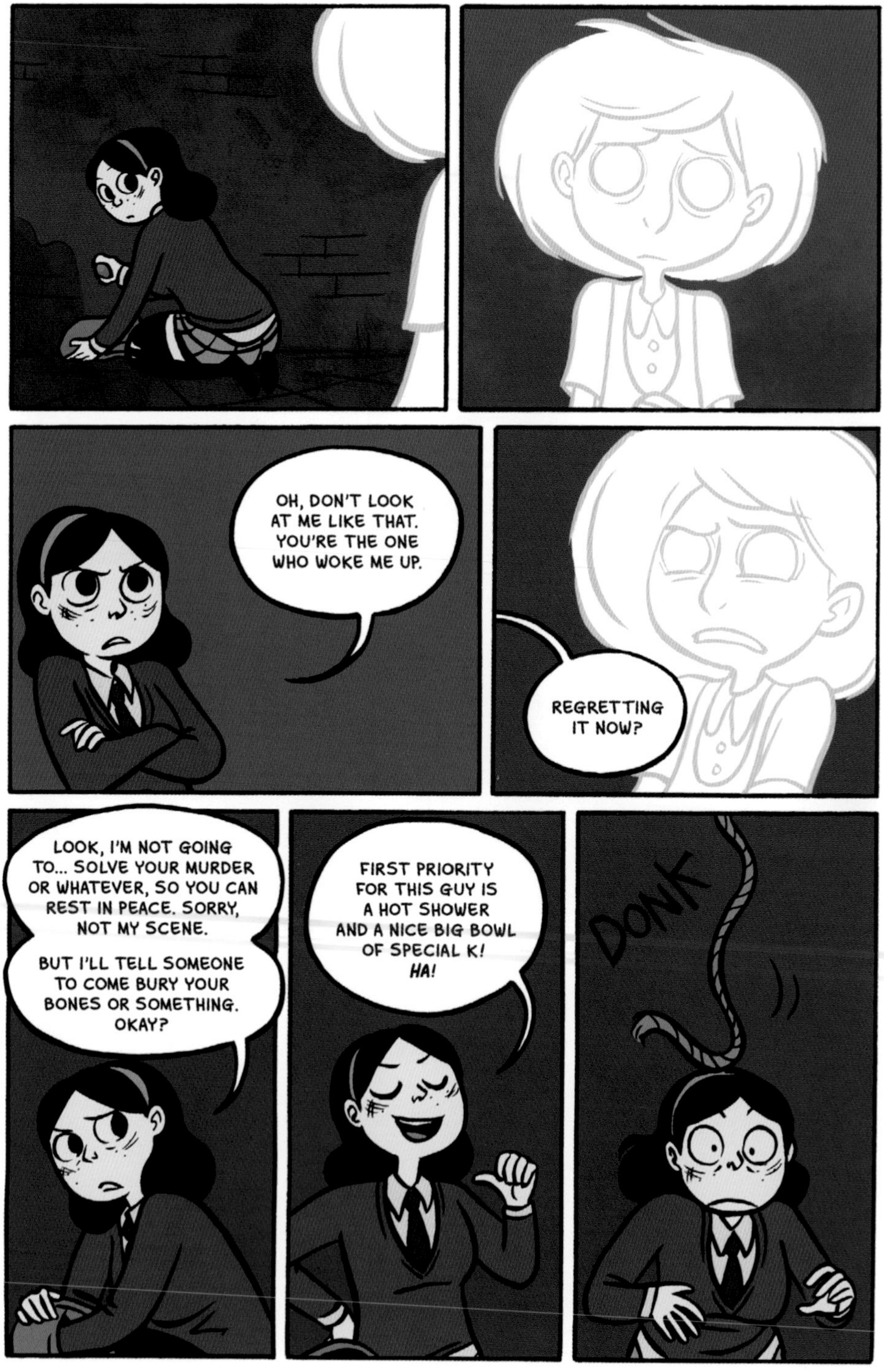

OH, DON'T LOOK AT ME LIKE THAT. YOU'RE THE ONE WHO WOKE ME UP.
REGRETTING IT NOW?
LOOK, I'M NOT GOING TO... SOLVE YOUR MURDER OR WHATEVER, SO YOU CAN REST IN PEACE. SORRY, NOT MY SCENE.
BUT I'LL TELL SOMEONE TO COME BURY YOUR BONES OR SOMETHING. OKAY?
FIRST PRIORITY FOR THIS GUY IS A HOT SHOWER AND A NICE BIG BOWL OF SPECIAL K! *HA!*
DONK

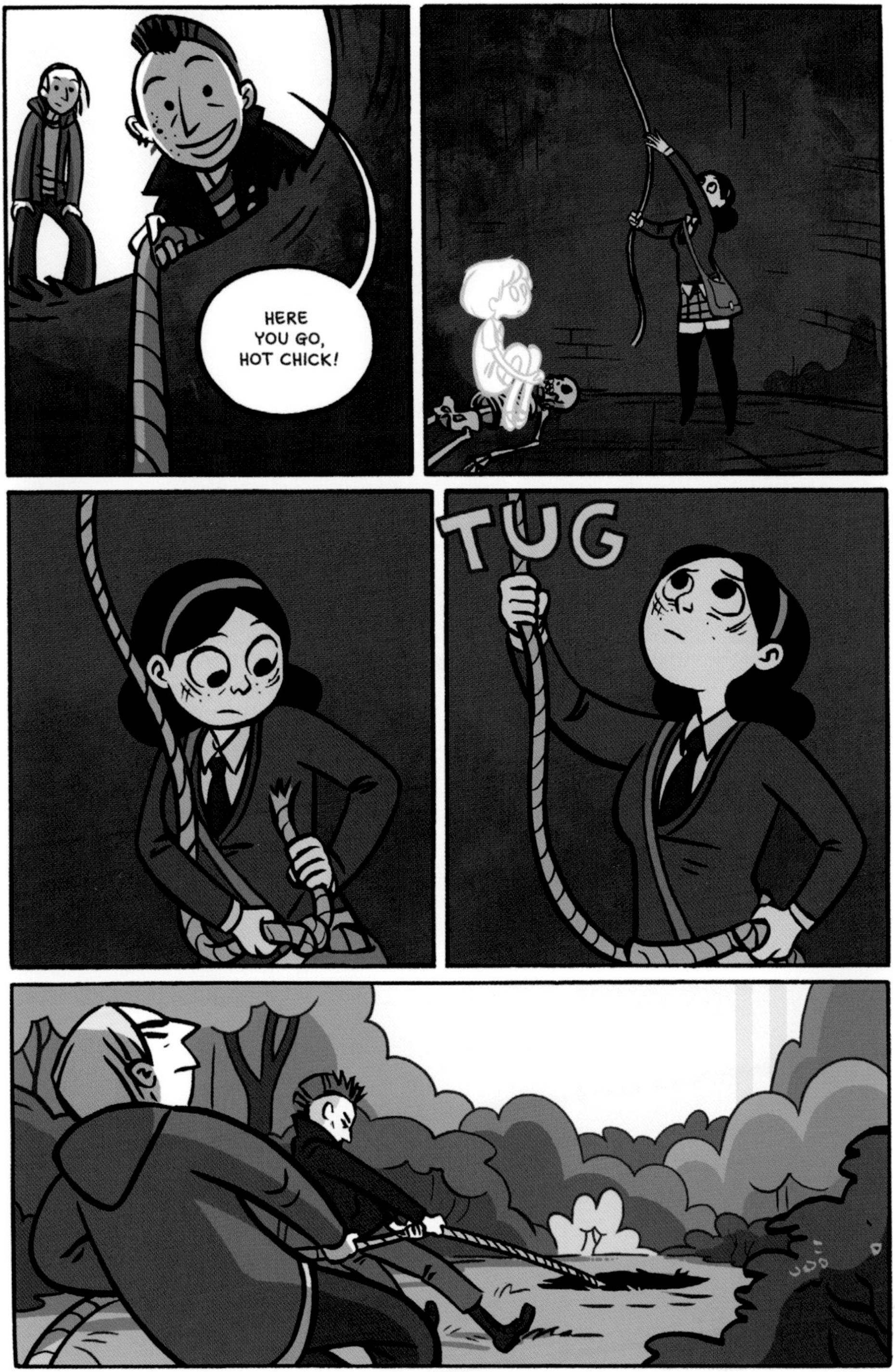
HERE YOU GO, HOT CHICK!
TUG

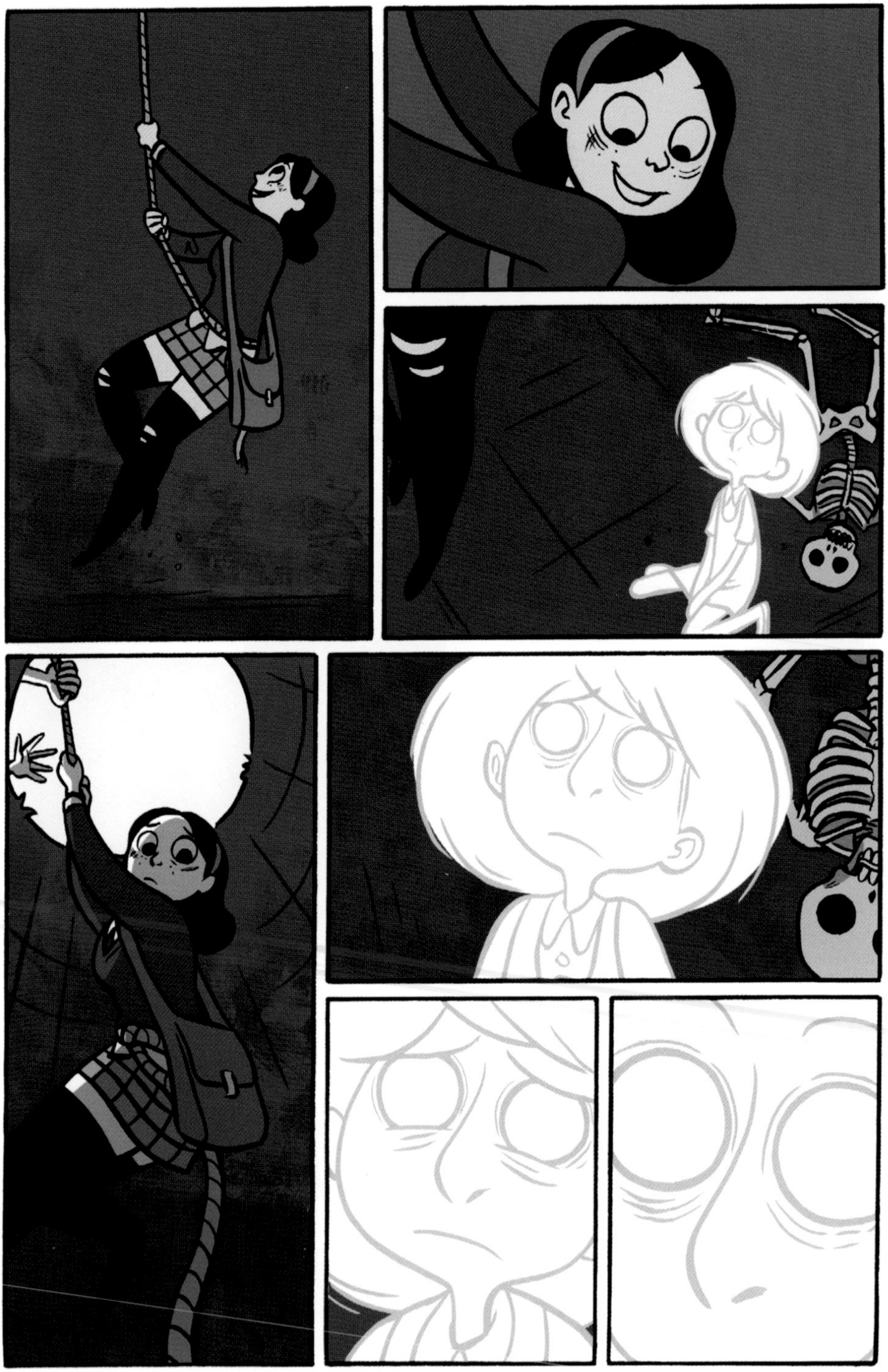

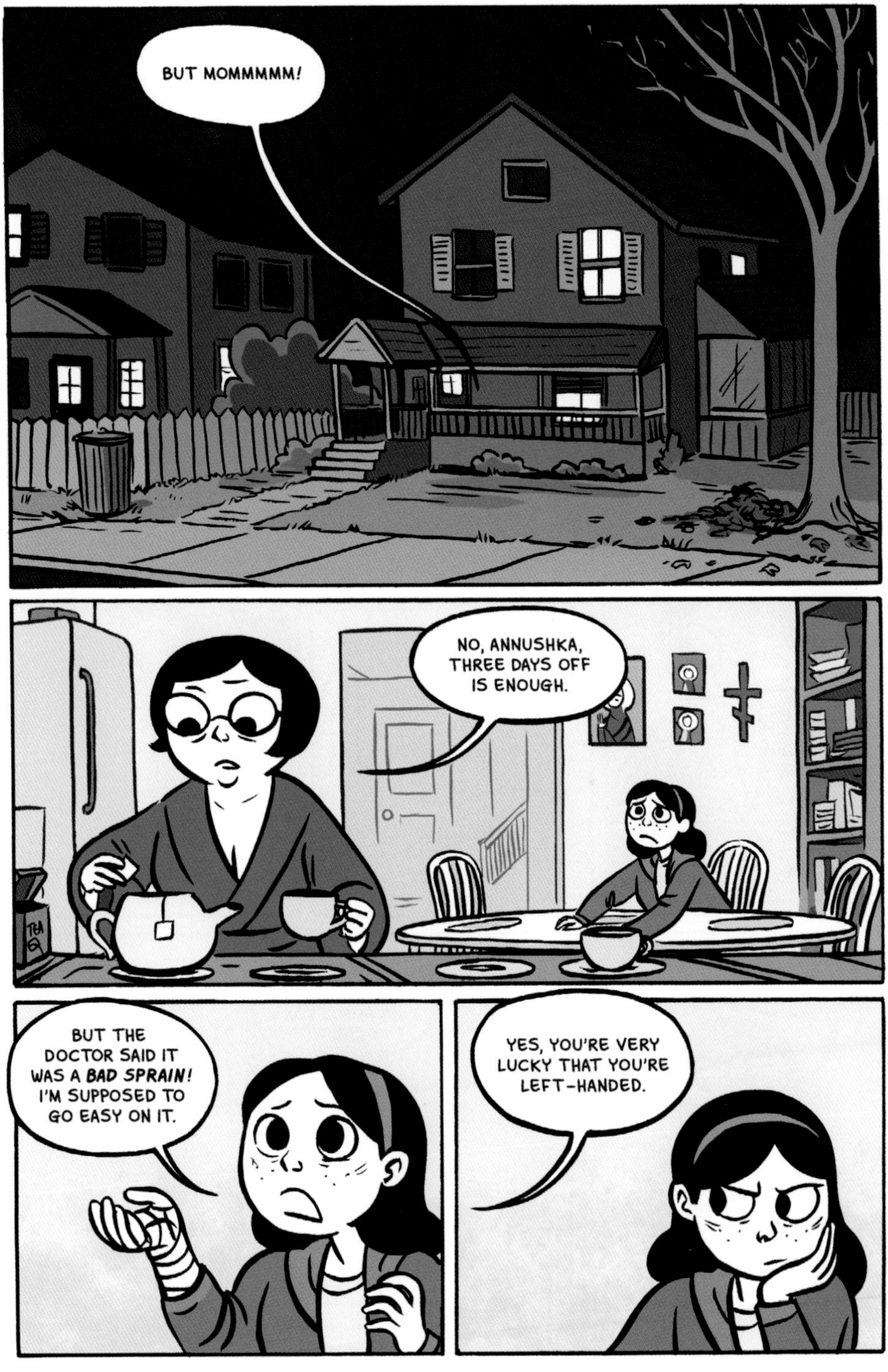
BUT MOMMMMM!
NO, ANNUSHKA, THREE DAYS OFF IS ENOUGH.
TEA
BUT THE DOCTOR SAID IT WAS A **BAD SPRAIN**! I'M SUPPOSED TO GO EASY ON IT.
YES, YOU'RE VERY LUCKY THAT YOU'RE LEFT-HANDED.

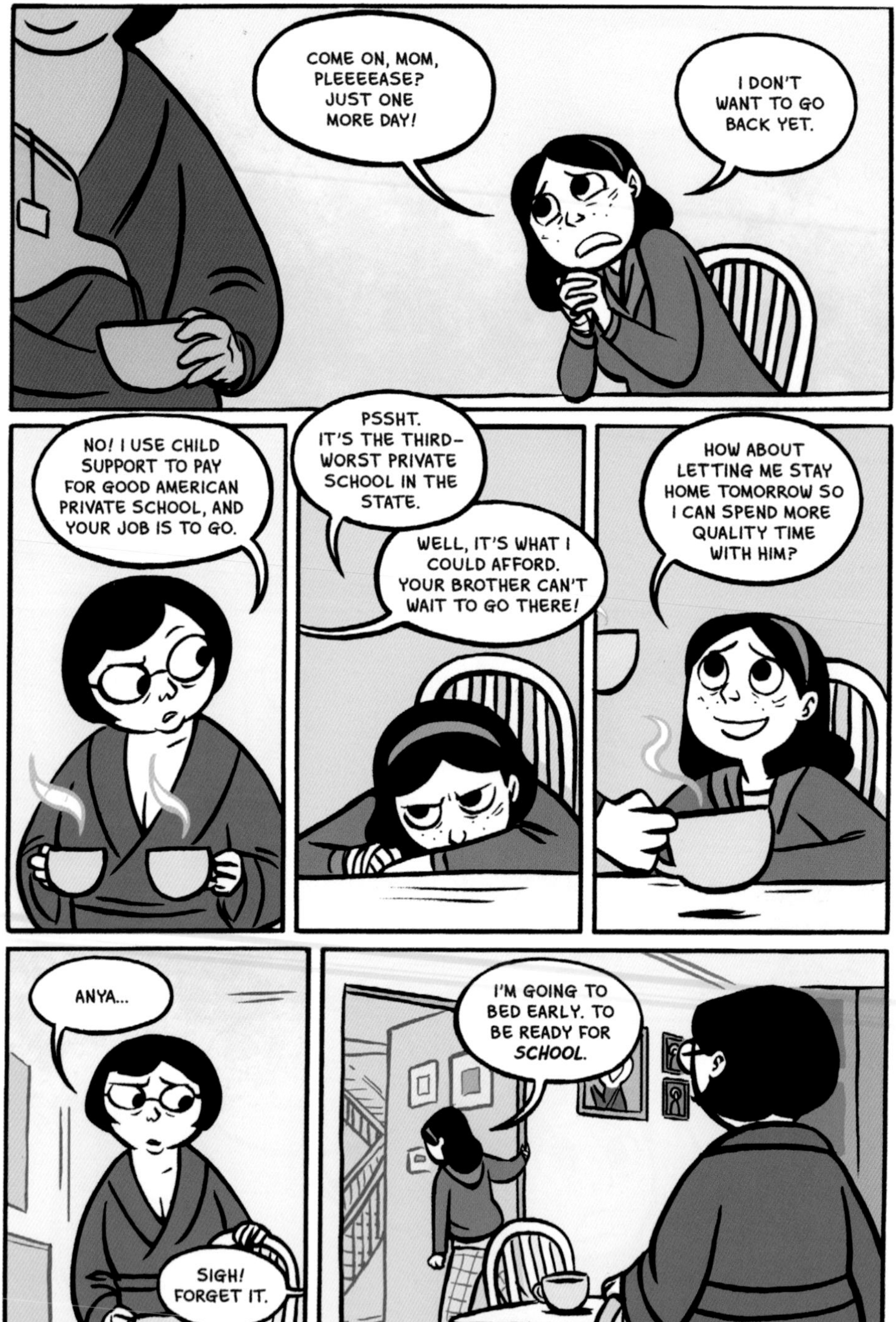
COME ON, MOM, PLEEEEASE? JUST ONE MORE DAY!
I DON'T WANT TO GO BACK YET.
NO! I USE CHILD SUPPORT TO PAY FOR GOOD AMERICAN PRIVATE SCHOOL, AND YOUR JOB IS TO GO.
PSSHT. IT'S THE THIRD-WORST PRIVATE SCHOOL IN THE STATE.
WELL, IT'S WHAT I COULD AFFORD. YOUR BROTHER CAN'T WAIT TO GO THERE!
HOW ABOUT LETTING ME STAY HOME TOMORROW SO I CAN SPEND MORE QUALITY TIME WITH HIM?
ANYA...
SIGH! FORGET IT.
I'M GOING TO BED EARLY. TO BE READY FOR *SCHOOL*.

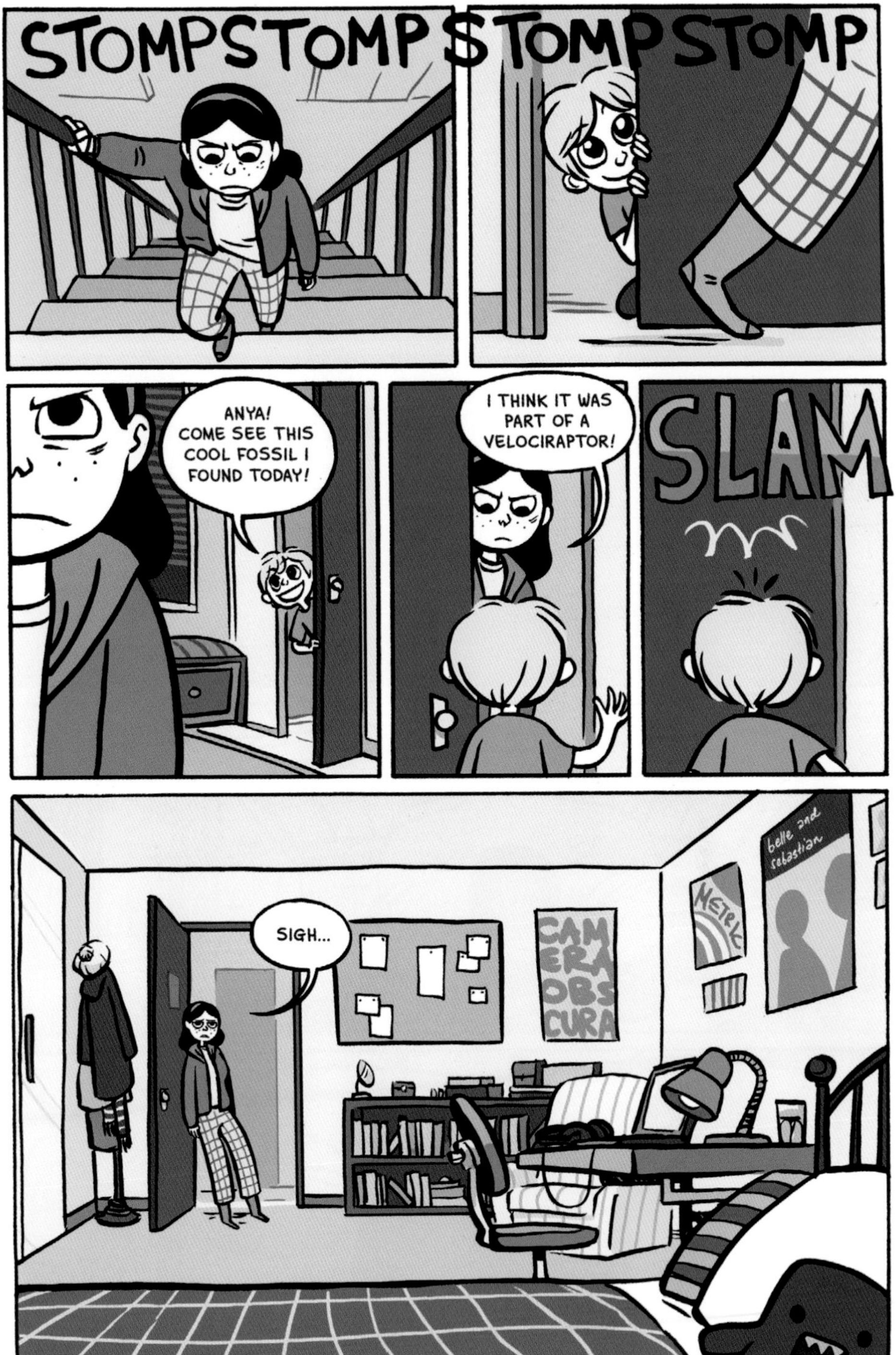
STOMPSTOMP STOMPSTOMP
ANYA!
COME SEE THIS
COOL FOSSIL I
FOUND TODAY!
I THINK IT WAS
PART OF A
VELOCIRAPTOR!
SLAM
SIGH...
CAMERA OBSCURA
belle and sebastian

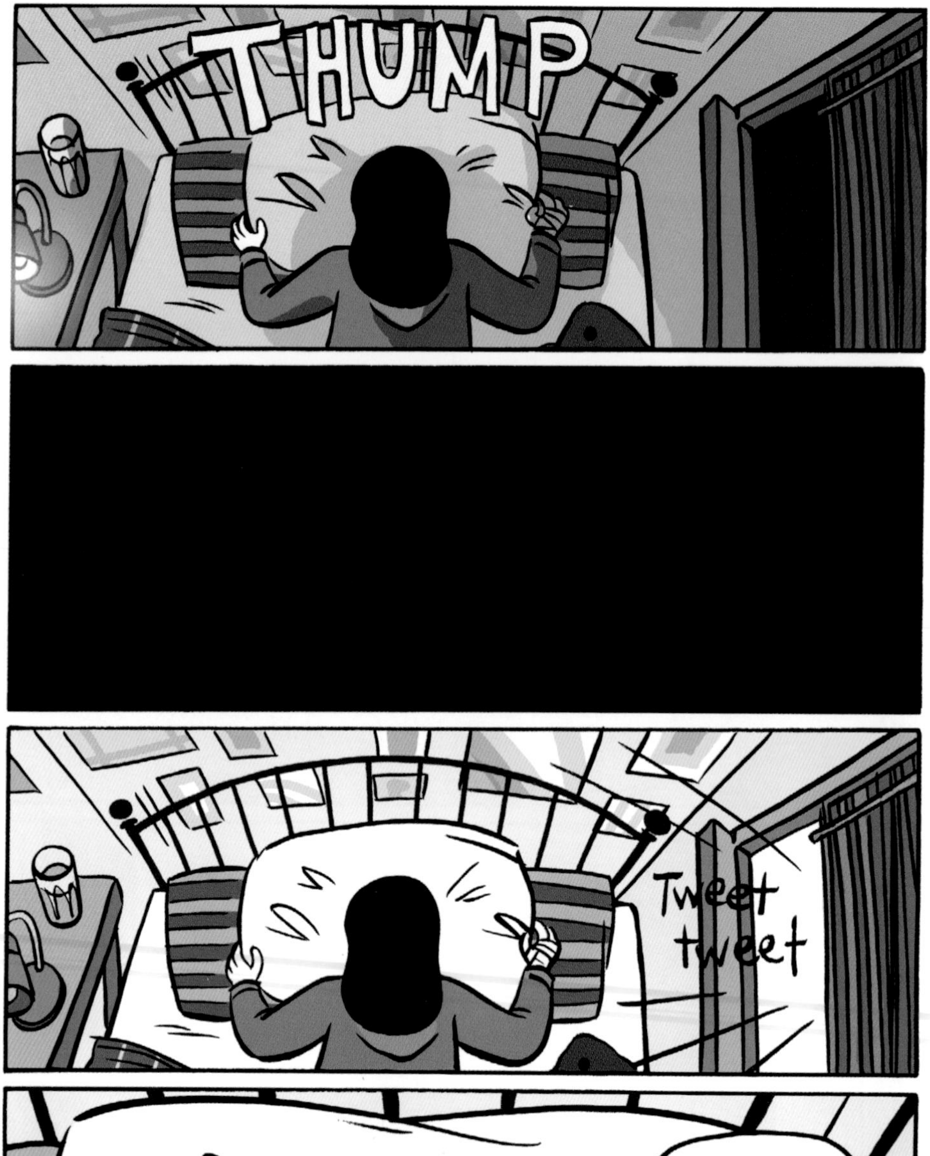
THUMP
Tweet
tweet
NUTS.

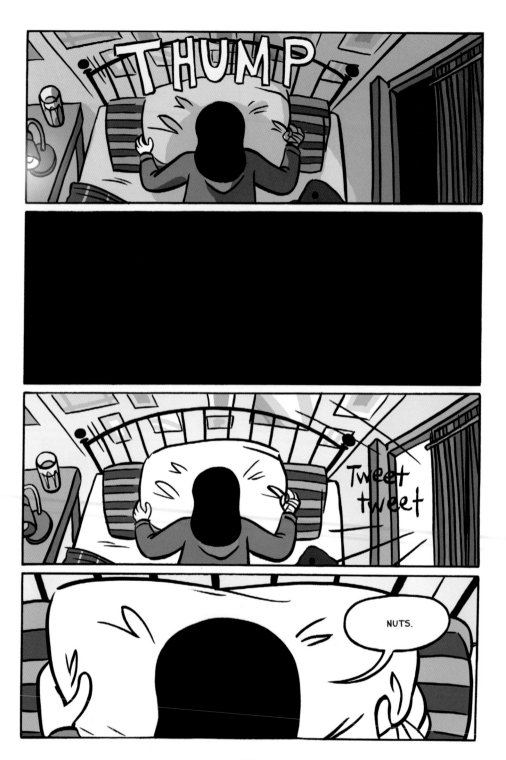

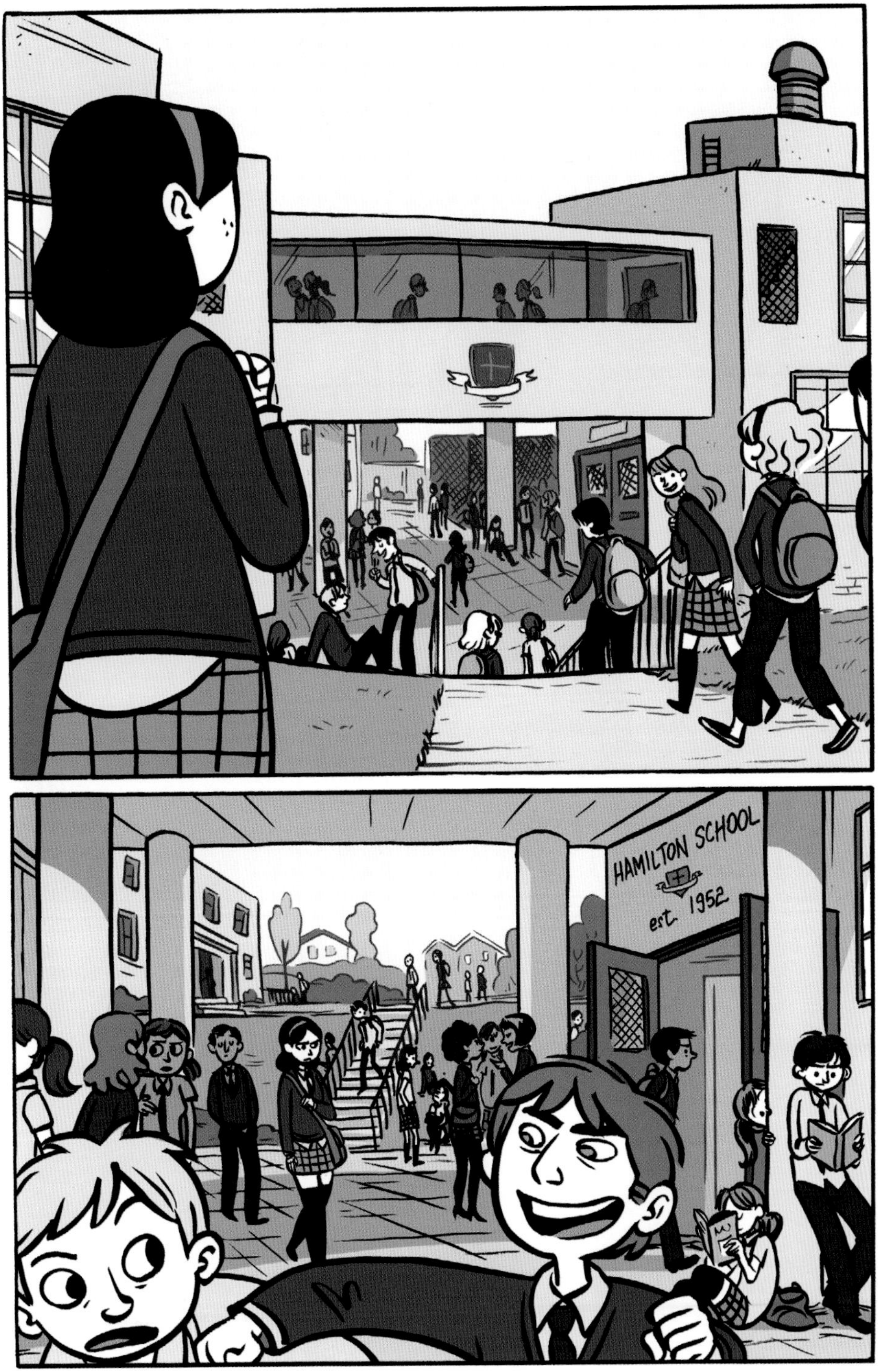
HAMILTON SCHOOL
est. 1952

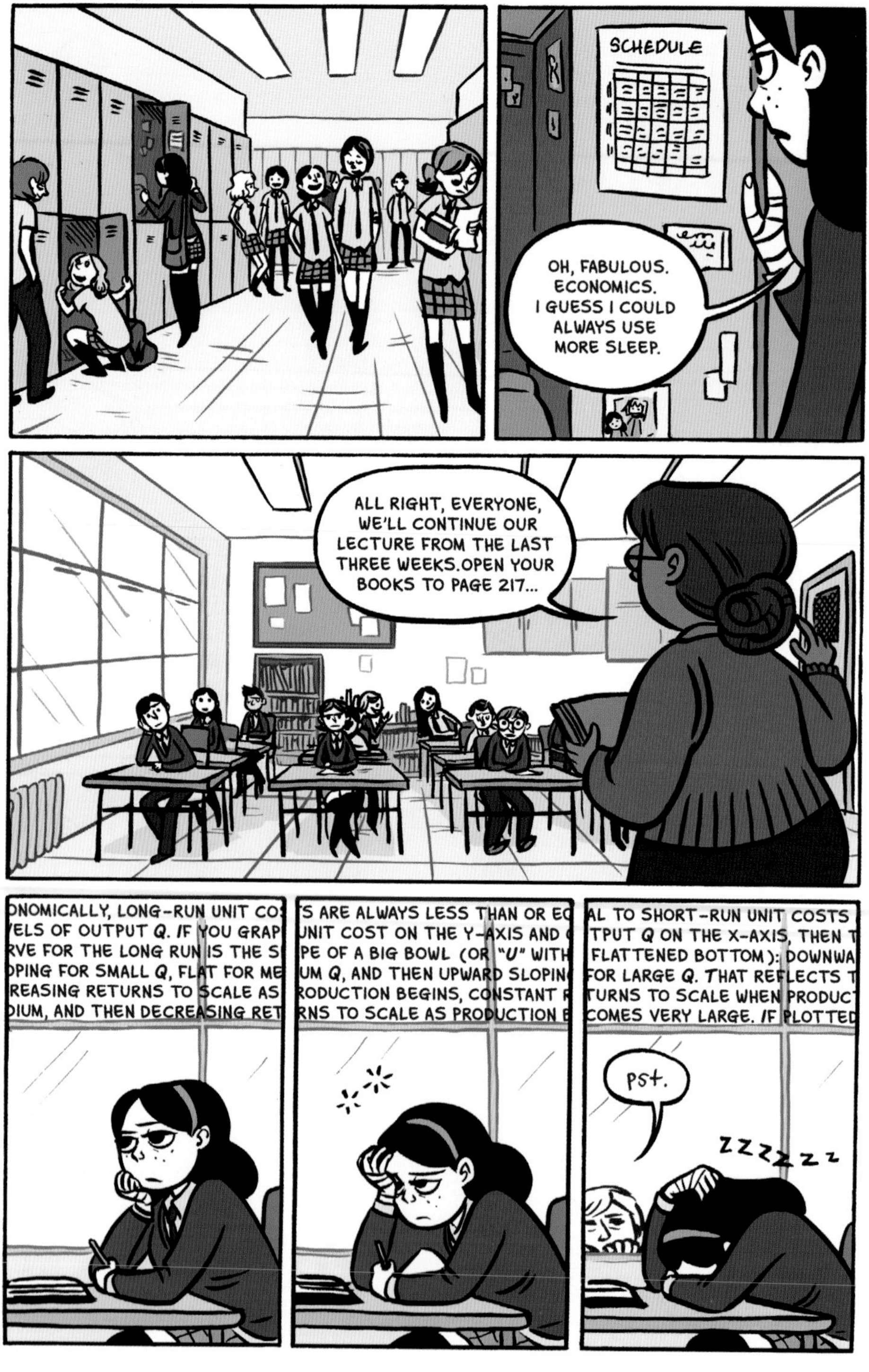
SCHEDULE
OH, FABULOUS. ECONOMICS. I GUESS I COULD ALWAYS USE MORE SLEEP.
ALL RIGHT, EVERYONE, WE'LL CONTINUE OUR LECTURE FROM THE LAST THREE WEEKS.OPEN YOUR BOOKS TO PAGE 217...
ONOMICALLY, LONG-RUN UNIT COS
VELS OF OUTPUT Q. IF YOU GRAP
RVE FOR THE LONG RUN IS THE S
OPING FOR SMALL Q, FLAT FOR ME
REASING RETURNS TO SCALE AS
DIUM, AND THEN DECREASING RET
S ARE ALWAYS LESS THAN OR EQ
UNIT COST ON THE Y-AXIS AND
PE OF A BIG BOWL (OR "U" WITH
UM Q, AND THEN UPWARD SLOPING
RODUCTION BEGINS, CONSTANT R
RNS TO SCALE AS PRODUCTION B
AL TO SHORT-RUN UNIT COSTS
TPUT Q ON THE X-AXIS, THEN T
FLATTENED BOTTOM): DOWNWA
FOR LARGE Q. THAT REFLECTS T
TURNS TO SCALE WHEN PRODUCT
COMES VERY LARGE. IF PLOTTED
pst.
ZZZZZZ

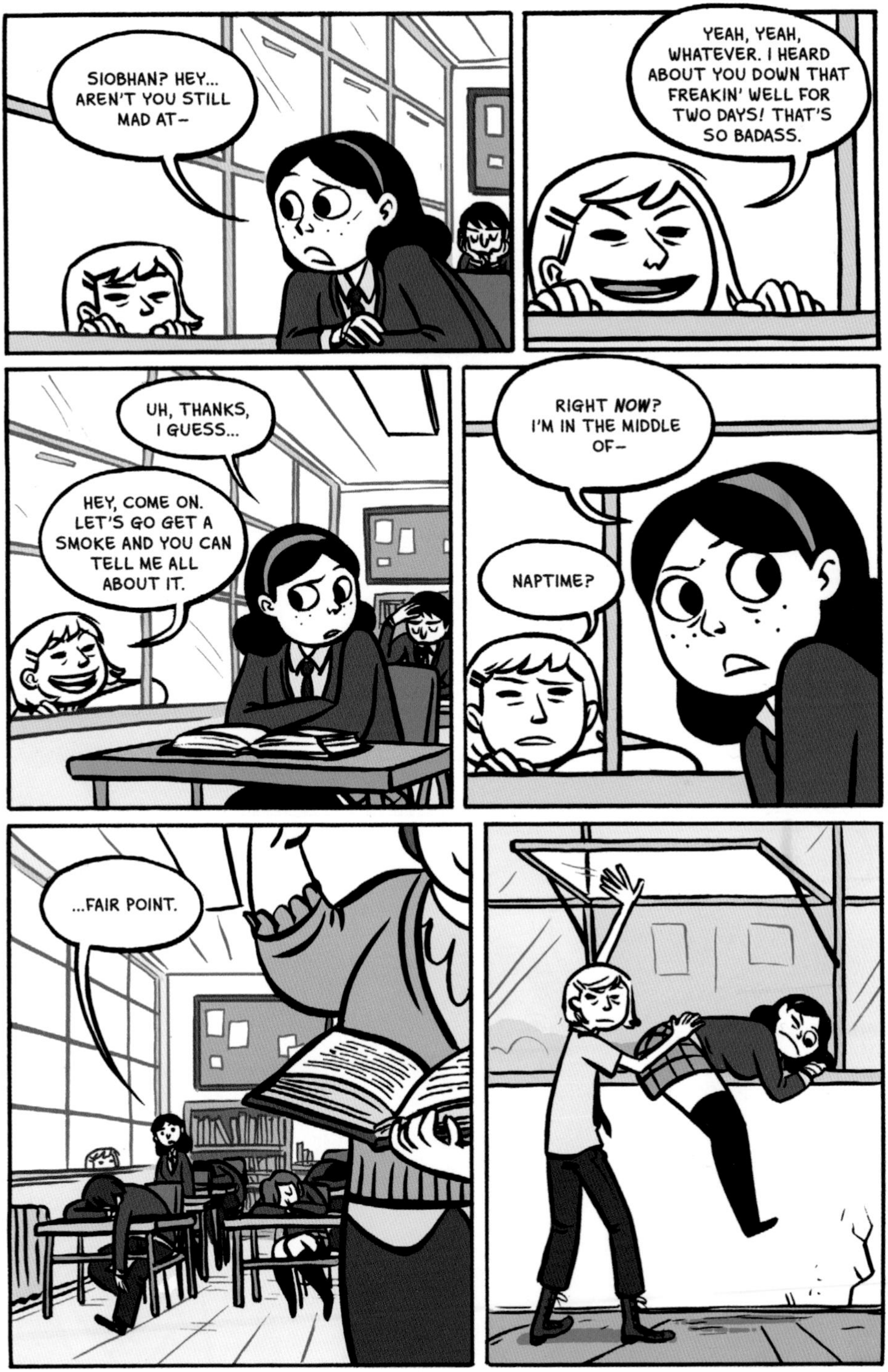
SIOBHAN? HEY... AREN'T YOU STILL MAD AT—
YEAH, YEAH, WHATEVER. I HEARD ABOUT YOU DOWN THAT FREAKIN' WELL FOR TWO DAYS! THAT'S SO BADASS.
UH, THANKS, I GUESS...
HEY, COME ON. LET'S GO GET A SMOKE AND YOU CAN TELL ME ALL ABOUT IT.
RIGHT *NOW*? I'M IN THE MIDDLE OF—
NAPTIME?
...FAIR POINT.

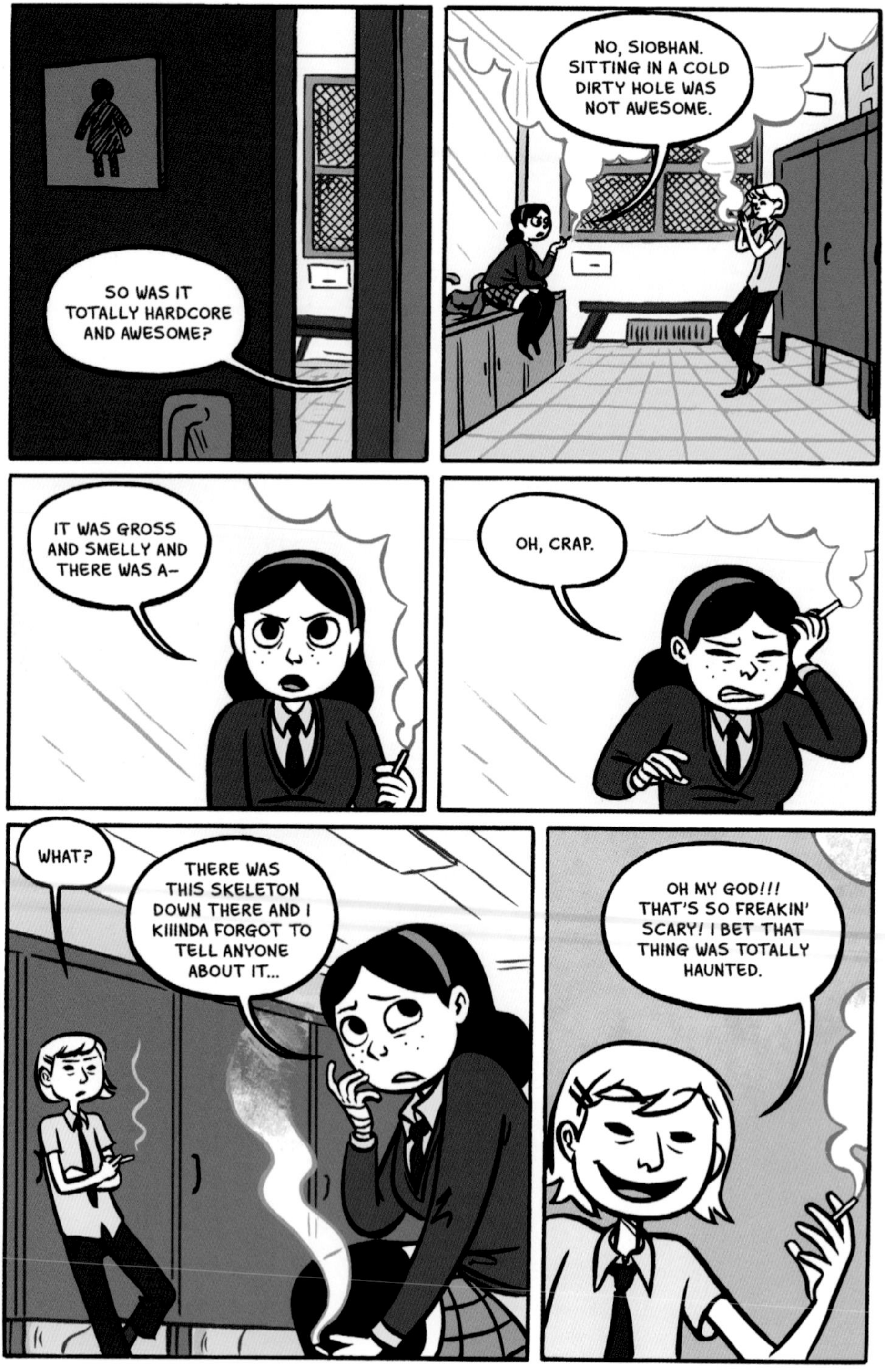
SO WAS IT TOTALLY HARDCORE AND AWESOME?
NO, SIOBHAN. SITTING IN A COLD DIRTY HOLE WAS NOT AWESOME.
IT WAS GROSS AND SMELLY AND THERE WAS A–
OH, CRAP.
WHAT?
THERE WAS THIS SKELETON DOWN THERE AND I KIIINDA FORGOT TO TELL ANYONE ABOUT IT...
OH MY GOD!!! THAT'S SO FREAKIN' SCARY! I BET THAT THING WAS TOTALLY HAUNTED.

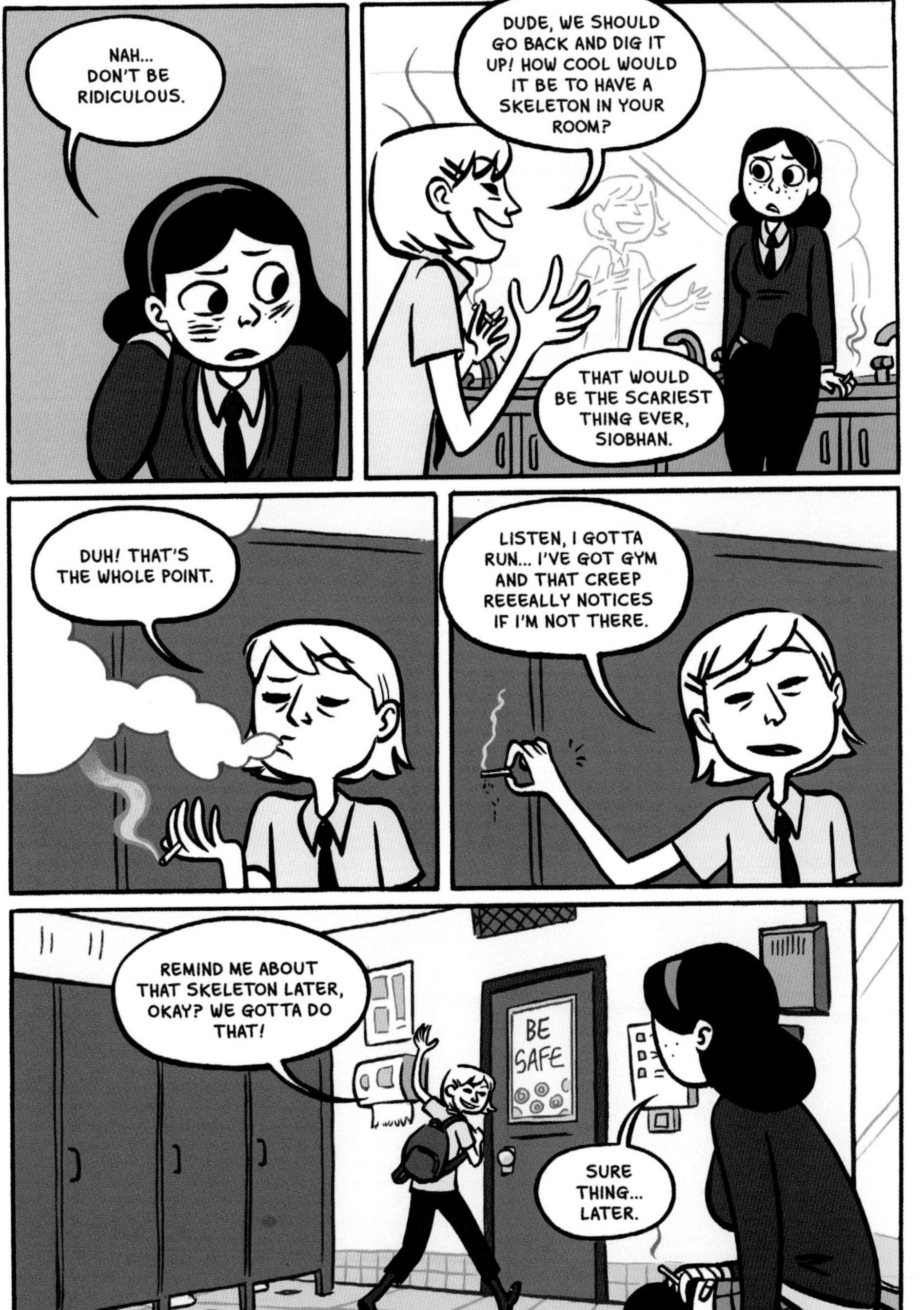
NAH... DON'T BE RIDICULOUS.
DUDE, WE SHOULD GO BACK AND DIG IT UP! HOW COOL WOULD IT BE TO HAVE A SKELETON IN YOUR ROOM?
THAT WOULD BE THE SCARIEST THING EVER, SIOBHAN.
DUH! THAT'S THE WHOLE POINT.
LISTEN, I GOTTA RUN... I'VE GOT GYM AND THAT CREEP REEEALLY NOTICES IF I'M NOT THERE.
REMIND ME ABOUT THAT SKELETON LATER, OKAY? WE GOTTA DO THAT!
BE SAFE
SURE THING... LATER.

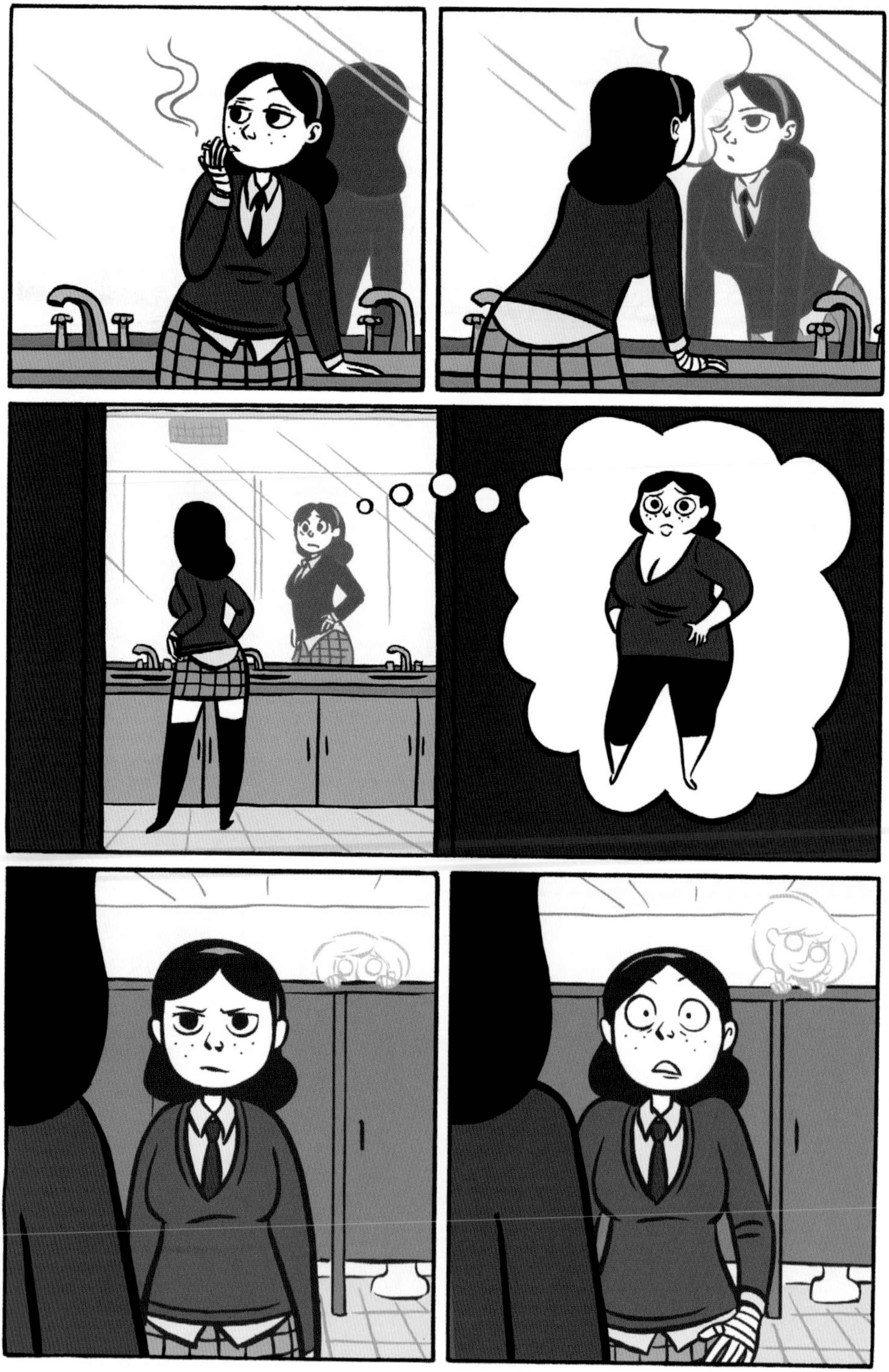

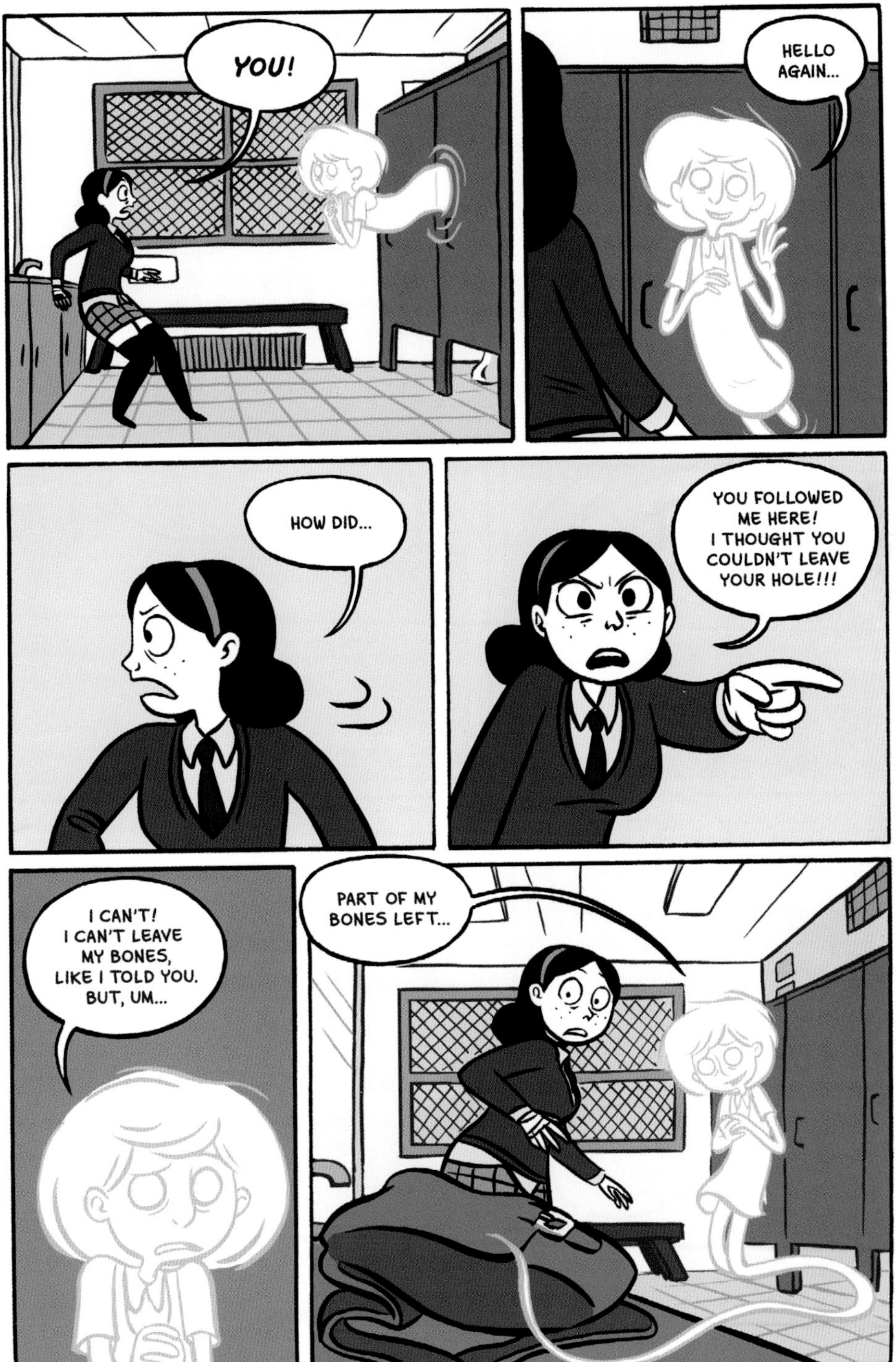
YOU!
HELLO AGAIN...
HOW DID...
YOU FOLLOWED ME HERE! I THOUGHT YOU COULDN'T LEAVE YOUR HOLE!!!
I CAN'T! I CAN'T LEAVE MY BONES, LIKE I TOLD YOU. BUT, UM...
PART OF MY BONES LEFT...

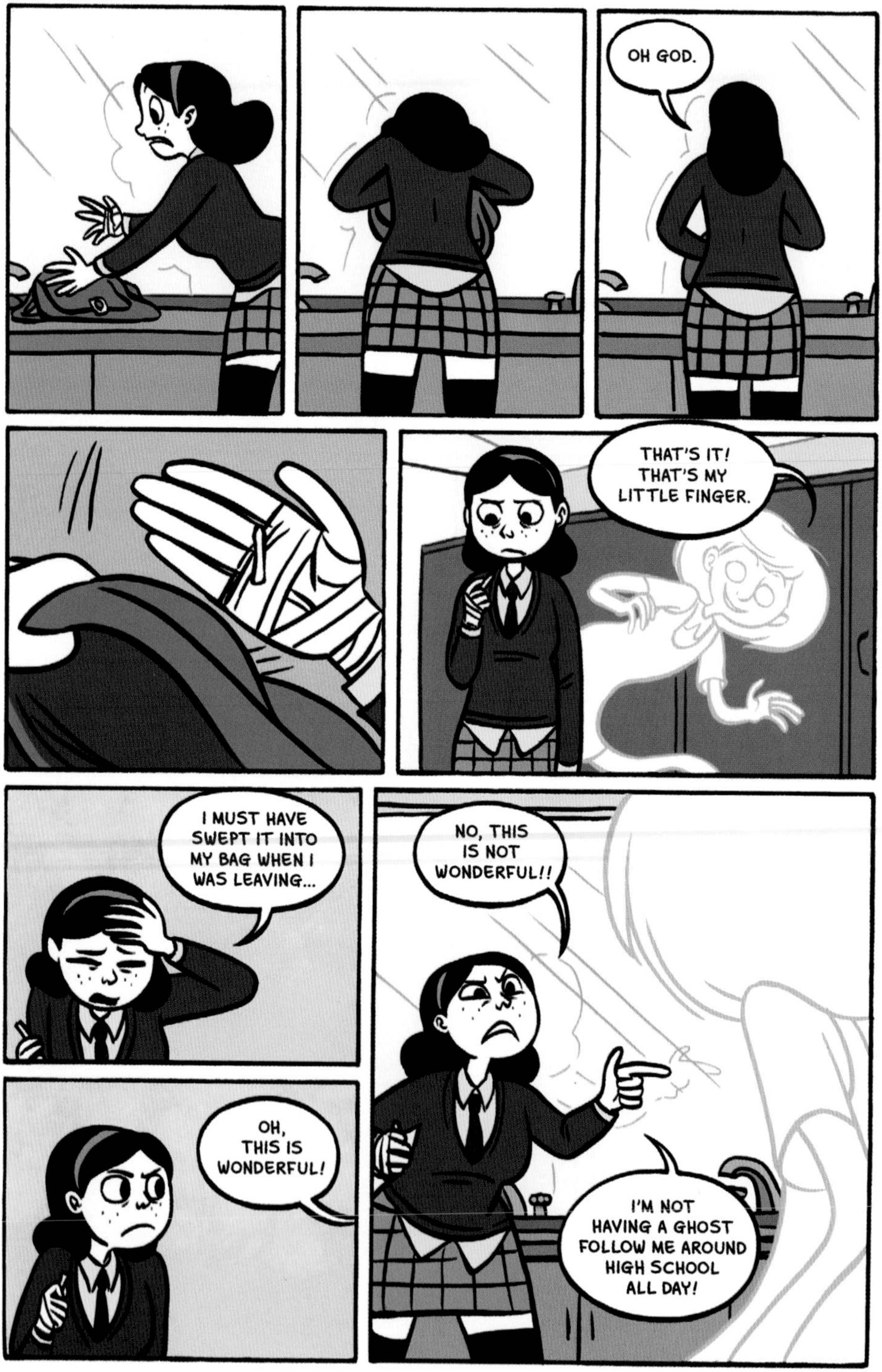
OH GOD.
THAT'S IT! THAT'S MY LITTLE FINGER.
I MUST HAVE SWEPT IT INTO MY BAG WHEN I WAS LEAVING...
OH, THIS IS WONDERFUL!
NO, THIS IS NOT WONDERFUL!!
I'M NOT HAVING A GHOST FOLLOW ME AROUND HIGH SCHOOL ALL DAY!

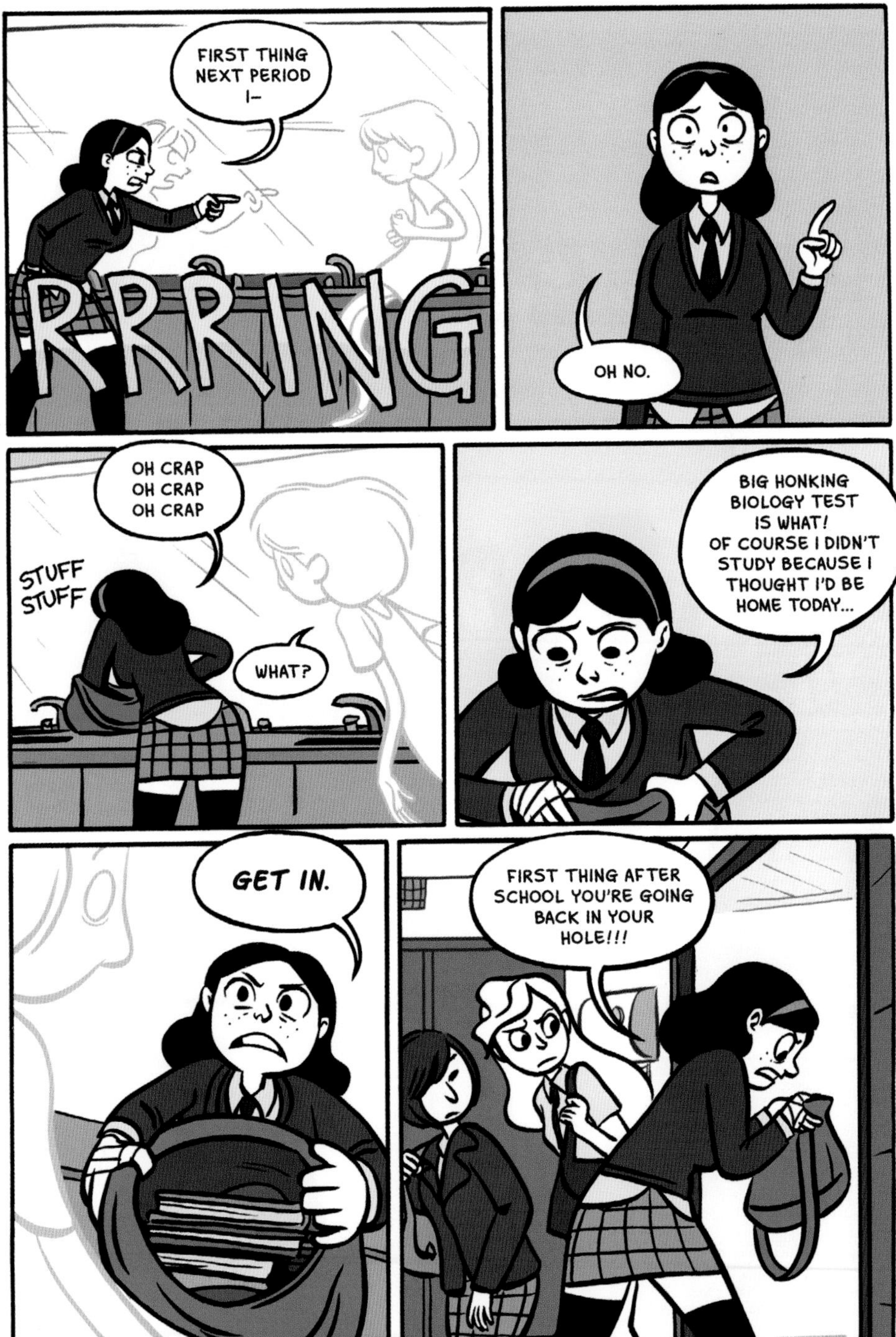
FIRST THING
NEXT PERIOD
I–
RRRING
OH NO.
OH CRAP
OH CRAP
OH CRAP
STUFF
STUFF
WHAT?
BIG HONKING BIOLOGY TEST IS WHAT! OF COURSE I DIDN'T STUDY BECAUSE I THOUGHT I'D BE HOME TODAY...
GET IN.
FIRST THING AFTER SCHOOL YOU'RE GOING BACK IN YOUR HOLE!!!

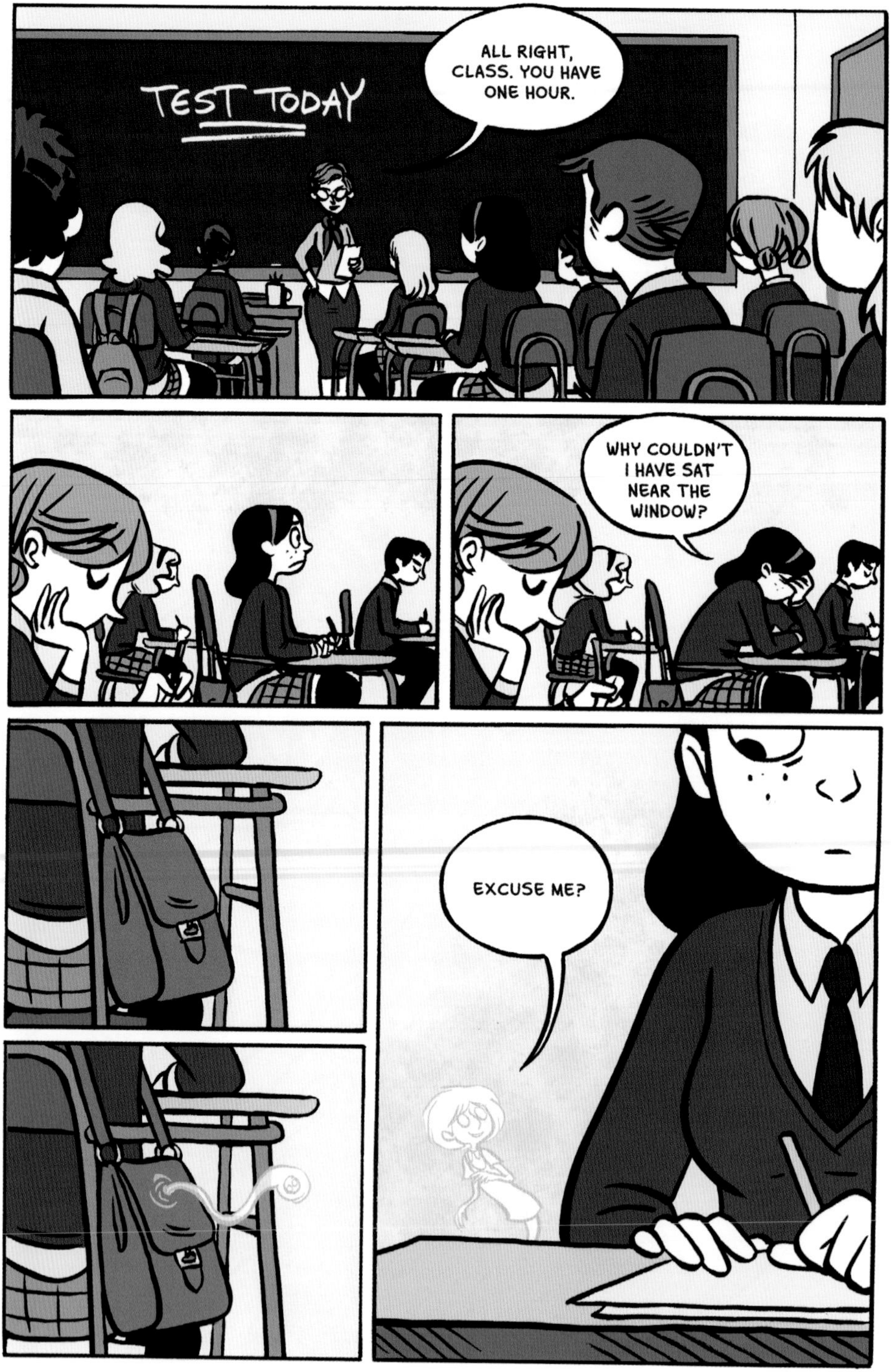
TEST TODAY
ALL RIGHT, CLASS. YOU HAVE ONE HOUR.
WHY COULDN'T I HAVE SAT NEAR THE WINDOW?
EXCUSE ME?

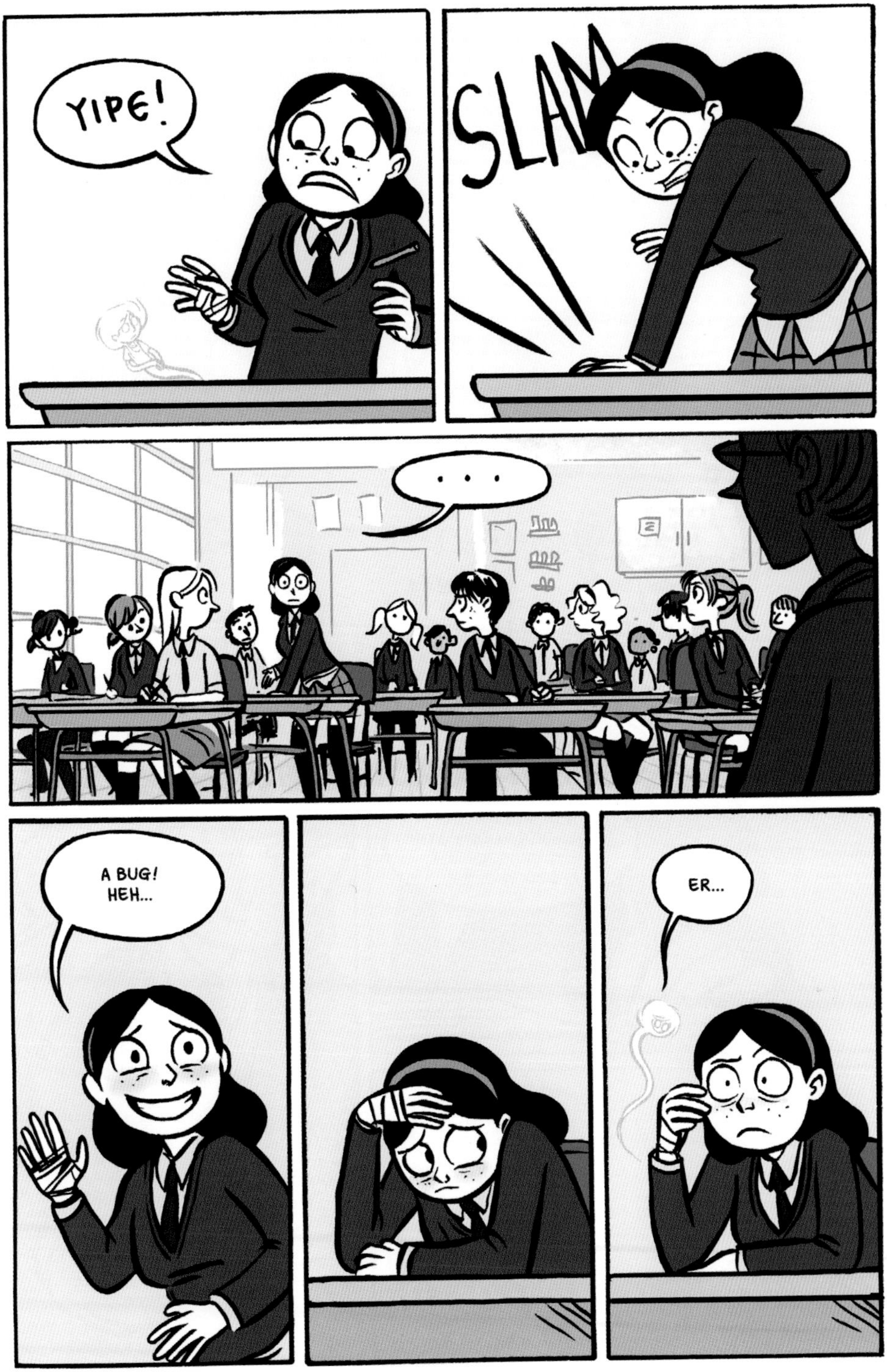
YIPE!
SLAM
. . .
A BUG! HEH...
ER...

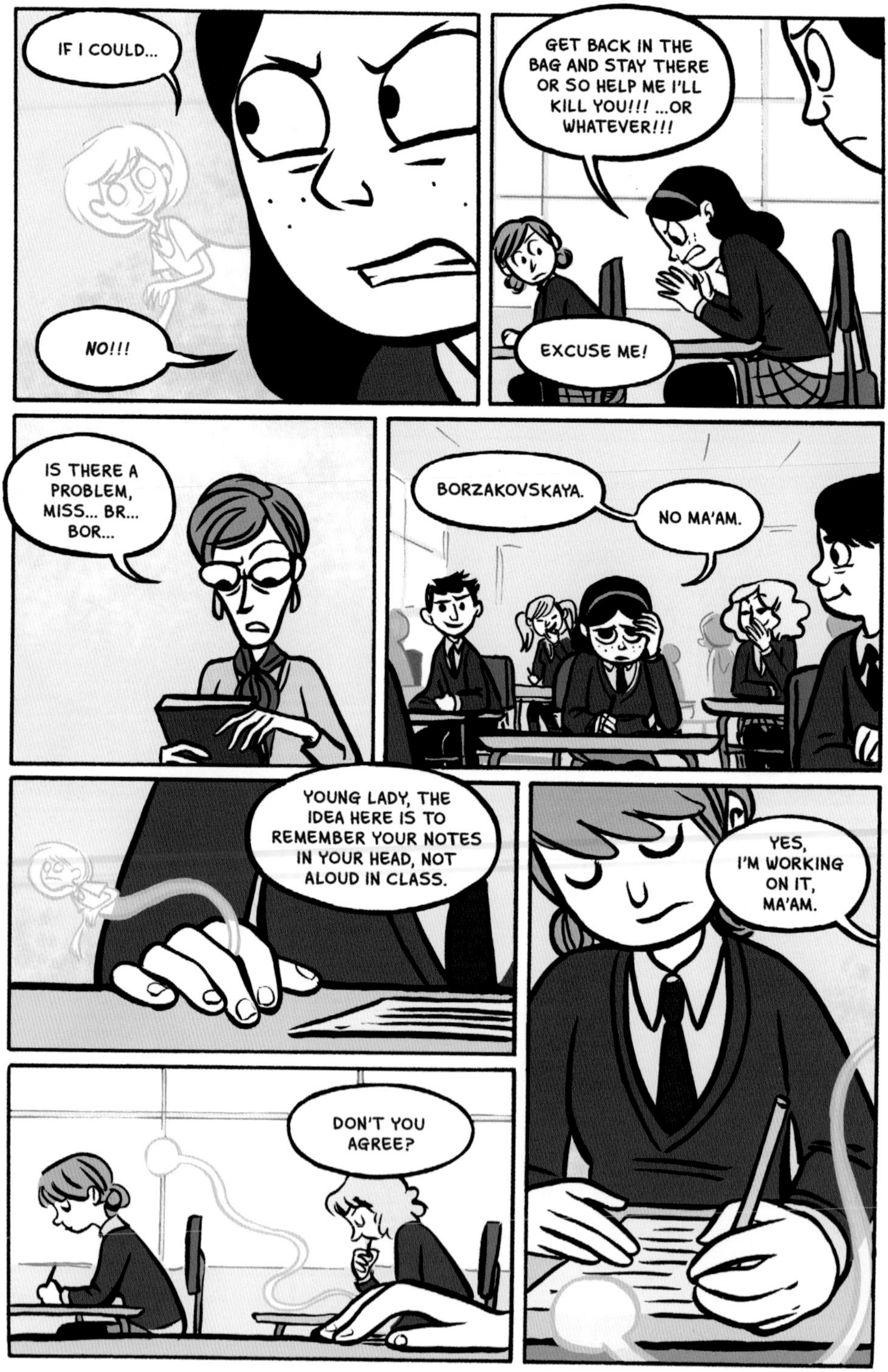
IF I COULD...
NO!!!
GET BACK IN THE BAG AND STAY THERE OR SO HELP ME I'LL KILL YOU!!! ...OR WHATEVER!!!
EXCUSE ME!
IS THERE A PROBLEM, MISS... BR... BOR...
BORZAKOVSKAYA.
NO MA'AM.
YOUNG LADY, THE IDEA HERE IS TO REMEMBER YOUR NOTES IN YOUR HEAD, NOT ALOUD IN CLASS.
YES, I'M WORKING ON IT, MA'AM.
DON'T YOU AGREE?

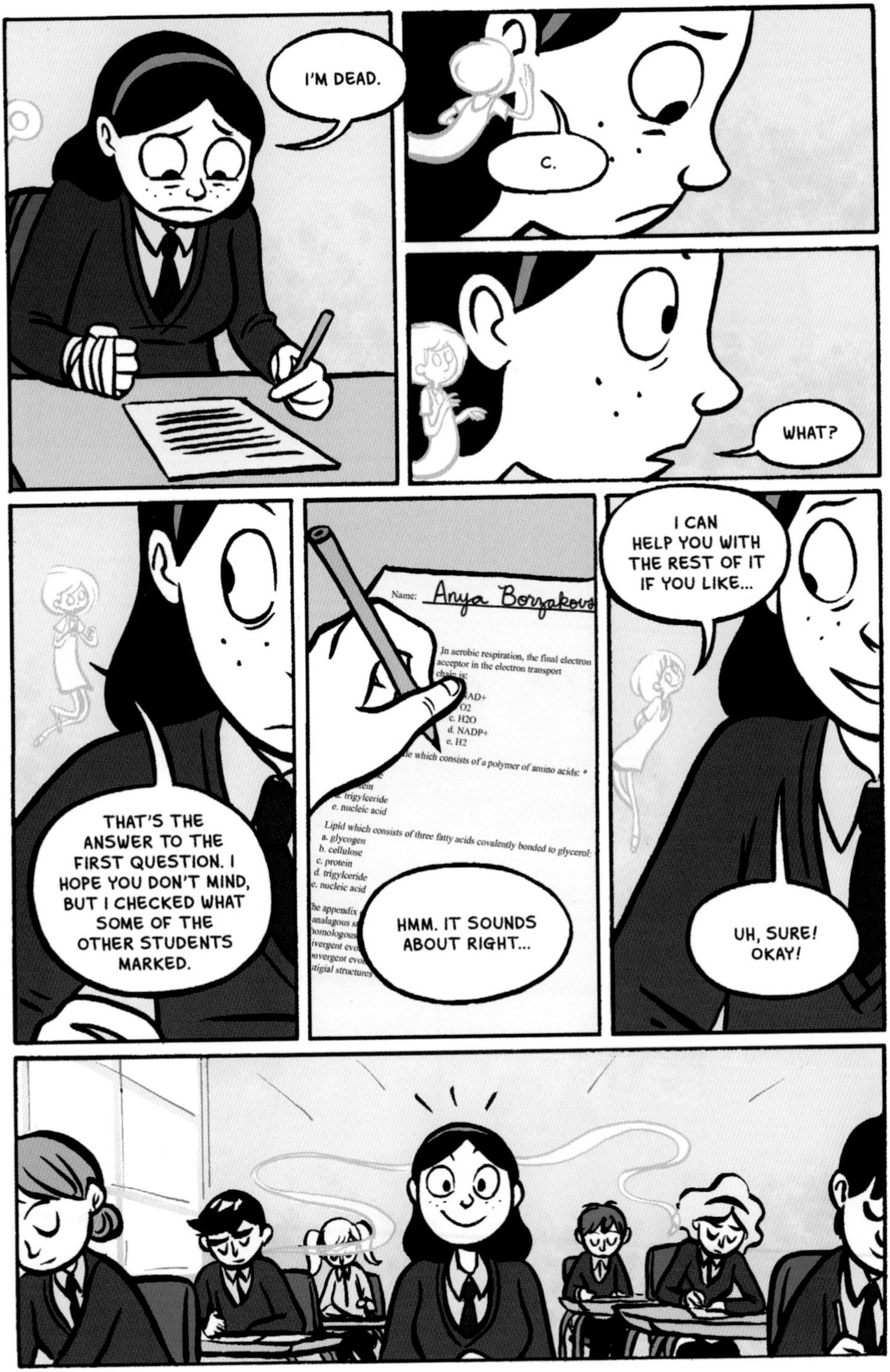

I'M DEAD.
C.
WHAT?
THAT'S THE ANSWER TO THE FIRST QUESTION. I HOPE YOU DON'T MIND, BUT I CHECKED WHAT SOME OF THE OTHER STUDENTS MARKED.
Name:
In aerobic respiration, the final electron
acceptor in the electron transport
c. H2O
d. NADP+
e. H2
which consists of a polymer of amino acids: *
e. nucleic acid
Lipid which consists of three fatty acids covalently bonded to glycerol:
a. glycogen
b. cellulose
c. protein
d. trigylceride
e. nucleic acid
HMM. IT SOUNDS ABOUT RIGHT...
I CAN HELP YOU WITH THE REST OF IT IF YOU LIKE...
UH, SURE! OKAY!

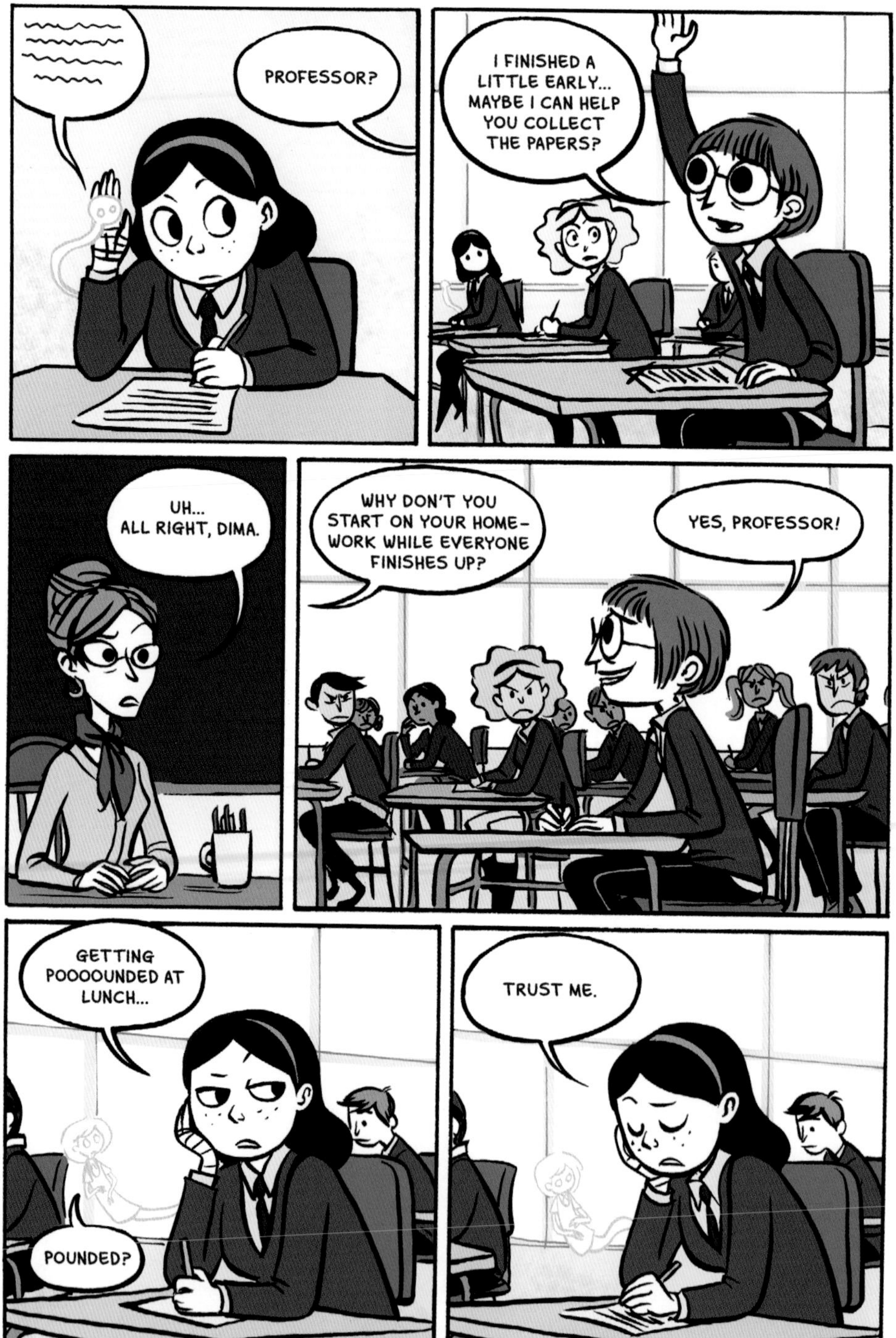
PROFESSOR?
I FINISHED A LITTLE EARLY... MAYBE I CAN HELP YOU COLLECT THE PAPERS?
UH... ALL RIGHT, DIMA.
WHY DON'T YOU START ON YOUR HOME-WORK WHILE EVERYONE FINISHES UP?
YES, PROFESSOR!
GETTING POOOOUNDED AT LUNCH...
POUNDED?
TRUST ME.

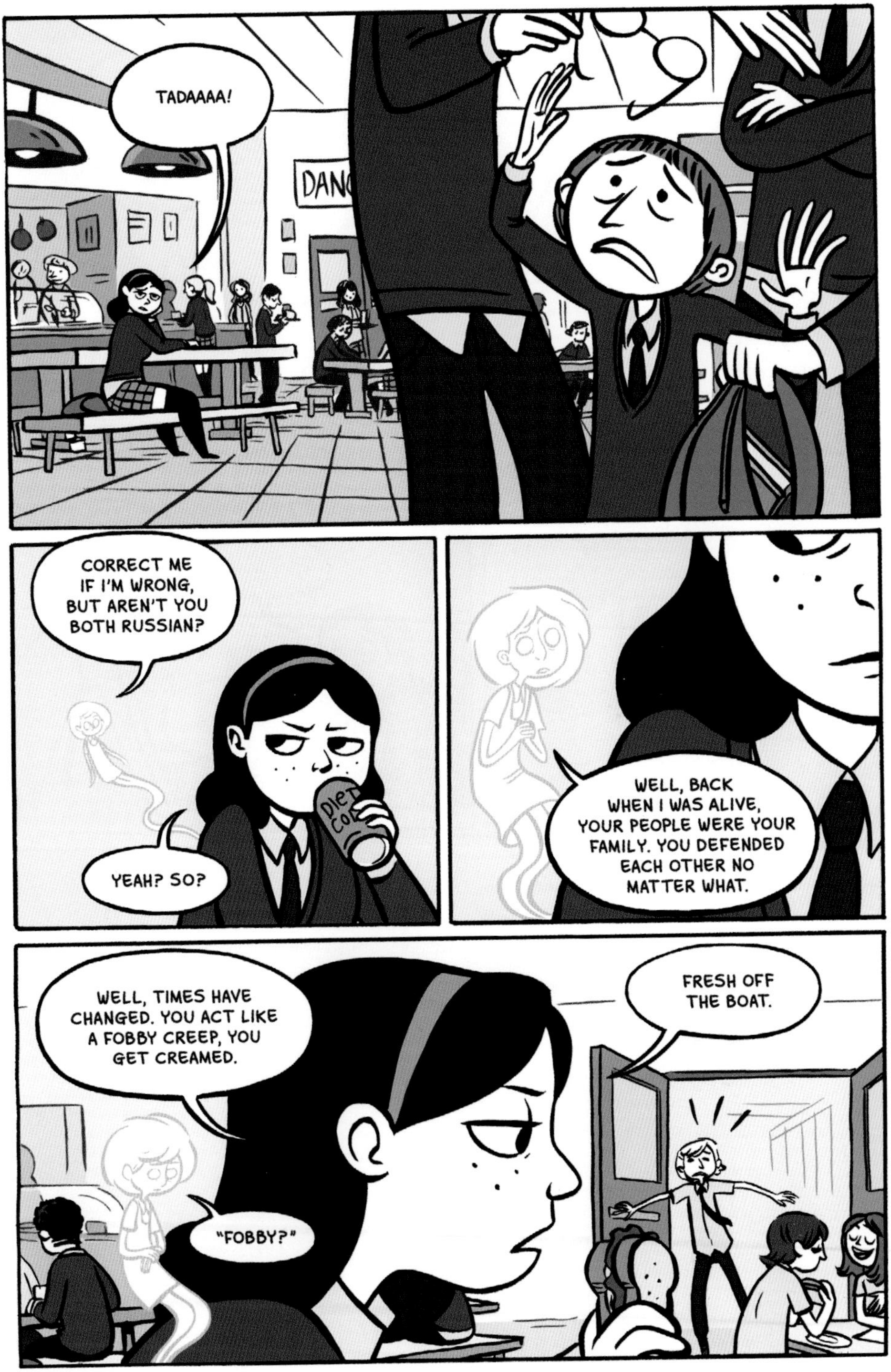
TADAAAA!
DANG
CORRECT ME IF I'M WRONG, BUT AREN'T YOU BOTH RUSSIAN?
YEAH? SO?
DIET COKE
WELL, BACK WHEN I WAS ALIVE, YOUR PEOPLE WERE YOUR FAMILY. YOU DEFENDED EACH OTHER NO MATTER WHAT.
WELL, TIMES HAVE CHANGED. YOU ACT LIKE A FOBBY CREEP, YOU GET CREAMED.
"FOBBY?"
FRESH OFF THE BOAT.

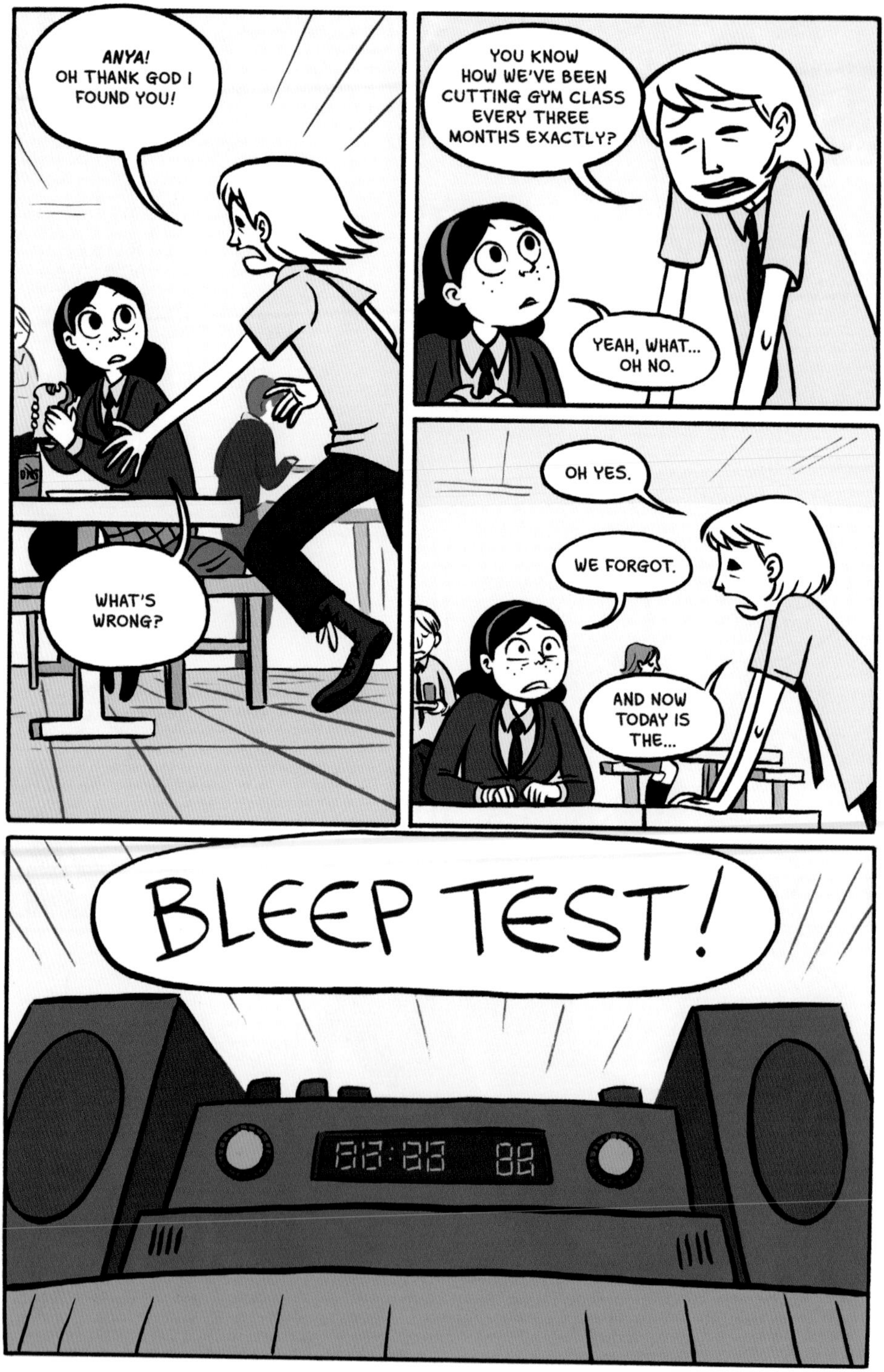
ANYA!
OH THANK GOD I FOUND YOU!
WHAT'S WRONG?
YOU KNOW HOW WE'VE BEEN CUTTING GYM CLASS EVERY THREE MONTHS EXACTLY?
YEAH, WHAT... OH NO.
OH YES.
WE FORGOT.
AND NOW TODAY IS THE...
BLEEP TEST!

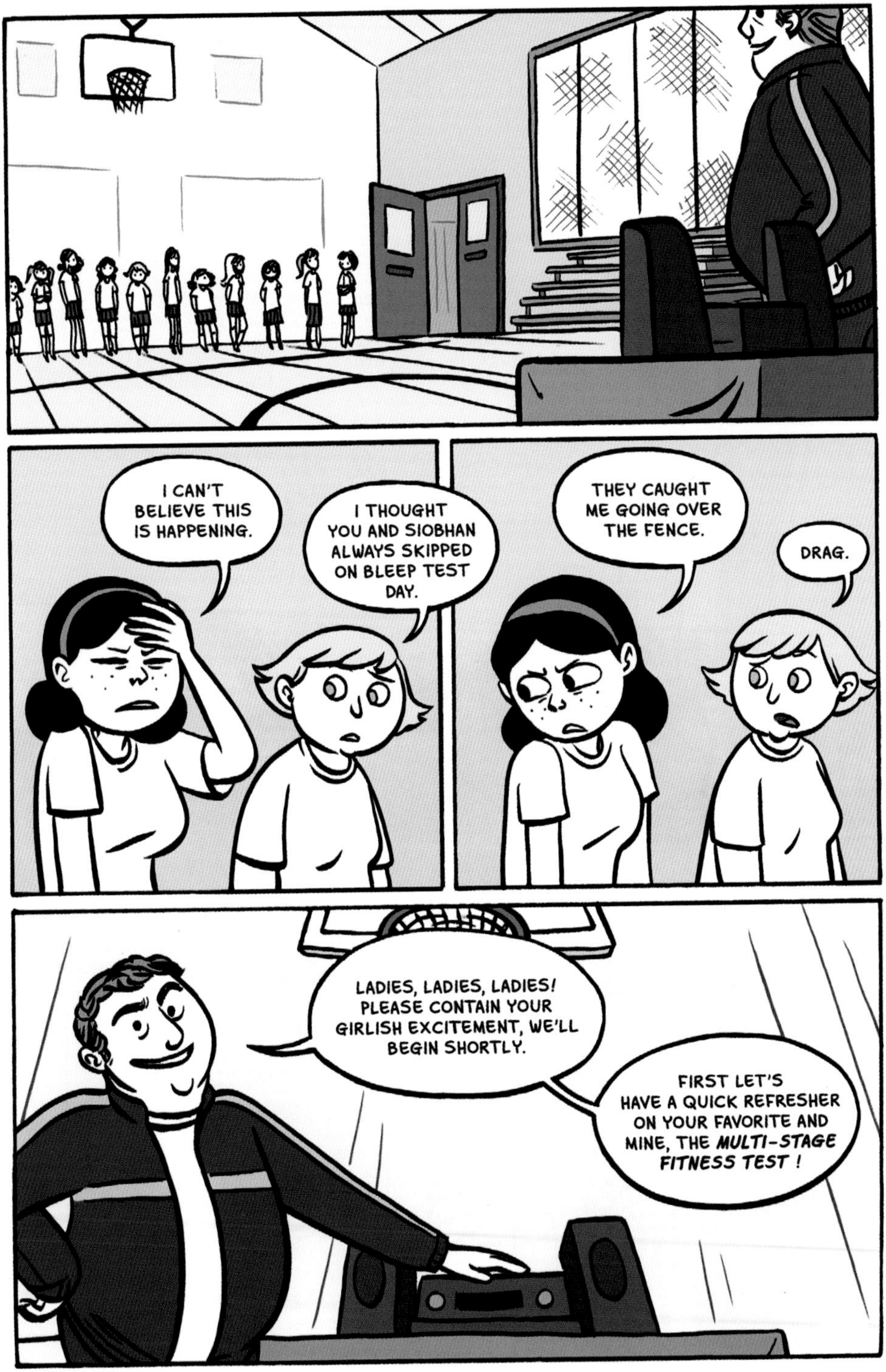
I CAN'T BELIEVE THIS IS HAPPENING.
I THOUGHT YOU AND SIOBHAN ALWAYS SKIPPED ON BLEEP TEST DAY.
THEY CAUGHT ME GOING OVER THE FENCE.
DRAG.
LADIES, LADIES, LADIES! PLEASE CONTAIN YOUR GIRLISH EXCITEMENT, WE'LL BEGIN SHORTLY.
FIRST LET'S HAVE A QUICK REFRESHER ON YOUR FAVORITE AND MINE, THE *MULTI-STAGE FITNESS TEST* !

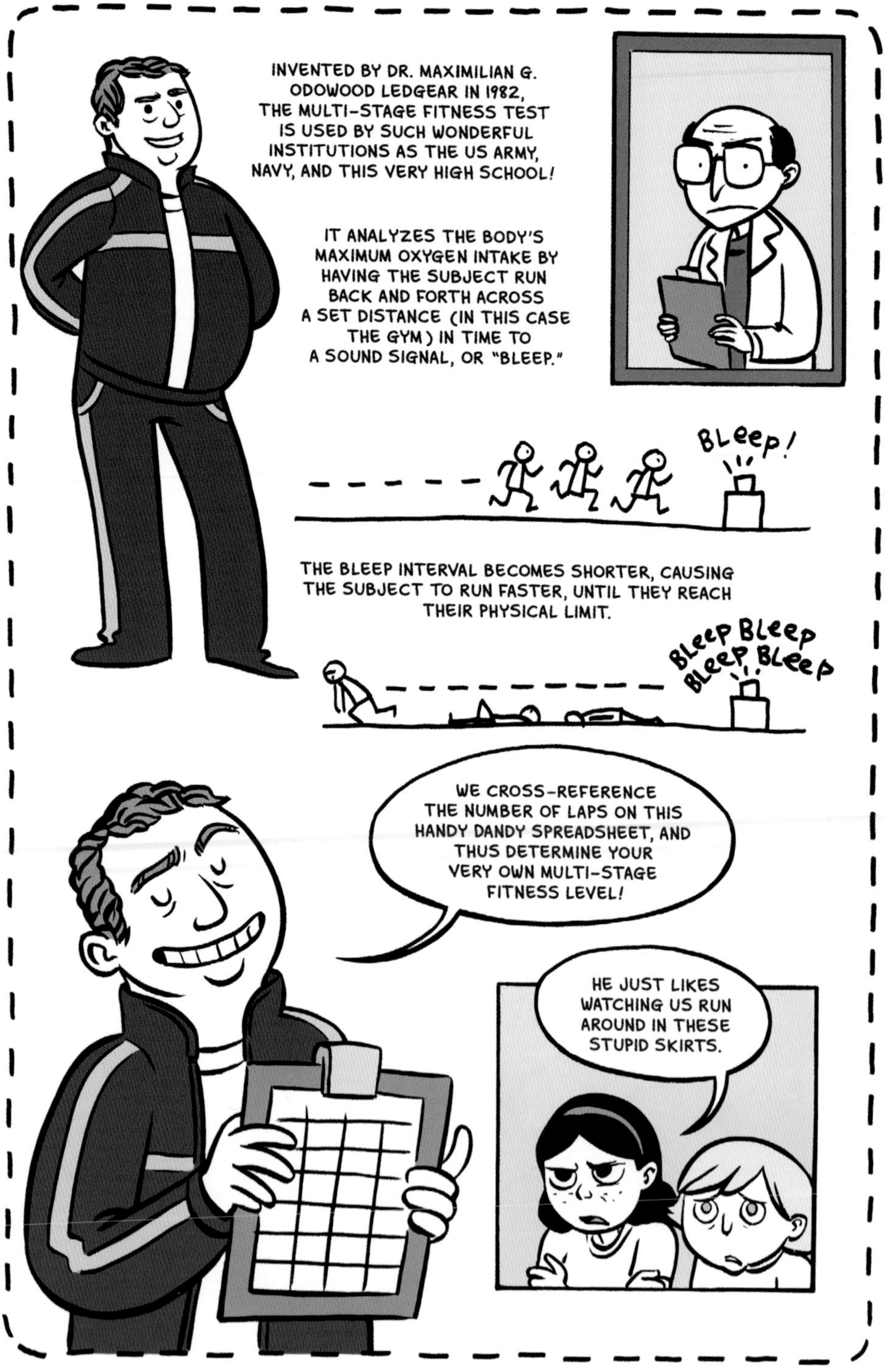
INVENTED BY DR. MAXIMILIAN G. ODOWOOD LEDGEAR IN 1982, THE MULTI-STAGE FITNESS TEST IS USED BY SUCH WONDERFUL INSTITUTIONS AS THE US ARMY, NAVY, AND THIS VERY HIGH SCHOOL!
IT ANALYZES THE BODY'S MAXIMUM OXYGEN INTAKE BY HAVING THE SUBJECT RUN BACK AND FORTH ACROSS A SET DISTANCE (IN THIS CASE THE GYM) IN TIME TO A SOUND SIGNAL, OR "BLEEP."
BLEEP!
THE BLEEP INTERVAL BECOMES SHORTER, CAUSING THE SUBJECT TO RUN FASTER, UNTIL THEY REACH THEIR PHYSICAL LIMIT.
BLEEP BLEEP BLEEP BLEEP
WE CROSS-REFERENCE THE NUMBER OF LAPS ON THIS HANDY DANDY SPREADSHEET, AND THUS DETERMINE YOUR VERY OWN MULTI-STAGE FITNESS LEVEL!
HE JUST LIKES WATCHING US RUN AROUND IN THESE STUPID SKIRTS.

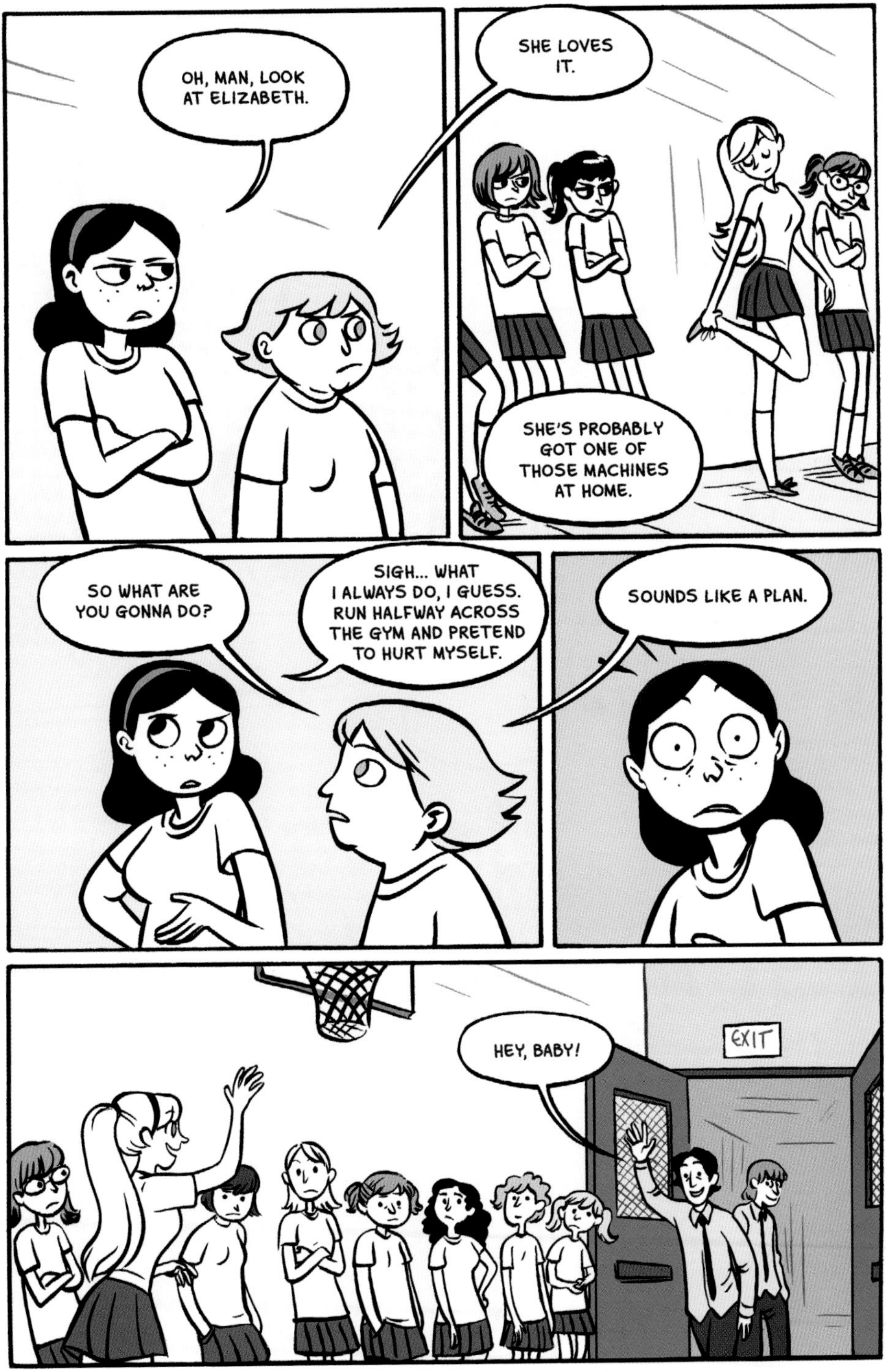
OH, MAN, LOOK AT ELIZABETH.
SHE LOVES IT.
SHE'S PROBABLY GOT ONE OF THOSE MACHINES AT HOME.
SO WHAT ARE YOU GONNA DO?
SIGH... WHAT I ALWAYS DO, I GUESS. RUN HALFWAY ACROSS THE GYM AND PRETEND TO HURT MYSELF.
SOUNDS LIKE A PLAN.
HEY, BABY!
EXIT

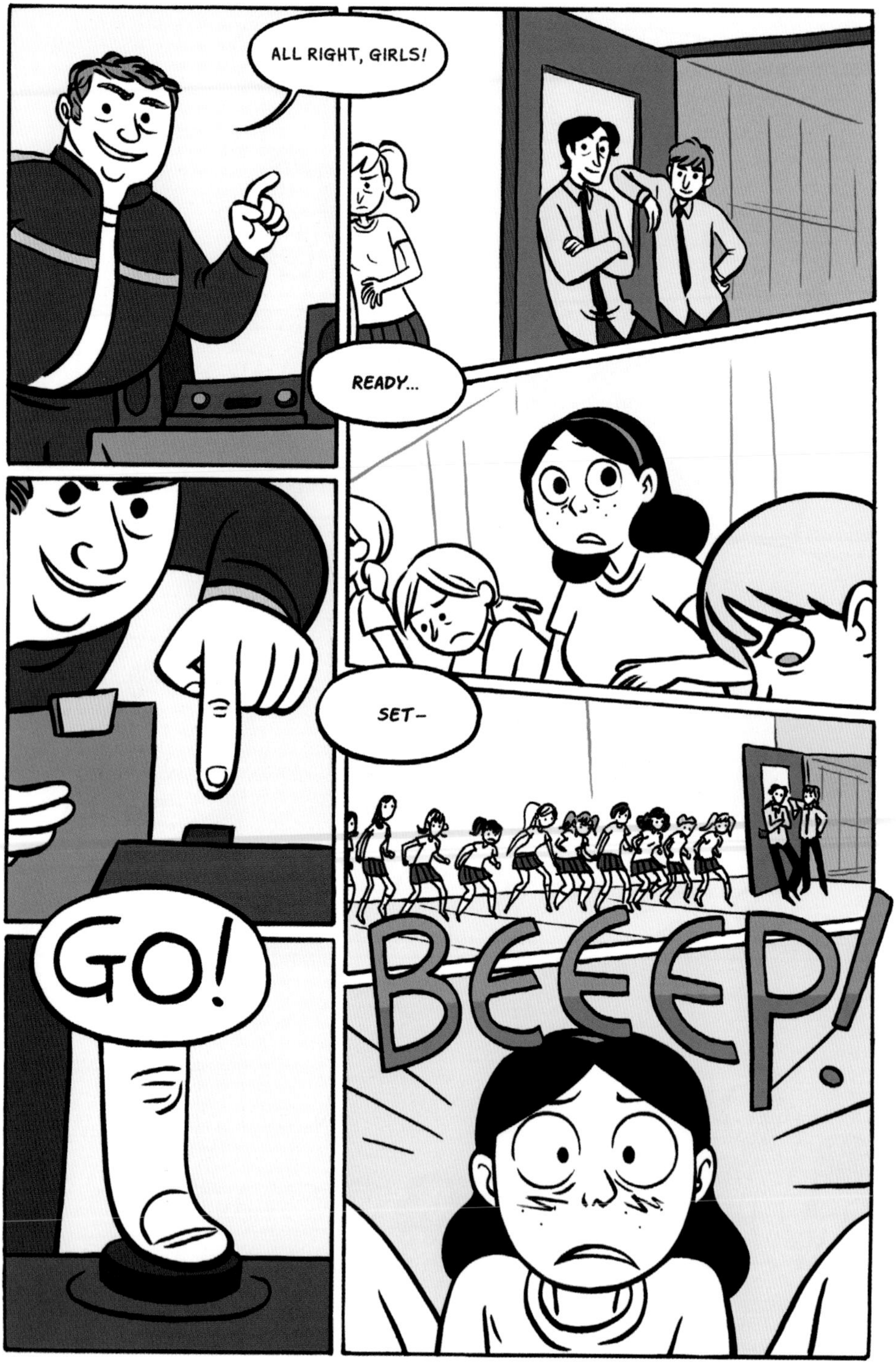
ALL RIGHT, GIRLS!
READY...
SET–
GO!
BEEEP!

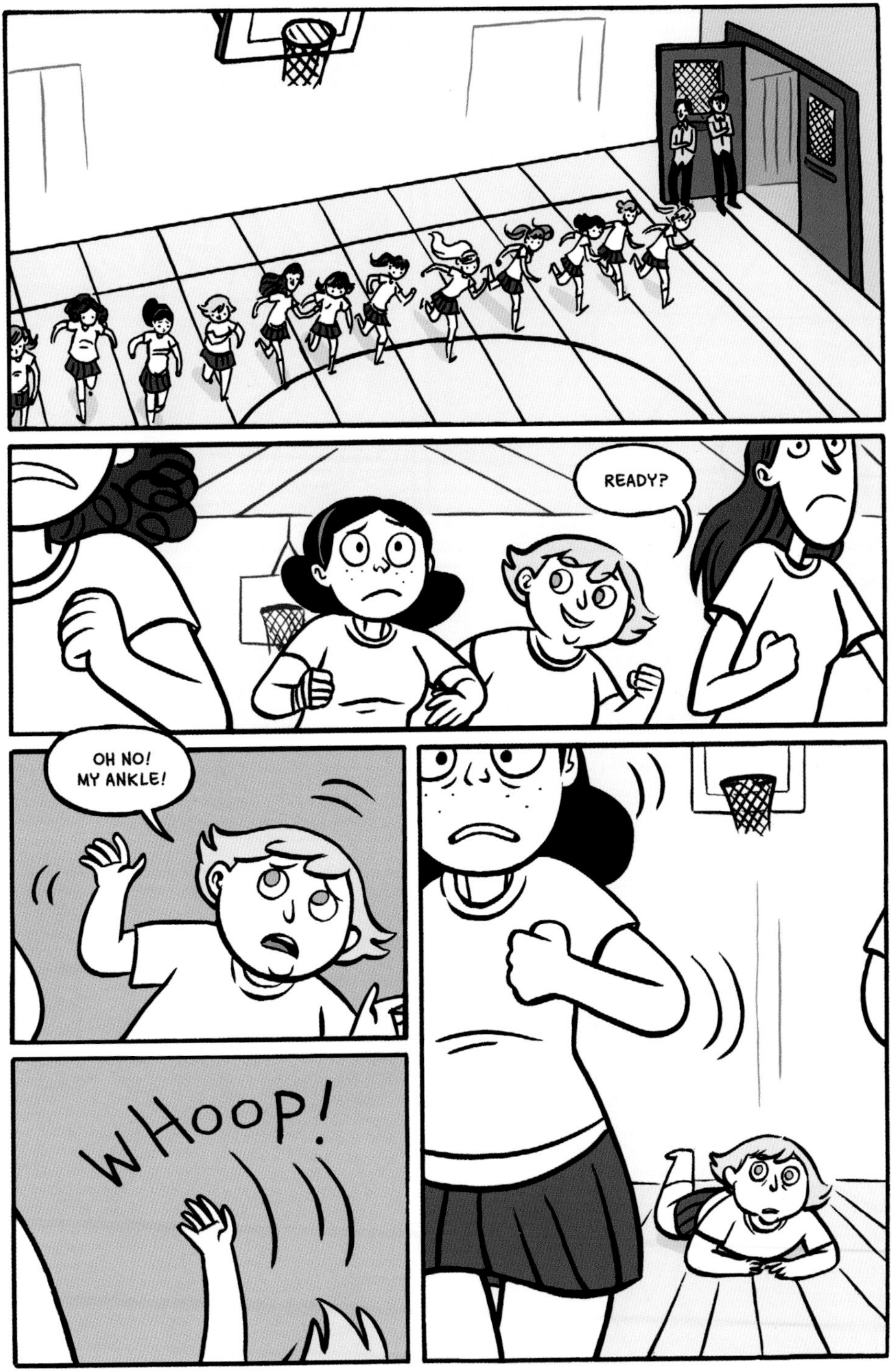
READY?
OH NO! MY ANKLE!
WHOOP!

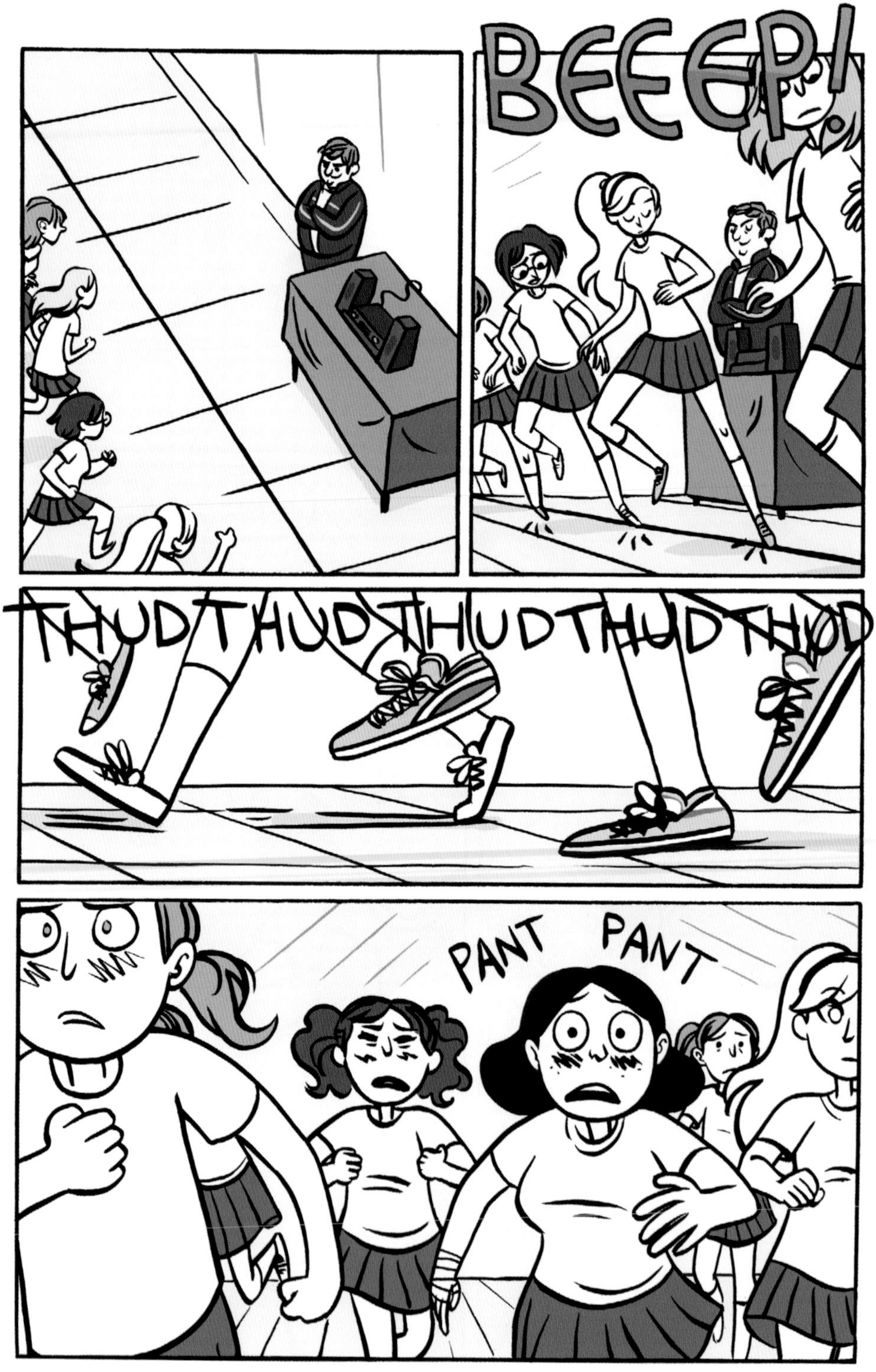
BEEEP!
THUDTHUDTHUDTHUDTHUD
PANT PANT

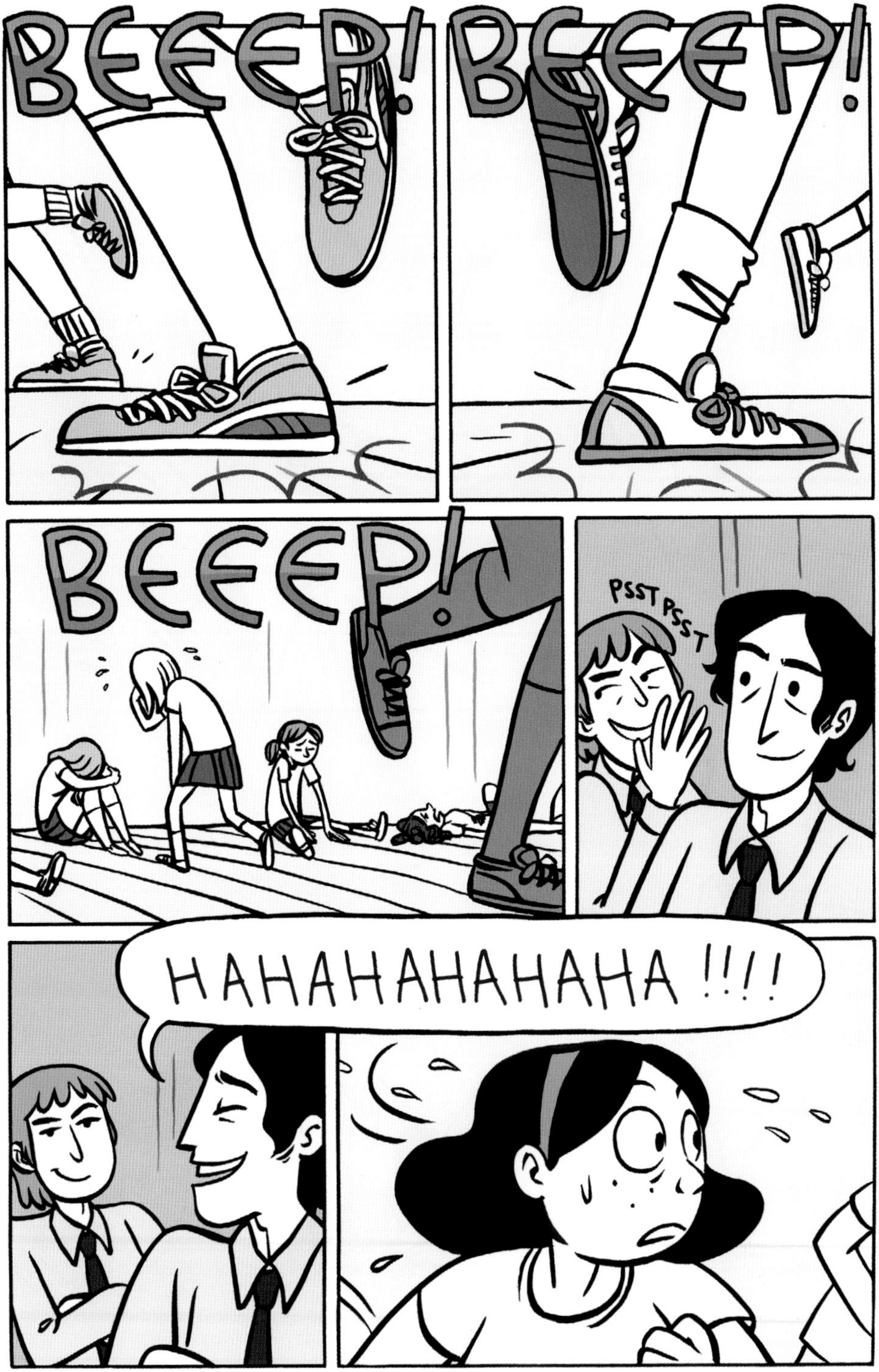
BEEEP!
BEEEP!
BEEEP!
PSST PSSST
HAHAHAHAHAHA !!!!

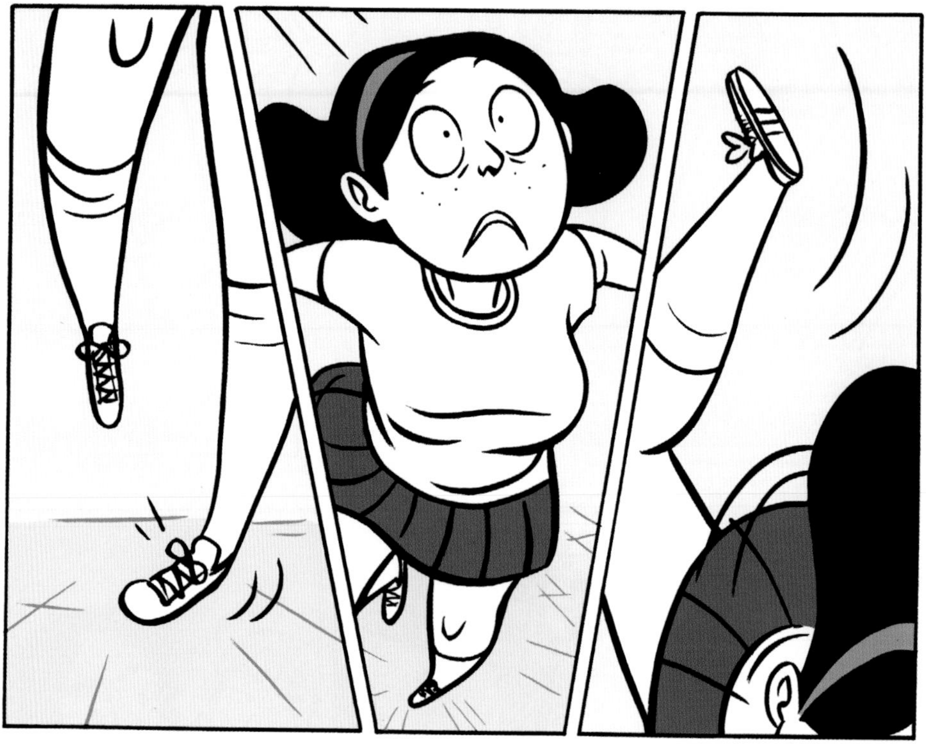

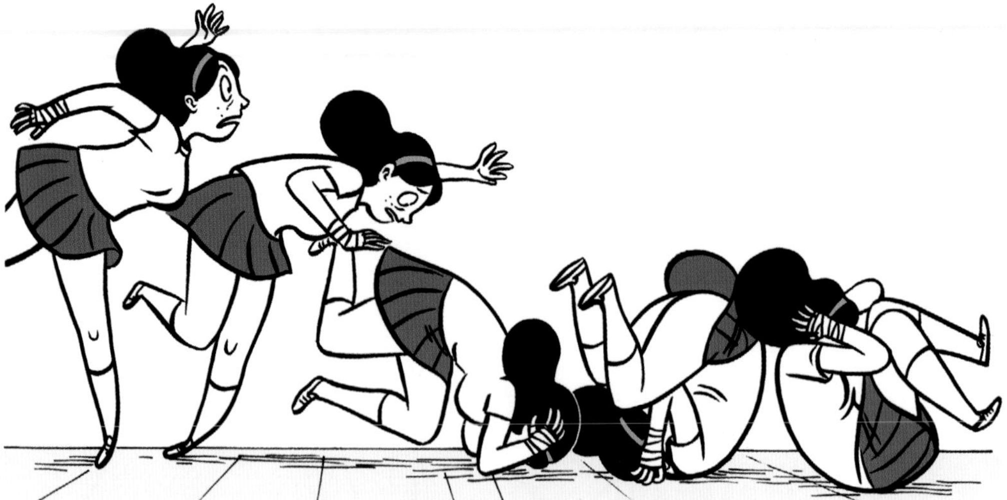

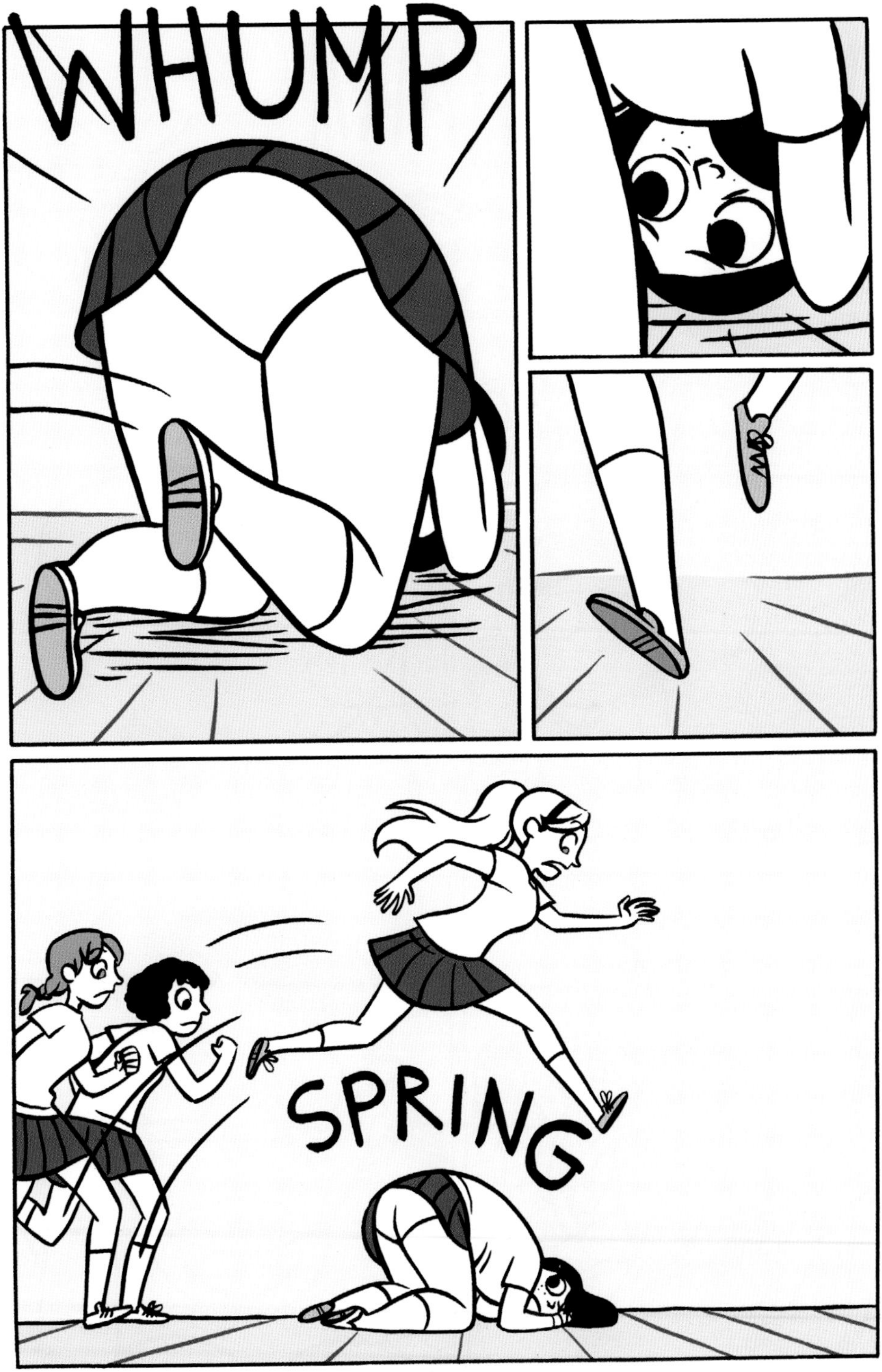
WHUMP
SPRING

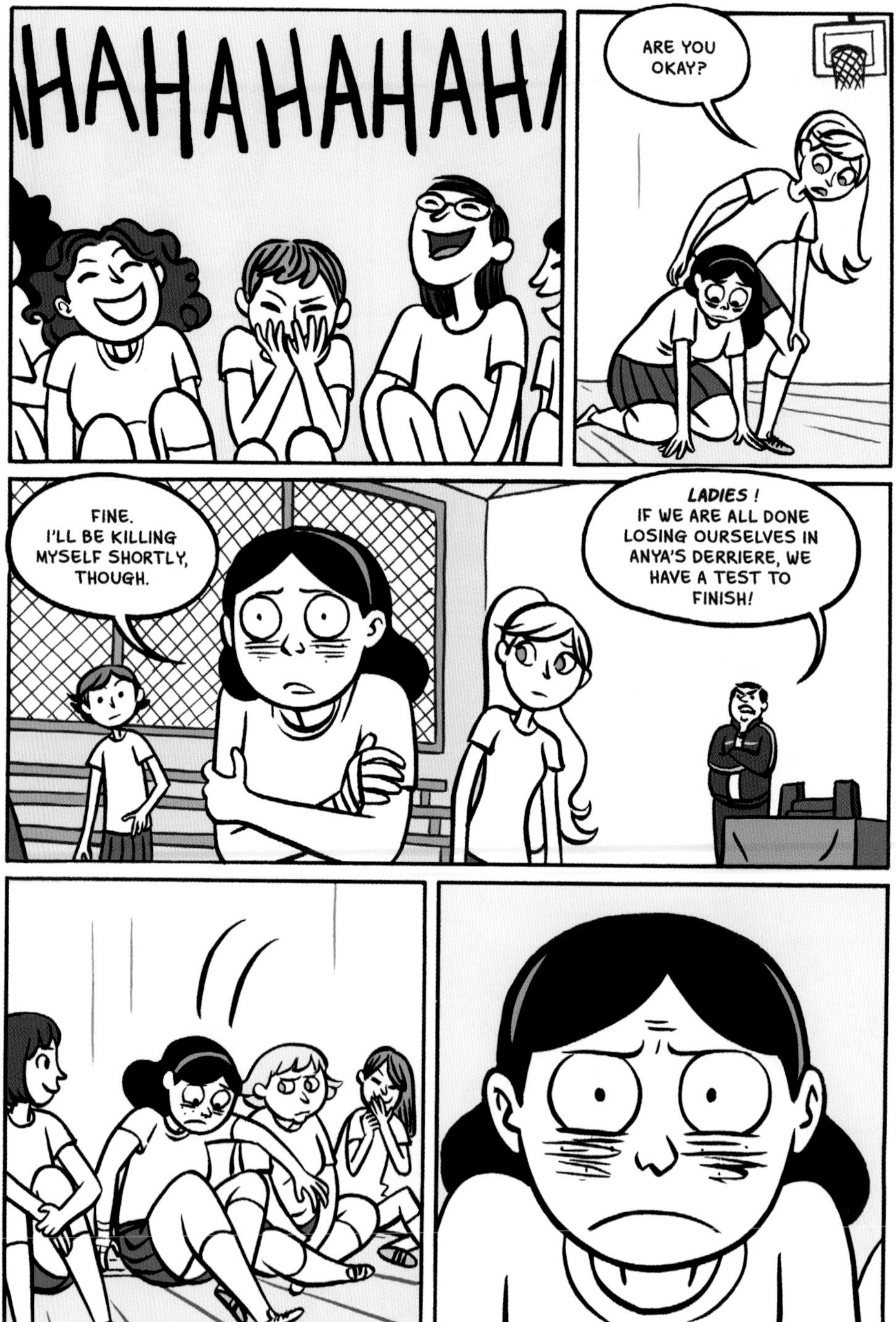
HAHAHAHAHAH
ARE YOU OKAY?
FINE. I'LL BE KILLING MYSELF SHORTLY, THOUGH.
LADIES ! IF WE ARE ALL DONE LOSING OURSELVES IN ANYA'S DERRIERE, WE HAVE A TEST TO FINISH!

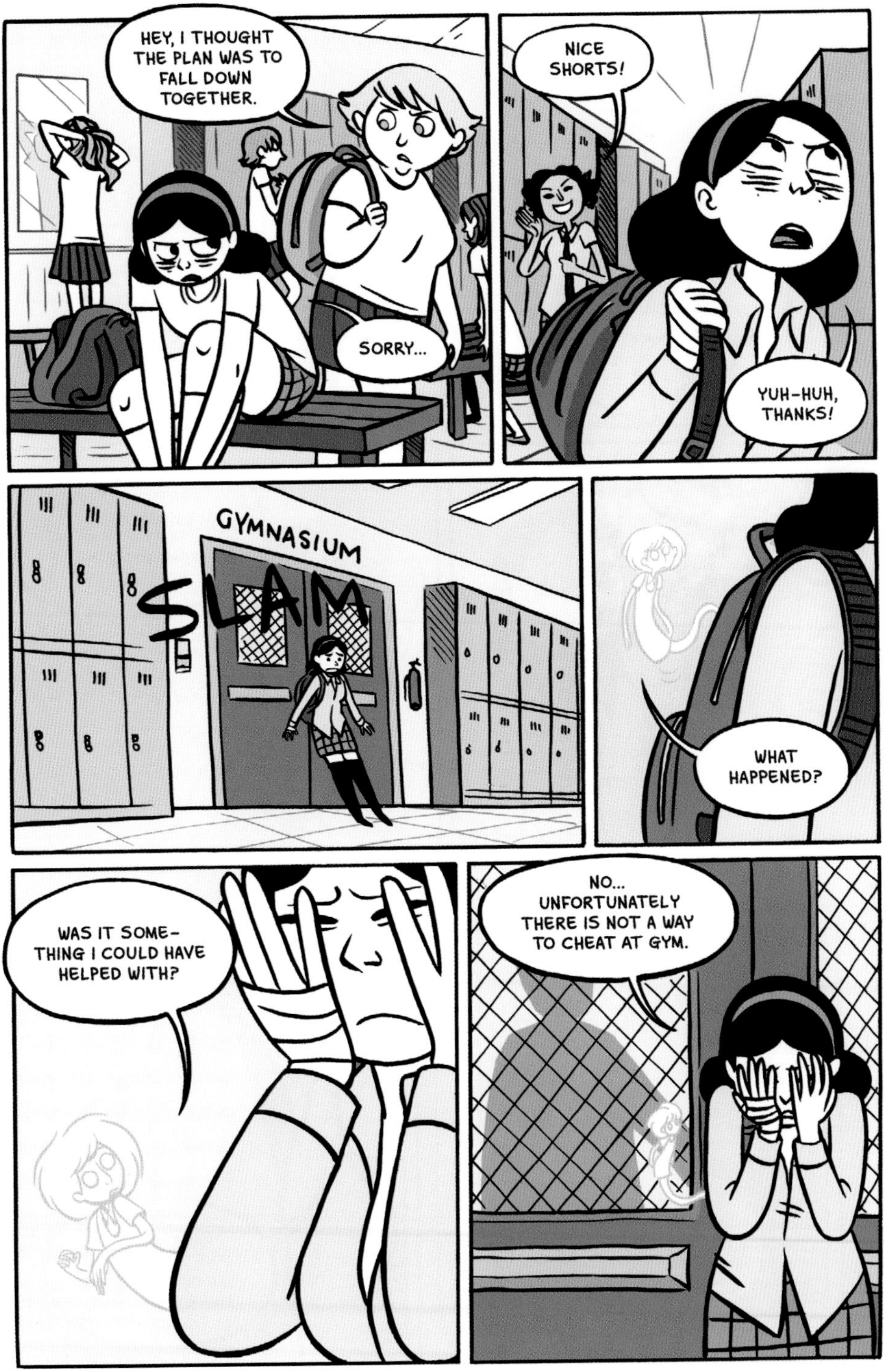
HEY, I THOUGHT THE PLAN WAS TO FALL DOWN TOGETHER.
SORRY...
NICE SHORTS!
YUH-HUH, THANKS!
GYMNASIUM
SLAM
WHAT HAPPENED?
WAS IT SOME-THING I COULD HAVE HELPED WITH?
NO... UNFORTUNATELY THERE IS NOT A WAY TO CHEAT AT GYM.

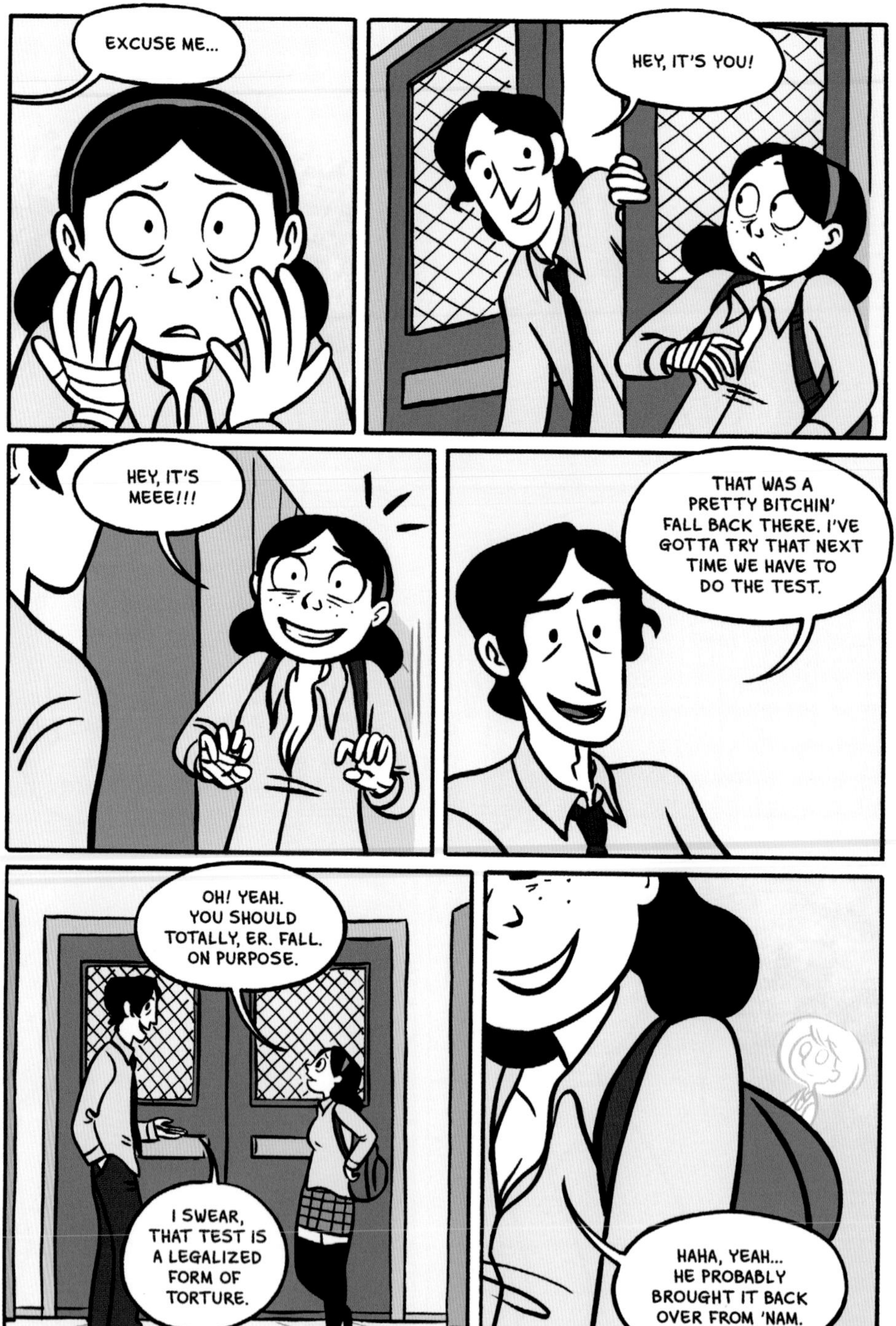
EXCUSE ME...
HEY, IT'S YOU!
HEY, IT'S MEEE!!!
THAT WAS A PRETTY BITCHIN' FALL BACK THERE. I'VE GOTTA TRY THAT NEXT TIME WE HAVE TO DO THE TEST.
OH! YEAH. YOU SHOULD TOTALLY, ER. FALL. ON PURPOSE.
I SWEAR, THAT TEST IS A LEGALIZED FORM OF TORTURE.
HAHA, YEAH... HE PROBABLY BROUGHT IT BACK OVER FROM 'NAM.

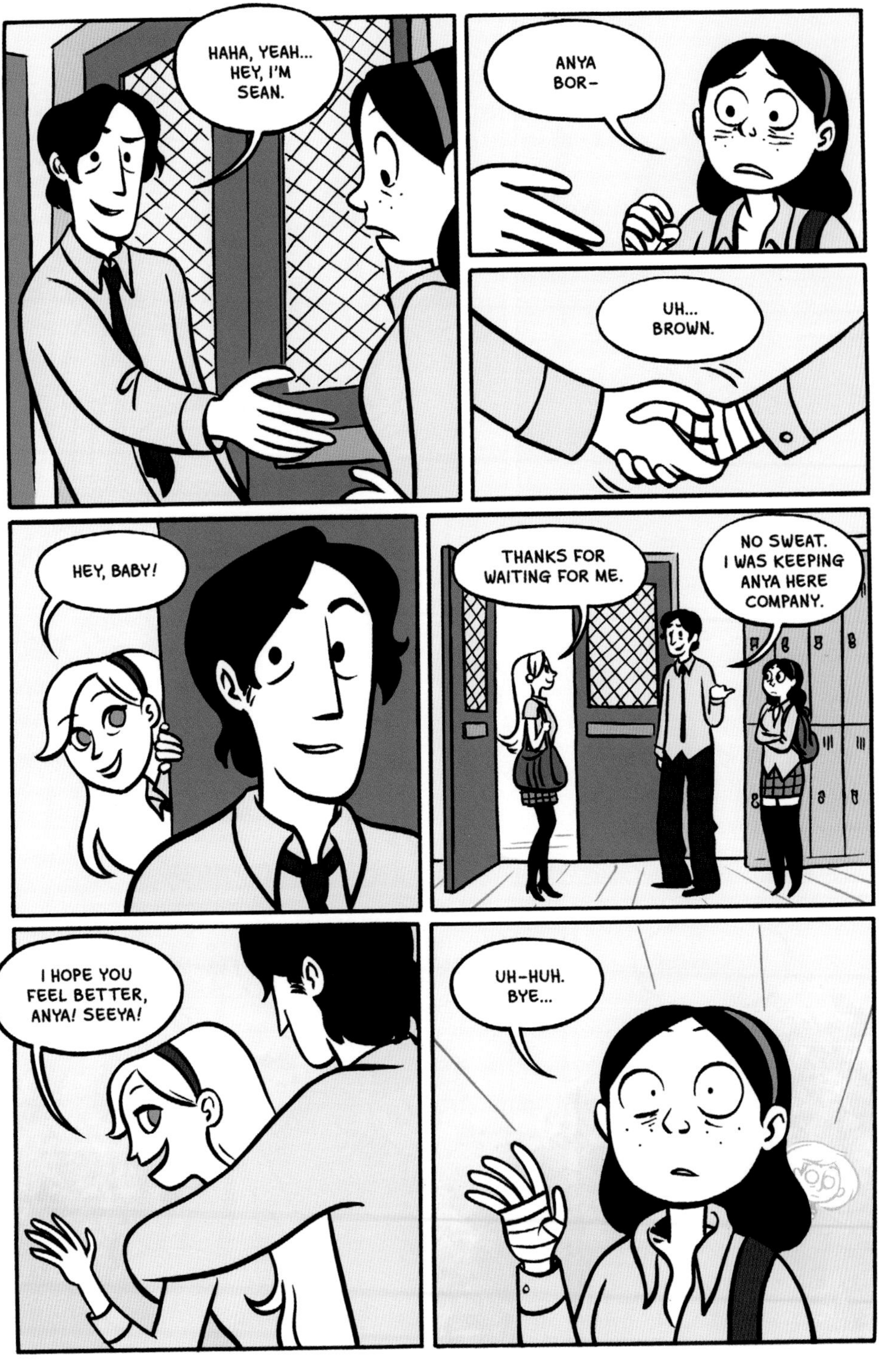
HAHA, YEAH... HEY, I'M SEAN.
ANYA BOR–
UH... BROWN.
HEY, BABY!
THANKS FOR WAITING FOR ME.
NO SWEAT. I WAS KEEPING ANYA HERE COMPANY.
I HOPE YOU FEEL BETTER, ANYA! SEEYA!
UH-HUH. BYE...

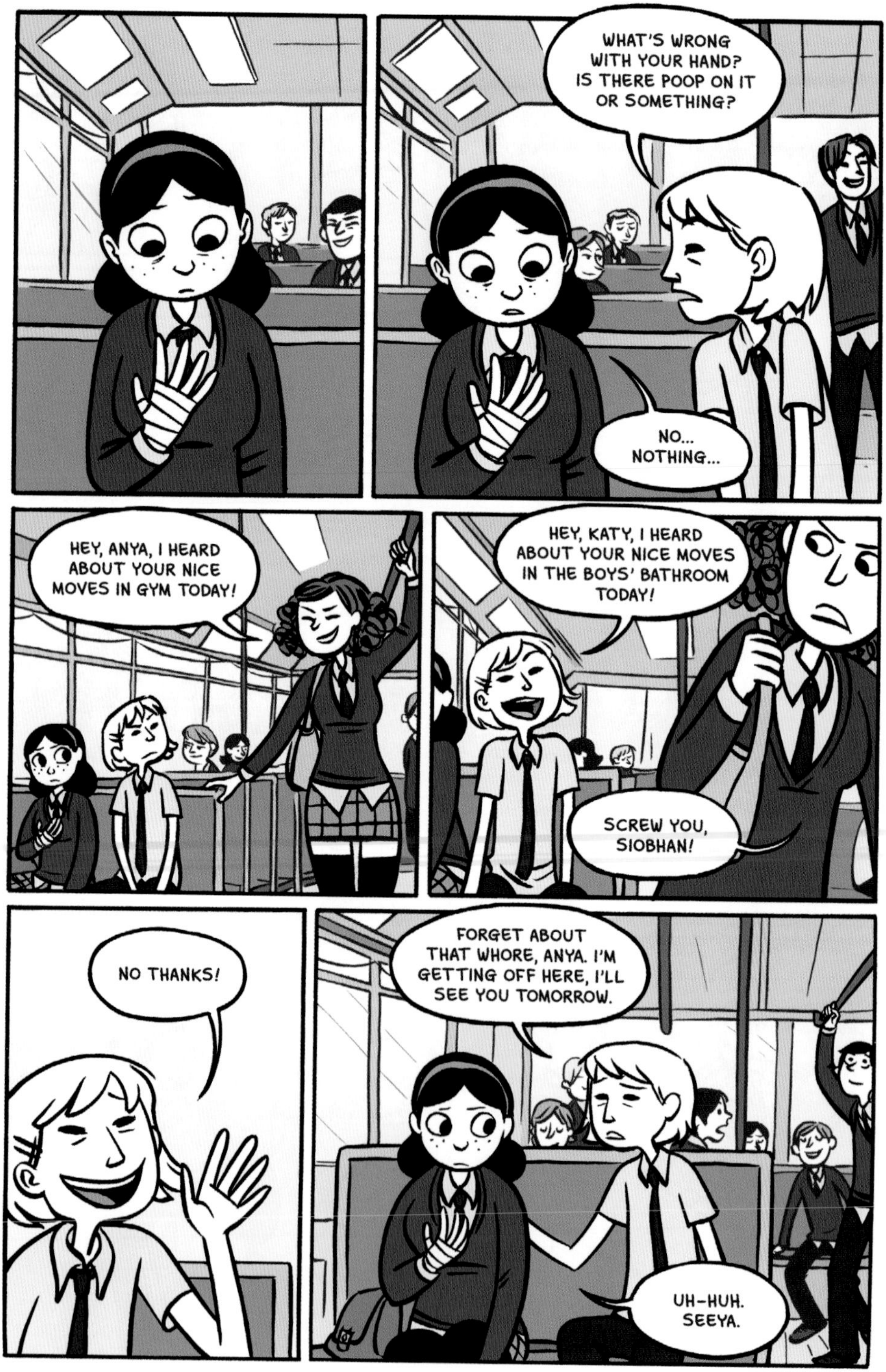
WHAT'S WRONG WITH YOUR HAND? IS THERE POOP ON IT OR SOMETHING?
NO... NOTHING...
HEY, ANYA, I HEARD ABOUT YOUR NICE MOVES IN GYM TODAY!
HEY, KATY, I HEARD ABOUT YOUR NICE MOVES IN THE BOYS' BATHROOM TODAY!
SCREW YOU, SIOBHAN!
NO THANKS!
FORGET ABOUT THAT WHORE, ANYA. I'M GETTING OFF HERE, I'LL SEE YOU TOMORROW.
UH-HUH. SEEYA.

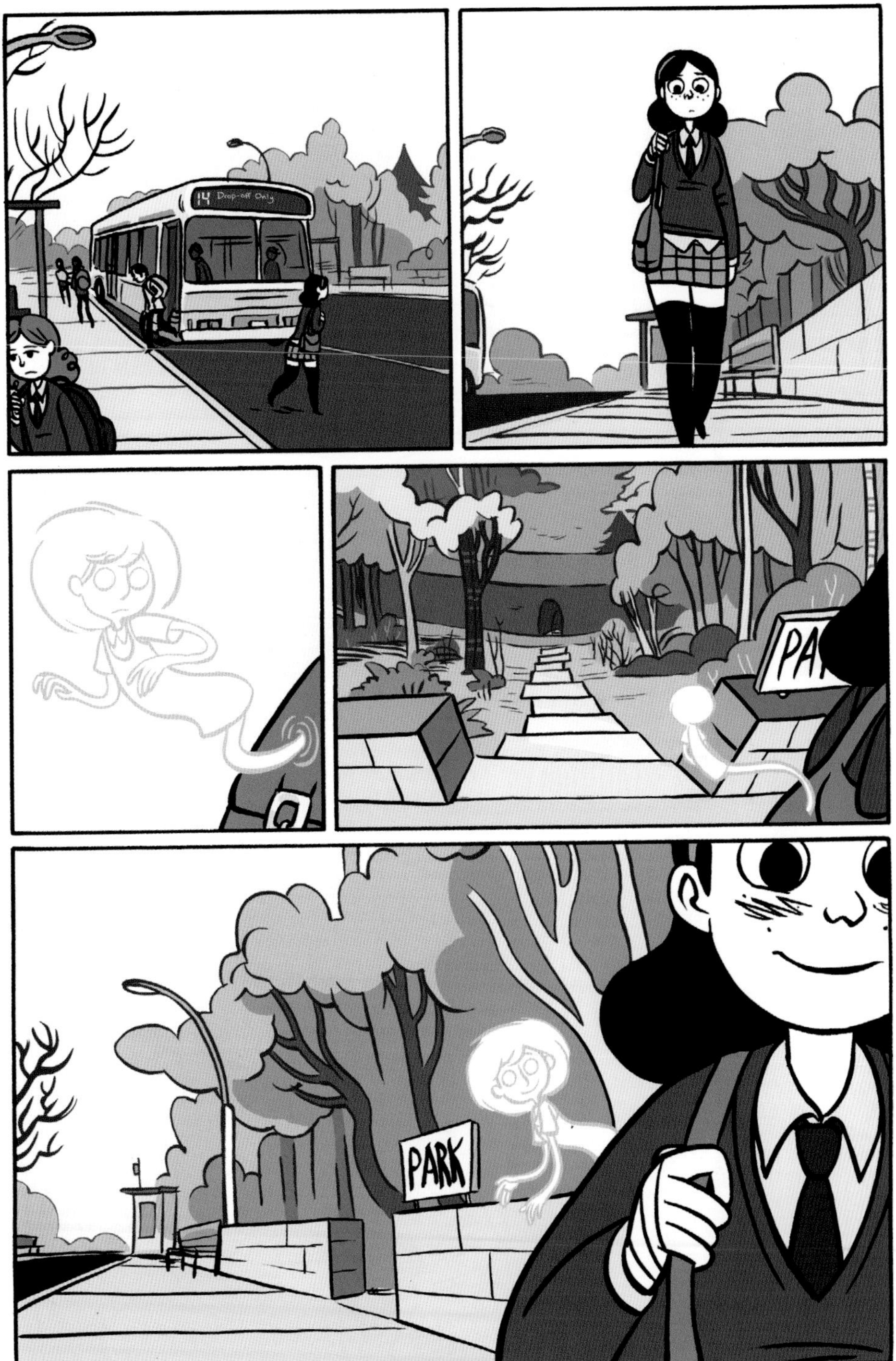
14 Drop-off Only
PARK
PARK

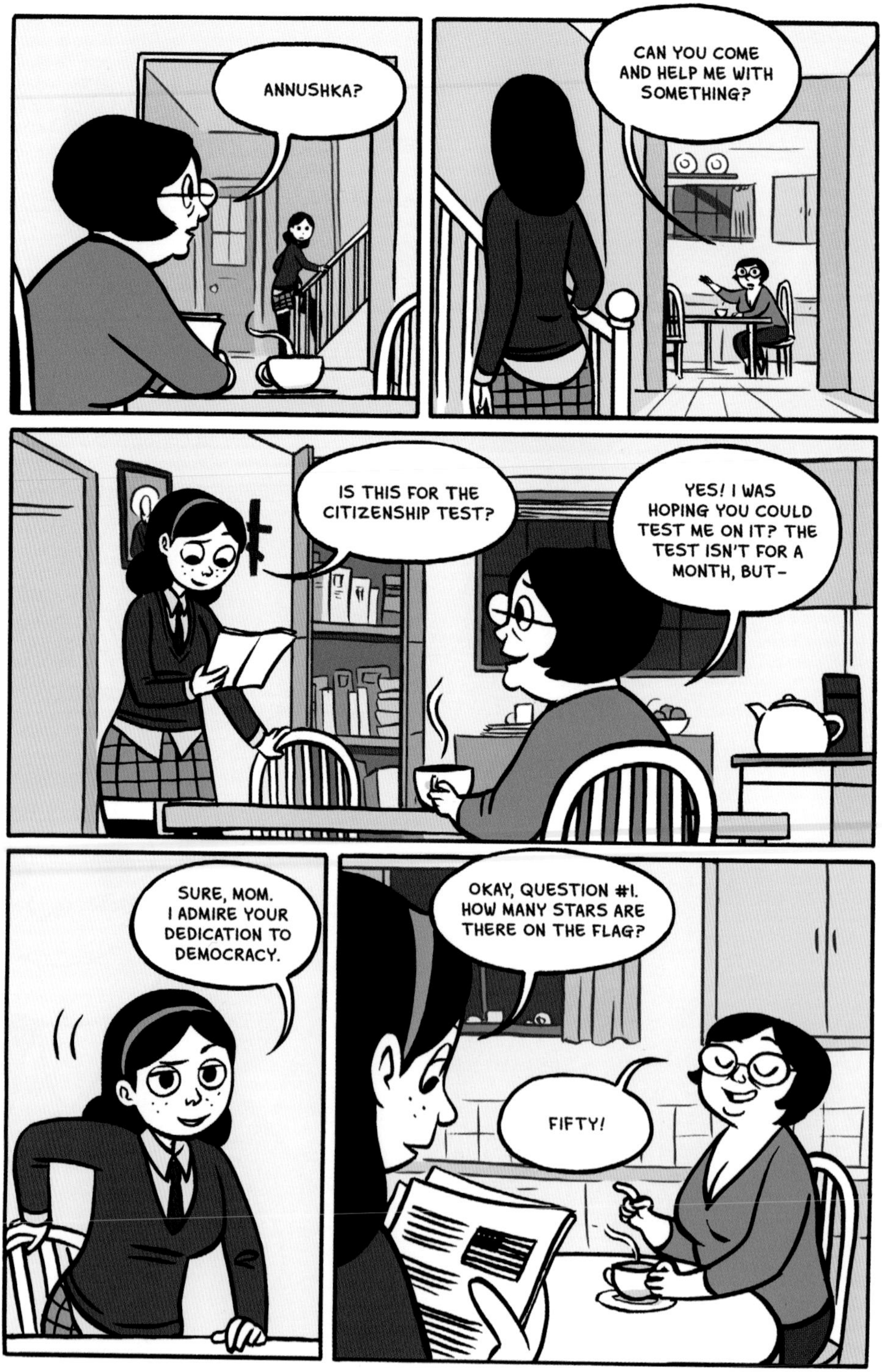
ANNUSHKA?
CAN YOU COME AND HELP ME WITH SOMETHING?
IS THIS FOR THE CITIZENSHIP TEST?
YES! I WAS HOPING YOU COULD TEST ME ON IT? THE TEST ISN'T FOR A MONTH, BUT-
SURE, MOM. I ADMIRE YOUR DEDICATION TO DEMOCRACY.
OKAY, QUESTION #1. HOW MANY STARS ARE THERE ON THE FLAG?
FIFTY!

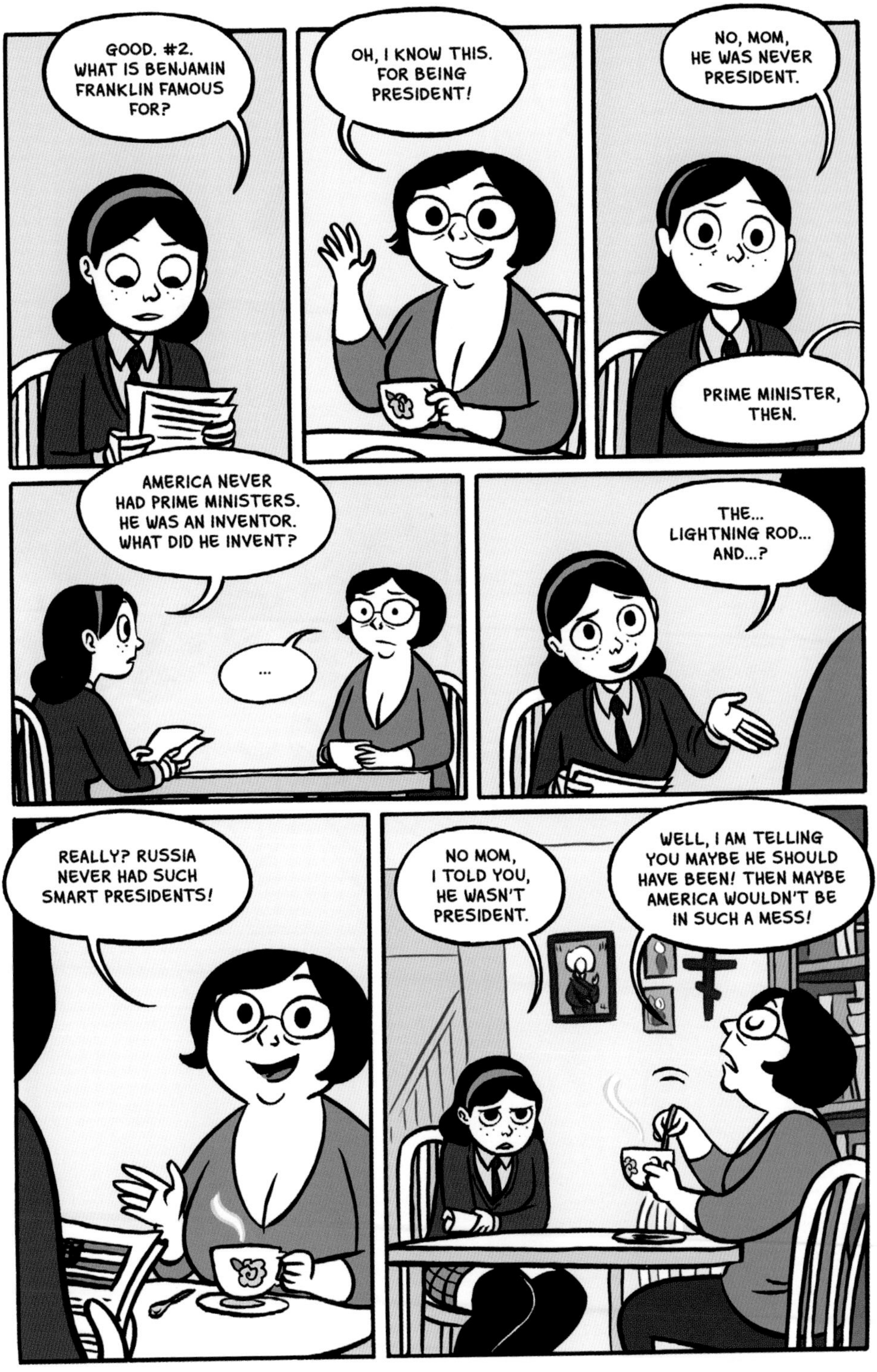
GOOD. #2. WHAT IS BENJAMIN FRANKLIN FAMOUS FOR?
OH, I KNOW THIS. FOR BEING PRESIDENT!
NO, MOM, HE WAS NEVER PRESIDENT.
PRIME MINISTER, THEN.
AMERICA NEVER HAD PRIME MINISTERS. HE WAS AN INVENTOR. WHAT DID HE INVENT?
...
THE... LIGHTNING ROD... AND...?
REALLY? RUSSIA NEVER HAD SUCH SMART PRESIDENTS!
NO MOM, I TOLD YOU, HE WASN'T PRESIDENT.
WELL, I AM TELLING YOU MAYBE HE SHOULD HAVE BEEN! THEN MAYBE AMERICA WOULDN'T BE IN SUCH A MESS!

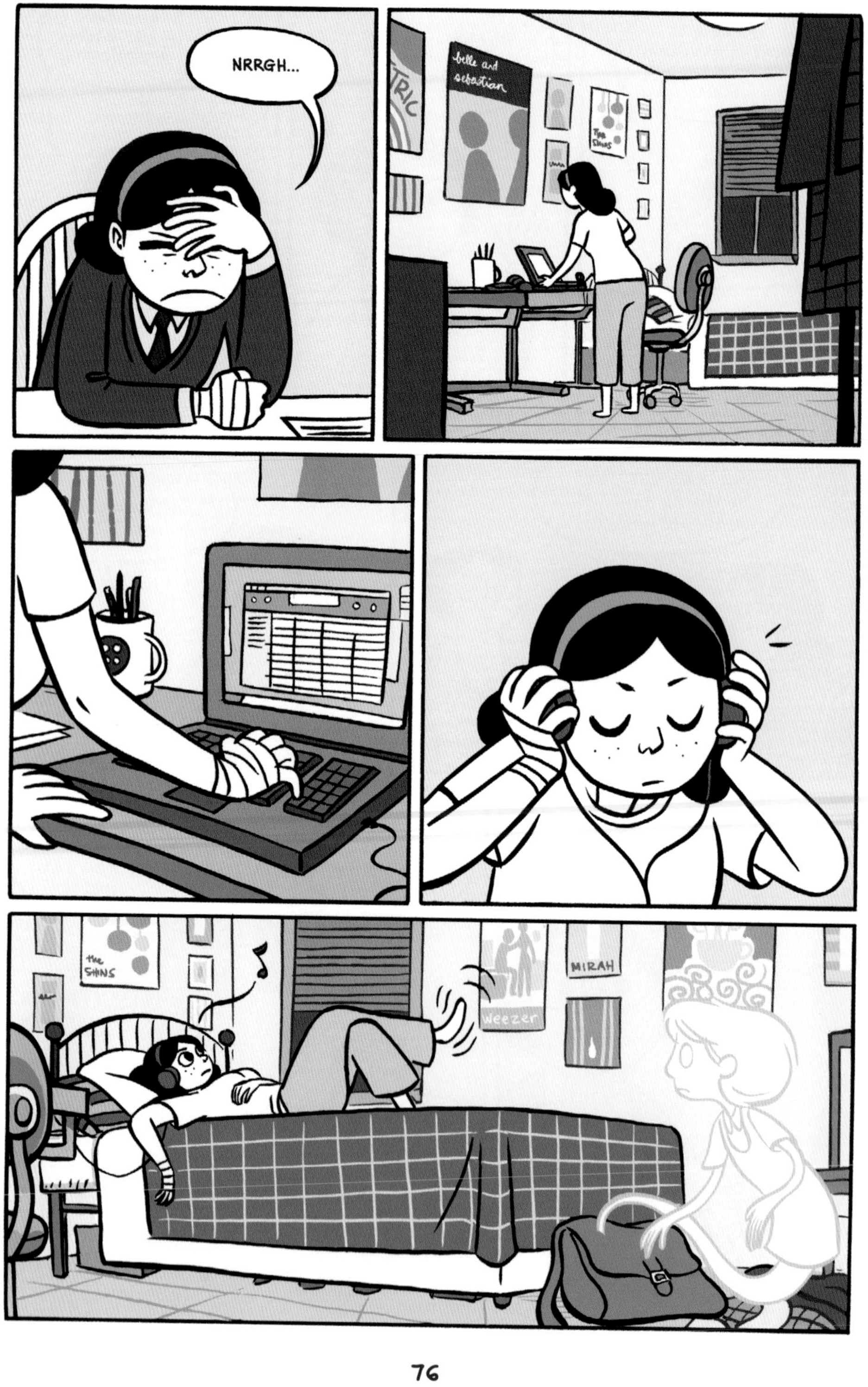
NRRGH...
belle and sebastian
The Shins
the SHINS
MIRAH
weezer

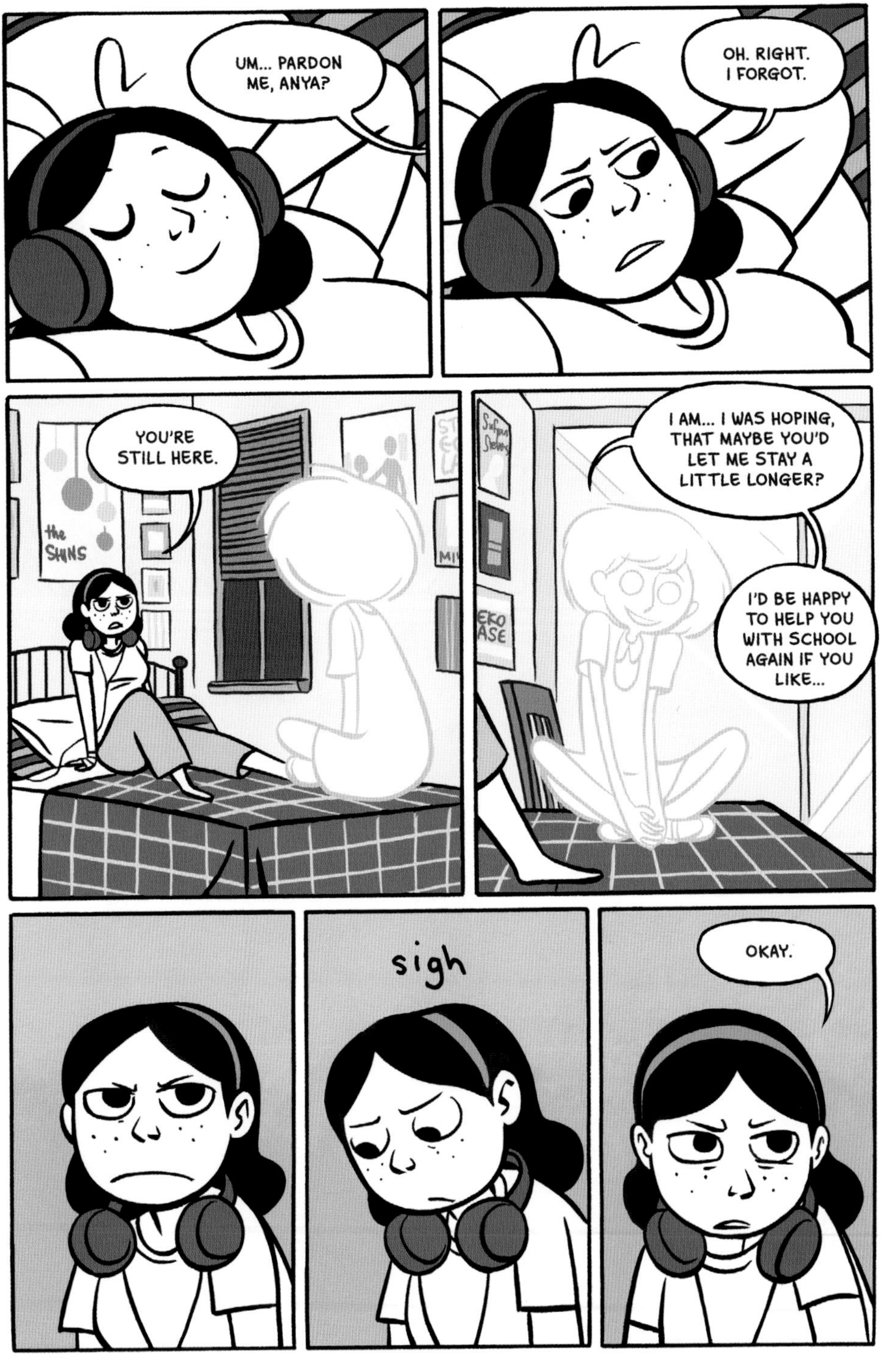
UM... PARDON ME, ANYA?
OH. RIGHT. I FORGOT.
YOU'RE STILL HERE.
the SHINS
I AM... I WAS HOPING, THAT MAYBE YOU'D LET ME STAY A LITTLE LONGER?
I'D BE HAPPY TO HELP YOU WITH SCHOOL AGAIN IF YOU LIKE...
sigh
OKAY.

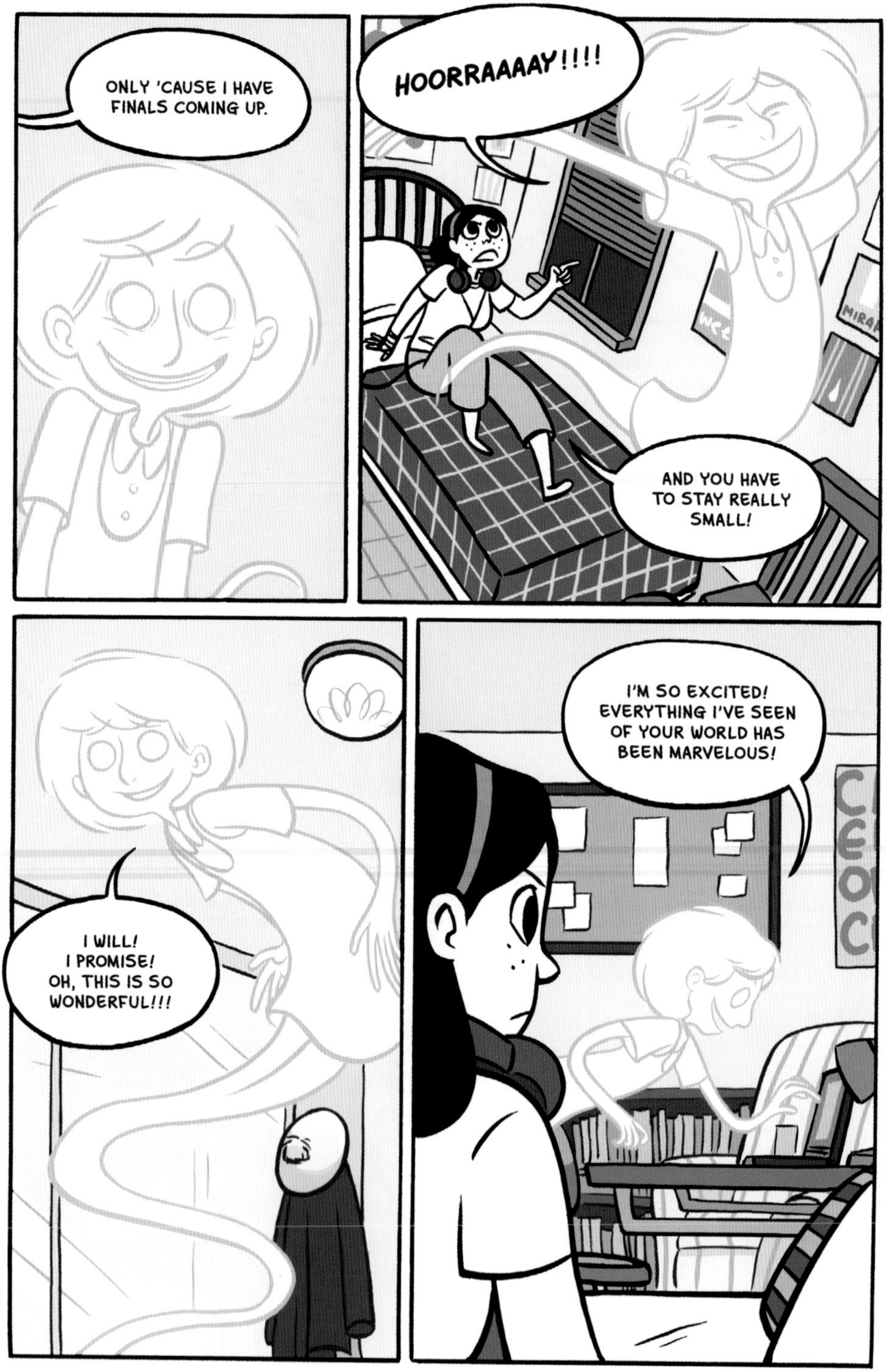
ONLY 'CAUSE I HAVE FINALS COMING UP.
HOORRAAAAY!!!!
AND YOU HAVE TO STAY REALLY SMALL!
I WILL! I PROMISE! OH, THIS IS SO WONDERFUL!!!
I'M SO EXCITED! EVERYTHING I'VE SEEN OF YOUR WORLD HAS BEEN MARVELOUS!

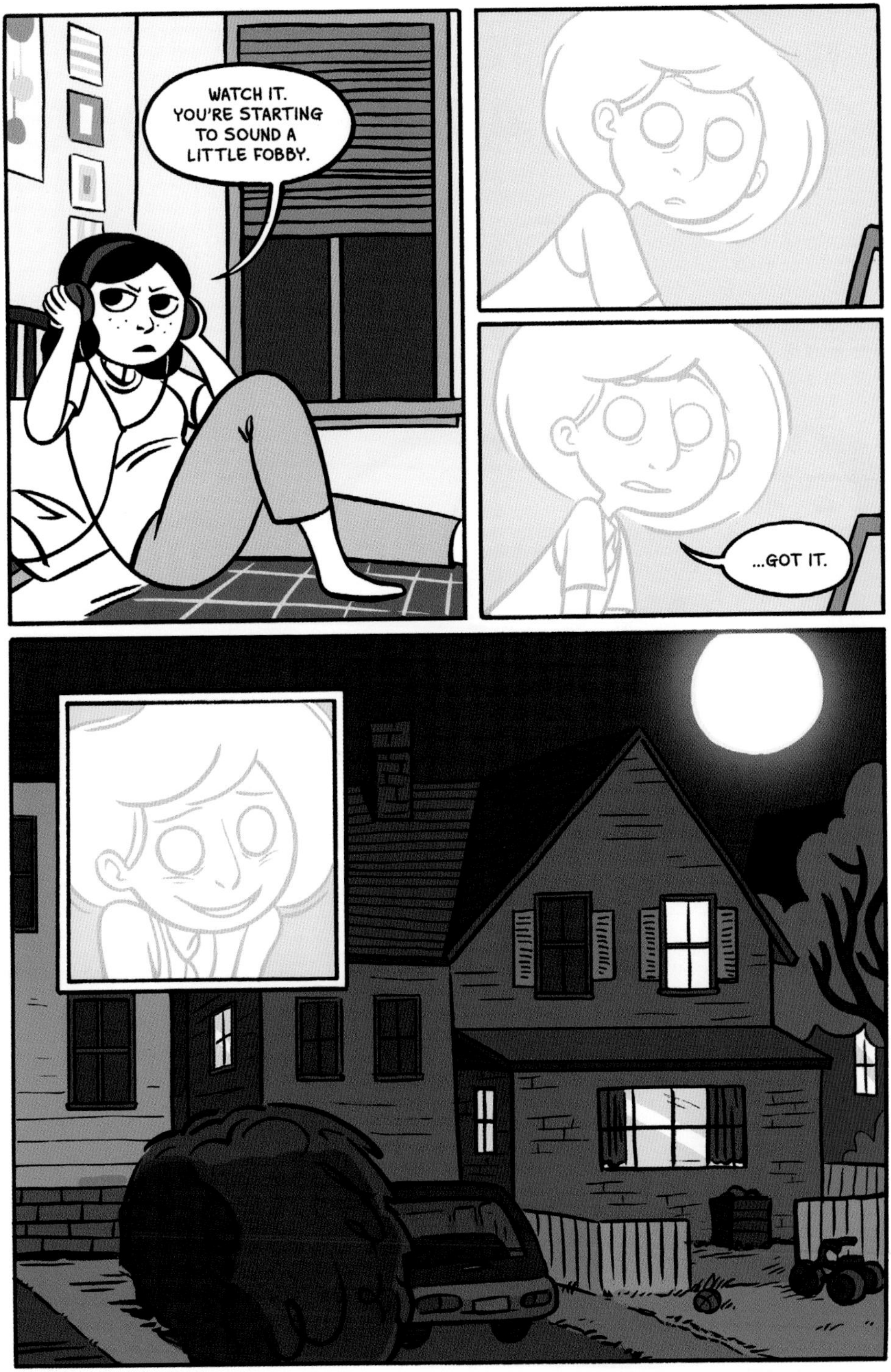
WATCH IT. YOU'RE STARTING TO SOUND A LITTLE FOBBY.
...GOT IT.

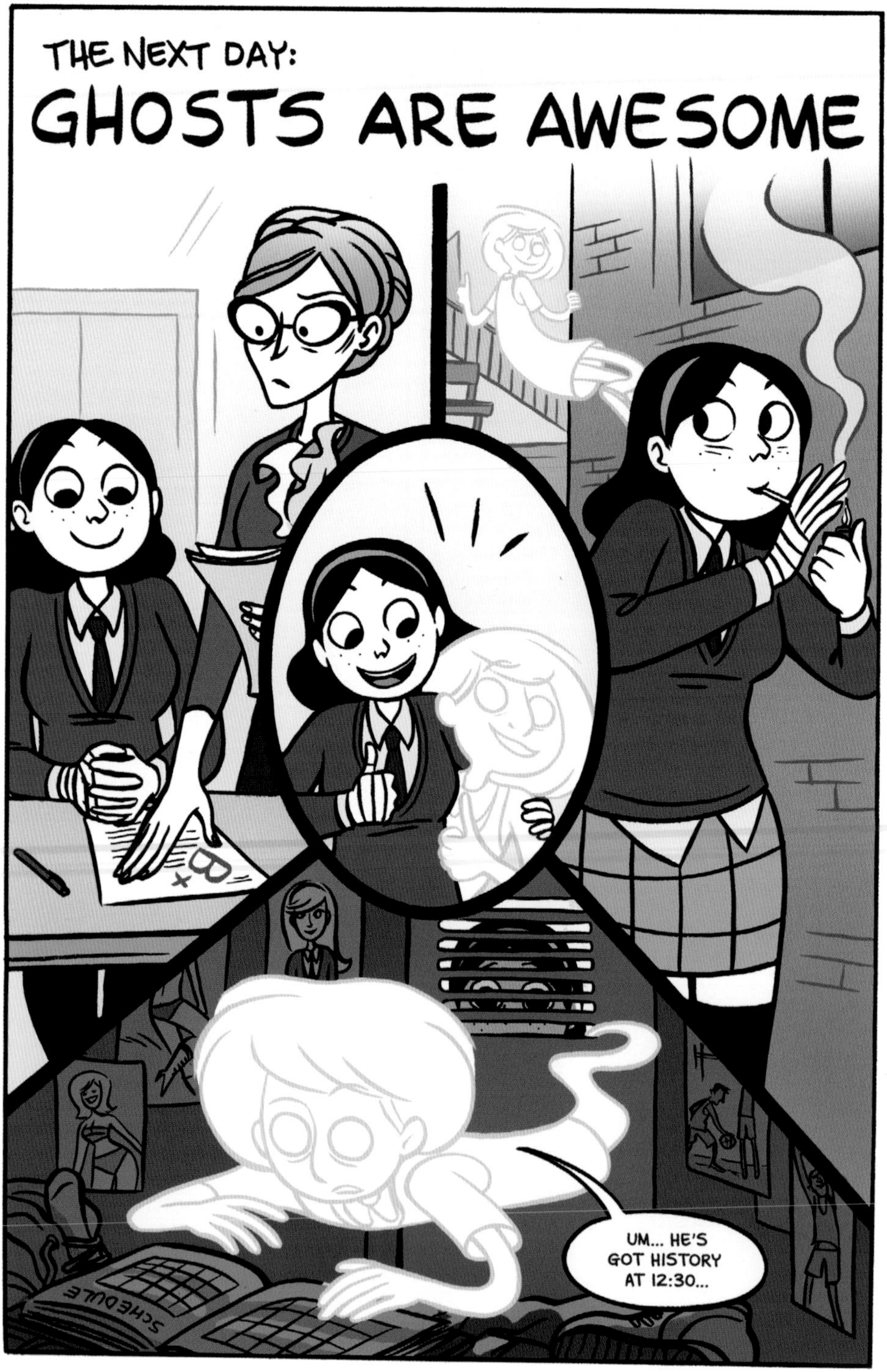
THE NEXT DAY:
GHOSTS ARE AWESOME
UM... HE'S GOT HISTORY AT 12:30...
SCHEDULE

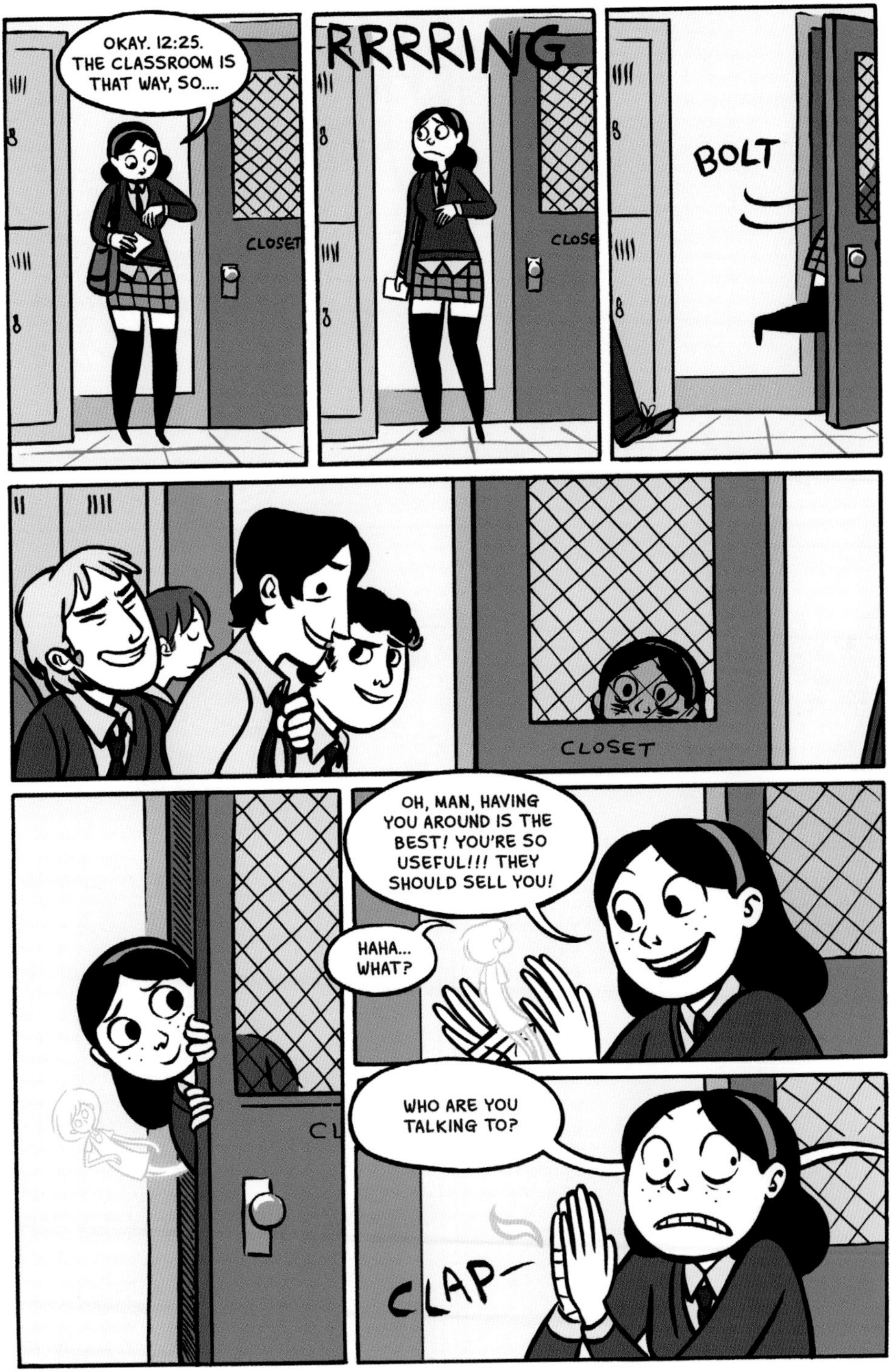
OKAY. 12:25.
THE CLASSROOM IS
THAT WAY, SO....
RRRRING
CLOSET
BOLT
CLOSET
OH, MAN, HAVING YOU AROUND IS THE BEST! YOU'RE SO USEFUL!!! THEY SHOULD SELL YOU!
HAHA... WHAT?
WHO ARE YOU TALKING TO?
CLAP-

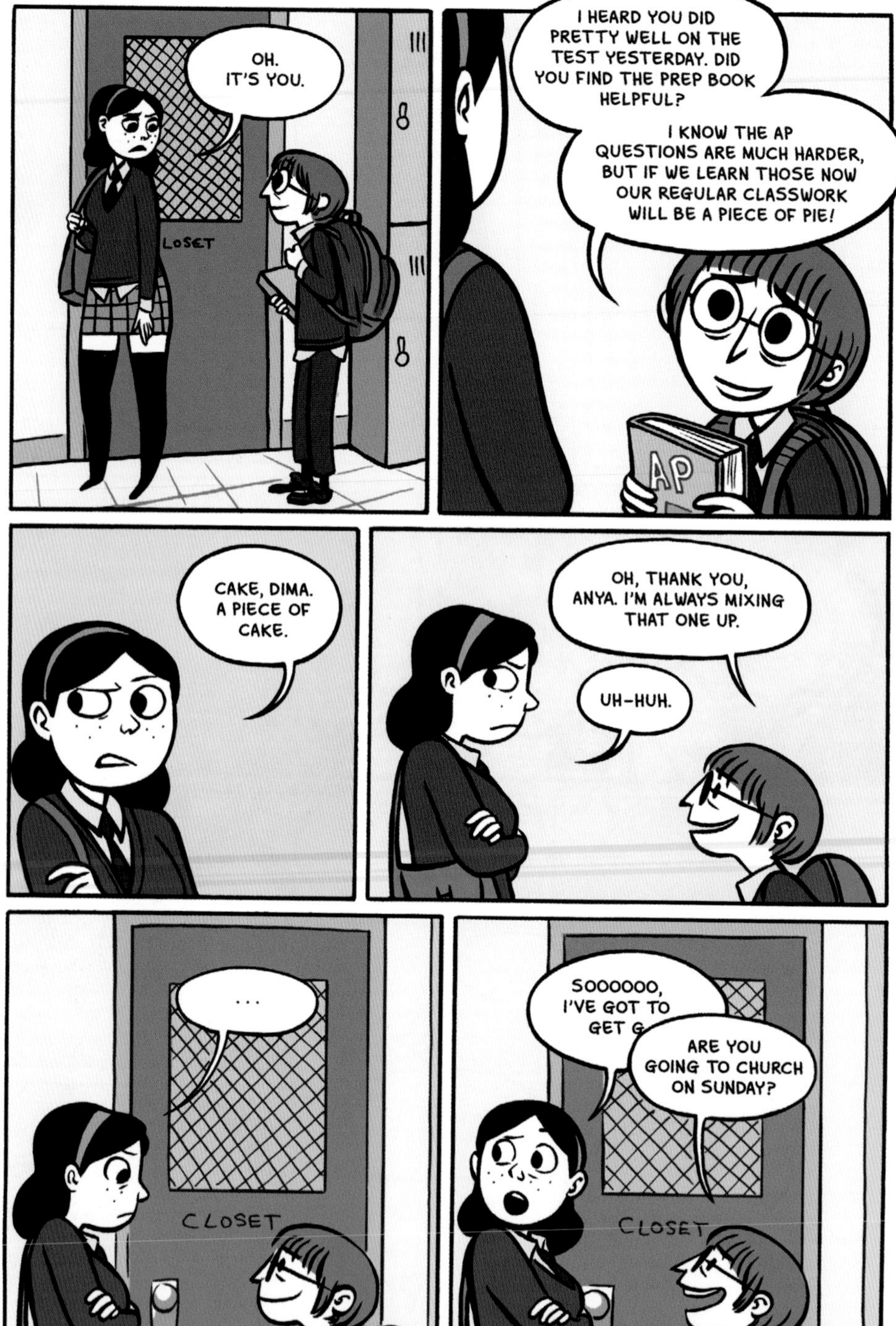
OH. IT'S YOU.
I HEARD YOU DID PRETTY WELL ON THE TEST YESTERDAY. DID YOU FIND THE PREP BOOK HELPFUL?
I KNOW THE AP QUESTIONS ARE MUCH HARDER, BUT IF WE LEARN THOSE NOW OUR REGULAR CLASSWORK WILL BE A PIECE OF PIE!
AP
CAKE, DIMA. A PIECE OF CAKE.
OH, THANK YOU, ANYA. I'M ALWAYS MIXING THAT ONE UP.
UH-HUH.
...
CLOSET
SOOOOOO, I'VE GOT TO GET G
ARE YOU GOING TO CHURCH ON SUNDAY?
CLOSET

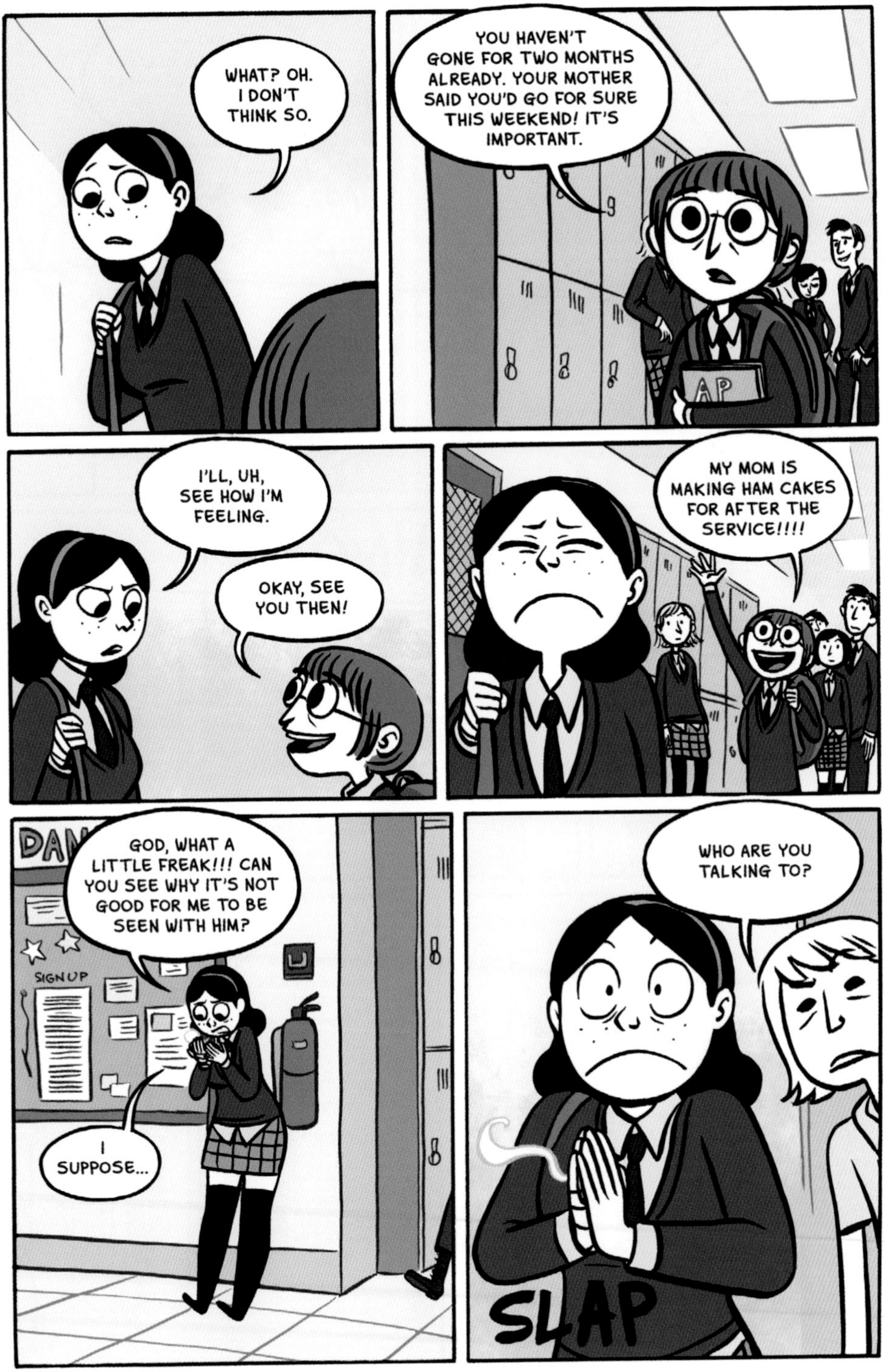
WHAT? OH. I DON'T THINK SO.
YOU HAVEN'T GONE FOR TWO MONTHS ALREADY. YOUR MOTHER SAID YOU'D GO FOR SURE THIS WEEKEND! IT'S IMPORTANT.
AP
I'LL, UH, SEE HOW I'M FEELING.
OKAY, SEE YOU THEN!
MY MOM IS MAKING HAM CAKES FOR AFTER THE SERVICE!!!!
GOD, WHAT A LITTLE FREAK!!! CAN YOU SEE WHY IT'S NOT GOOD FOR ME TO BE SEEN WITH HIM?
SIGN UP
I SUPPOSE...
WHO ARE YOU TALKING TO?
SLAP

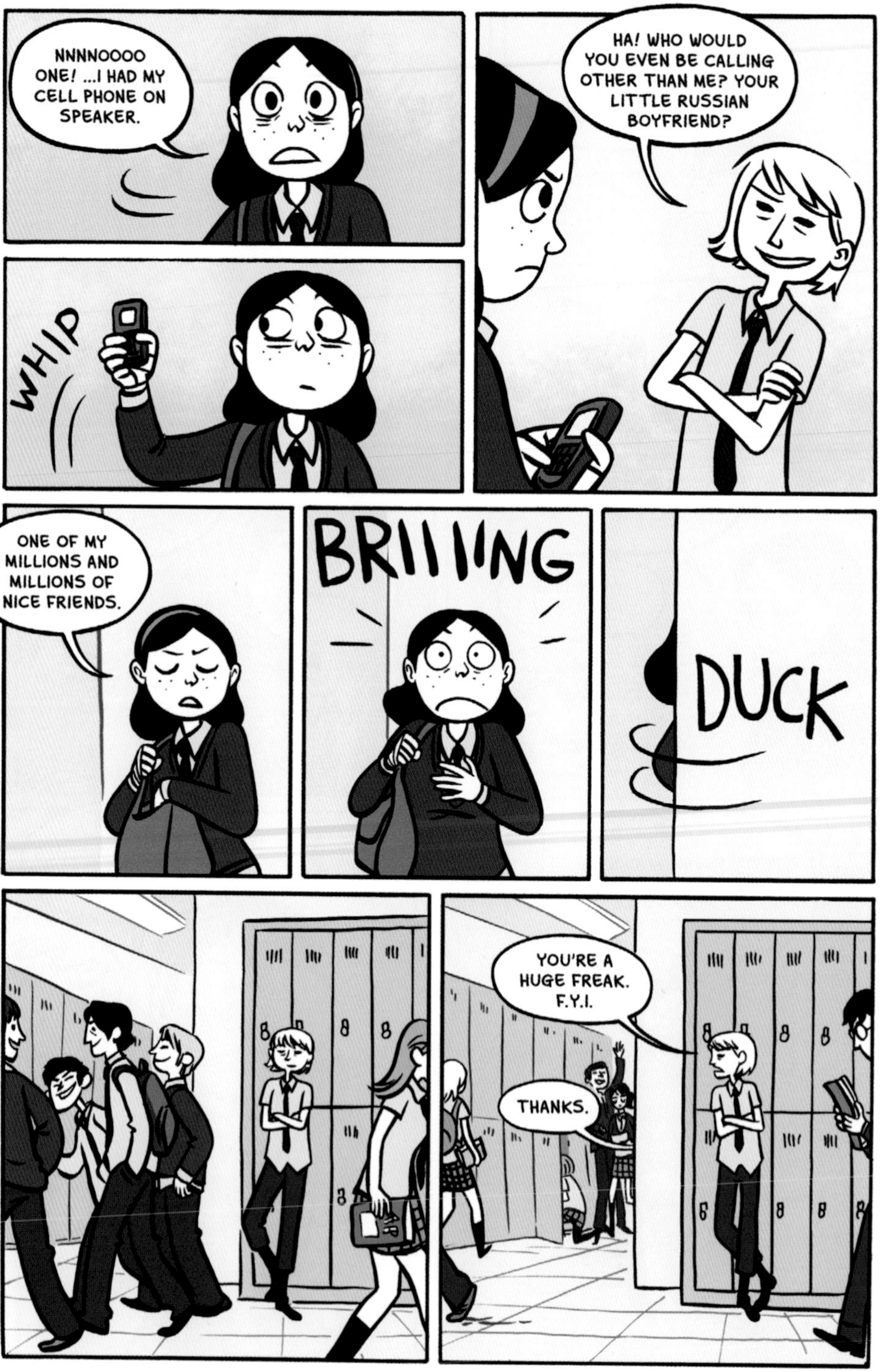
NNNNOOOO ONE! ...I HAD MY CELL PHONE ON SPEAKER.
HA! WHO WOULD YOU EVEN BE CALLING OTHER THAN ME? YOUR LITTLE RUSSIAN BOYFRIEND?
WHIP
ONE OF MY MILLIONS AND MILLIONS OF NICE FRIENDS.
BRIIIING
DUCK
YOU'RE A HUGE FREAK. F.Y.I.
THANKS.

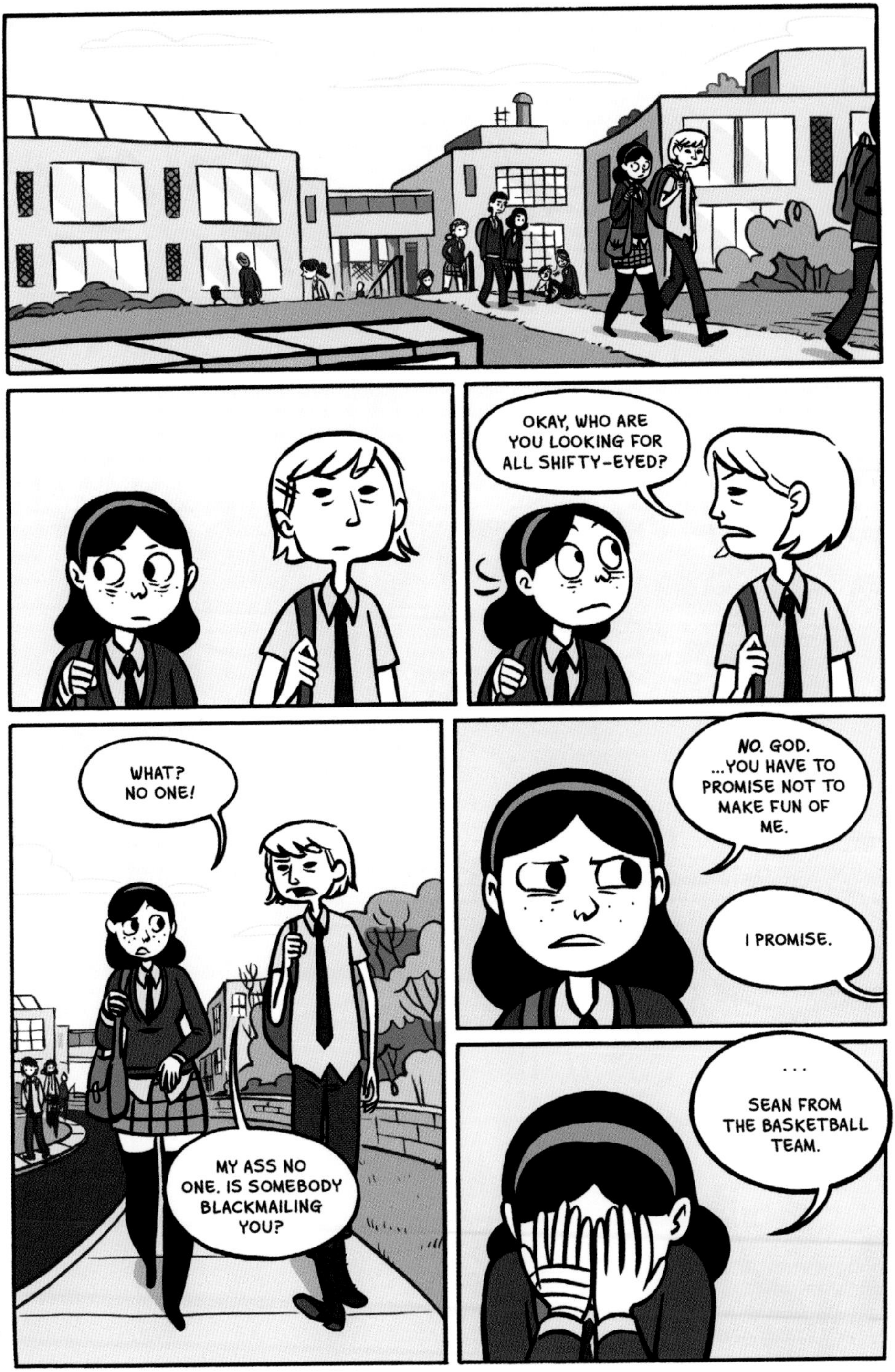
OKAY, WHO ARE YOU LOOKING FOR ALL SHIFTY-EYED?
WHAT? NO ONE!
MY ASS NO ONE. IS SOMEBODY BLACKMAILING YOU?
NO. GOD. ...YOU HAVE TO PROMISE NOT TO MAKE FUN OF ME.
I PROMISE.
...
SEAN FROM THE BASKETBALL TEAM.

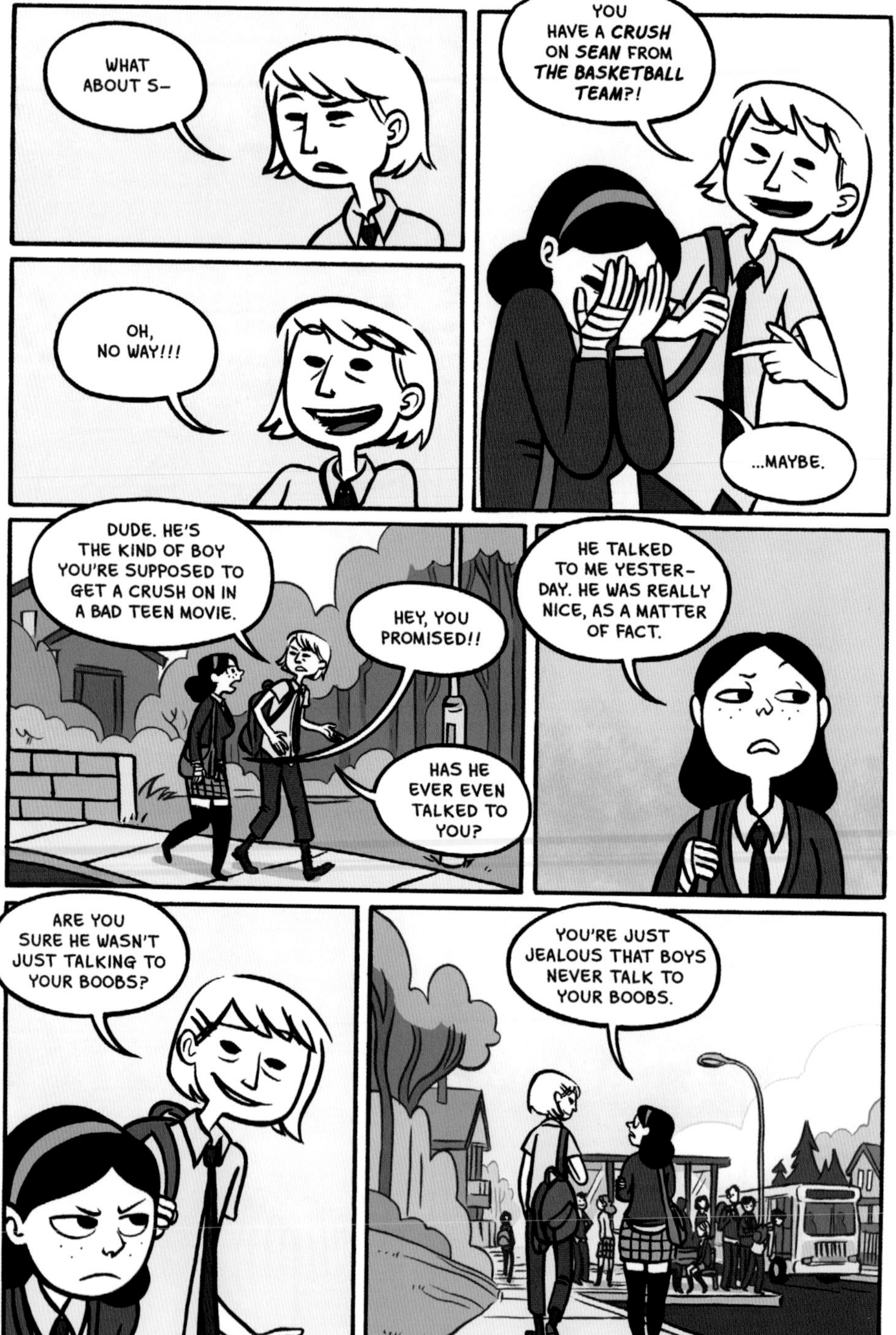
WHAT ABOUT S–
YOU HAVE A CRUSH ON SEAN FROM THE BASKETBALL TEAM?!
OH, NO WAY!!!
...MAYBE.
DUDE. HE'S THE KIND OF BOY YOU'RE SUPPOSED TO GET A CRUSH ON IN A BAD TEEN MOVIE.
HEY, YOU PROMISED!!
HAS HE EVER EVEN TALKED TO YOU?
HE TALKED TO ME YESTER-DAY. HE WAS REALLY NICE, AS A MATTER OF FACT.
ARE YOU SURE HE WASN'T JUST TALKING TO YOUR BOOBS?
YOU'RE JUST JEALOUS THAT BOYS NEVER TALK TO YOUR BOOBS.

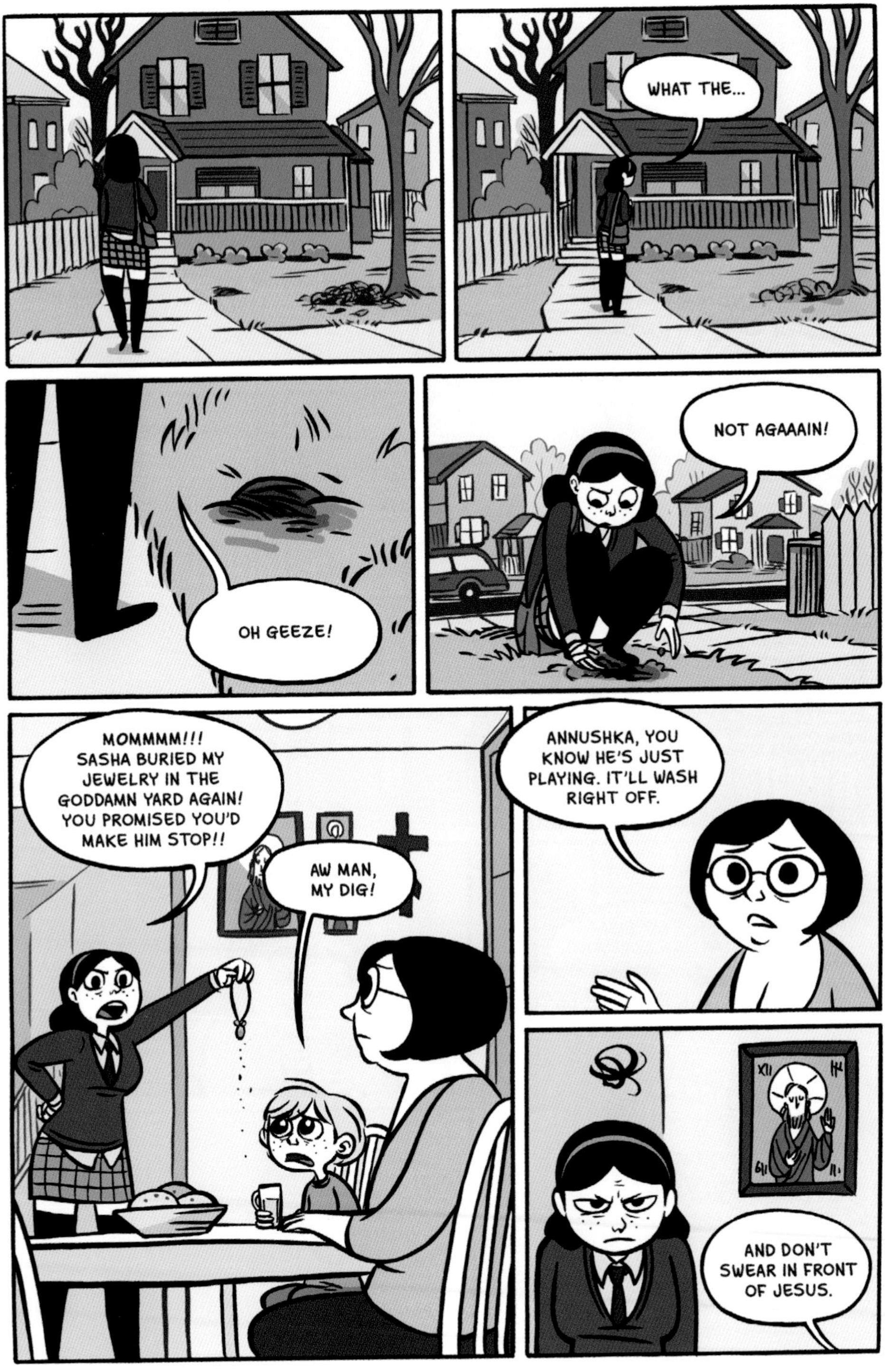
WHAT THE...
OH GEEZE!
NOT AGAAAIN!
MOMMMM!!! SASHA BURIED MY JEWELRY IN THE GODDAMN YARD AGAIN! YOU PROMISED YOU'D MAKE HIM STOP!!
AW MAN, MY DIG!
ANNUSHKA, YOU KNOW HE'S JUST PLAYING. IT'LL WASH RIGHT OFF.
AND DON'T SWEAR IN FRONT OF JESUS.

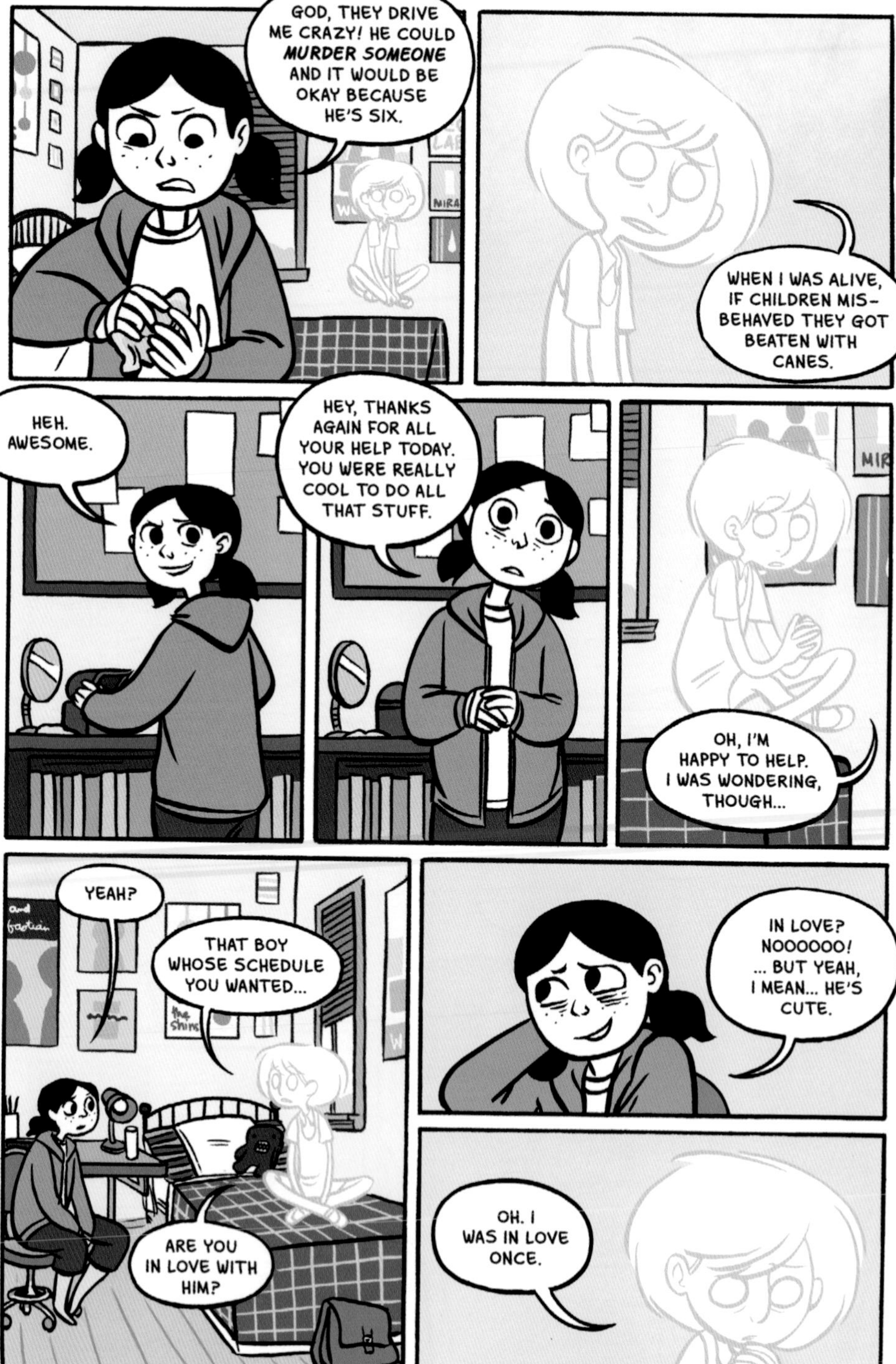
GOD, THEY DRIVE ME CRAZY! HE COULD *MURDER SOMEONE* AND IT WOULD BE OKAY BECAUSE HE'S SIX.
WHEN I WAS ALIVE, IF CHILDREN MIS-BEHAVED THEY GOT BEATEN WITH CANES.
HEH. AWESOME.
HEY, THANKS AGAIN FOR ALL YOUR HELP TODAY. YOU WERE REALLY COOL TO DO ALL THAT STUFF.
OH, I'M HAPPY TO HELP. I WAS WONDERING, THOUGH...
YEAH?
THAT BOY WHOSE SCHEDULE YOU WANTED...
ARE YOU IN LOVE WITH HIM?
IN LOVE? NOOOOOO! ... BUT YEAH, I MEAN... HE'S CUTE.
OH. I WAS IN LOVE ONCE.

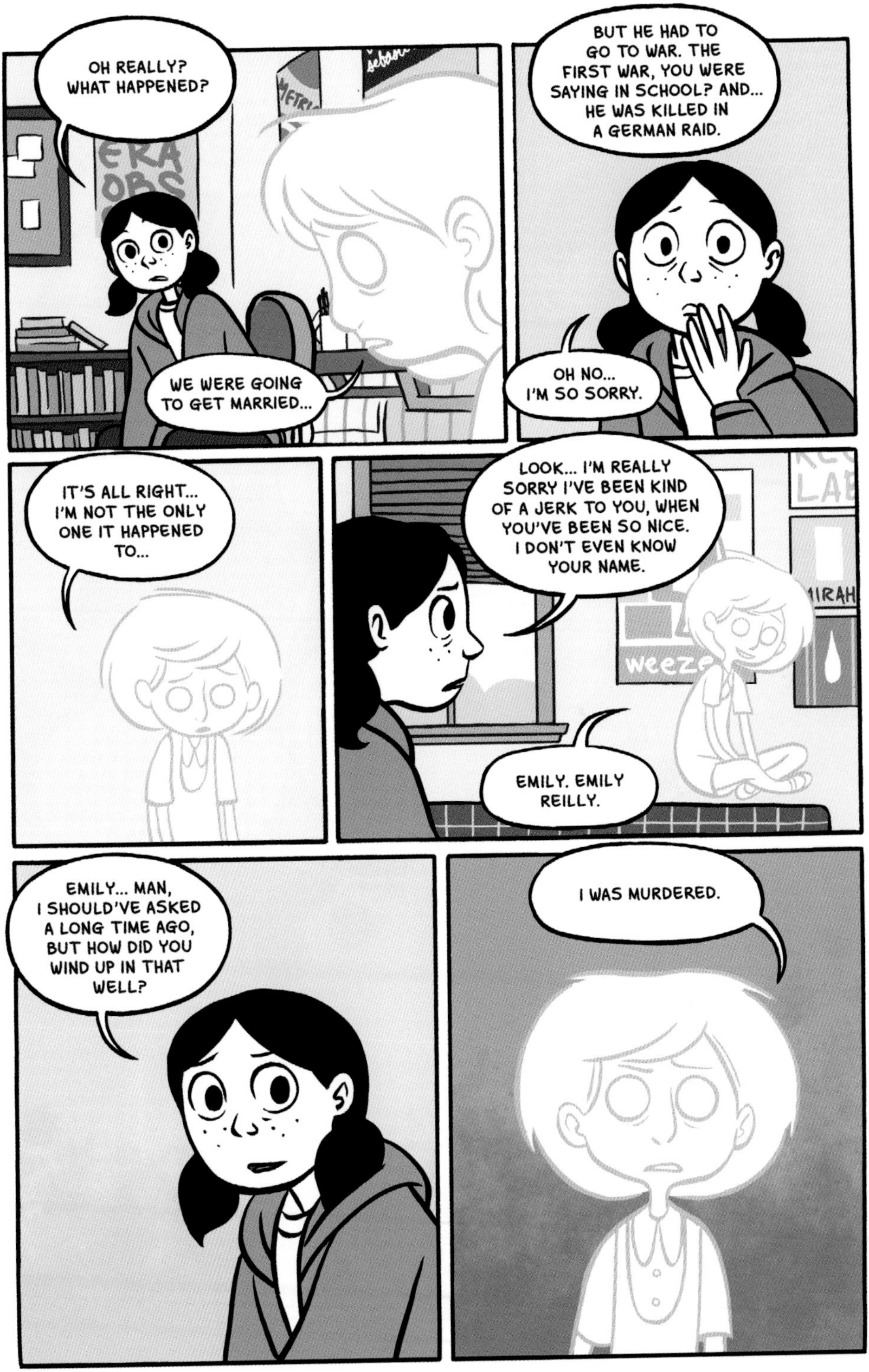
OH REALLY? WHAT HAPPENED?
WE WERE GOING TO GET MARRIED...
BUT HE HAD TO GO TO WAR. THE FIRST WAR, YOU WERE SAYING IN SCHOOL? AND... HE WAS KILLED IN A GERMAN RAID.
OH NO... I'M SO SORRY.
IT'S ALL RIGHT... I'M NOT THE ONLY ONE IT HAPPENED TO...
LOOK... I'M REALLY SORRY I'VE BEEN KIND OF A JERK TO YOU, WHEN YOU'VE BEEN SO NICE. I DON'T EVEN KNOW YOUR NAME.
EMILY. EMILY REILLY.
EMILY... MAN, I SHOULD'VE ASKED A LONG TIME AGO, BUT HOW DID YOU WIND UP IN THAT WELL?
I WAS MURDERED.

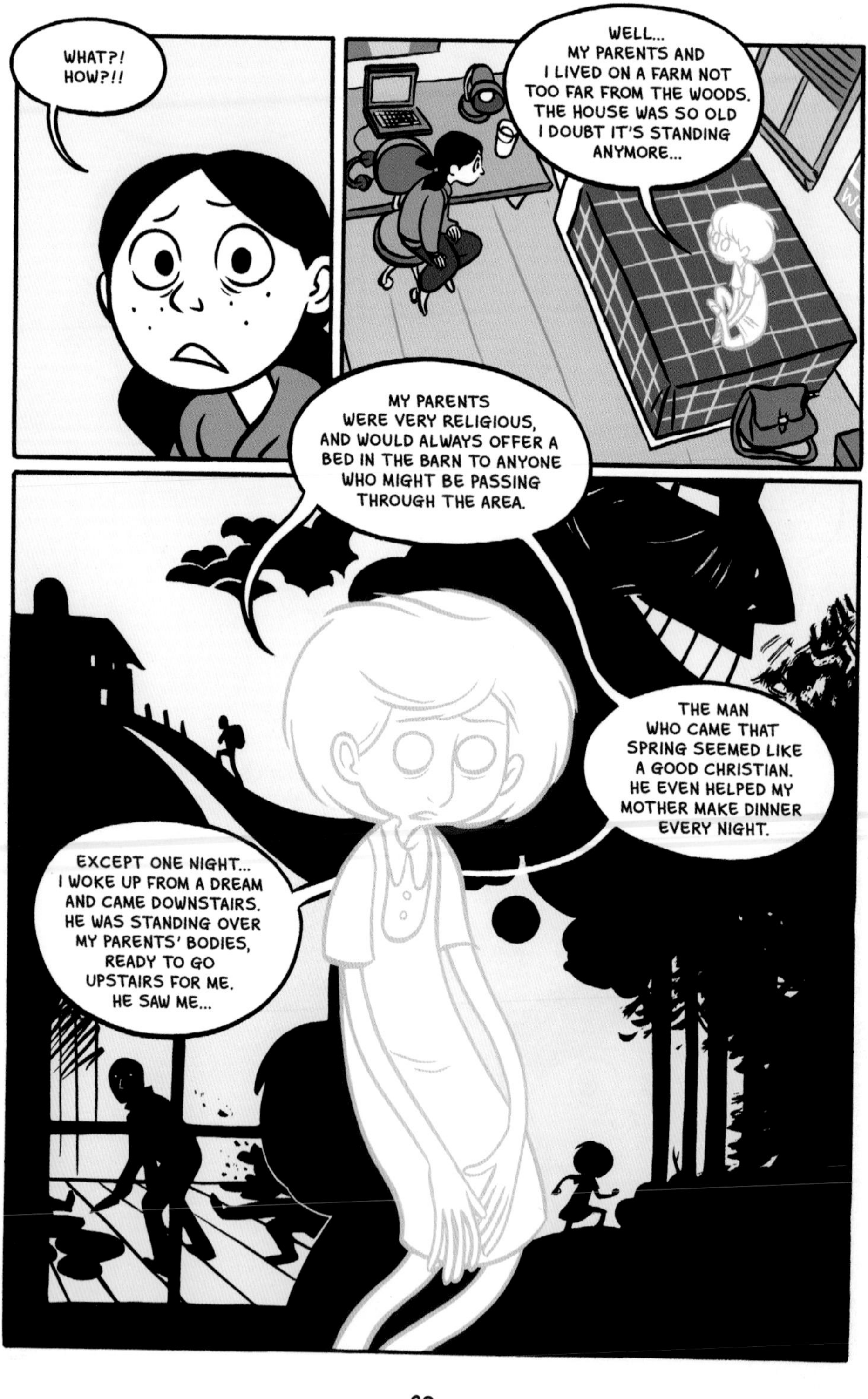
WHAT?! HOW?!!
WELL... MY PARENTS AND I LIVED ON A FARM NOT TOO FAR FROM THE WOODS. THE HOUSE WAS SO OLD I DOUBT IT'S STANDING ANYMORE...
MY PARENTS WERE VERY RELIGIOUS, AND WOULD ALWAYS OFFER A BED IN THE BARN TO ANYONE WHO MIGHT BE PASSING THROUGH THE AREA.
THE MAN WHO CAME THAT SPRING SEEMED LIKE A GOOD CHRISTIAN. HE EVEN HELPED MY MOTHER MAKE DINNER EVERY NIGHT.
EXCEPT ONE NIGHT... I WOKE UP FROM A DREAM AND CAME DOWNSTAIRS. HE WAS STANDING OVER MY PARENTS' BODIES, READY TO GO UPSTAIRS FOR ME. HE SAW ME...

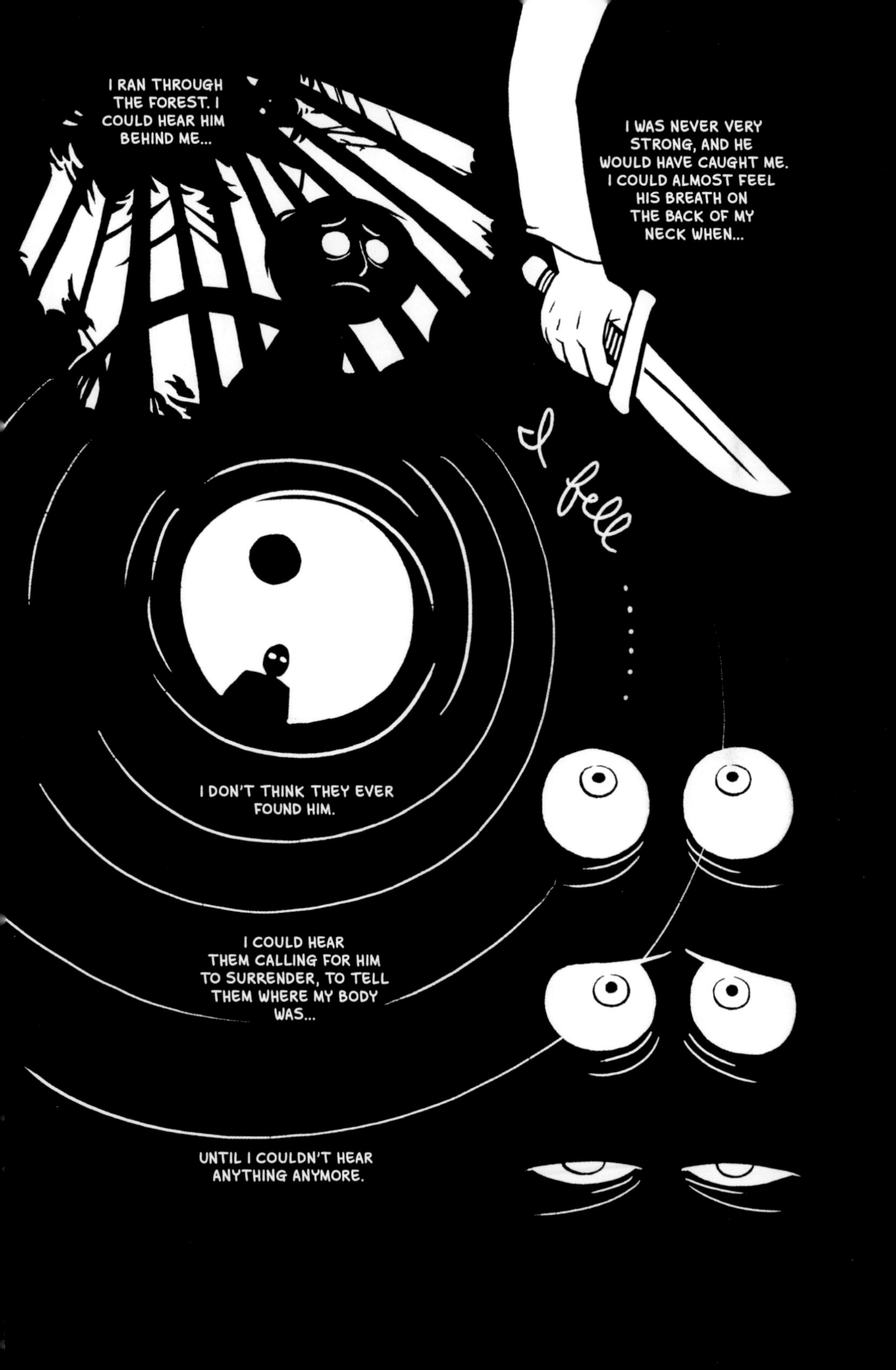
I RAN THROUGH THE FOREST. I COULD HEAR HIM BEHIND ME...
I WAS NEVER VERY STRONG, AND HE WOULD HAVE CAUGHT ME. I COULD ALMOST FEEL HIS BREATH ON THE BACK OF MY NECK WHEN...
I fell
I DON'T THINK THEY EVER FOUND HIM.
I COULD HEAR THEM CALLING FOR HIM TO SURRENDER, TO TELL THEM WHERE MY BODY WAS...
UNTIL I COULDN'T HEAR ANYTHING ANYMORE.

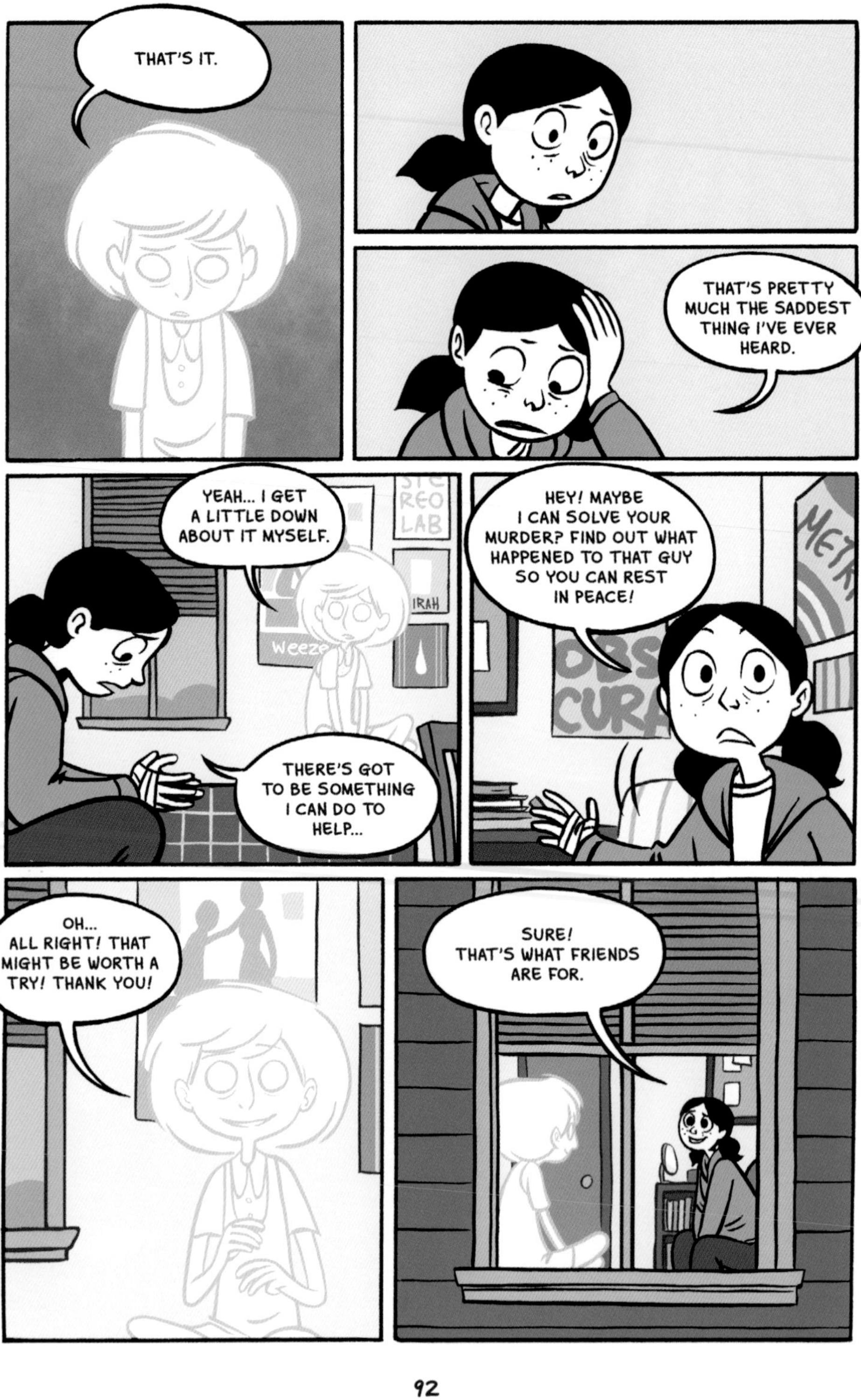
THAT'S IT.
THAT'S PRETTY MUCH THE SADDEST THING I'VE EVER HEARD.
YEAH... I GET A LITTLE DOWN ABOUT IT MYSELF.
STEREO LAB
weeze
THERE'S GOT TO BE SOMETHING I CAN DO TO HELP...
HEY! MAYBE I CAN SOLVE YOUR MURDER? FIND OUT WHAT HAPPENED TO THAT GUY SO YOU CAN REST IN PEACE!
OBSCURA
OH... ALL RIGHT! THAT MIGHT BE WORTH A TRY! THANK YOU!
SURE! THAT'S WHAT FRIENDS ARE FOR.

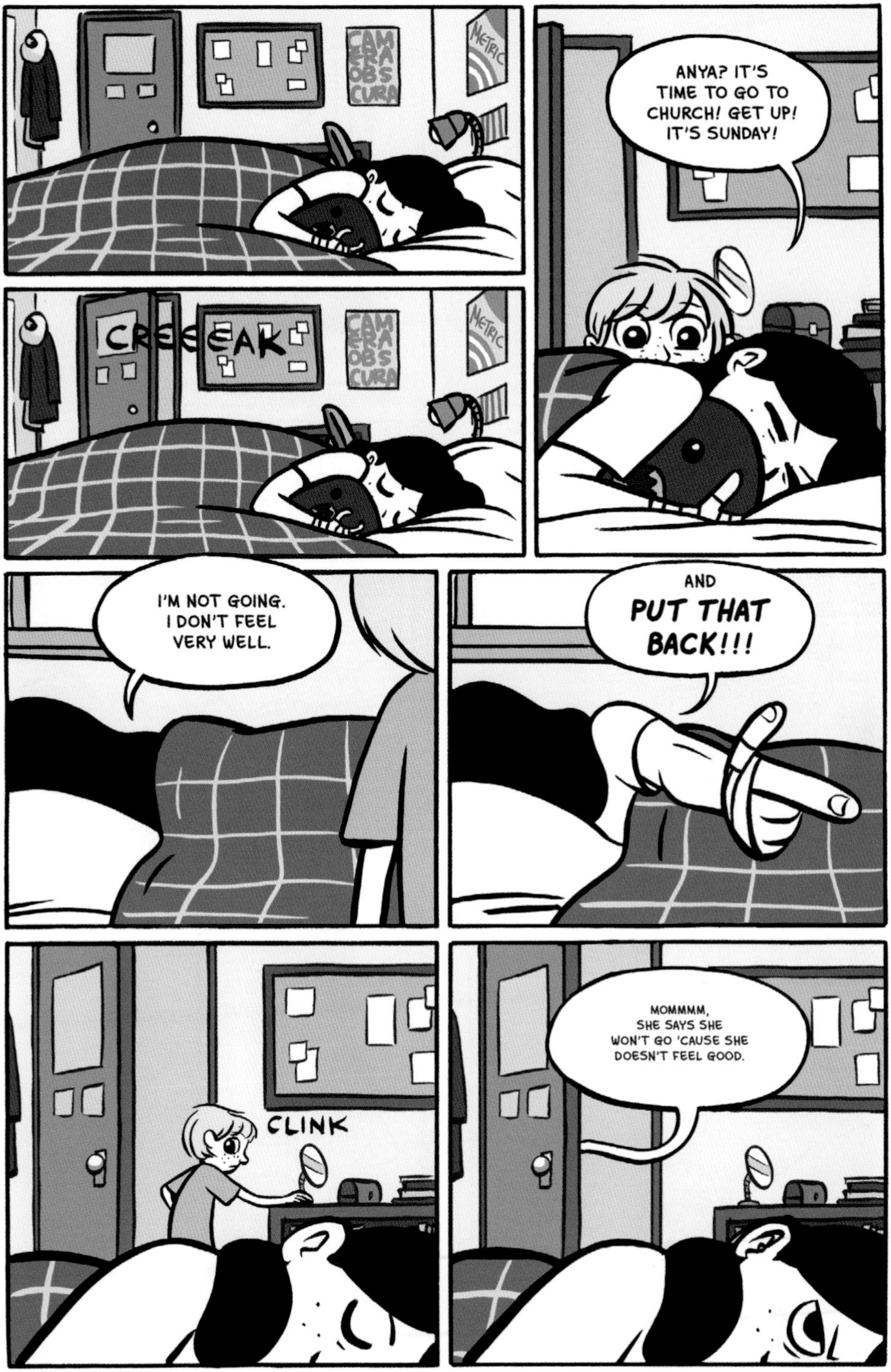
CAMERA OBSCURA
METRIC
CREEEAK
ANYA? IT'S TIME TO GO TO CHURCH! GET UP! IT'S SUNDAY!
I'M NOT GOING. I DON'T FEEL VERY WELL.
AND PUT THAT BACK!!!
CLINK
MOMMMM, SHE SAYS SHE WON'T GO 'CAUSE SHE DOESN'T FEEL GOOD.

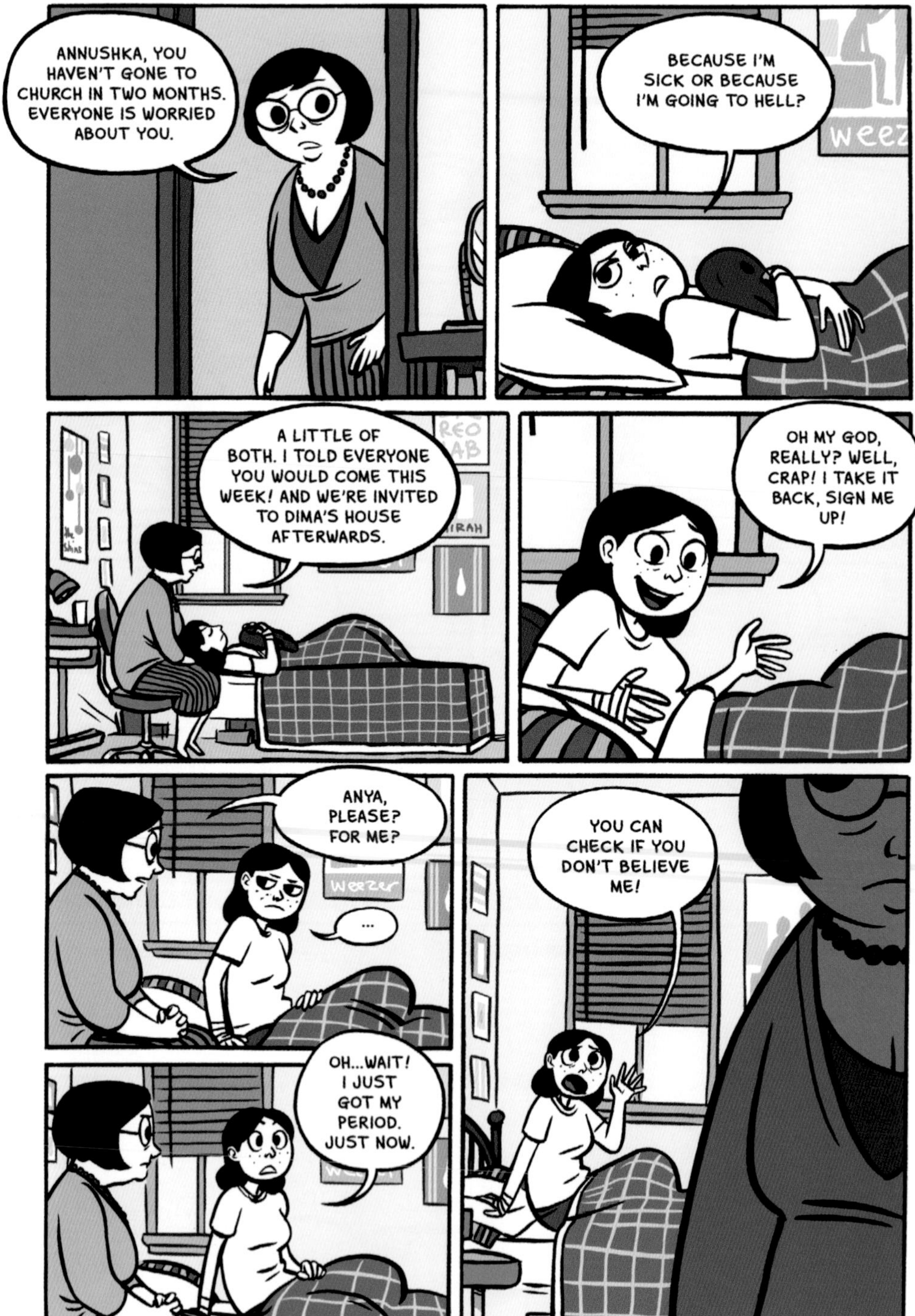
ANNUSHKA, YOU HAVEN'T GONE TO CHURCH IN TWO MONTHS. EVERYONE IS WORRIED ABOUT YOU.
BECAUSE I'M SICK OR BECAUSE I'M GOING TO HELL?
weez
A LITTLE OF BOTH. I TOLD EVERYONE YOU WOULD COME THIS WEEK! AND WE'RE INVITED TO DIMA'S HOUSE AFTERWARDS.
OH MY GOD, REALLY? WELL, CRAP! I TAKE IT BACK, SIGN ME UP!
ANYA, PLEASE? FOR ME?
...
weezer
OH...WAIT! I JUST GOT MY PERIOD. JUST NOW.
YOU CAN CHECK IF YOU DON'T BELIEVE ME!

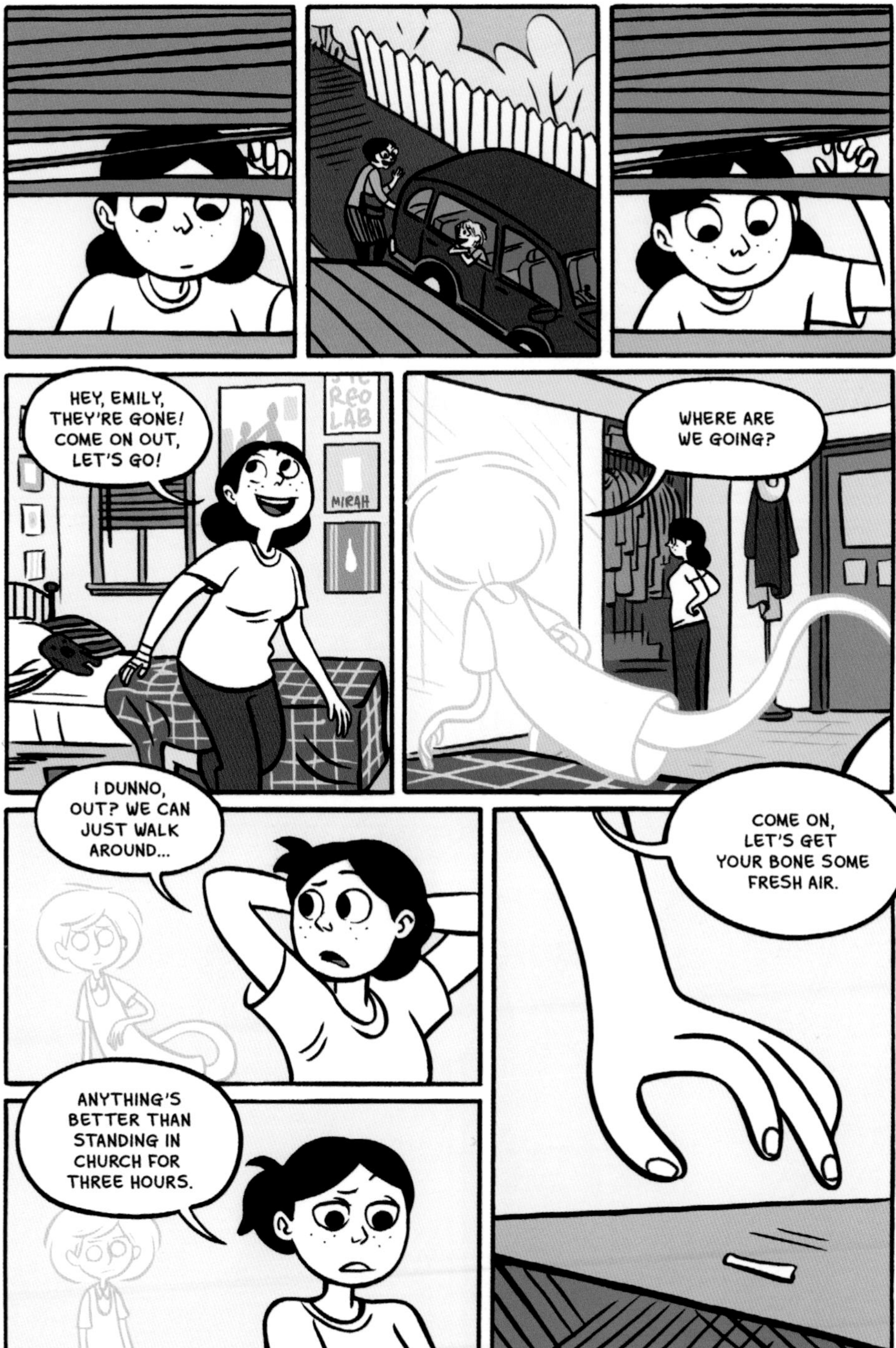
HEY, EMILY, THEY'RE GONE! COME ON OUT, LET'S GO!
MIRAH
WHERE ARE WE GOING?
I DUNNO, OUT? WE CAN JUST WALK AROUND...
COME ON, LET'S GET YOUR BONE SOME FRESH AIR.
ANYTHING'S BETTER THAN STANDING IN CHURCH FOR THREE HOURS.

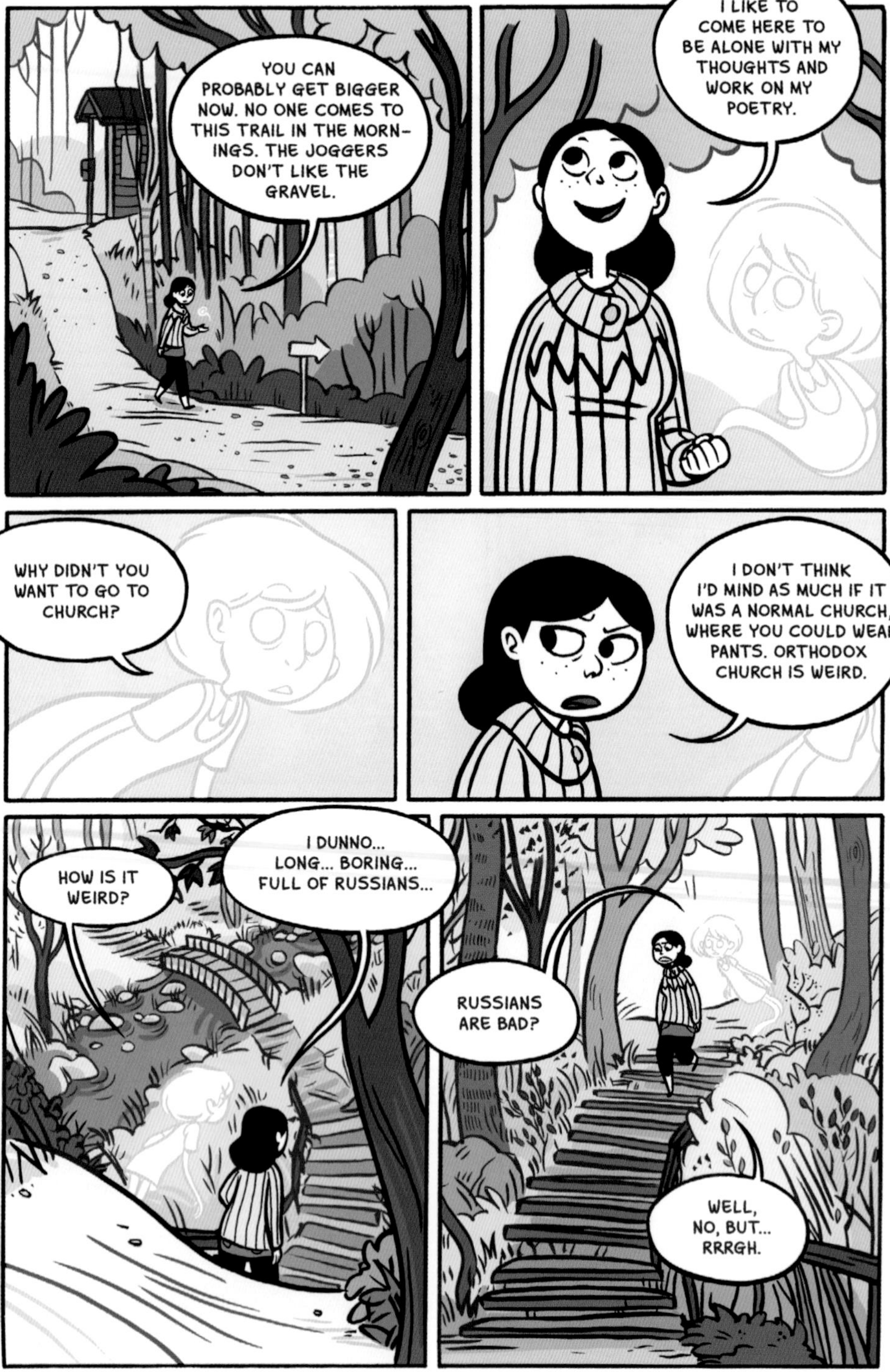
YOU CAN PROBABLY GET BIGGER NOW. NO ONE COMES TO THIS TRAIL IN THE MORNINGS. THE JOGGERS DON'T LIKE THE GRAVEL.
I LIKE TO COME HERE TO BE ALONE WITH MY THOUGHTS AND WORK ON MY POETRY.
WHY DIDN'T YOU WANT TO GO TO CHURCH?
I DON'T THINK I'D MIND AS MUCH IF IT WAS A NORMAL CHURCH, WHERE YOU COULD WEAR PANTS. ORTHODOX CHURCH IS WEIRD.
HOW IS IT WEIRD?
I DUNNO... LONG... BORING... FULL OF RUSSIANS...
RUSSIANS ARE BAD?
WELL, NO, BUT... RRRGH.

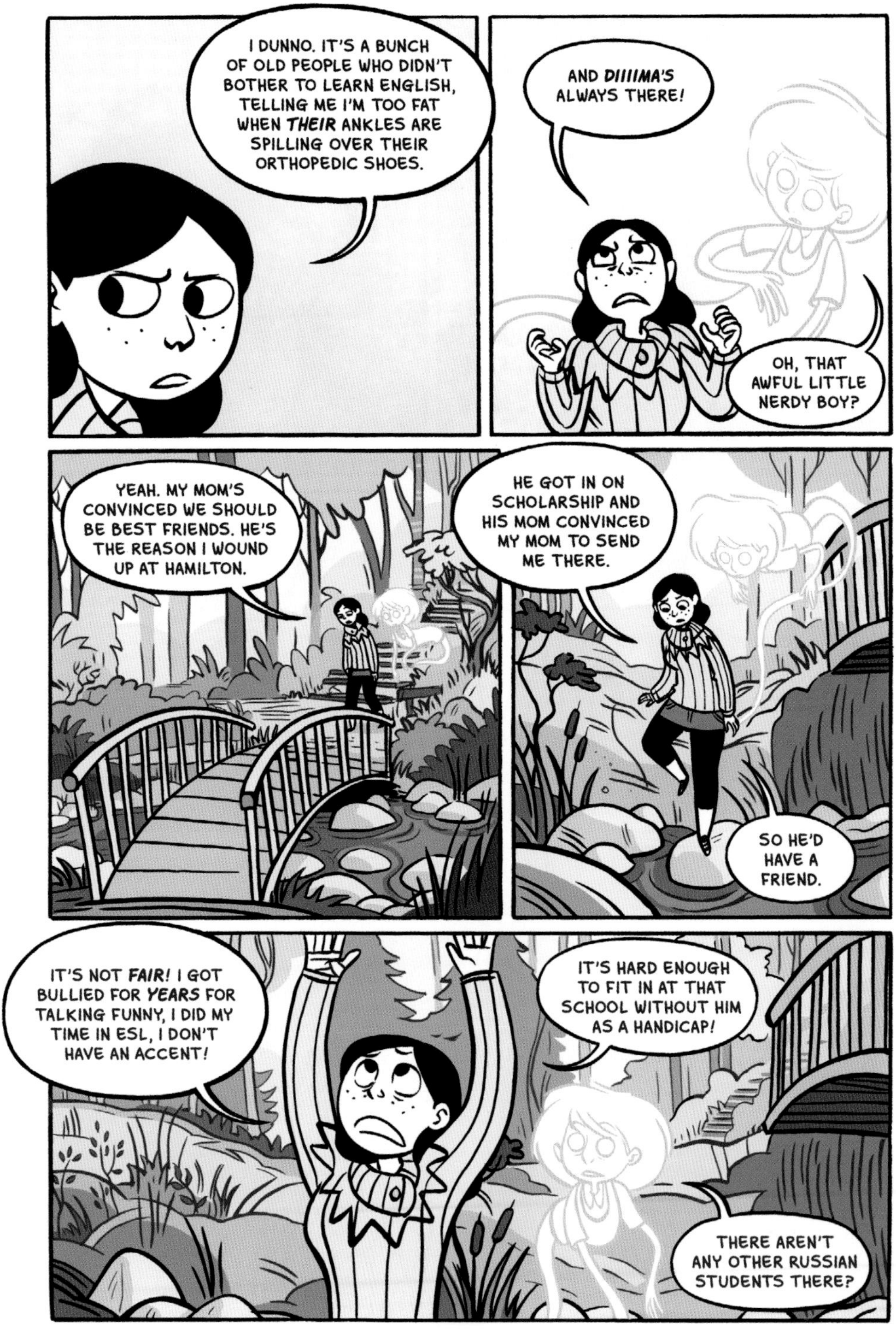
I DUNNO. IT'S A BUNCH OF OLD PEOPLE WHO DIDN'T BOTHER TO LEARN ENGLISH, TELLING ME I'M TOO FAT WHEN *THEIR* ANKLES ARE SPILLING OVER THEIR ORTHOPEDIC SHOES.
AND *DIIIIMA'S* ALWAYS THERE!
OH, THAT AWFUL LITTLE NERDY BOY?
YEAH. MY MOM'S CONVINCED WE SHOULD BE BEST FRIENDS. HE'S THE REASON I WOUND UP AT HAMILTON.
HE GOT IN ON SCHOLARSHIP AND HIS MOM CONVINCED MY MOM TO SEND ME THERE.
SO HE'D HAVE A FRIEND.
IT'S NOT *FAIR!* I GOT BULLIED FOR *YEARS* FOR TALKING FUNNY, I DID MY TIME IN ESL, I DON'T HAVE AN ACCENT!
IT'S HARD ENOUGH TO FIT IN AT THAT SCHOOL WITHOUT HIM AS A HANDICAP!
THERE AREN'T ANY OTHER RUSSIAN STUDENTS THERE?

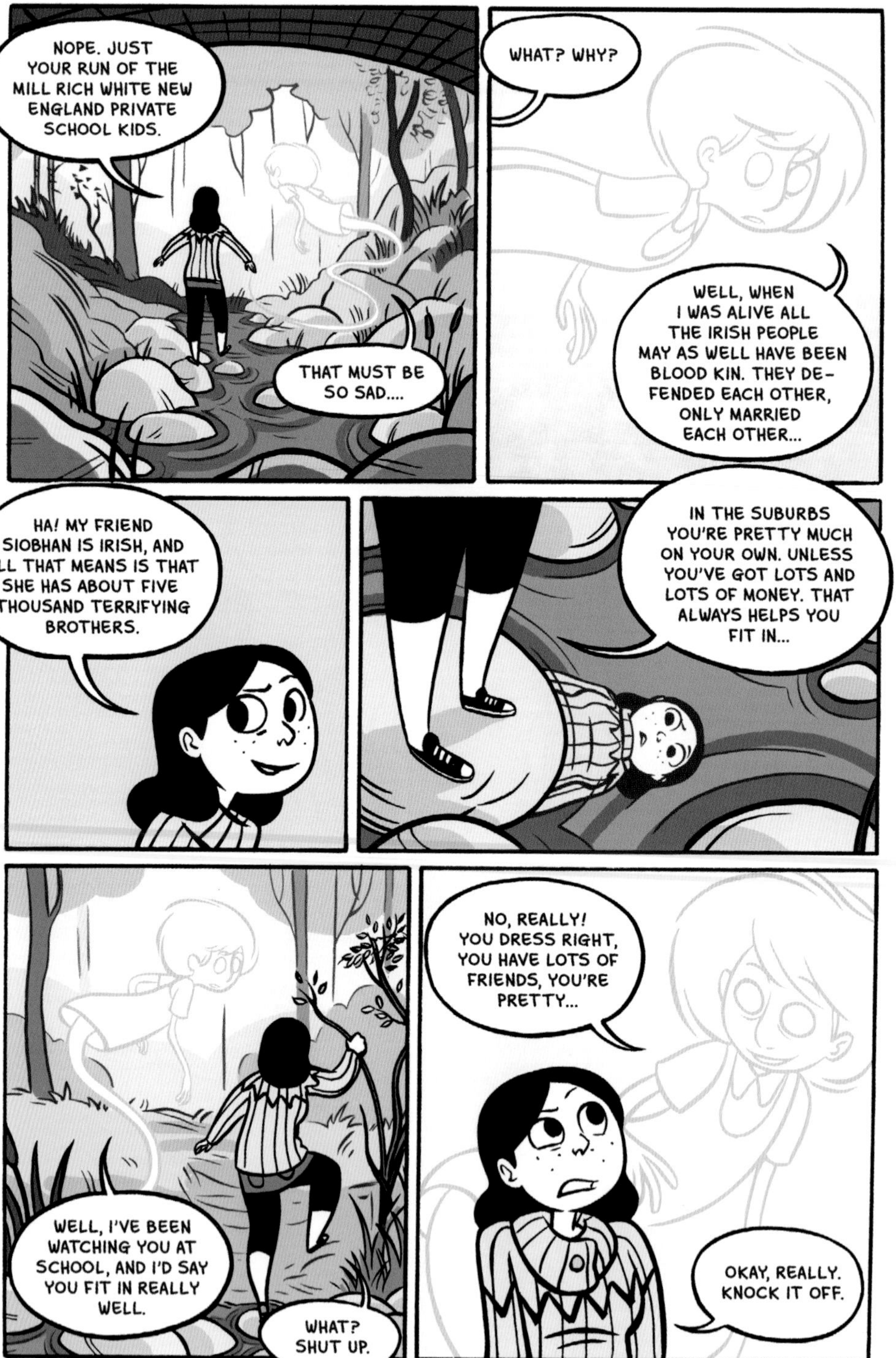
NOPE. JUST YOUR RUN OF THE MILL RICH WHITE NEW ENGLAND PRIVATE SCHOOL KIDS.
THAT MUST BE SO SAD....
WHAT? WHY?
WELL, WHEN I WAS ALIVE ALL THE IRISH PEOPLE MAY AS WELL HAVE BEEN BLOOD KIN. THEY DE-FENDED EACH OTHER, ONLY MARRIED EACH OTHER...
HA! MY FRIEND SIOBHAN IS IRISH, AND ALL THAT MEANS IS THAT SHE HAS ABOUT FIVE THOUSAND TERRIFYING BROTHERS.
IN THE SUBURBS YOU'RE PRETTY MUCH ON YOUR OWN. UNLESS YOU'VE GOT LOTS AND LOTS OF MONEY. THAT ALWAYS HELPS YOU FIT IN...
WELL, I'VE BEEN WATCHING YOU AT SCHOOL, AND I'D SAY YOU FIT IN REALLY WELL.
WHAT? SHUT UP.
NO, REALLY! YOU DRESS RIGHT, YOU HAVE LOTS OF FRIENDS, YOU'RE PRETTY...
OKAY, REALLY. KNOCK IT OFF.

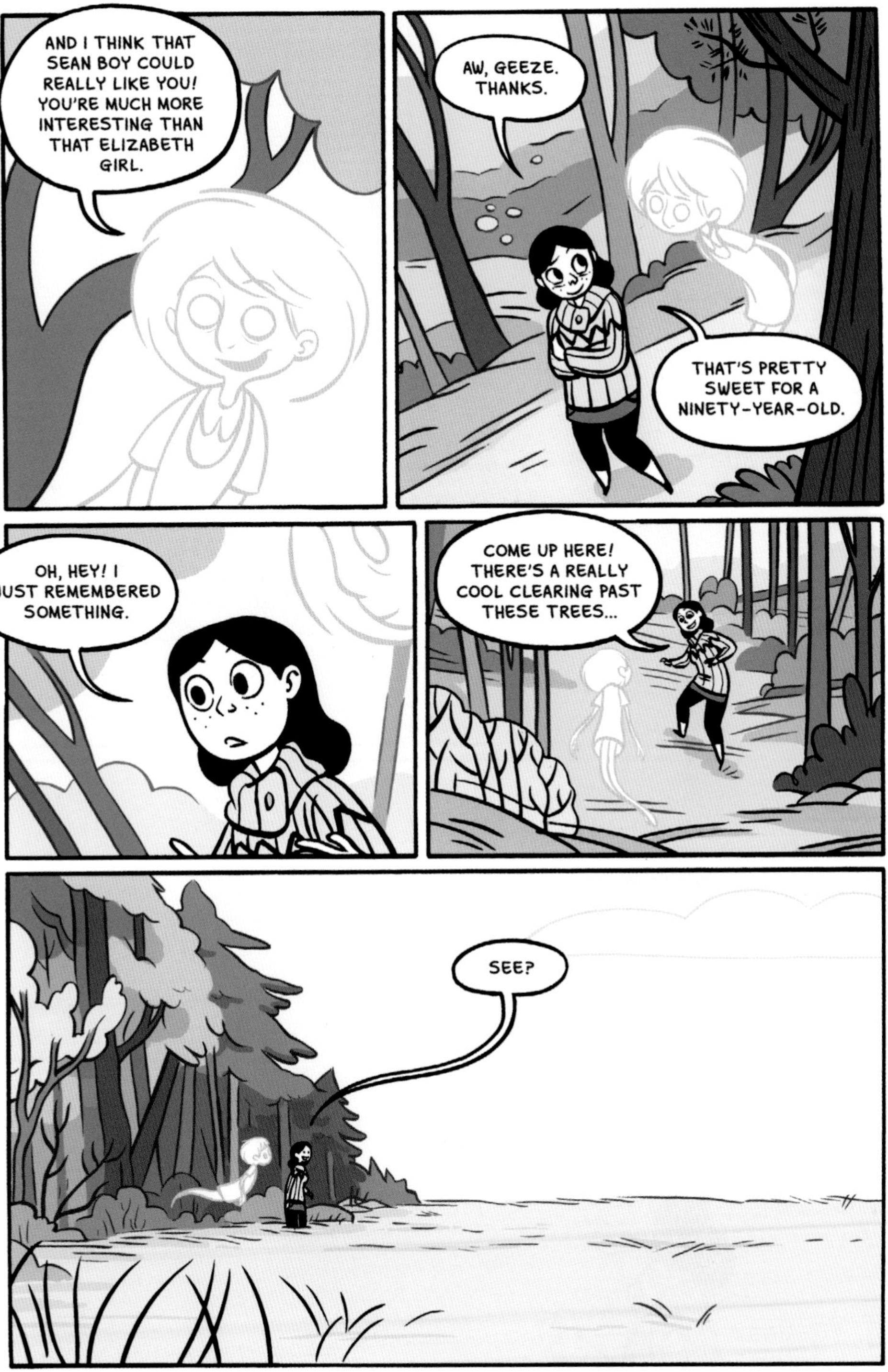
AND I THINK THAT SEAN BOY COULD REALLY LIKE YOU! YOU'RE MUCH MORE INTERESTING THAN THAT ELIZABETH GIRL.
AW, GEEZE. THANKS.
THAT'S PRETTY SWEET FOR A NINETY-YEAR-OLD.
OH, HEY! I JUST REMEMBERED SOMETHING.
COME UP HERE! THERE'S A REALLY COOL CLEARING PAST THESE TREES...
SEE?

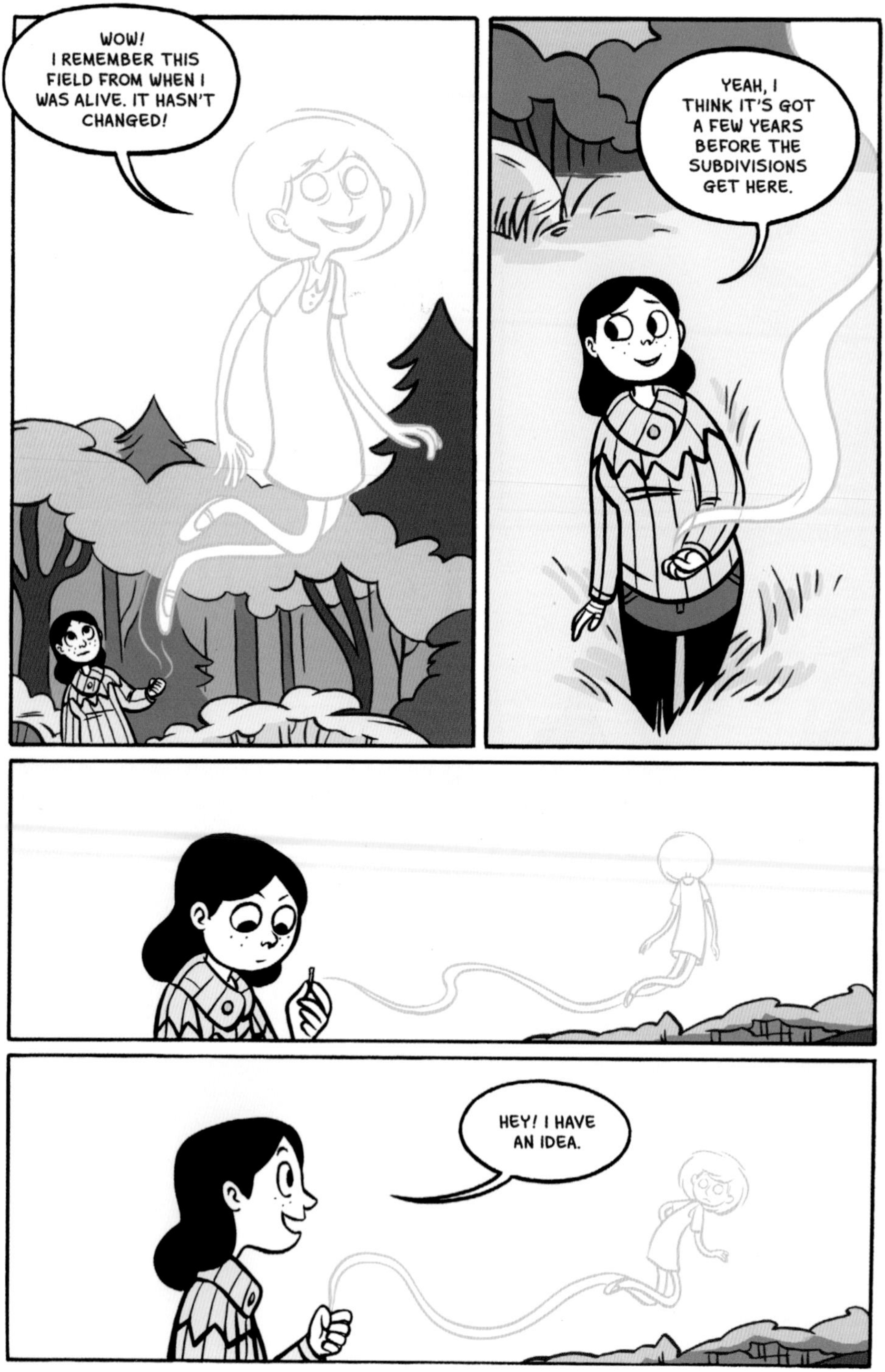
WOW! I REMEMBER THIS FIELD FROM WHEN I WAS ALIVE. IT HASN'T CHANGED!
YEAH, I THINK IT'S GOT A FEW YEARS BEFORE THE SUBDIVISIONS GET HERE.
HEY! I HAVE AN IDEA.

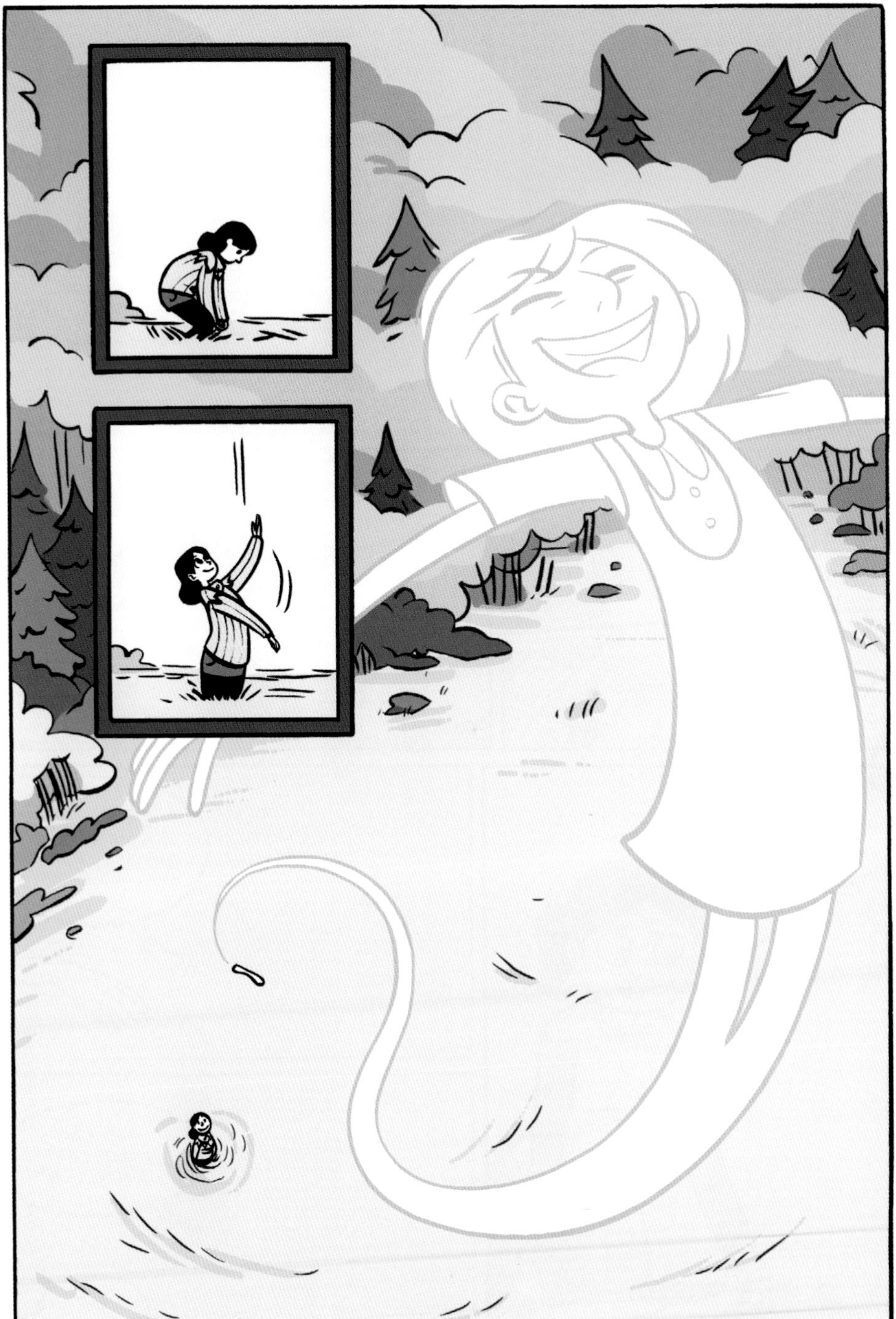

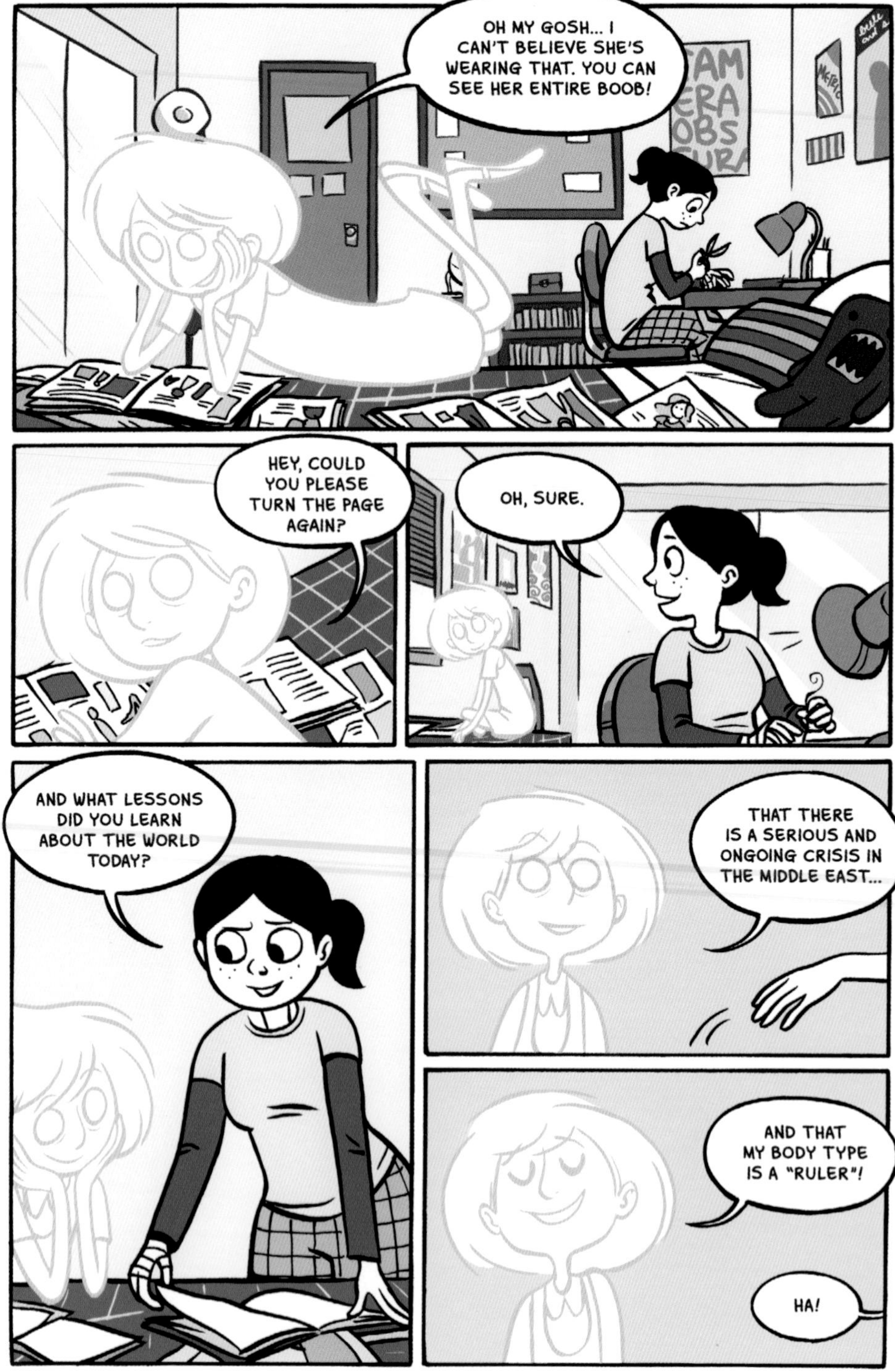
OH MY GOSH... I CAN'T BELIEVE SHE'S WEARING THAT. YOU CAN SEE HER ENTIRE BOOB!
HEY, COULD YOU PLEASE TURN THE PAGE AGAIN?
OH, SURE.
AND WHAT LESSONS DID YOU LEARN ABOUT THE WORLD TODAY?
THAT THERE IS A SERIOUS AND ONGOING CRISIS IN THE MIDDLE EAST...
AND THAT MY BODY TYPE IS A "RULER"!
HA!

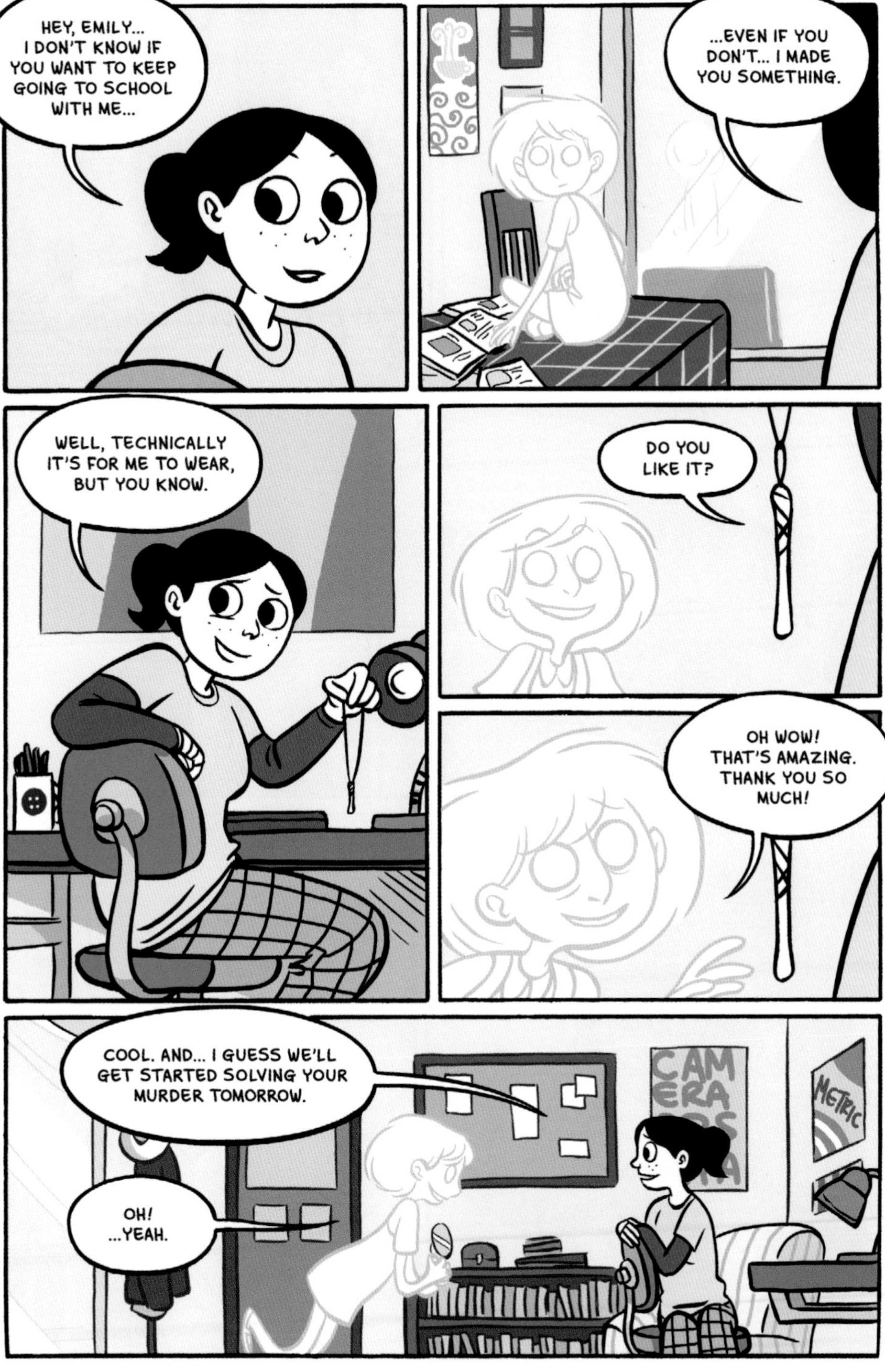
HEY, EMILY... I DON'T KNOW IF YOU WANT TO KEEP GOING TO SCHOOL WITH ME...
...EVEN IF YOU DON'T... I MADE YOU SOMETHING.
WELL, TECHNICALLY IT'S FOR ME TO WEAR, BUT YOU KNOW.
DO YOU LIKE IT?
OH WOW! THAT'S AMAZING. THANK YOU SO MUCH!
COOL. AND... I GUESS WE'LL GET STARTED SOLVING YOUR MURDER TOMORROW.
OH! ...YEAH.
CAM ERA
METRIC

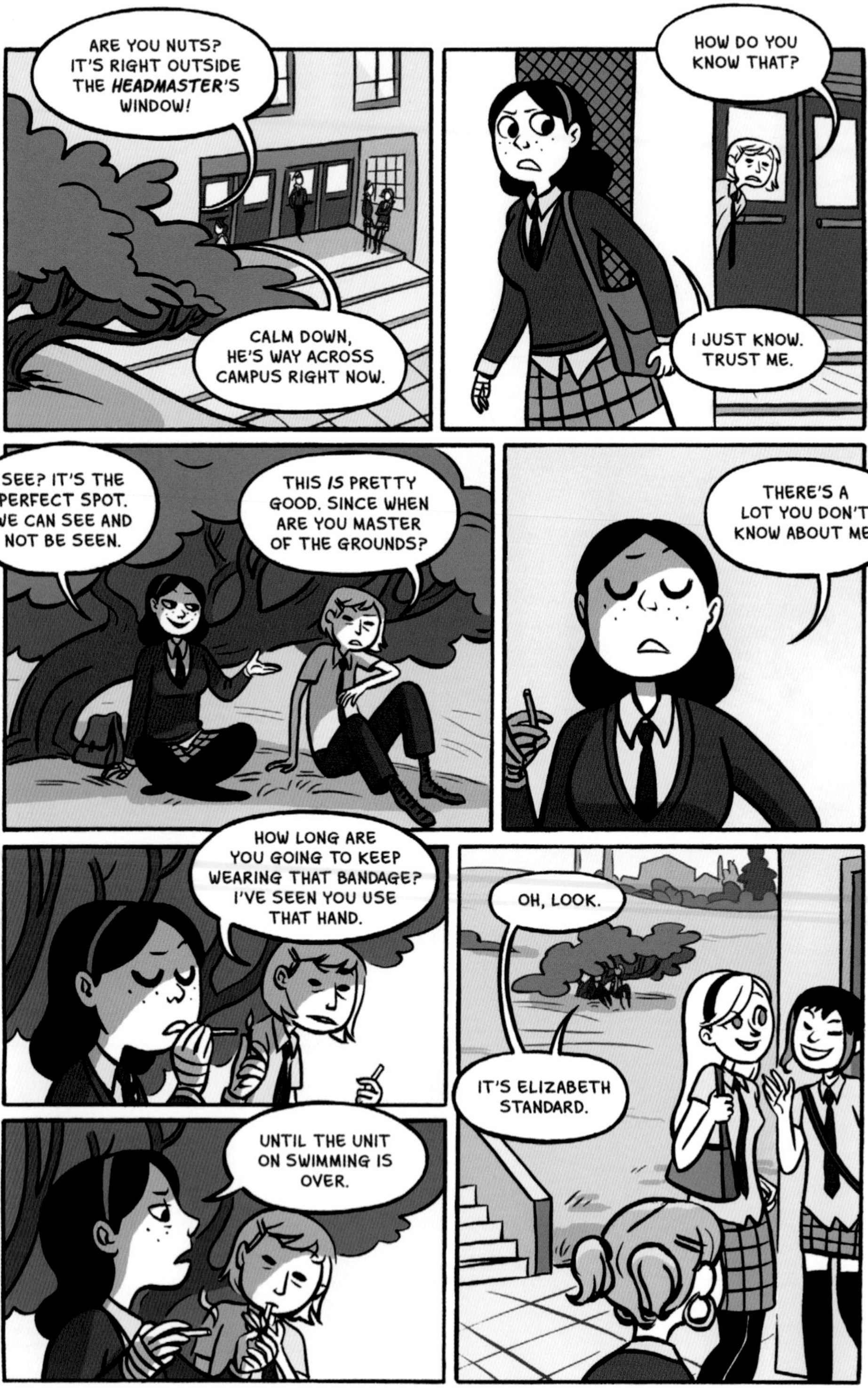
ARE YOU NUTS? IT'S RIGHT OUTSIDE THE *HEADMASTER*'S WINDOW!
CALM DOWN, HE'S WAY ACROSS CAMPUS RIGHT NOW.
HOW DO YOU KNOW THAT?
I JUST KNOW. TRUST ME.
SEE? IT'S THE PERFECT SPOT. WE CAN SEE AND NOT BE SEEN.
THIS *IS* PRETTY GOOD. SINCE WHEN ARE YOU MASTER OF THE GROUNDS?
THERE'S A LOT YOU DON'T KNOW ABOUT ME.
HOW LONG ARE YOU GOING TO KEEP WEARING THAT BANDAGE? I'VE SEEN YOU USE THAT HAND.
UNTIL THE UNIT ON SWIMMING IS OVER.
OH, LOOK.
IT'S ELIZABETH STANDARD.

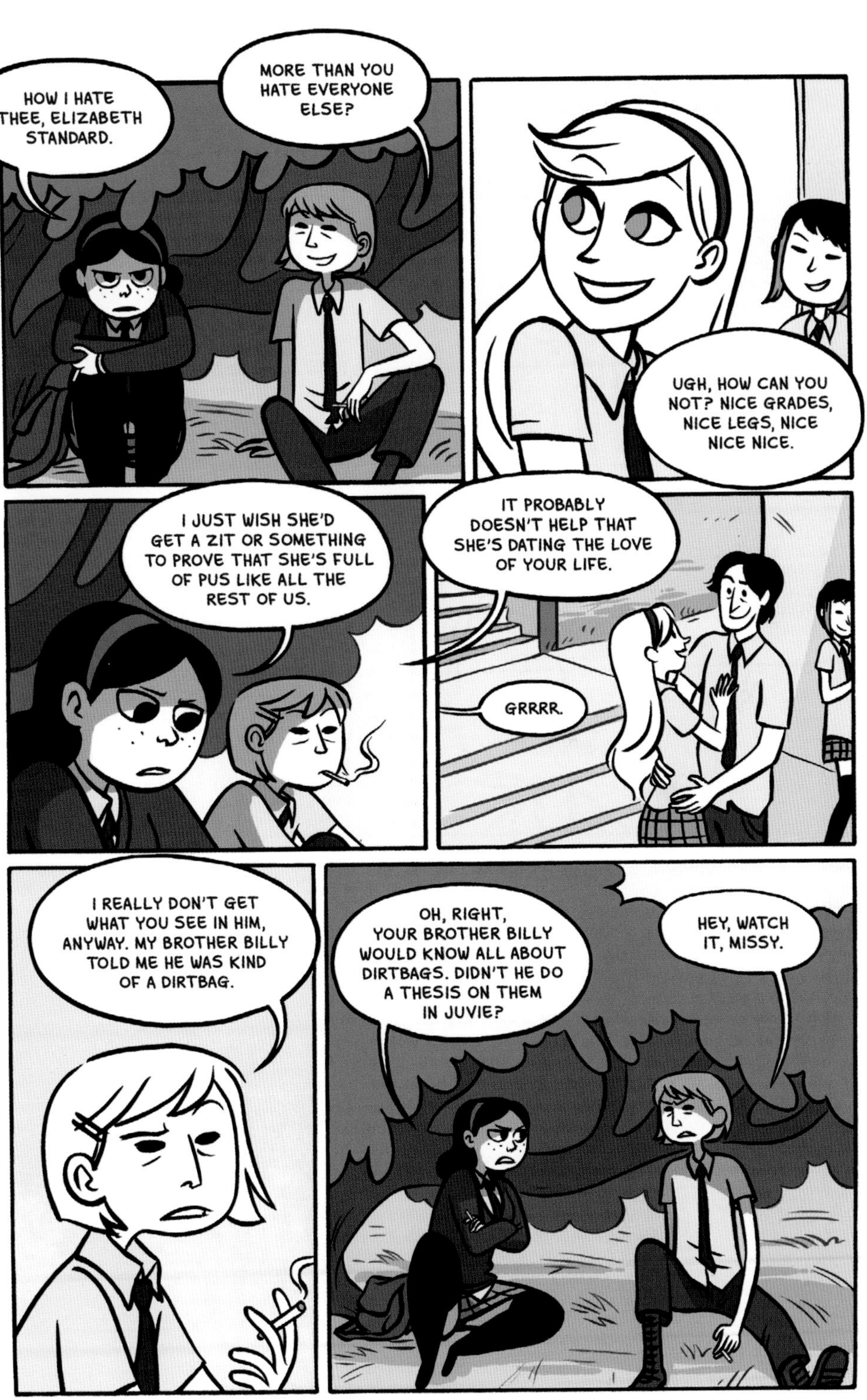
HOW I HATE THEE, ELIZABETH STANDARD.
MORE THAN YOU HATE EVERYONE ELSE?
UGH, HOW CAN YOU NOT? NICE GRADES, NICE LEGS, NICE NICE NICE.
I JUST WISH SHE'D GET A ZIT OR SOMETHING TO PROVE THAT SHE'S FULL OF PUS LIKE ALL THE REST OF US.
IT PROBABLY DOESN'T HELP THAT SHE'S DATING THE LOVE OF YOUR LIFE.
GRRRR.
I REALLY DON'T GET WHAT YOU SEE IN HIM, ANYWAY. MY BROTHER BILLY TOLD ME HE WAS KIND OF A DIRTBAG.
OH, RIGHT, YOUR BROTHER BILLY WOULD KNOW ALL ABOUT DIRTBAGS. DIDN'T HE DO A THESIS ON THEM IN JUVIE?
HEY, WATCH IT, MISSY.

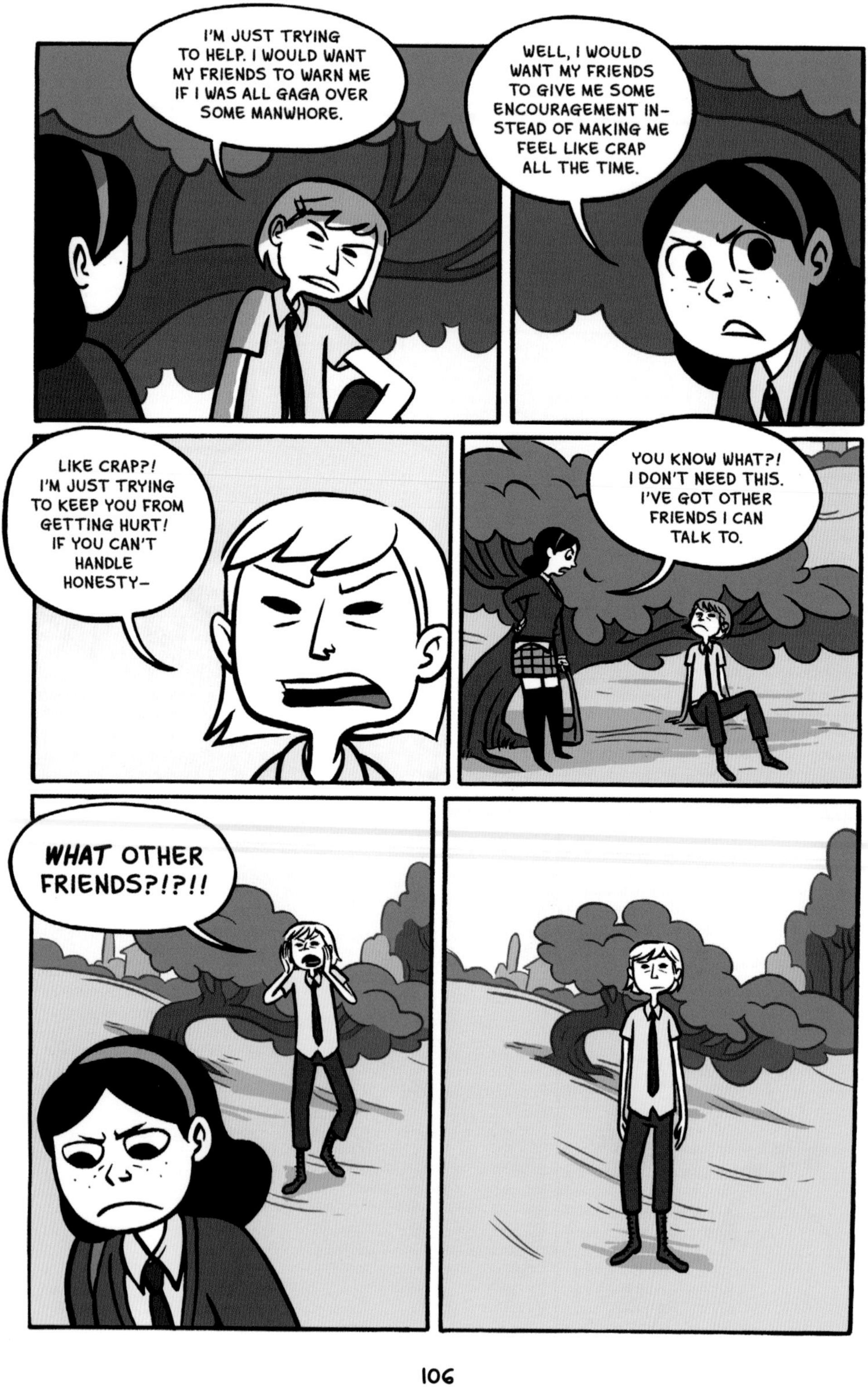
I'M JUST TRYING TO HELP. I WOULD WANT MY FRIENDS TO WARN ME IF I WAS ALL GAGA OVER SOME MANWHORE.
WELL, I WOULD WANT MY FRIENDS TO GIVE ME SOME ENCOURAGEMENT IN-STEAD OF MAKING ME FEEL LIKE CRAP ALL THE TIME.
LIKE CRAP?! I'M JUST TRYING TO KEEP YOU FROM GETTING HURT! IF YOU CAN'T HANDLE HONESTY–
YOU KNOW WHAT?! I DON'T NEED THIS. I'VE GOT OTHER FRIENDS I CAN TALK TO.
WHAT OTHER FRIENDS?!?!!

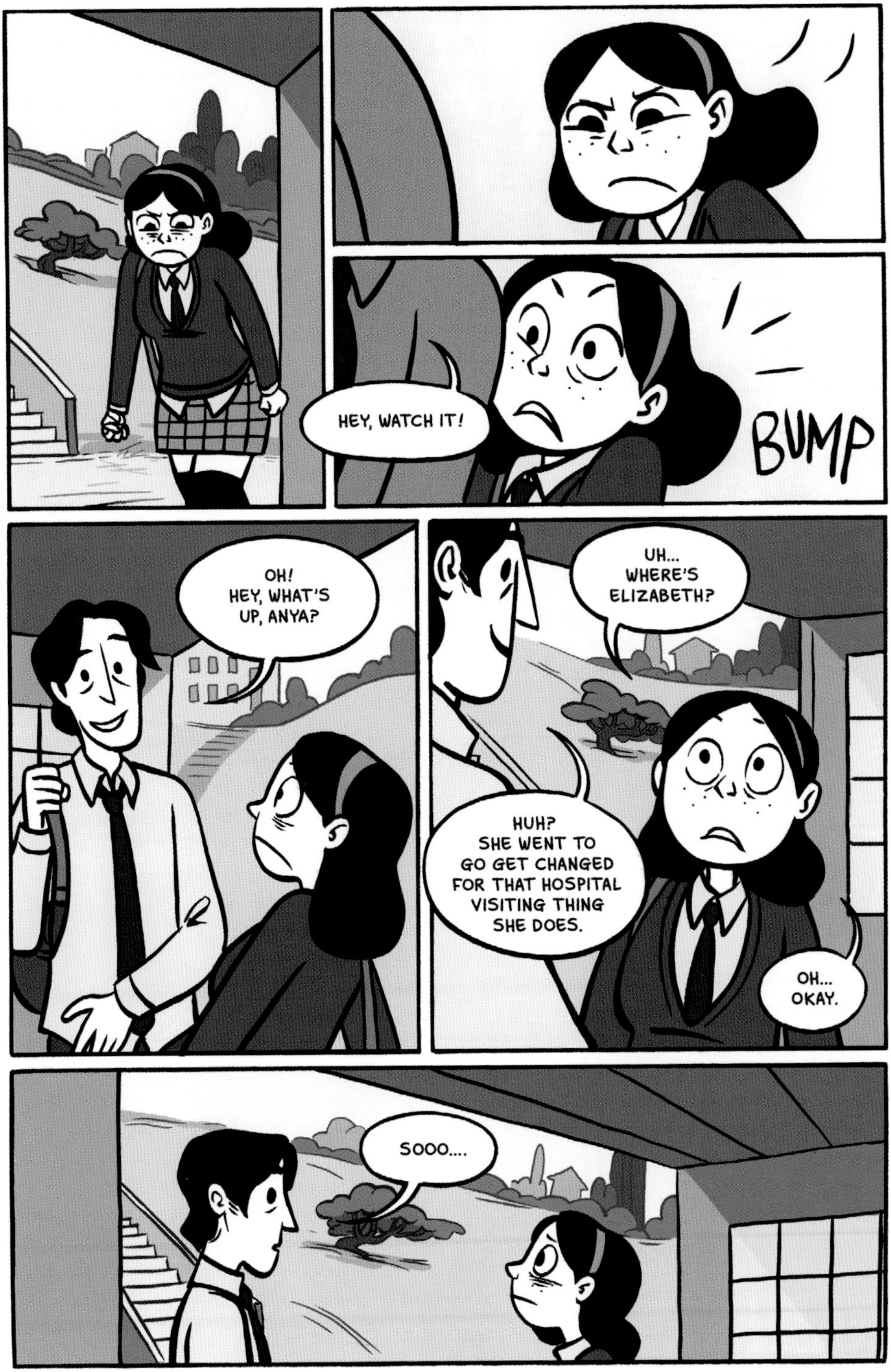
HEY, WATCH IT!
BUMP
OH! HEY, WHAT'S UP, ANYA?
UH... WHERE'S ELIZABETH?
HUH? SHE WENT TO GO GET CHANGED FOR THAT HOSPITAL VISITING THING SHE DOES.
OH... OKAY.
SOOO....

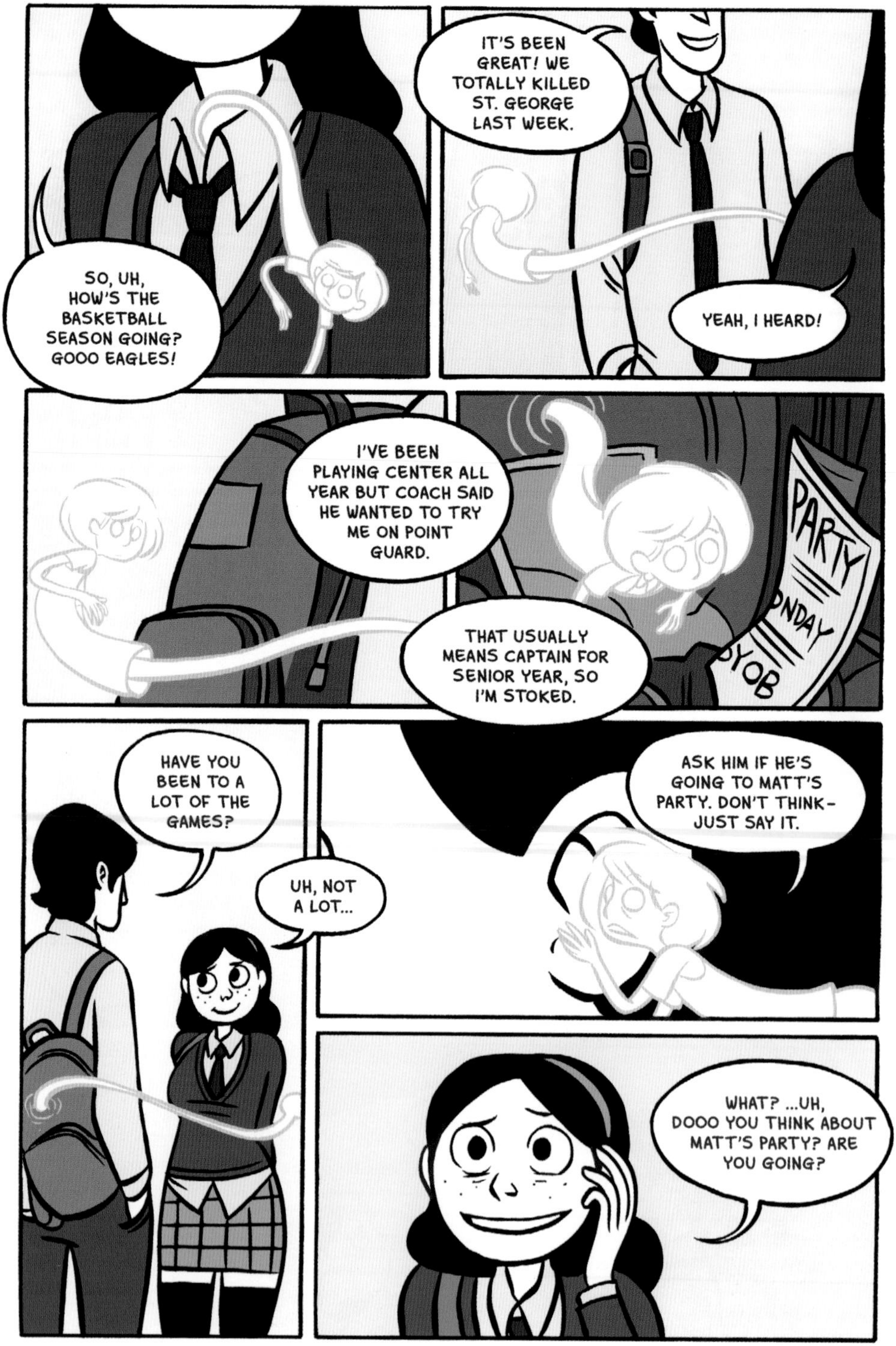
SO, UH, HOW'S THE BASKETBALL SEASON GOING? GOOO EAGLES!
IT'S BEEN GREAT! WE TOTALLY KILLED ST. GEORGE LAST WEEK.
YEAH, I HEARD!
I'VE BEEN PLAYING CENTER ALL YEAR BUT COACH SAID HE WANTED TO TRY ME ON POINT GUARD.
PARTY
ONDAY
BYOB
THAT USUALLY MEANS CAPTAIN FOR SENIOR YEAR, SO I'M STOKED.
HAVE YOU BEEN TO A LOT OF THE GAMES?
UH, NOT A LOT...
ASK HIM IF HE'S GOING TO MATT'S PARTY. DON'T THINK- JUST SAY IT.
WHAT? ...UH, DOOO YOU THINK ABOUT MATT'S PARTY? ARE YOU GOING?

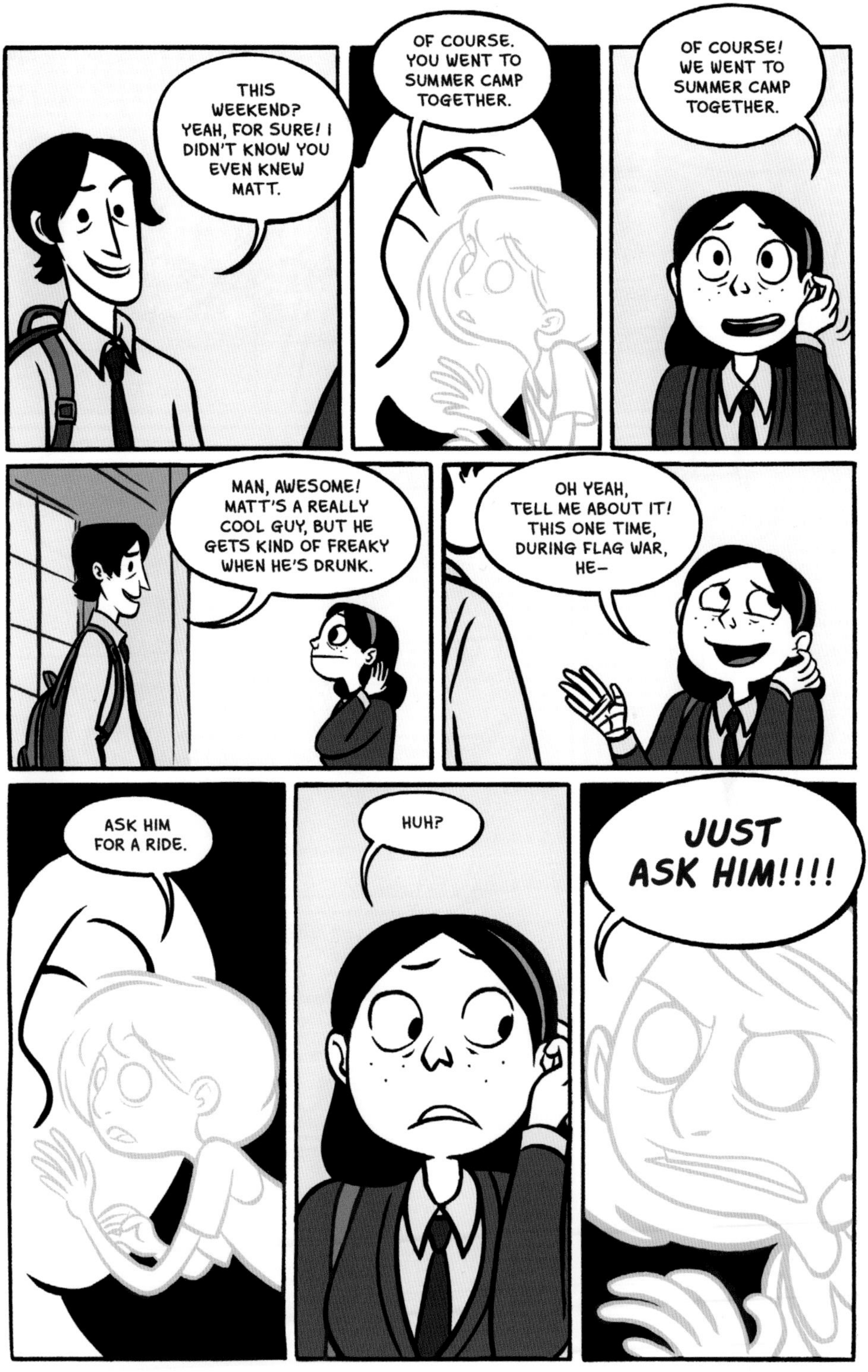
THIS WEEKEND? YEAH, FOR SURE! I DIDN'T KNOW YOU EVEN KNEW MATT.
OF COURSE. YOU WENT TO SUMMER CAMP TOGETHER.
OF COURSE! WE WENT TO SUMMER CAMP TOGETHER.
MAN, AWESOME! MATT'S A REALLY COOL GUY, BUT HE GETS KIND OF FREAKY WHEN HE'S DRUNK.
OH YEAH, TELL ME ABOUT IT! THIS ONE TIME, DURING FLAG WAR, HE–
ASK HIM FOR A RIDE.
HUH?
JUST ASK HIM!!!!

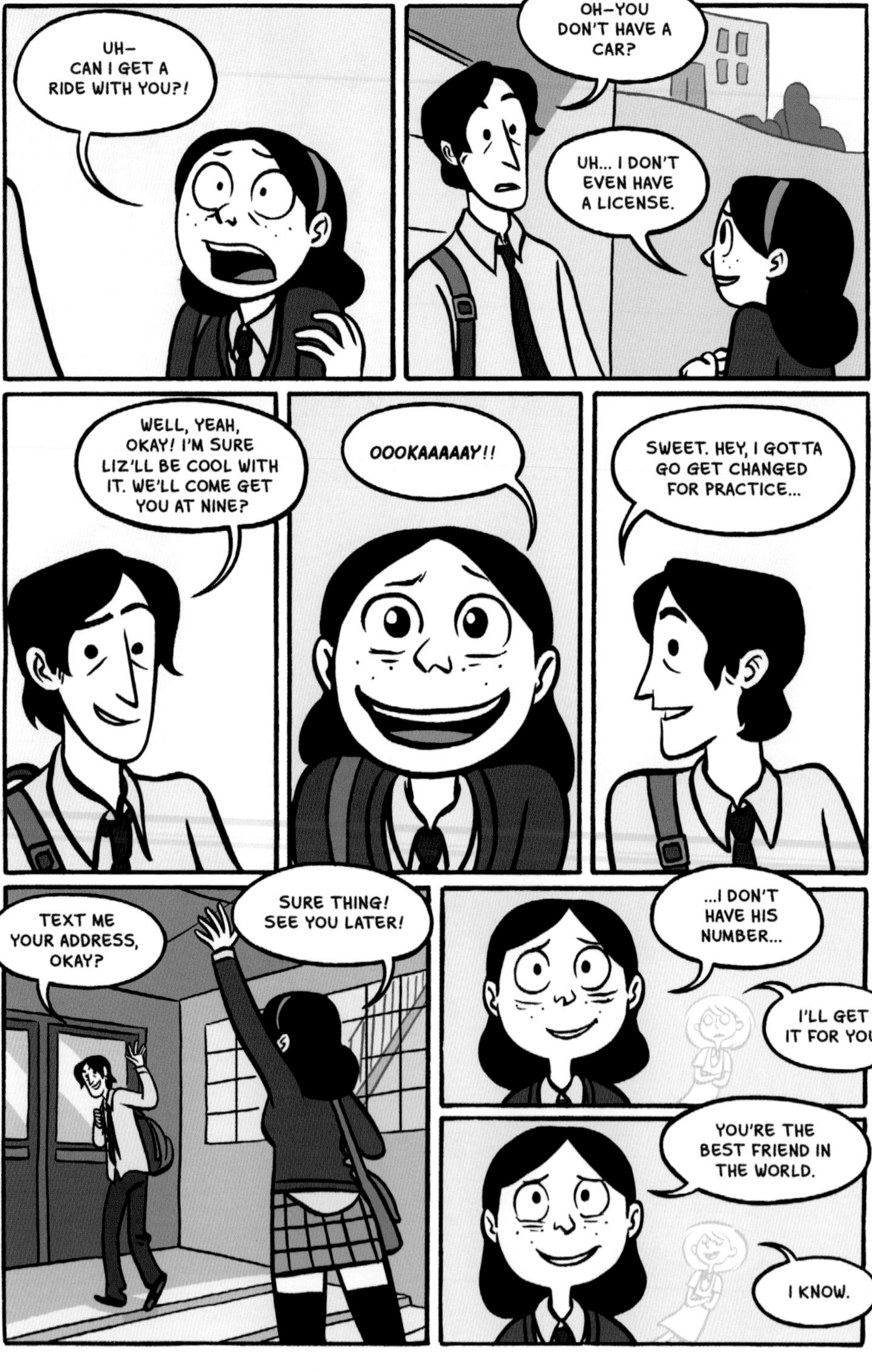
UH— CAN I GET A RIDE WITH YOU?!
OH—YOU DON'T HAVE A CAR?
UH... I DON'T EVEN HAVE A LICENSE.
WELL, YEAH, OKAY! I'M SURE LIZ'LL BE COOL WITH IT. WE'LL COME GET YOU AT NINE?
OOOKAAAAAY!!
SWEET. HEY, I GOTTA GO GET CHANGED FOR PRACTICE...
TEXT ME YOUR ADDRESS, OKAY?
SURE THING! SEE YOU LATER!
...I DON'T HAVE HIS NUMBER...
I'LL GET IT FOR YOU.
YOU'RE THE BEST FRIEND IN THE WORLD.
I KNOW.

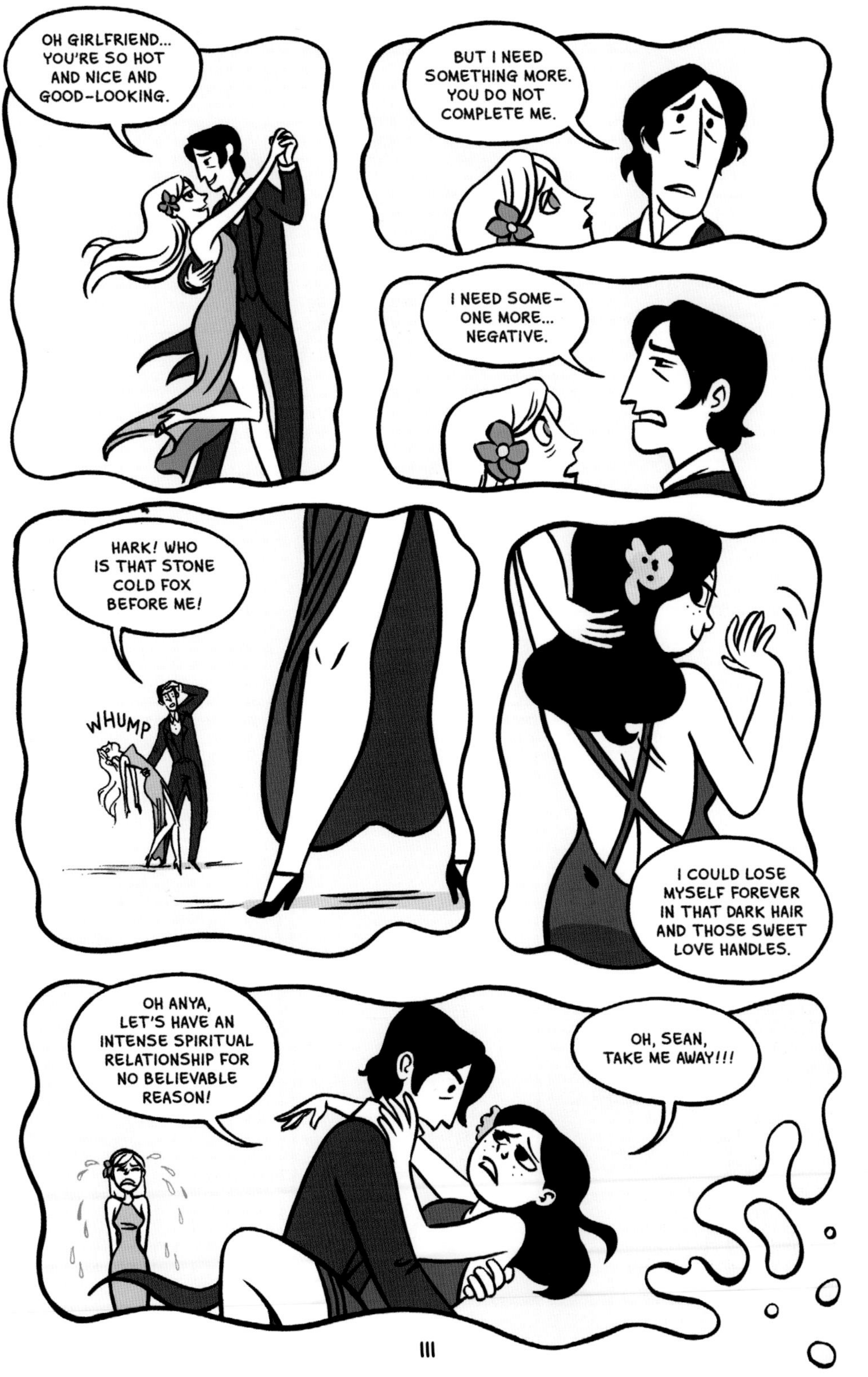
OH GIRLFRIEND... YOU'RE SO HOT AND NICE AND GOOD-LOOKING.
BUT I NEED SOMETHING MORE. YOU DO NOT COMPLETE ME.
I NEED SOME-ONE MORE... NEGATIVE.
HARK! WHO IS THAT STONE COLD FOX BEFORE ME!
WHUMP
I COULD LOSE MYSELF FOREVER IN THAT DARK HAIR AND THOSE SWEET LOVE HANDLES.
OH ANYA, LET'S HAVE AN INTENSE SPIRITUAL RELATIONSHIP FOR NO BELIEVABLE REASON!
OH, SEAN, TAKE ME AWAY!!!

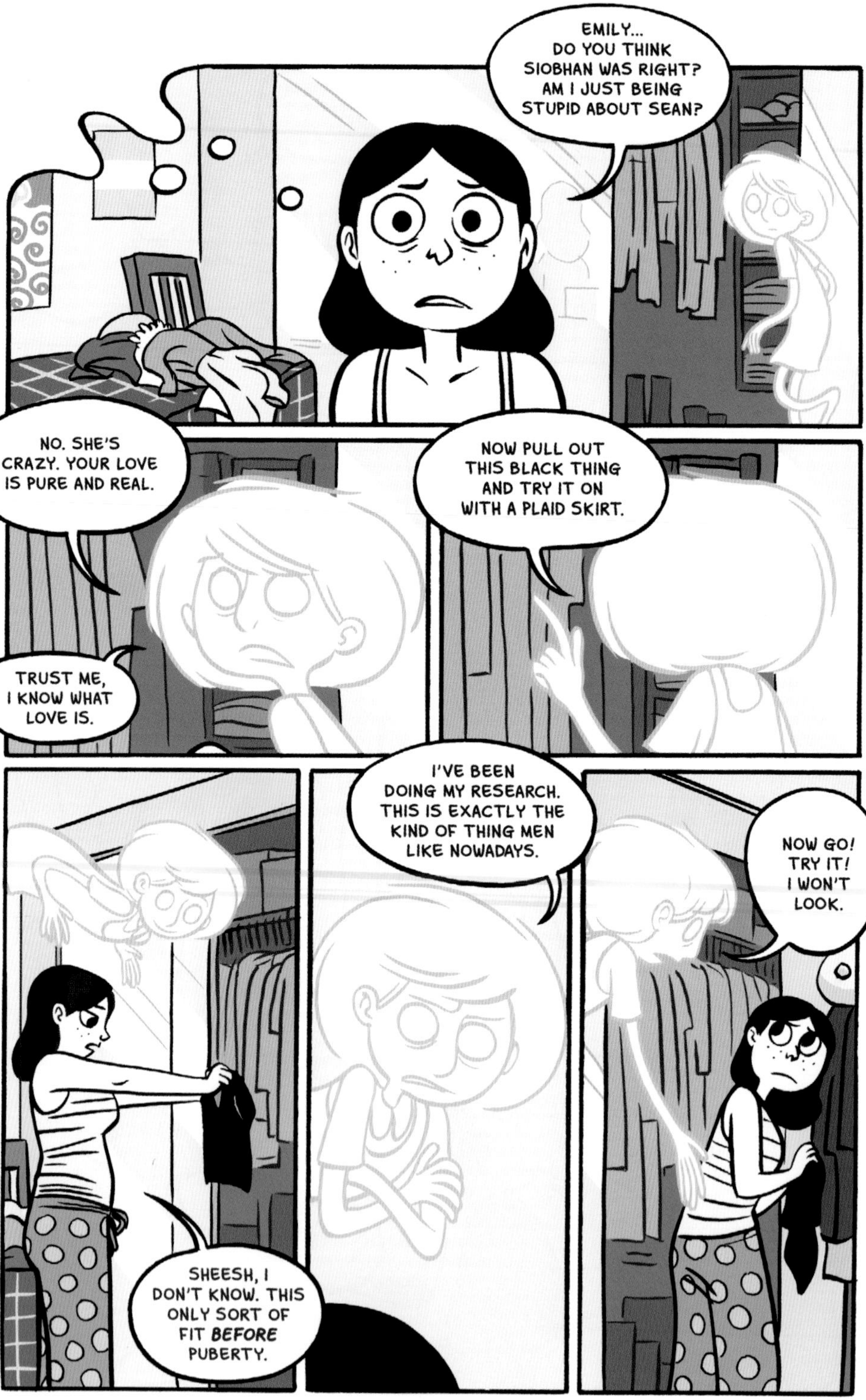
EMILY...
DO YOU THINK SIOBHAN WAS RIGHT? AM I JUST BEING STUPID ABOUT SEAN?
NO. SHE'S CRAZY. YOUR LOVE IS PURE AND REAL.
TRUST ME, I KNOW WHAT LOVE IS.
NOW PULL OUT THIS BLACK THING AND TRY IT ON WITH A PLAID SKIRT.
SHEESH, I DON'T KNOW. THIS ONLY SORT OF FIT *BEFORE* PUBERTY.
I'VE BEEN DOING MY RESEARCH. THIS IS EXACTLY THE KIND OF THING MEN LIKE NOWADAYS.
NOW GO! TRY IT! I WON'T LOOK.

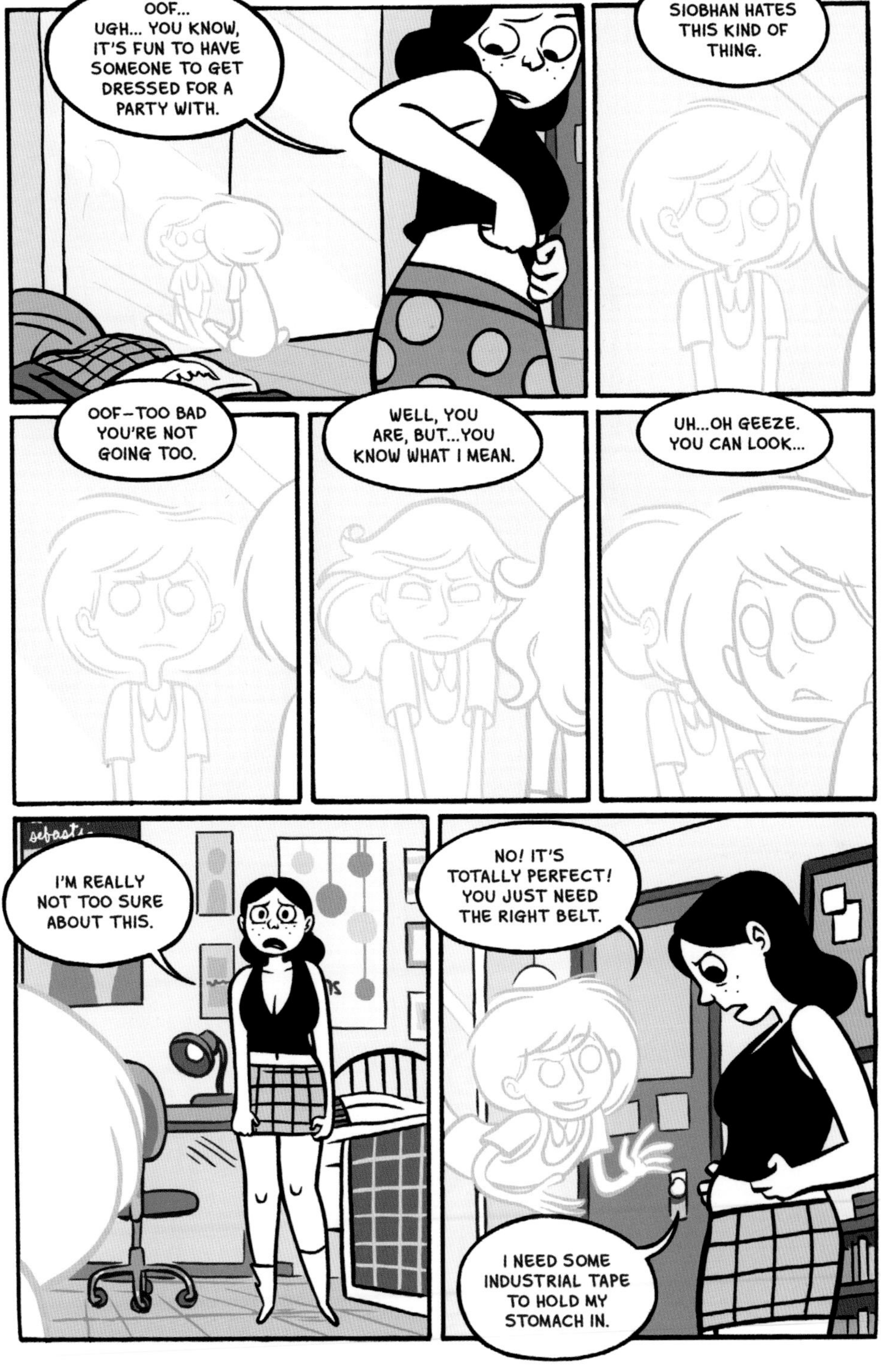
OOF... UGH... YOU KNOW, IT'S FUN TO HAVE SOMEONE TO GET DRESSED FOR A PARTY WITH.
SIOBHAN HATES THIS KIND OF THING.
OOF—TOO BAD YOU'RE NOT GOING TOO.
WELL, YOU ARE, BUT...YOU KNOW WHAT I MEAN.
UH...OH GEEZE. YOU CAN LOOK...
I'M REALLY NOT TOO SURE ABOUT THIS.
NO! IT'S TOTALLY PERFECT! YOU JUST NEED THE RIGHT BELT.
I NEED SOME INDUSTRIAL TAPE TO HOLD MY STOMACH IN.

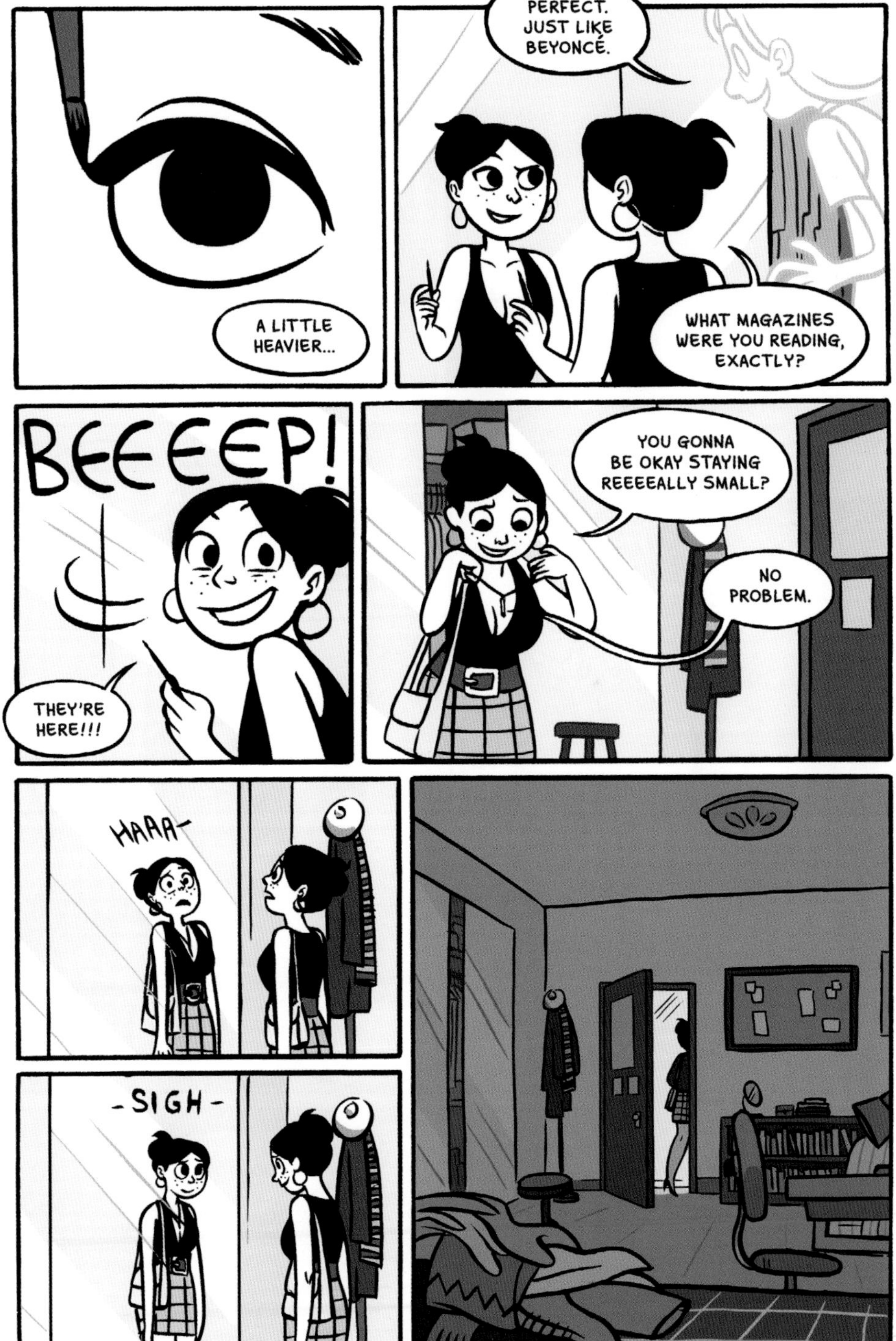
A LITTLE HEAVIER...
PERFECT. JUST LIKE BEYONCÉ.
WHAT MAGAZINES WERE YOU READING, EXACTLY?
BEEEEP!
THEY'RE HERE!!!
YOU GONNA BE OKAY STAYING REEEEALLY SMALL?
NO PROBLEM.
HAAA-
-SIGH-

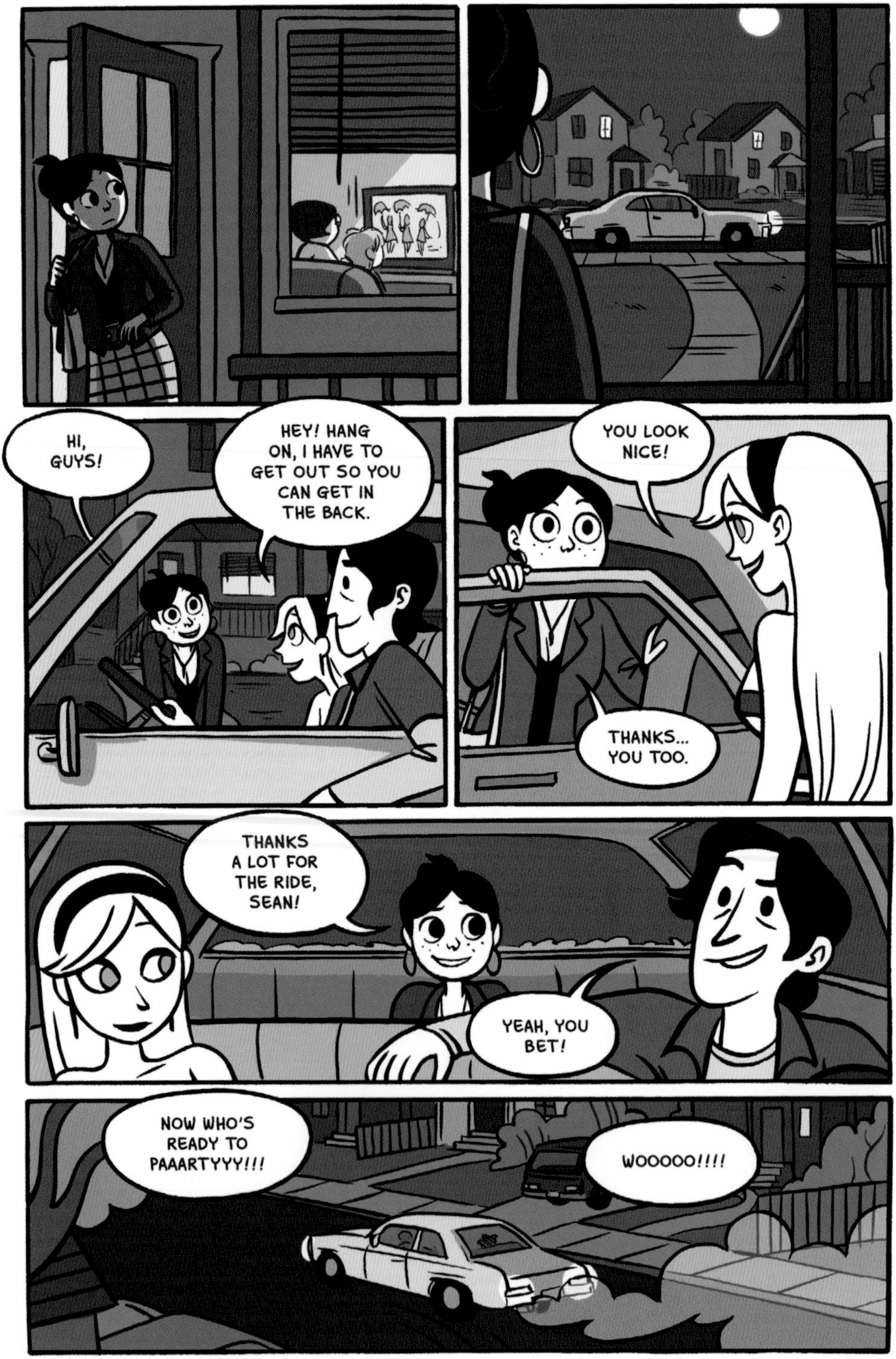
HI, GUYS!
HEY! HANG ON, I HAVE TO GET OUT SO YOU CAN GET IN THE BACK.
YOU LOOK NICE!
THANKS... YOU TOO.
THANKS A LOT FOR THE RIDE, SEAN!
YEAH, YOU BET!
NOW WHO'S READY TO PAAARTYYY!!!
WOOOOO!!!!

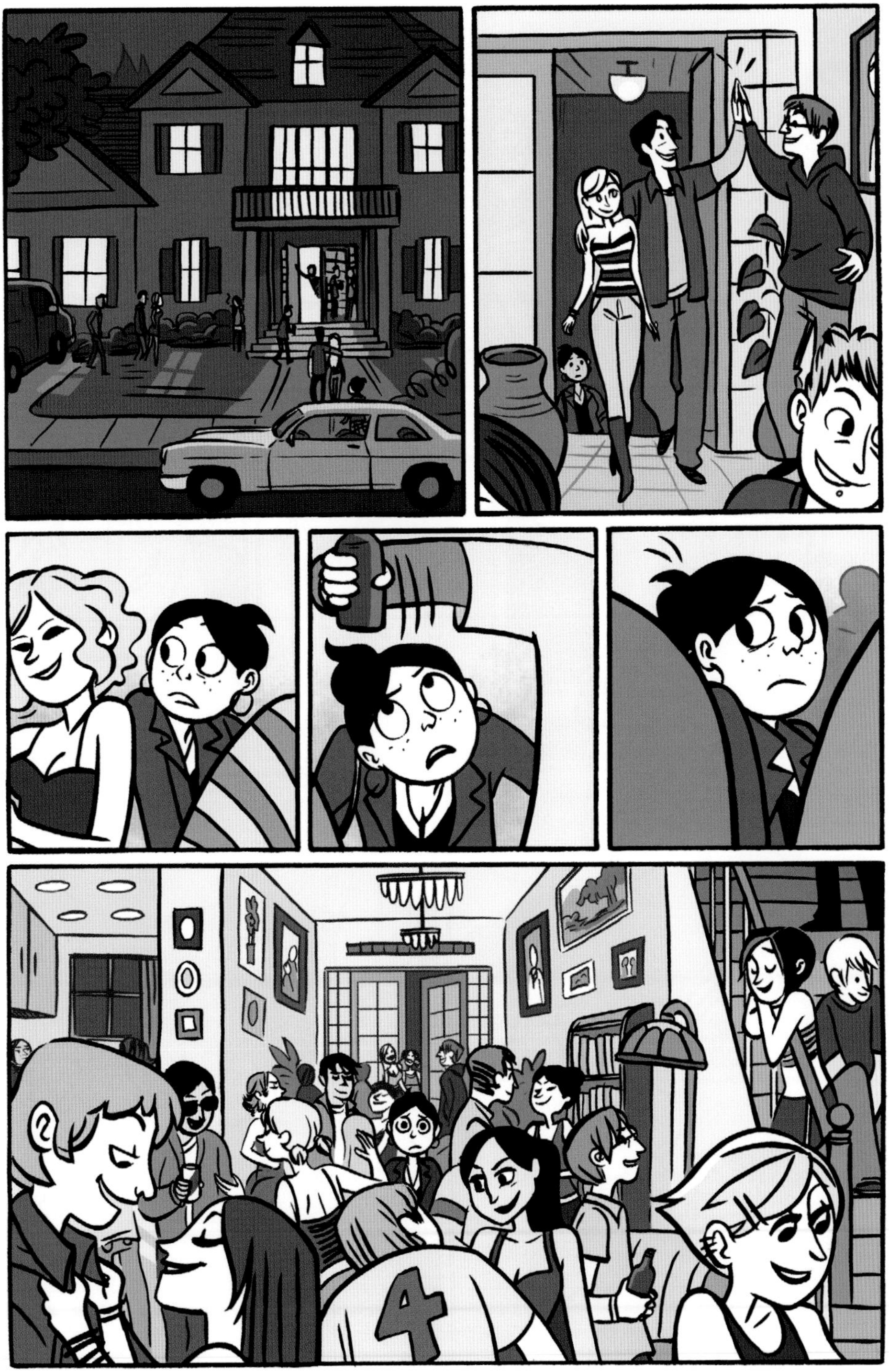
4

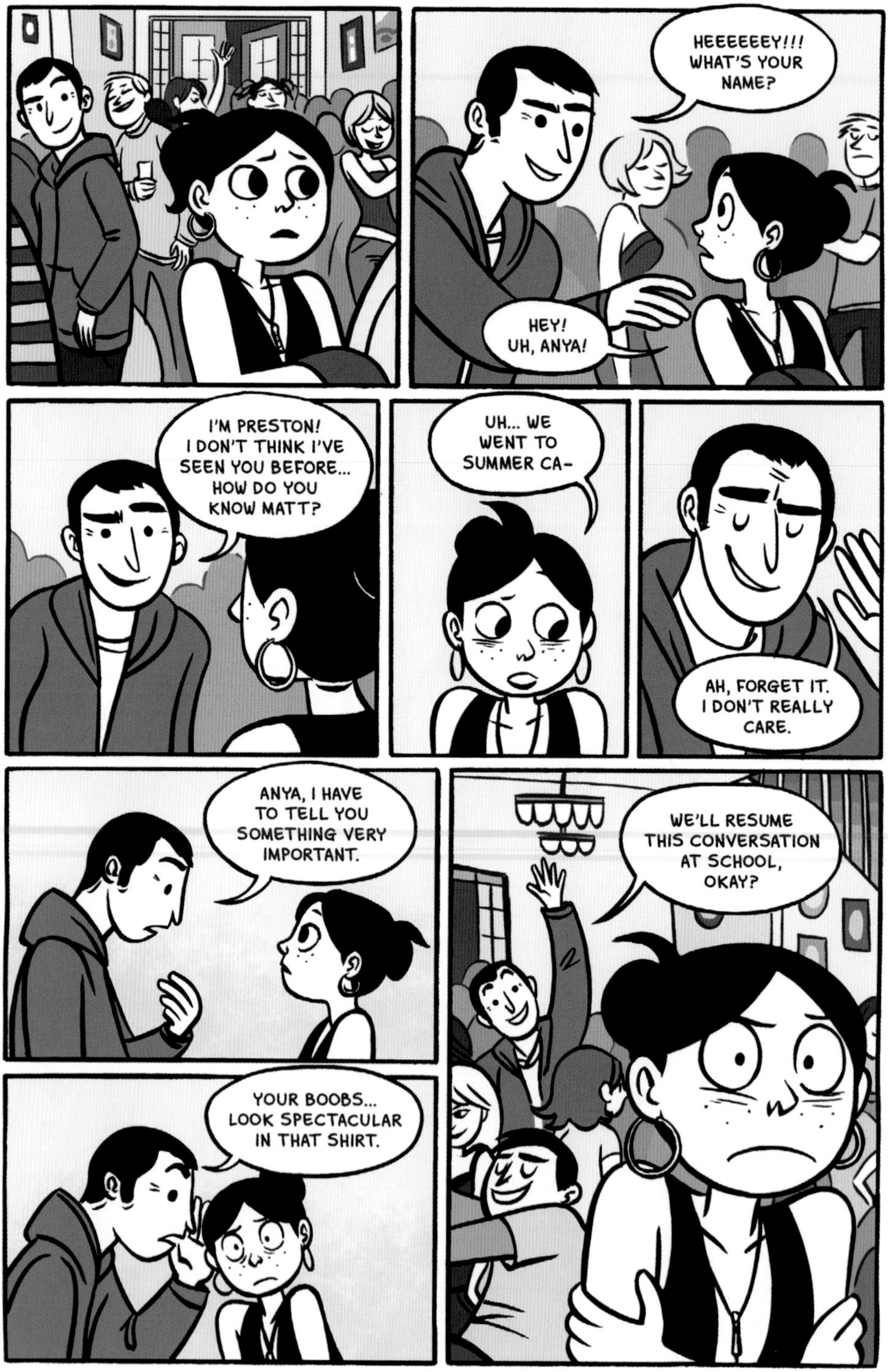
HEEEEEEY!!! WHAT'S YOUR NAME?
HEY! UH, ANYA!
I'M PRESTON! I DON'T THINK I'VE SEEN YOU BEFORE... HOW DO YOU KNOW MATT?
UH... WE WENT TO SUMMER CA-
AH, FORGET IT. I DON'T REALLY CARE.
ANYA, I HAVE TO TELL YOU SOMETHING VERY IMPORTANT.
YOUR BOOBS... LOOK SPECTACULAR IN THAT SHIRT.
WE'LL RESUME THIS CONVERSATION AT SCHOOL, OKAY?

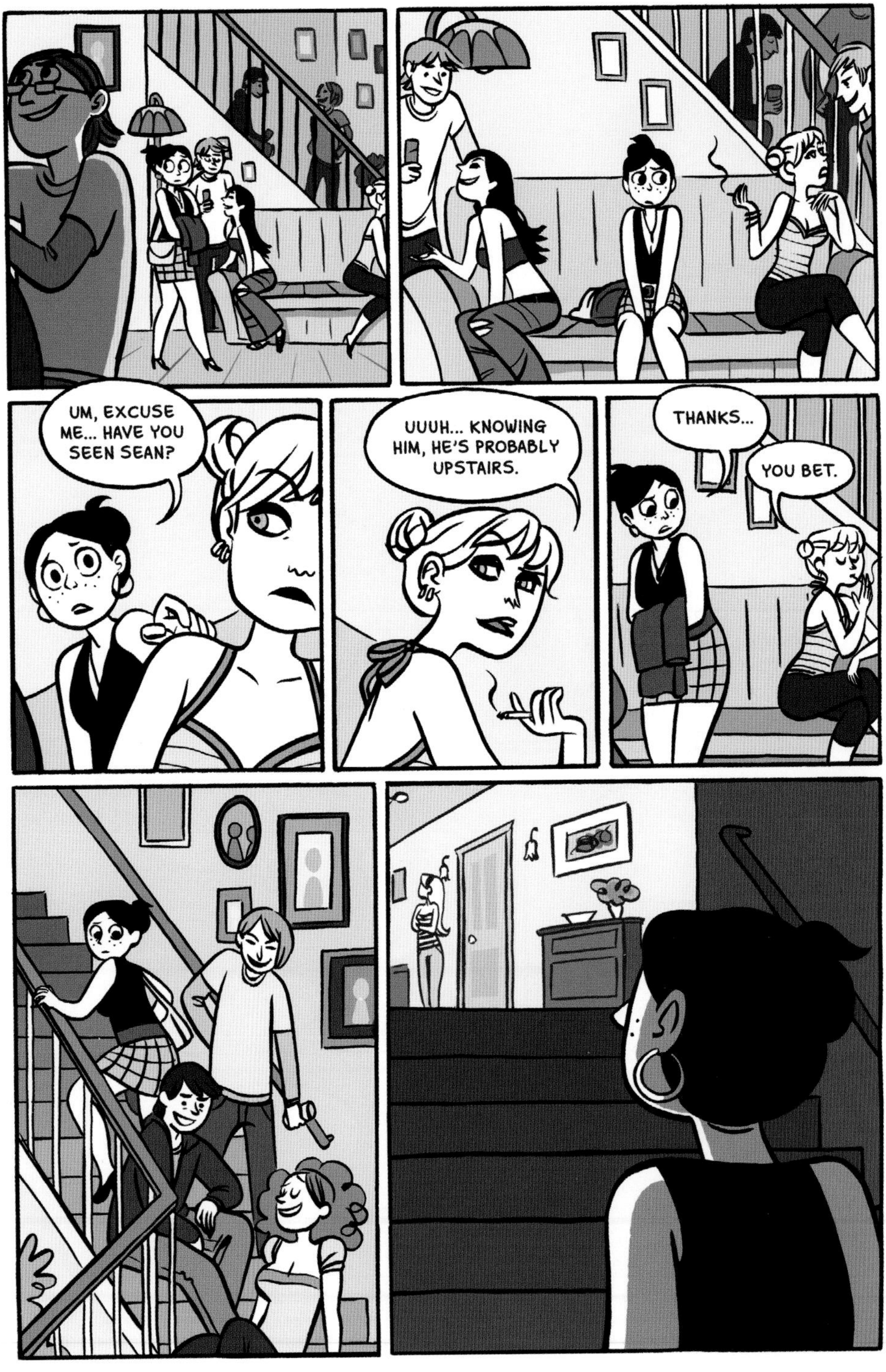
UM, EXCUSE ME... HAVE YOU SEEN SEAN?
UUUH... KNOWING HIM, HE'S PROBABLY UPSTAIRS.
THANKS...
YOU BET.

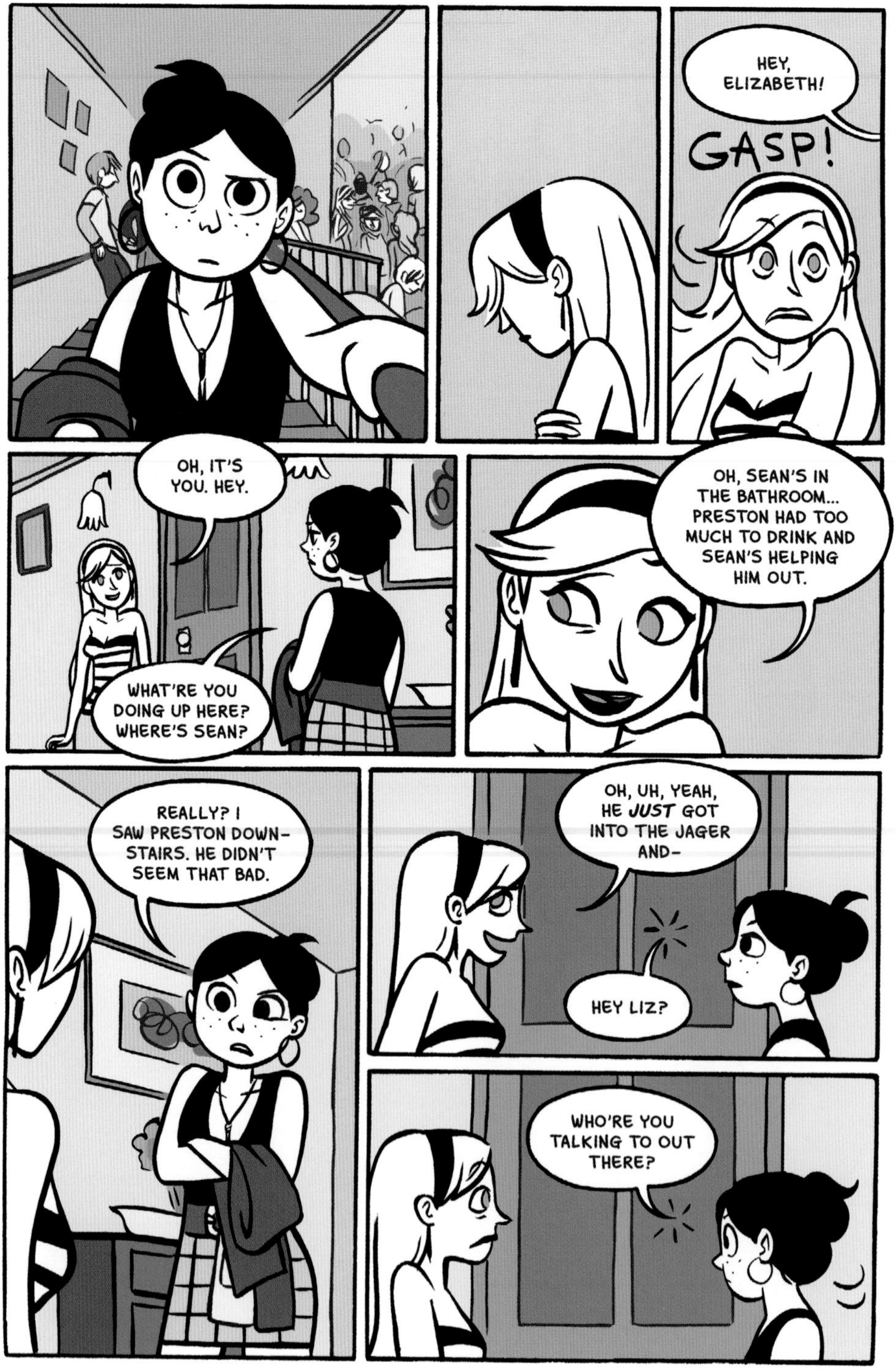
HEY, ELIZABETH!
GASP!
OH, IT'S YOU. HEY.
WHAT'RE YOU DOING UP HERE? WHERE'S SEAN?
OH, SEAN'S IN THE BATHROOM... PRESTON HAD TOO MUCH TO DRINK AND SEAN'S HELPING HIM OUT.
REALLY? I SAW PRESTON DOWN-STAIRS. HE DIDN'T SEEM THAT BAD.
OH, UH, YEAH, HE *JUST* GOT INTO THE JAGER AND-
HEY LIZ?
WHO'RE YOU TALKING TO OUT THERE?

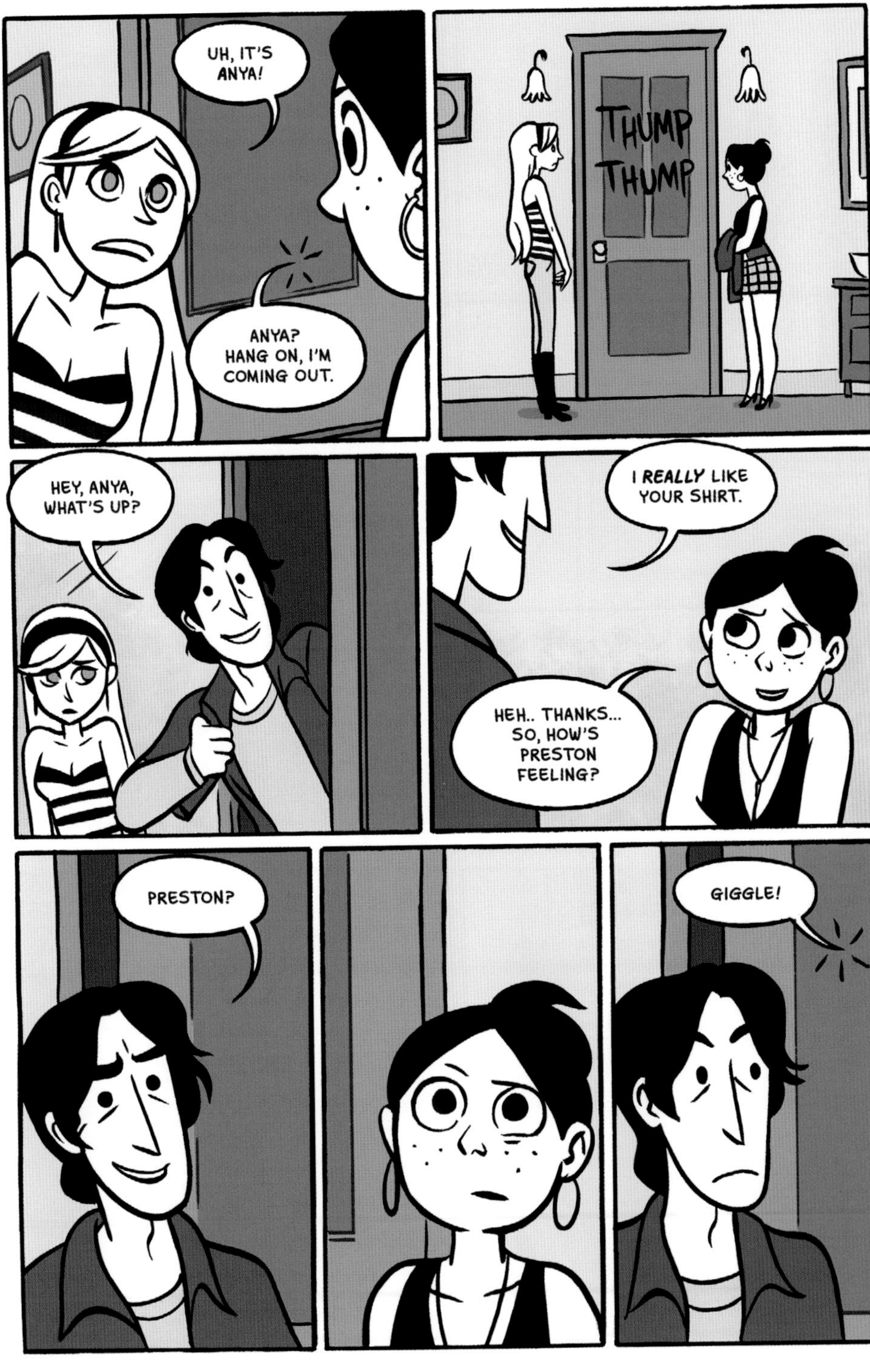
UH, IT'S ANYA!
ANYA? HANG ON, I'M COMING OUT.
THUMP THUMP
HEY, ANYA, WHAT'S UP?
I *REALLY* LIKE YOUR SHIRT.
HEH.. THANKS... SO, HOW'S PRESTON FEELING?
PRESTON?
GIGGLE!

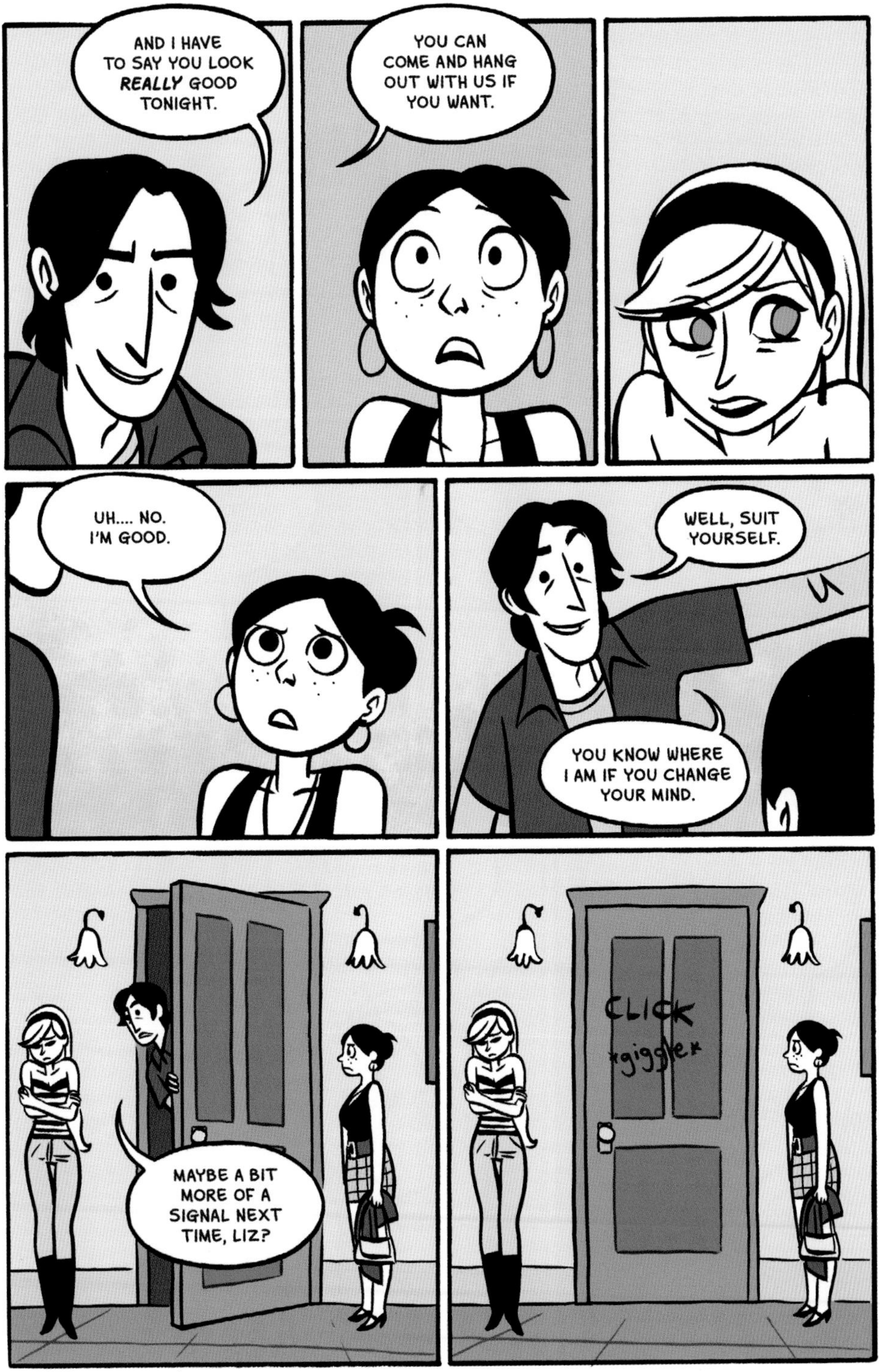
AND I HAVE TO SAY YOU LOOK *REALLY* GOOD TONIGHT.
YOU CAN COME AND HANG OUT WITH US IF YOU WANT.
UH.... NO. I'M GOOD.
WELL, SUIT YOURSELF.
YOU KNOW WHERE I AM IF YOU CHANGE YOUR MIND.
MAYBE A BIT MORE OF A SIGNAL NEXT TIME, LIZ?
CLICK
giggle

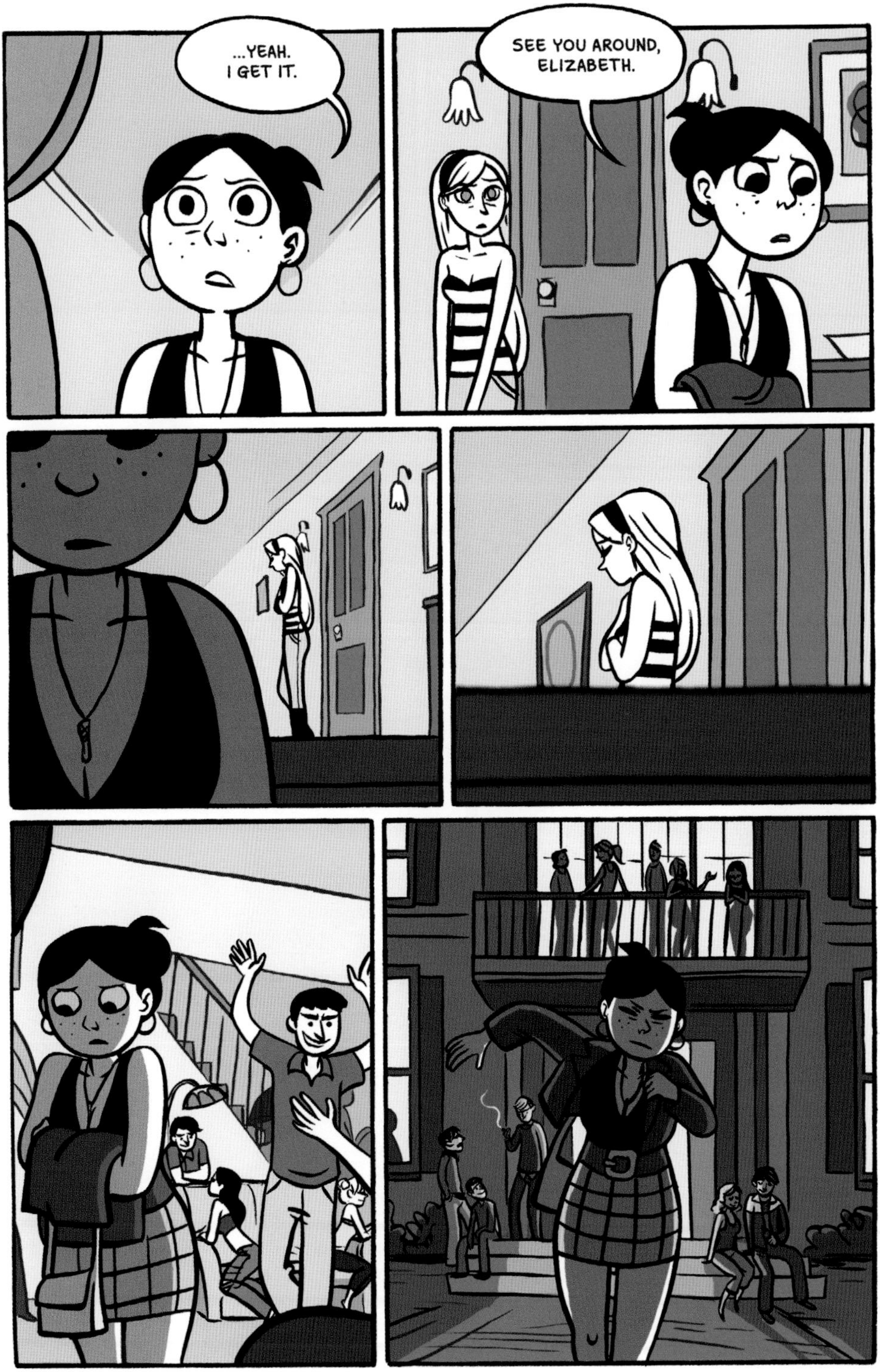
...YEAH.
I GET IT.
SEE YOU AROUND,
ELIZABETH.

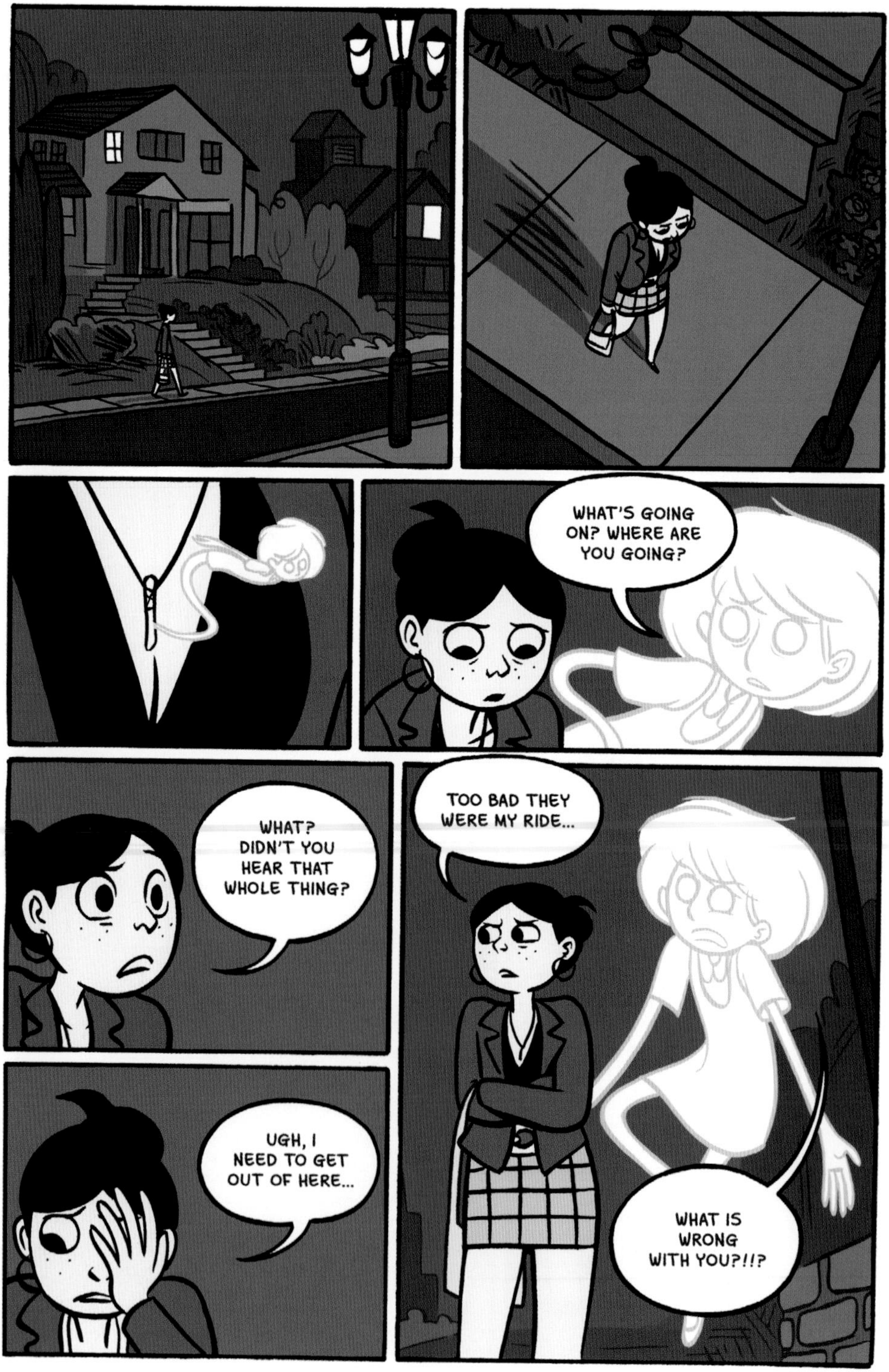
WHAT'S GOING ON? WHERE ARE YOU GOING?
WHAT? DIDN'T YOU HEAR THAT WHOLE THING?
UGH, I NEED TO GET OUT OF HERE...
TOO BAD THEY WERE MY RIDE...
WHAT IS WRONG WITH YOU?!!?

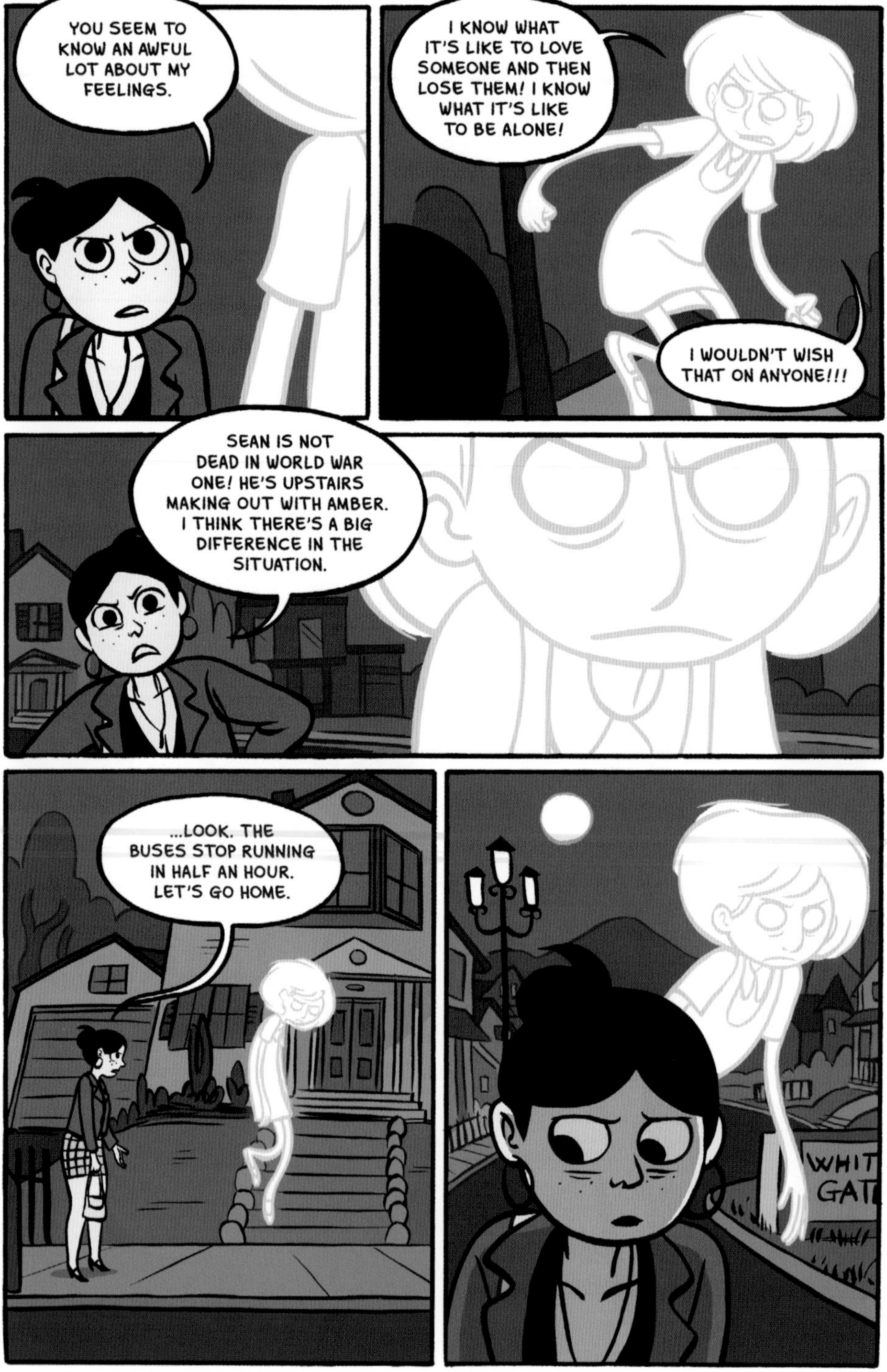
YOU SEEM TO KNOW AN AWFUL LOT ABOUT MY FEELINGS.
I KNOW WHAT IT'S LIKE TO LOVE SOMEONE AND THEN LOSE THEM! I KNOW WHAT IT'S LIKE TO BE ALONE!
I WOULDN'T WISH THAT ON ANYONE!!!
SEAN IS NOT DEAD IN WORLD WAR ONE! HE'S UPSTAIRS MAKING OUT WITH AMBER. I THINK THERE'S A BIG DIFFERENCE IN THE SITUATION.
...LOOK. THE BUSES STOP RUNNING IN HALF AN HOUR. LET'S GO HOME.
WHIT
GAT

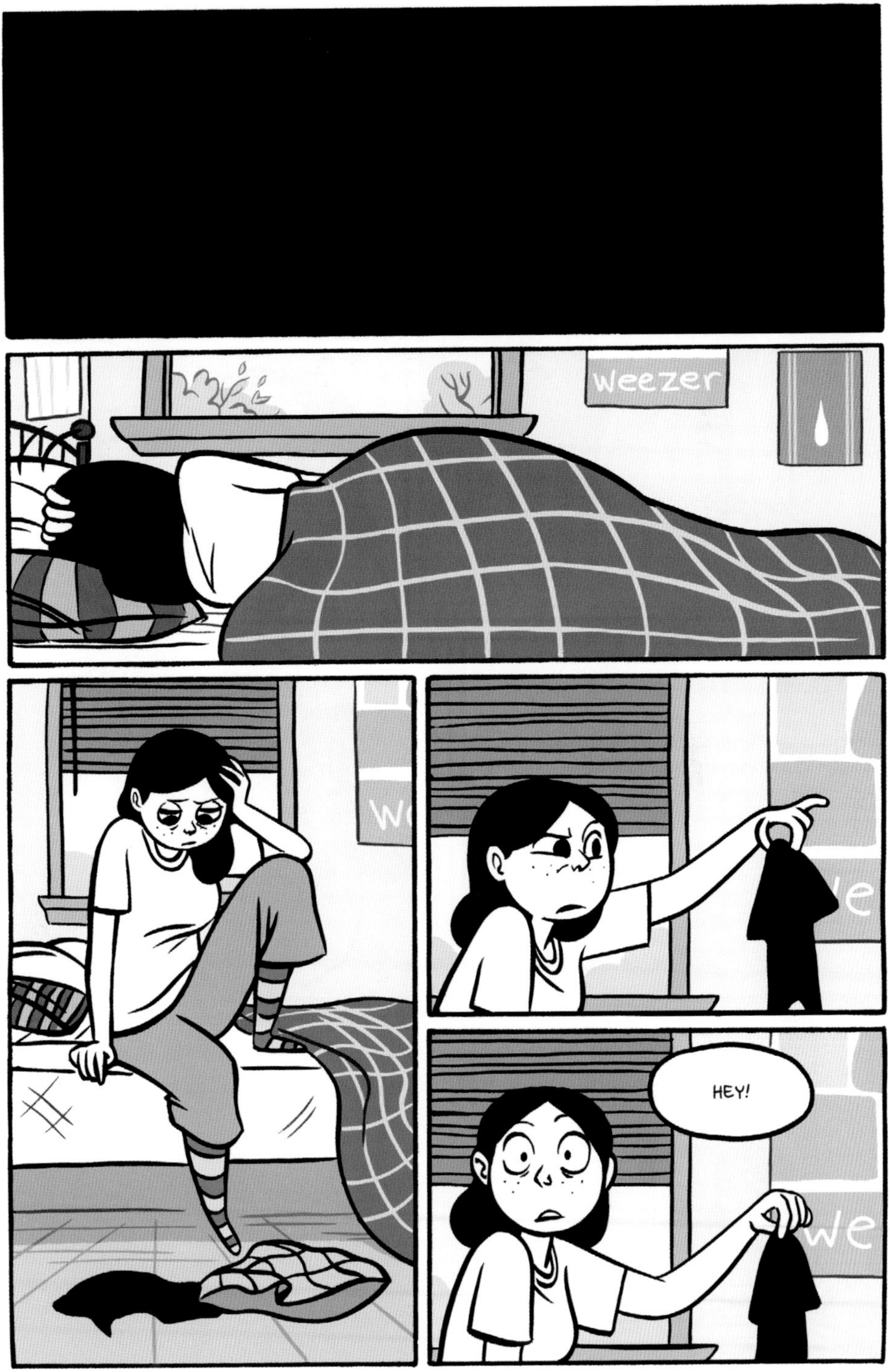
weezer
HEY!

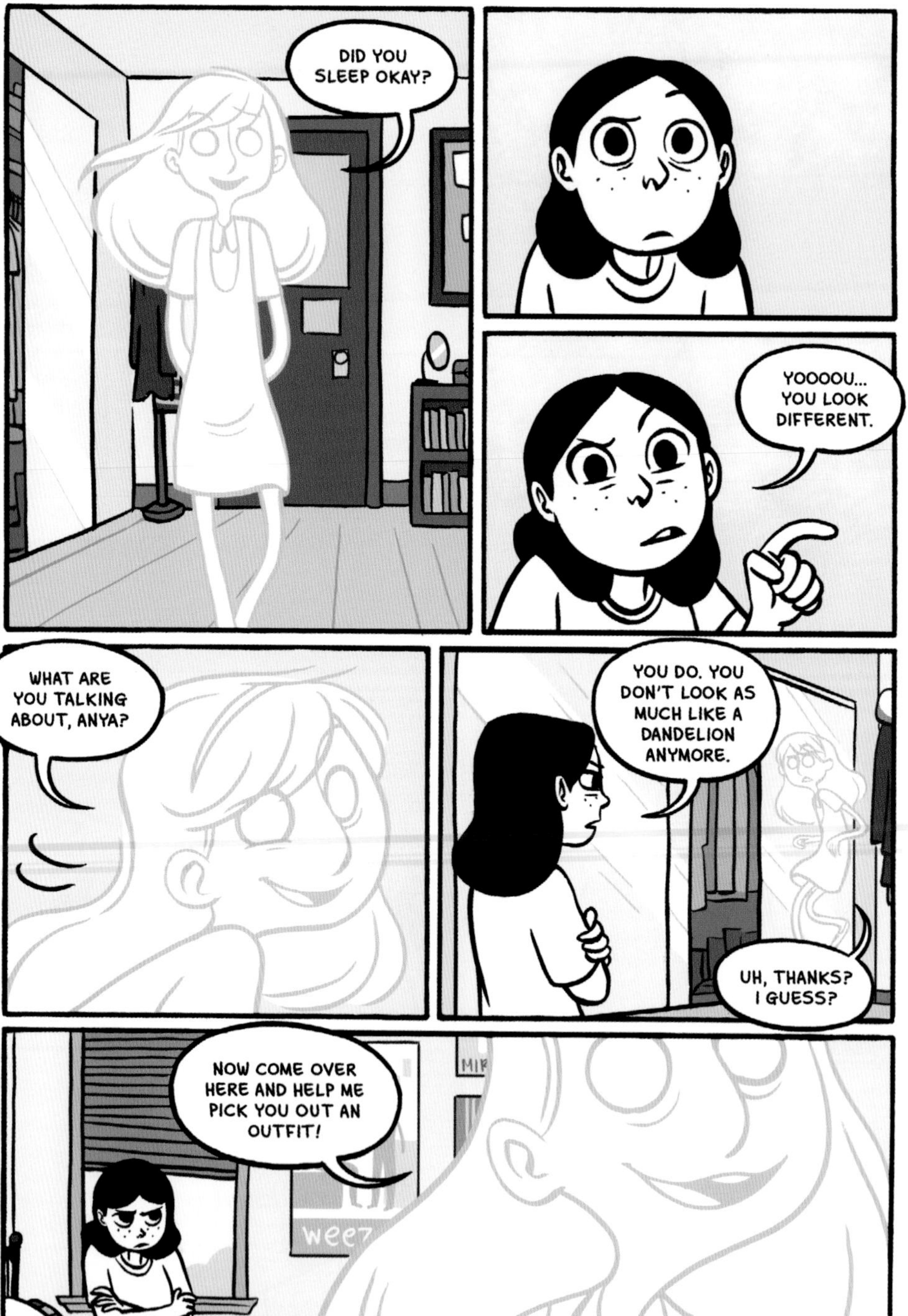
DID YOU SLEEP OKAY?
YOOOOU... YOU LOOK DIFFERENT.
WHAT ARE YOU TALKING ABOUT, ANYA?
YOU DO. YOU DON'T LOOK AS MUCH LIKE A DANDELION ANYMORE.
UH, THANKS? I GUESS?
NOW COME OVER HERE AND HELP ME PICK YOU OUT AN OUTFIT!

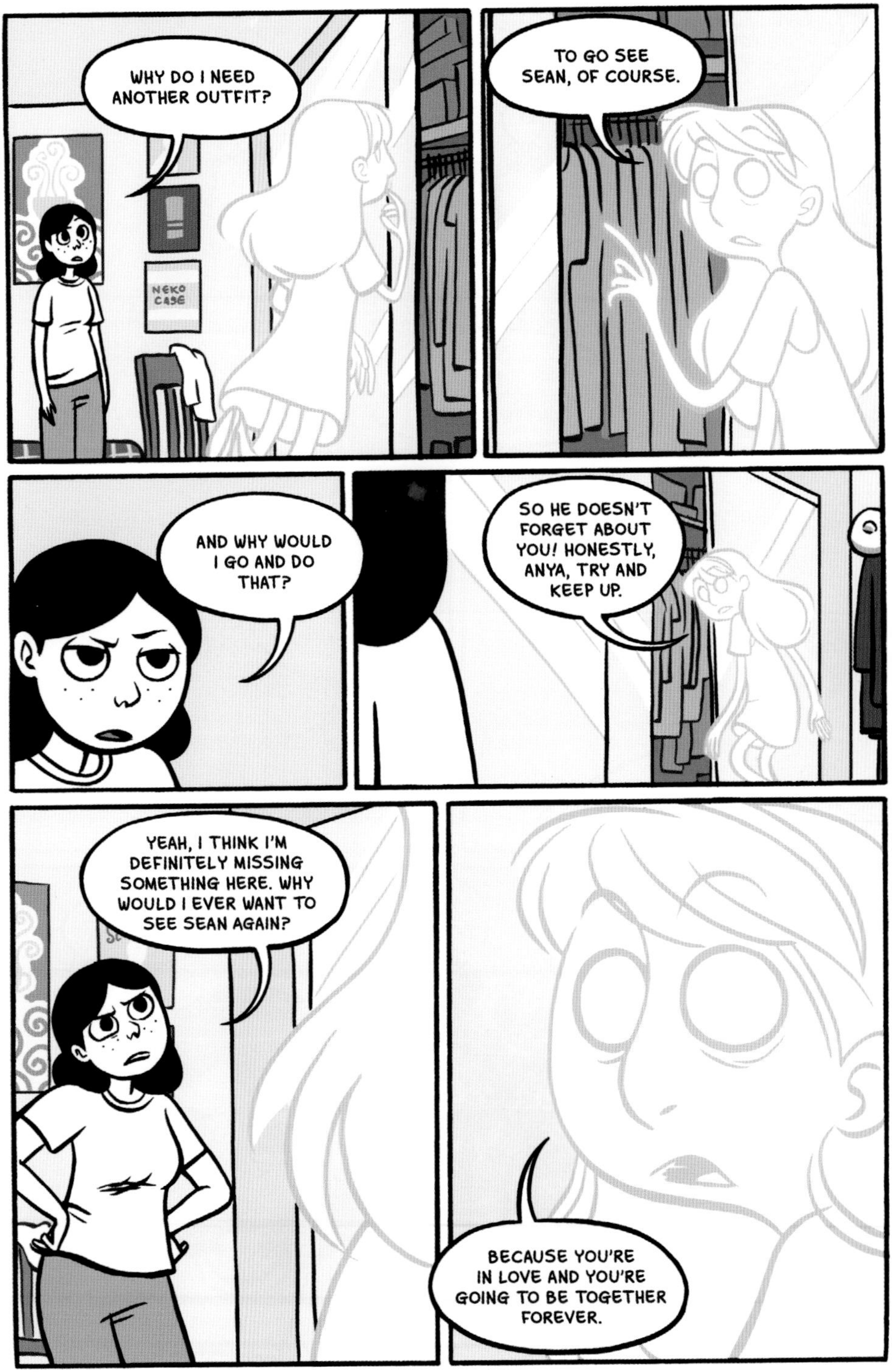
WHY DO I NEED ANOTHER OUTFIT?
NEKO CASE
TO GO SEE SEAN, OF COURSE.
AND WHY WOULD I GO AND DO THAT?
SO HE DOESN'T FORGET ABOUT YOU! HONESTLY, ANYA, TRY AND KEEP UP.
YEAH, I THINK I'M DEFINITELY MISSING SOMETHING HERE. WHY WOULD I EVER WANT TO SEE SEAN AGAIN?
BECAUSE YOU'RE IN LOVE AND YOU'RE GOING TO BE TOGETHER FOREVER.

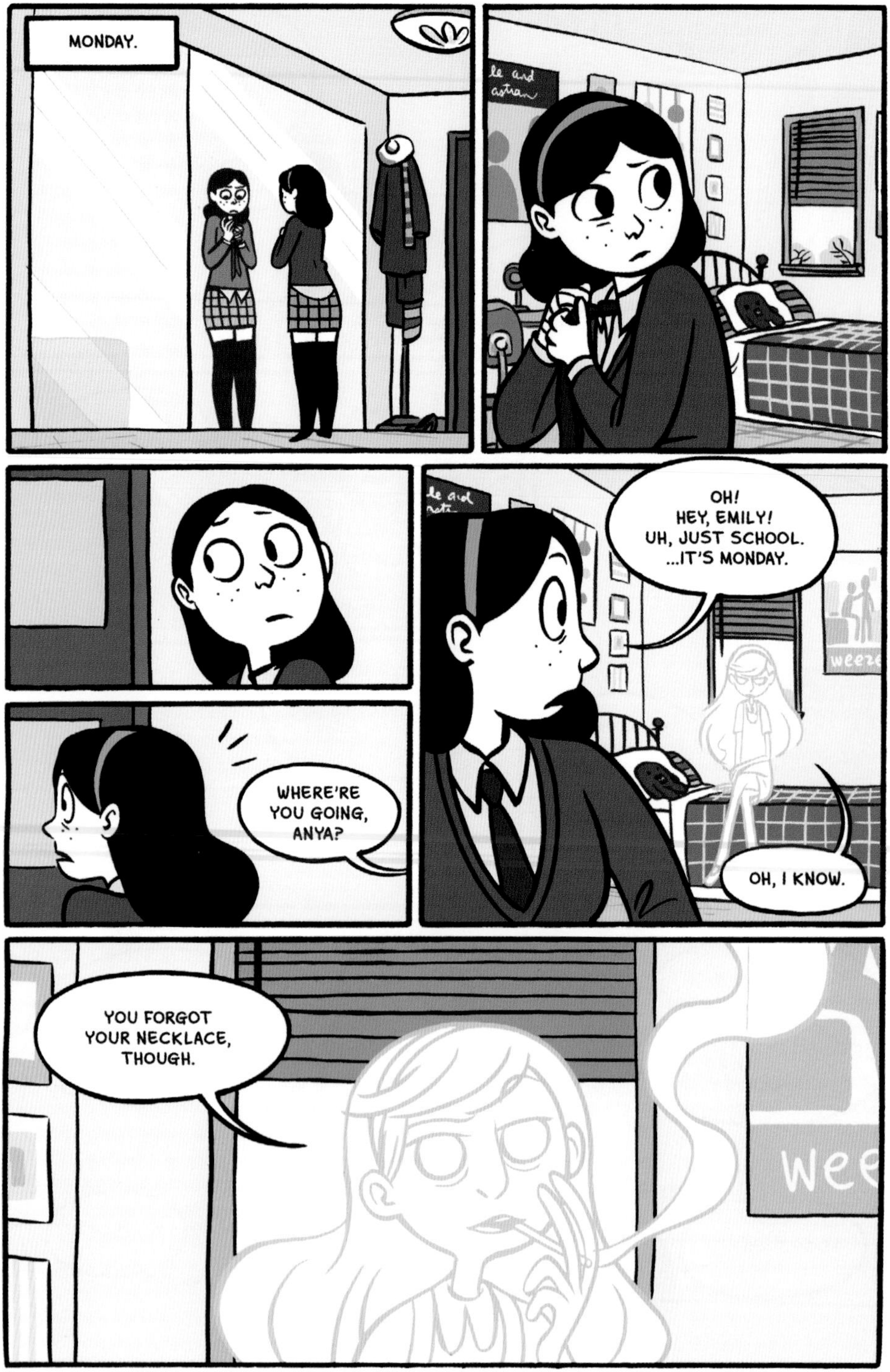
MONDAY.
WHERE'RE YOU GOING, ANYA?
OH! HEY, EMILY! UH, JUST SCHOOL. ...IT'S MONDAY.
OH, I KNOW.
YOU FORGOT YOUR NECKLACE, THOUGH.

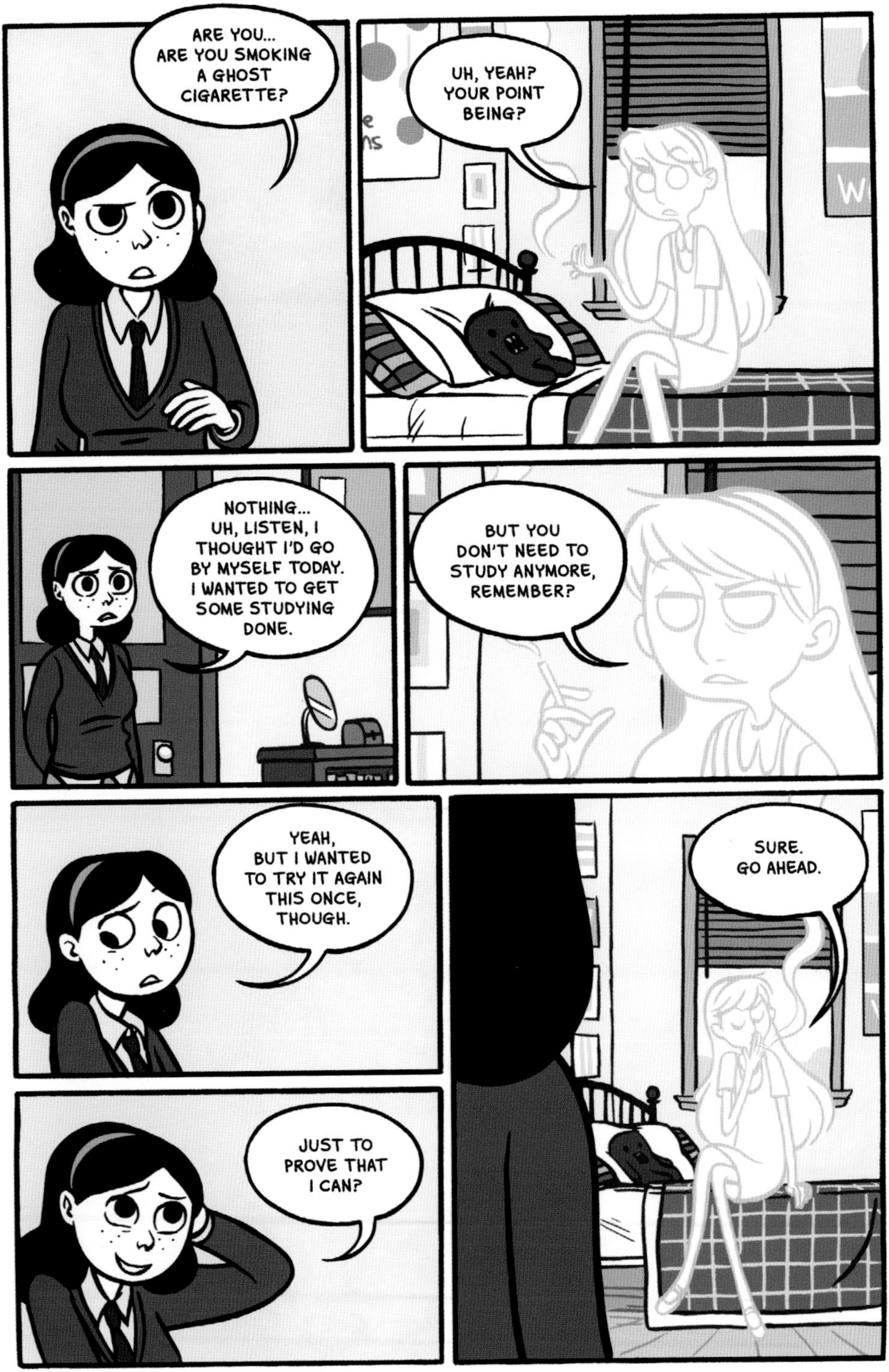

ARE YOU... ARE YOU SMOKING A GHOST CIGARETTE?
UH, YEAH? YOUR POINT BEING?
NOTHING... UH, LISTEN, I THOUGHT I'D GO BY MYSELF TODAY. I WANTED TO GET SOME STUDYING DONE.
BUT YOU DON'T NEED TO STUDY ANYMORE, REMEMBER?
YEAH, BUT I WANTED TO TRY IT AGAIN THIS ONCE, THOUGH.
JUST TO PROVE THAT I CAN?
SURE. GO AHEAD.

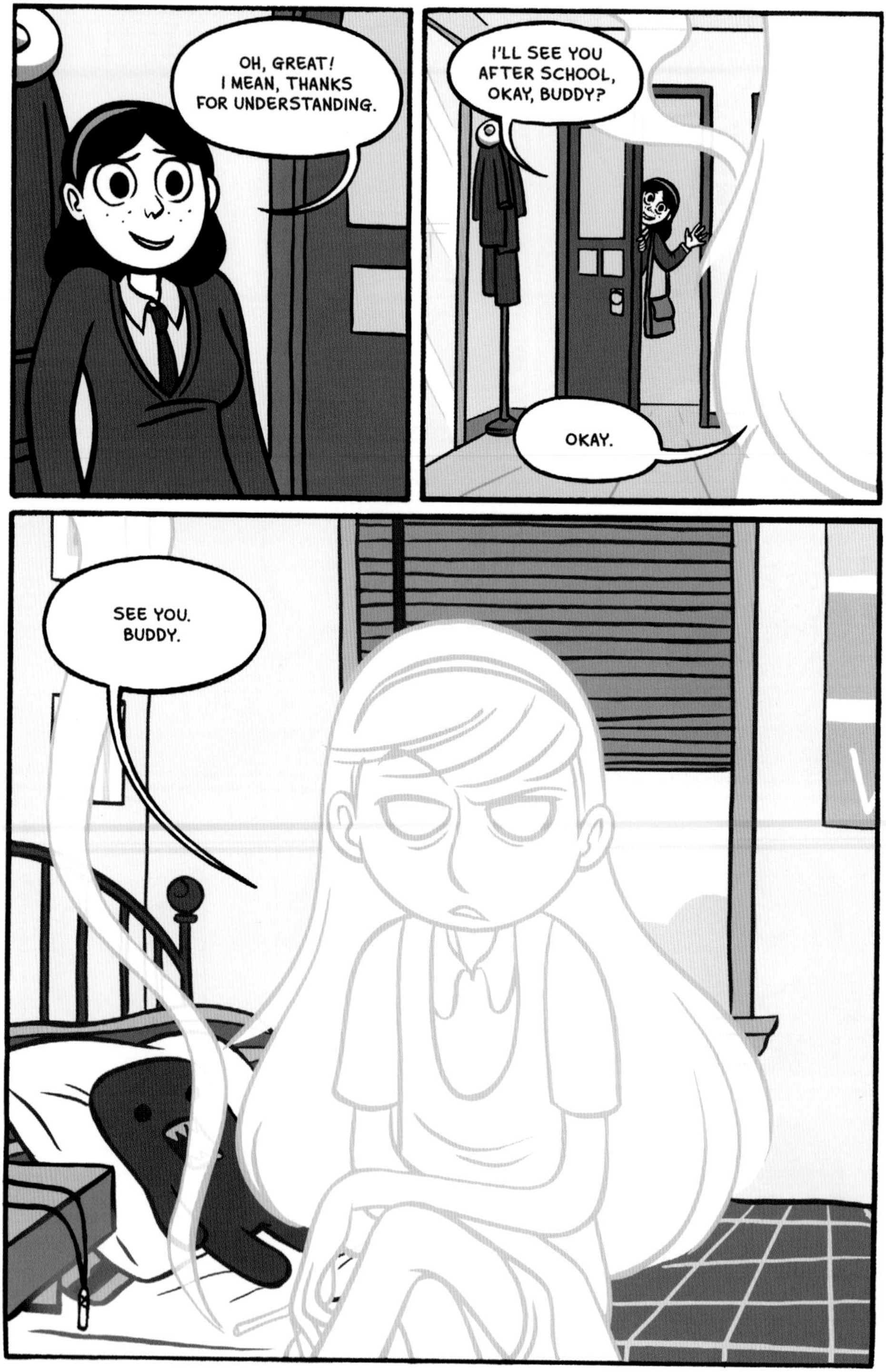
OH, GREAT! I MEAN, THANKS FOR UNDERSTANDING.
I'LL SEE YOU AFTER SCHOOL, OKAY, BUDDY?
OKAY.
SEE YOU. BUDDY.

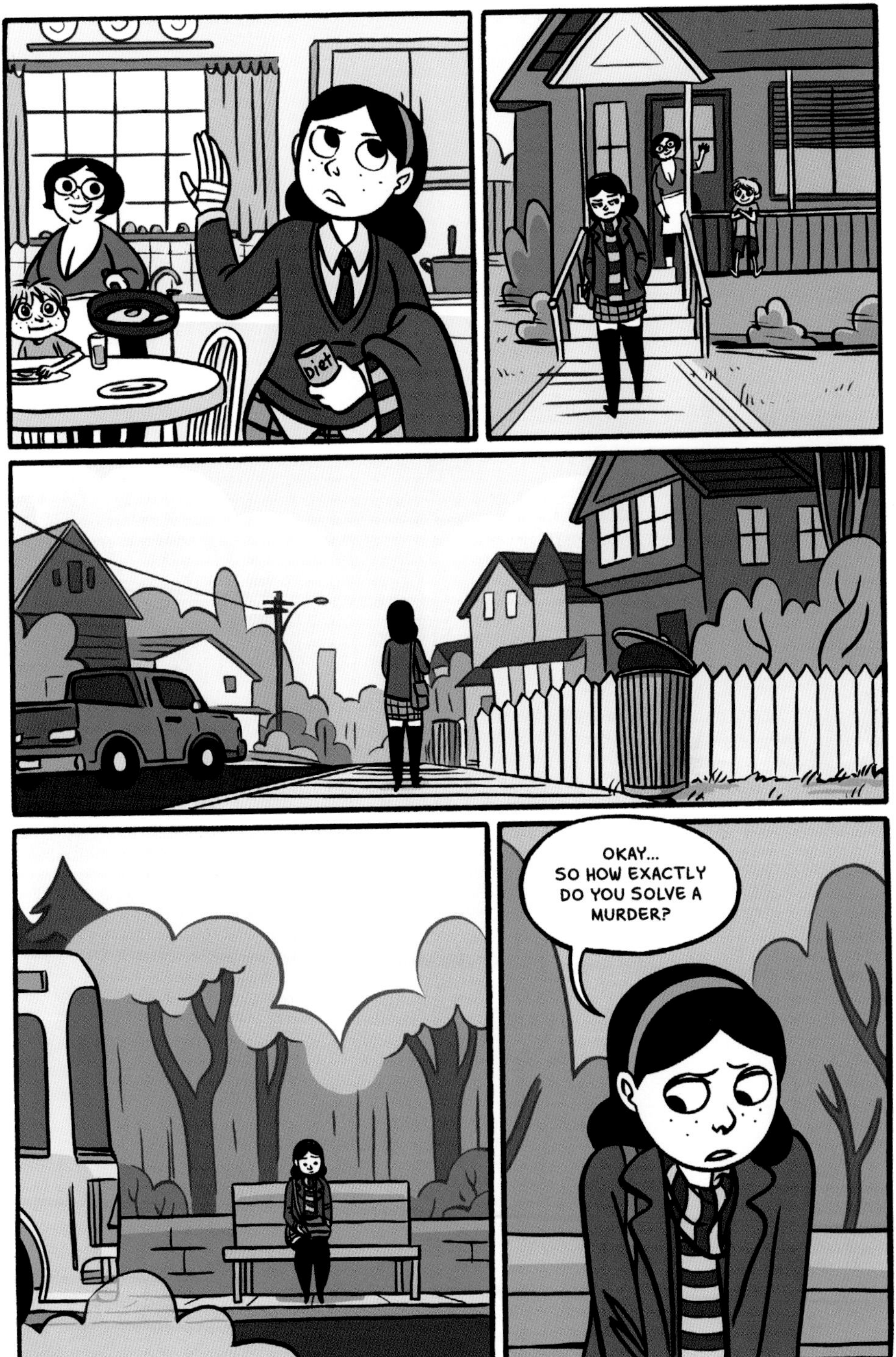
Diet
OKAY... SO HOW EXACTLY DO YOU SOLVE A MURDER?

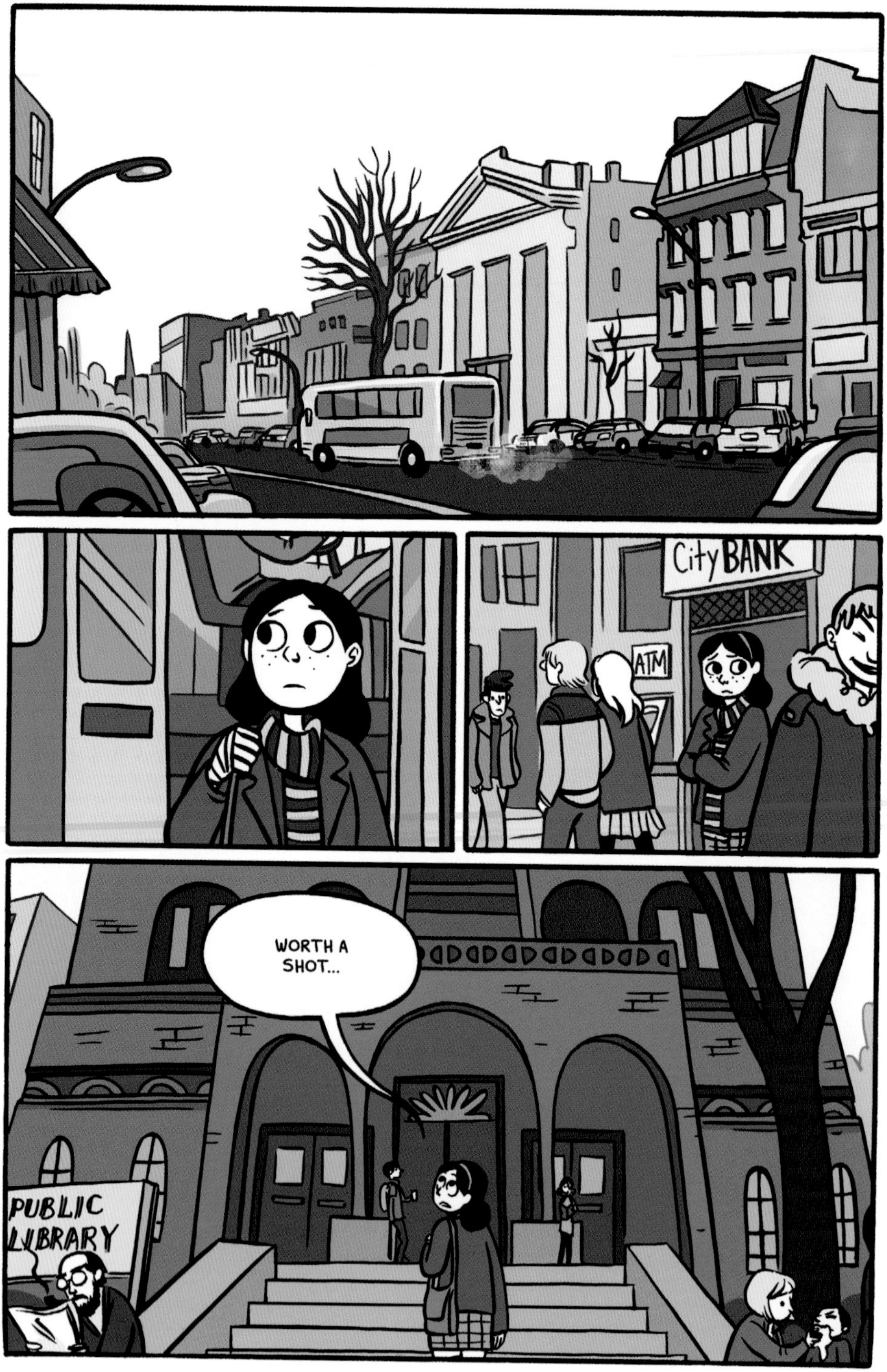
City BANK
ATM
WORTH A SHOT...
PUBLIC LIBRARY

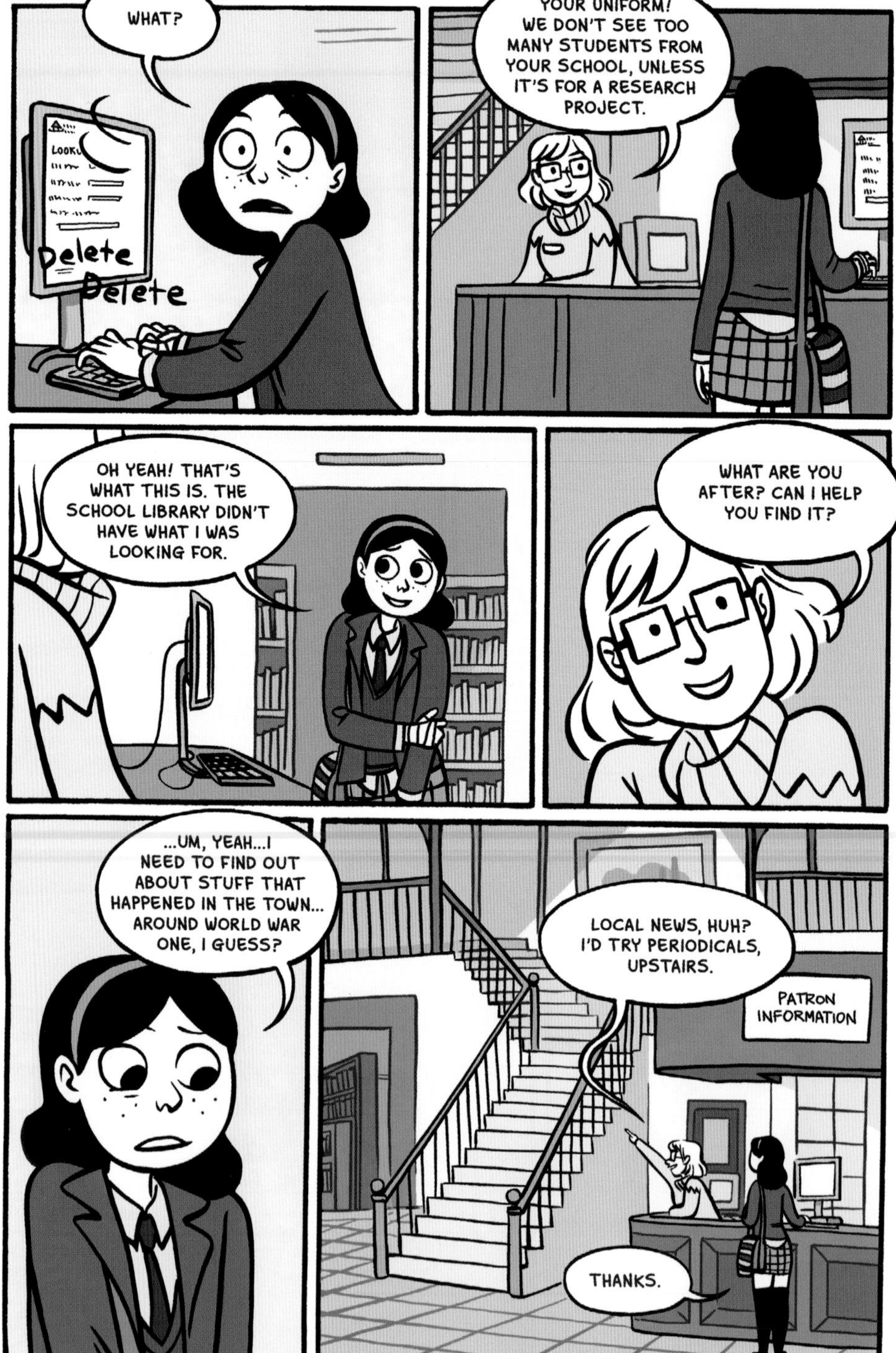
WHAT?
Delete
Delete
YOUR UNIFORM! WE DON'T SEE TOO MANY STUDENTS FROM YOUR SCHOOL, UNLESS IT'S FOR A RESEARCH PROJECT.
OH YEAH! THAT'S WHAT THIS IS. THE SCHOOL LIBRARY DIDN'T HAVE WHAT I WAS LOOKING FOR.
WHAT ARE YOU AFTER? CAN I HELP YOU FIND IT?
...UM, YEAH...I NEED TO FIND OUT ABOUT STUFF THAT HAPPENED IN THE TOWN... AROUND WORLD WAR ONE, I GUESS?
LOCAL NEWS, HUH? I'D TRY PERIODICALS, UPSTAIRS.
PATRON INFORMATION
THANKS.

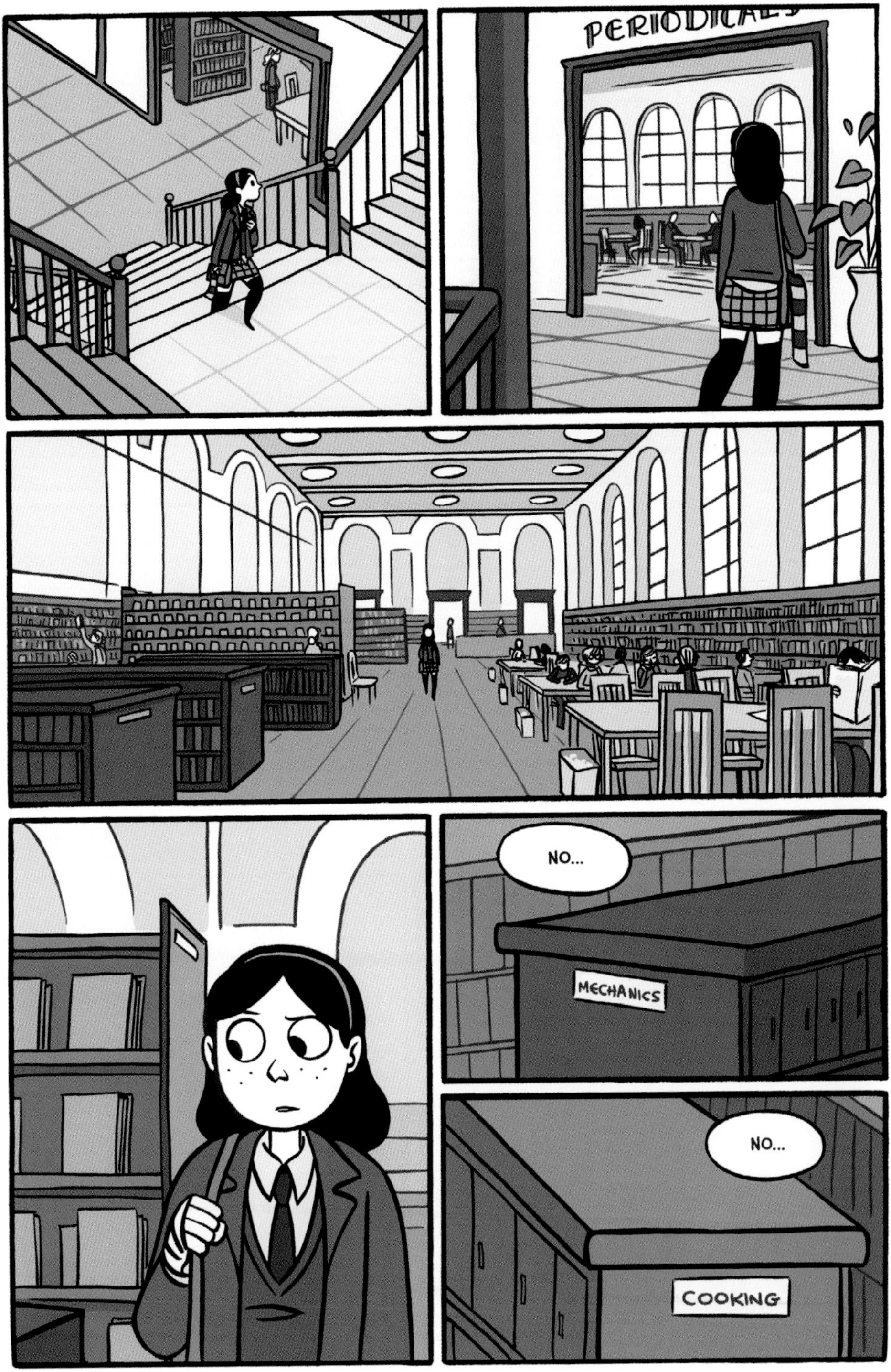
PERIODICALS
NO...
MECHANICS
NO...
COOKING

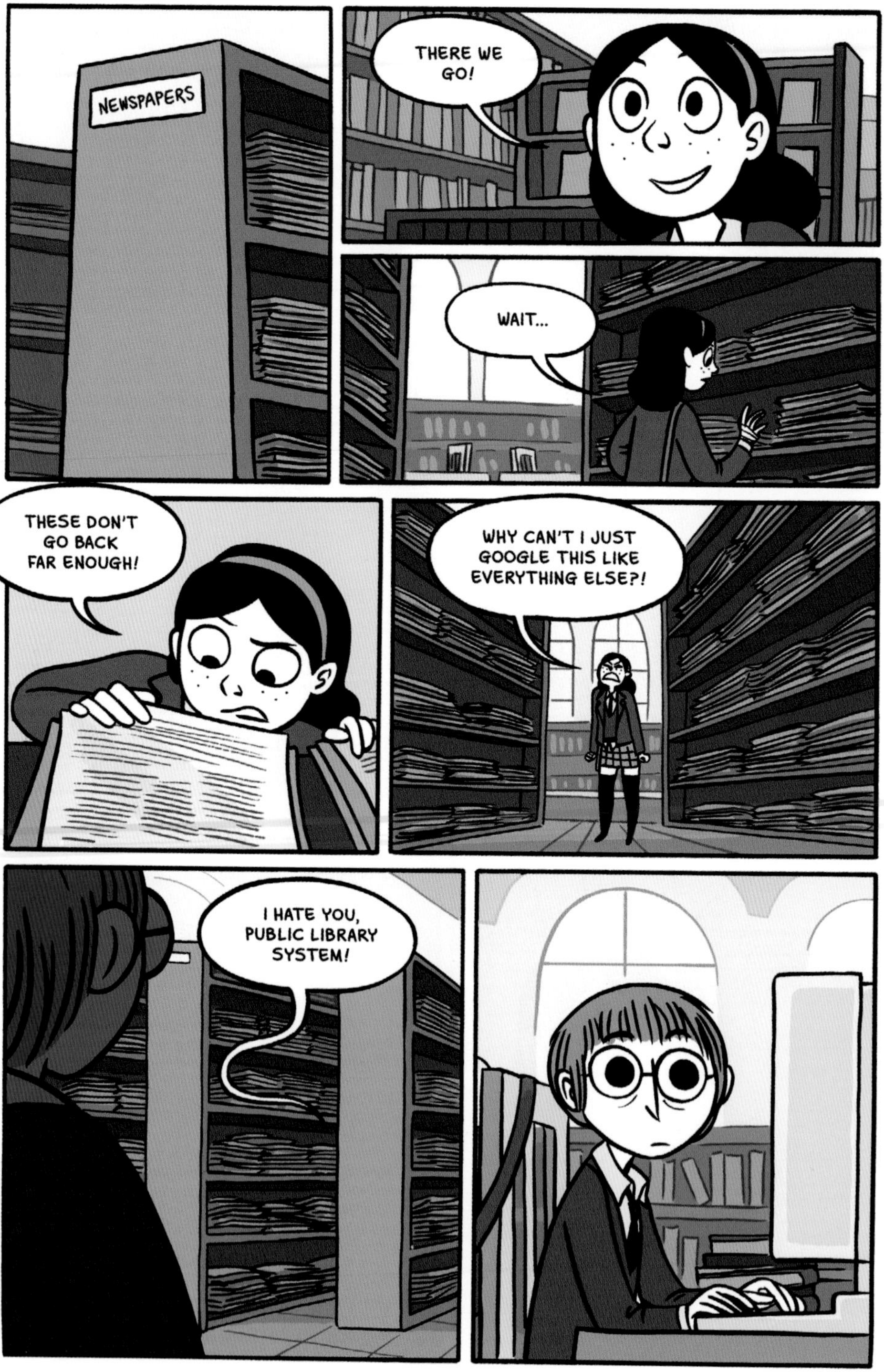
NEWSPAPERS
THERE WE GO!
WAIT...
THESE DON'T GO BACK FAR ENOUGH!
WHY CAN'T I JUST GOOGLE THIS LIKE EVERYTHING ELSE?!
I HATE YOU, PUBLIC LIBRARY SYSTEM!

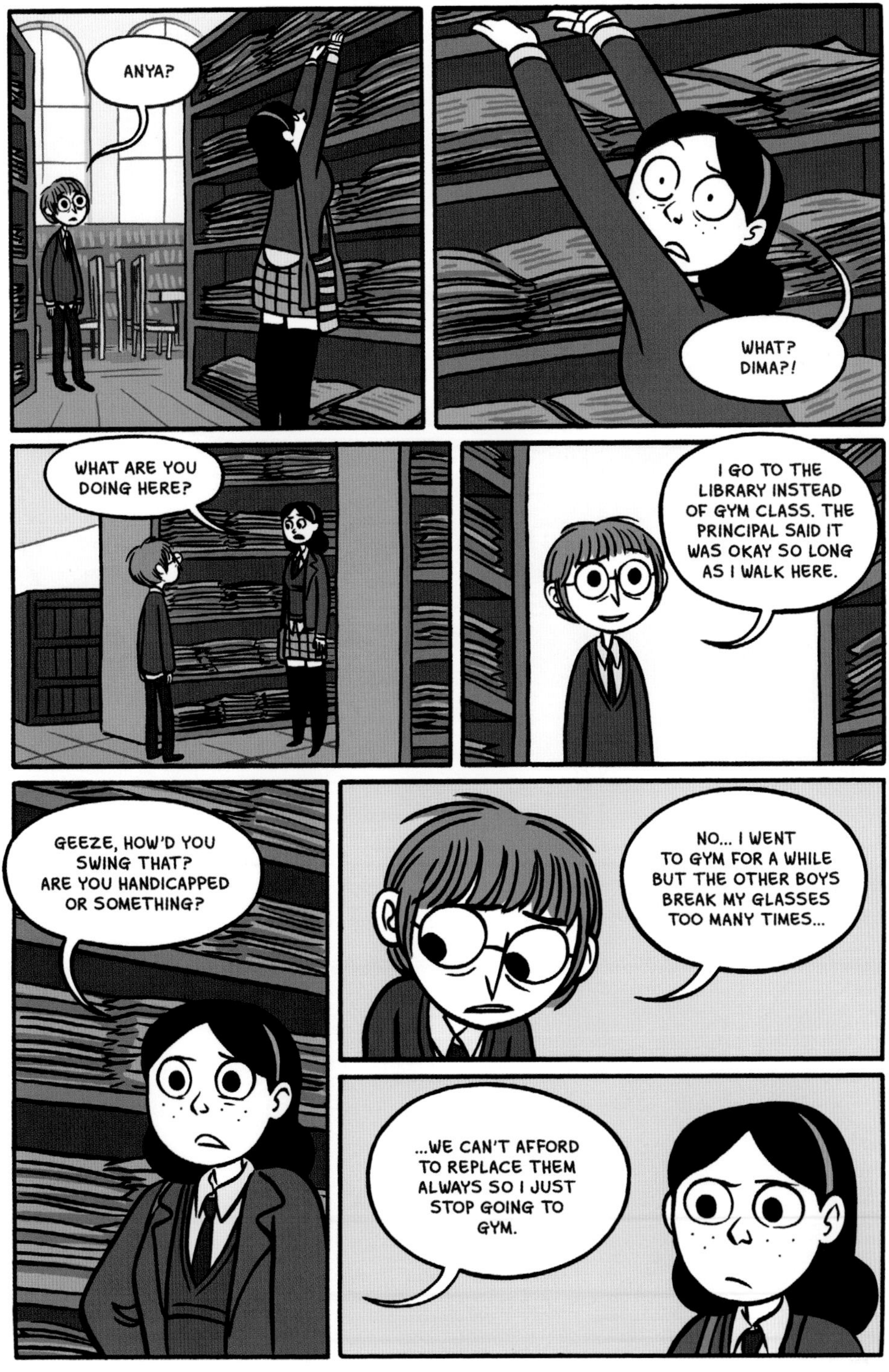
ANYA?
WHAT? DIMA?!
WHAT ARE YOU DOING HERE?
I GO TO THE LIBRARY INSTEAD OF GYM CLASS. THE PRINCIPAL SAID IT WAS OKAY SO LONG AS I WALK HERE.
GEEZE, HOW'D YOU SWING THAT? ARE YOU HANDICAPPED OR SOMETHING?
NO... I WENT TO GYM FOR A WHILE BUT THE OTHER BOYS BREAK MY GLASSES TOO MANY TIMES...
...WE CAN'T AFFORD TO REPLACE THEM ALWAYS SO I JUST STOP GOING TO GYM.

145

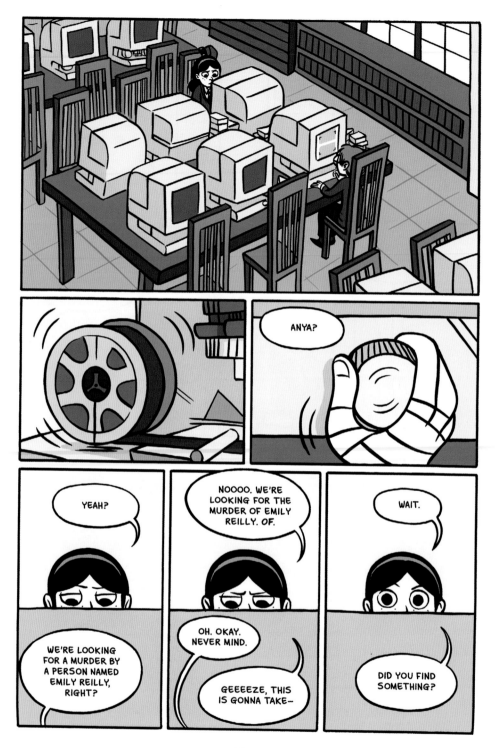

153

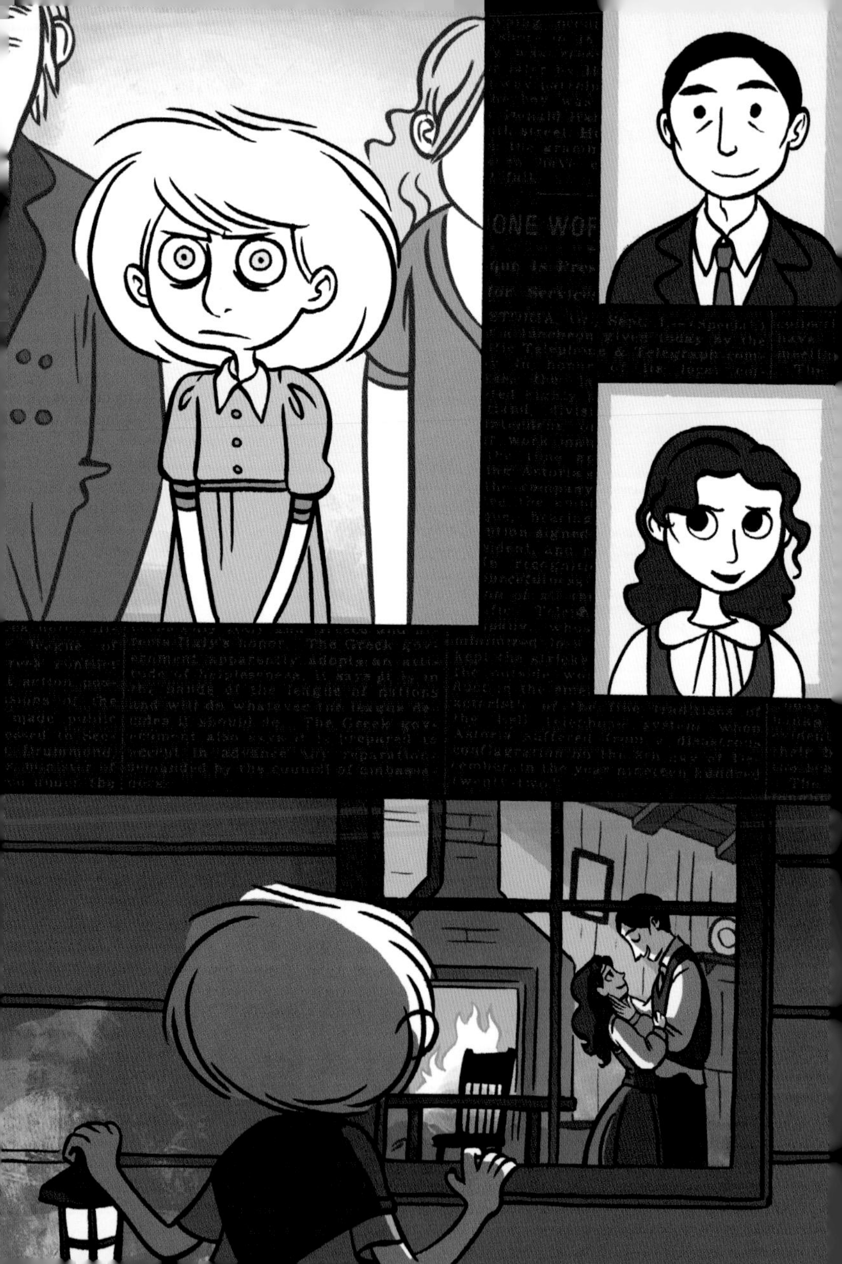

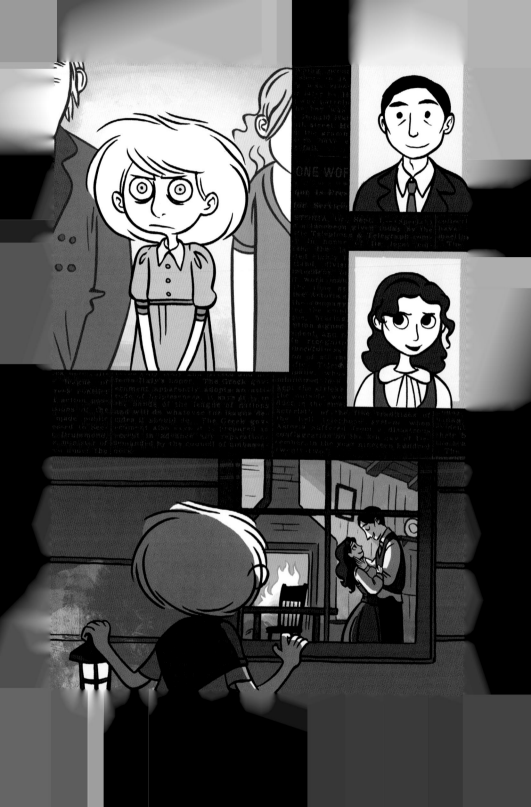

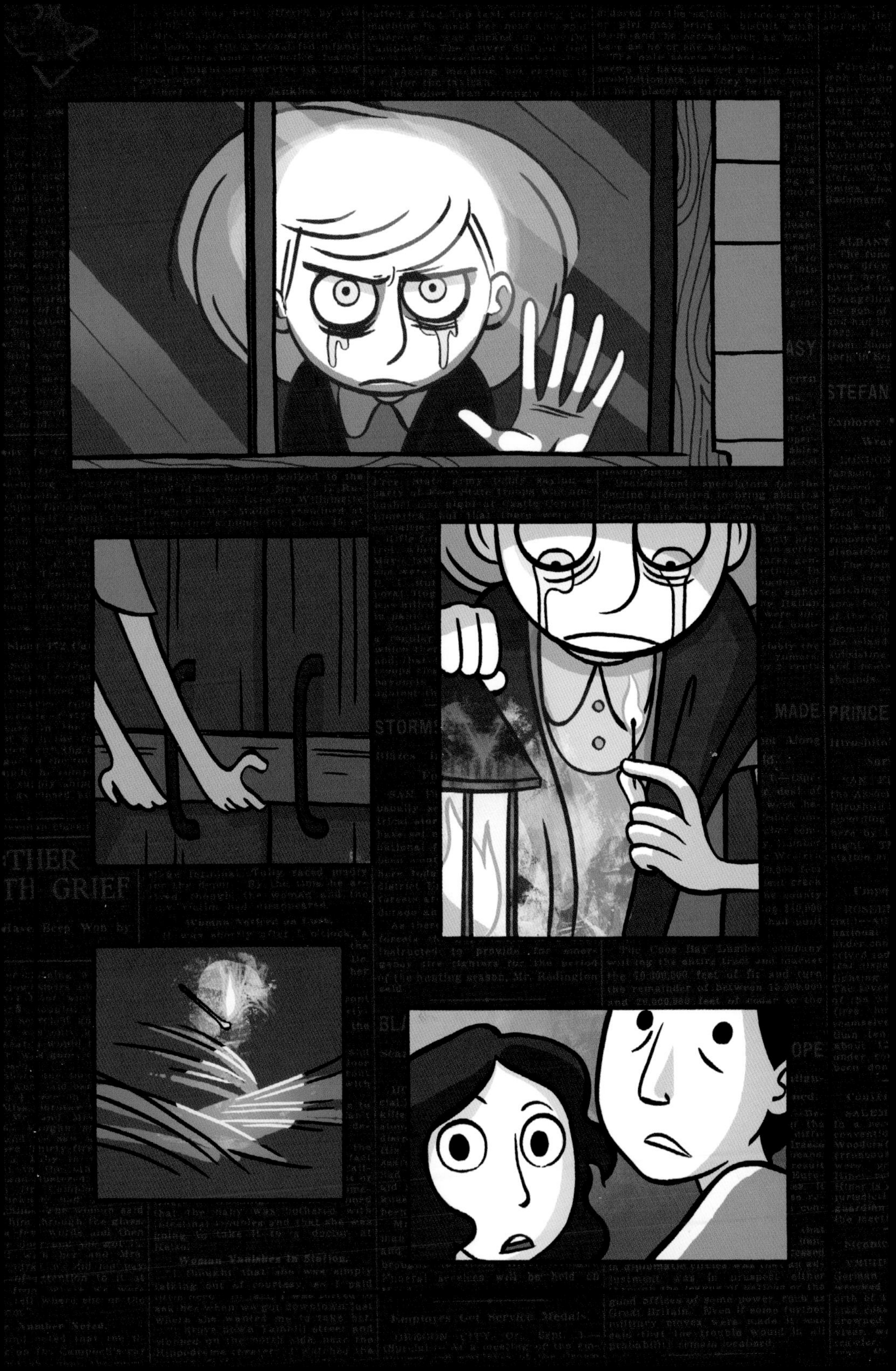

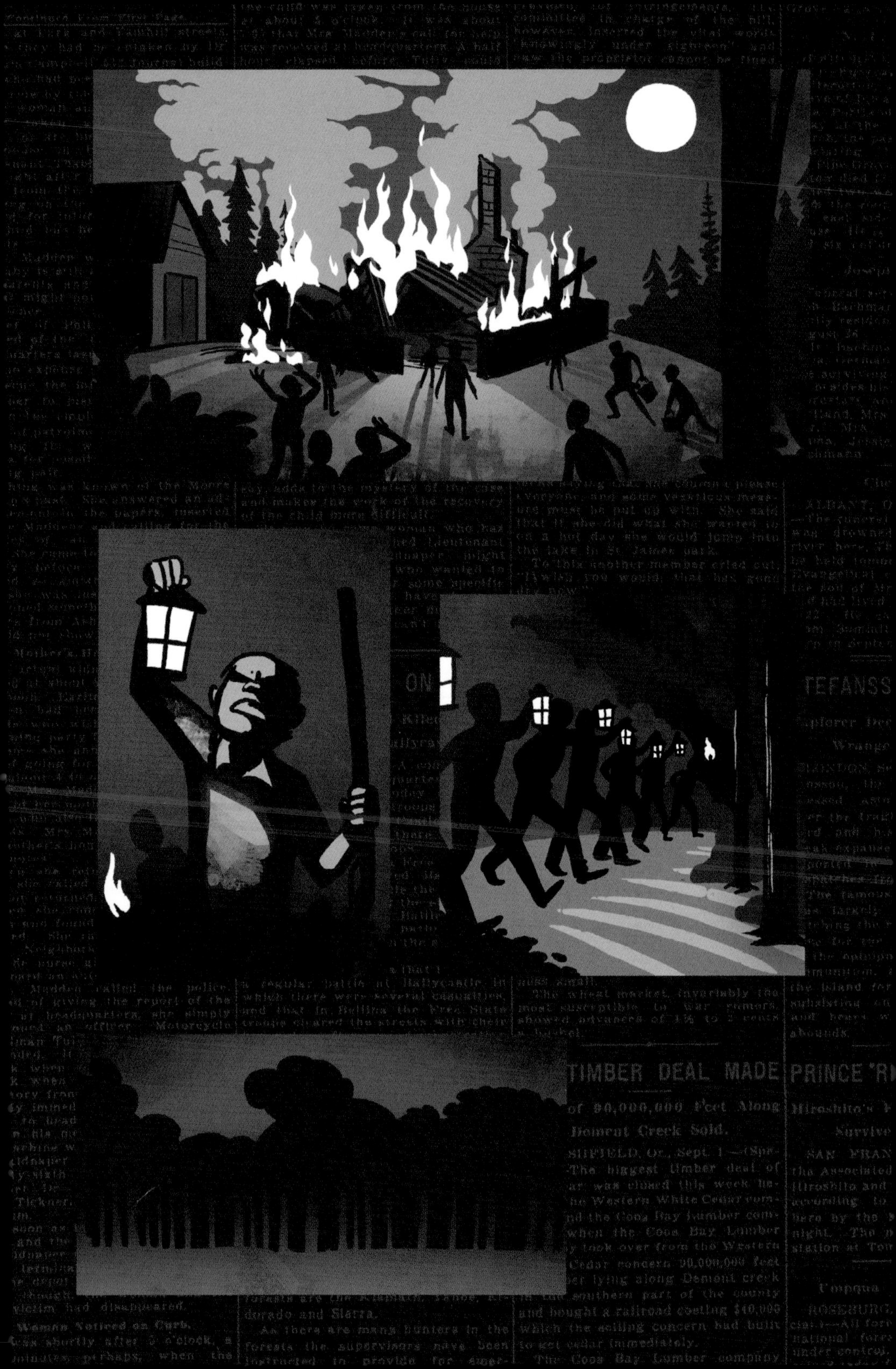
TIMBER DEAL MADE

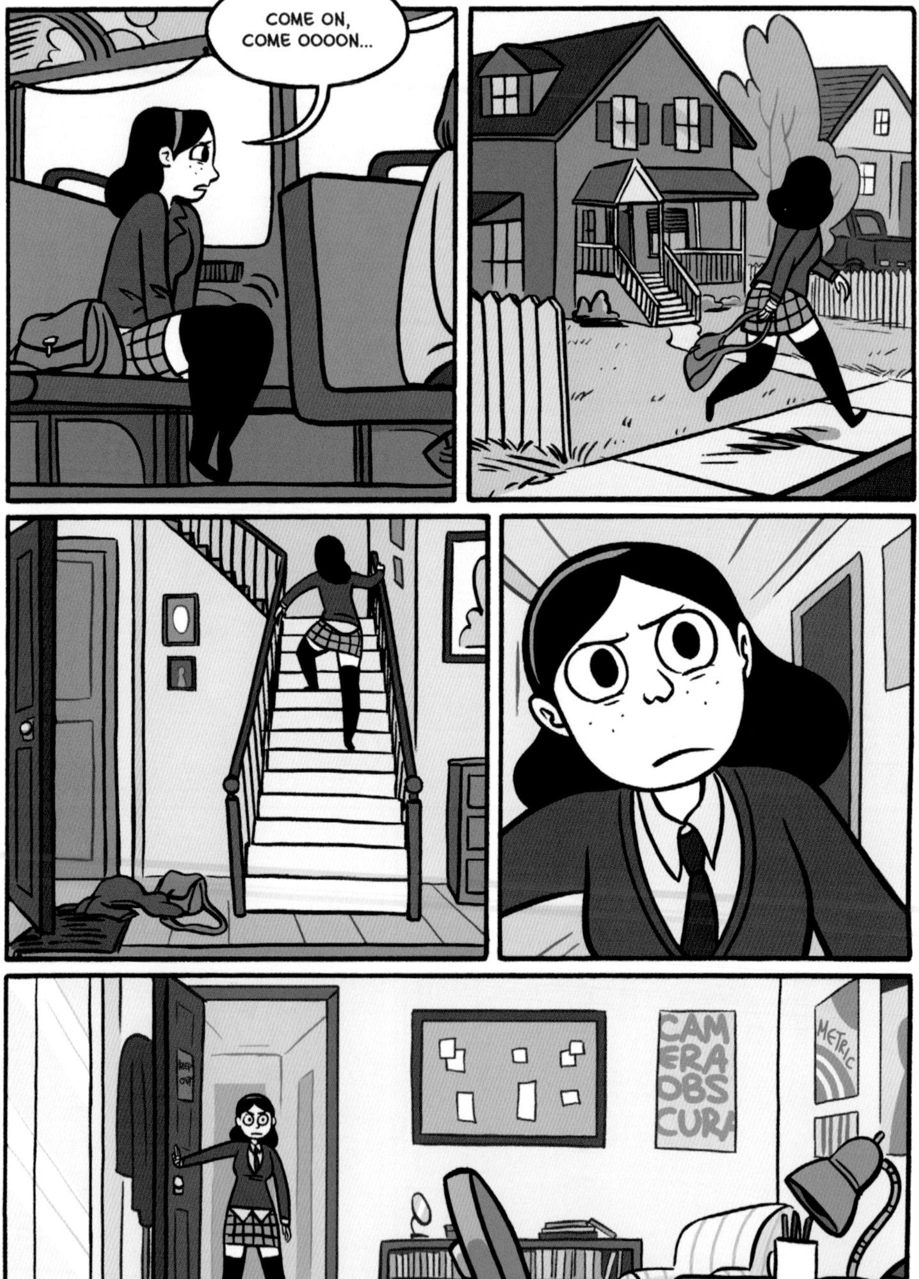
COME ON,
COME OOOON...
CAMERA OBSCURA
METRIC

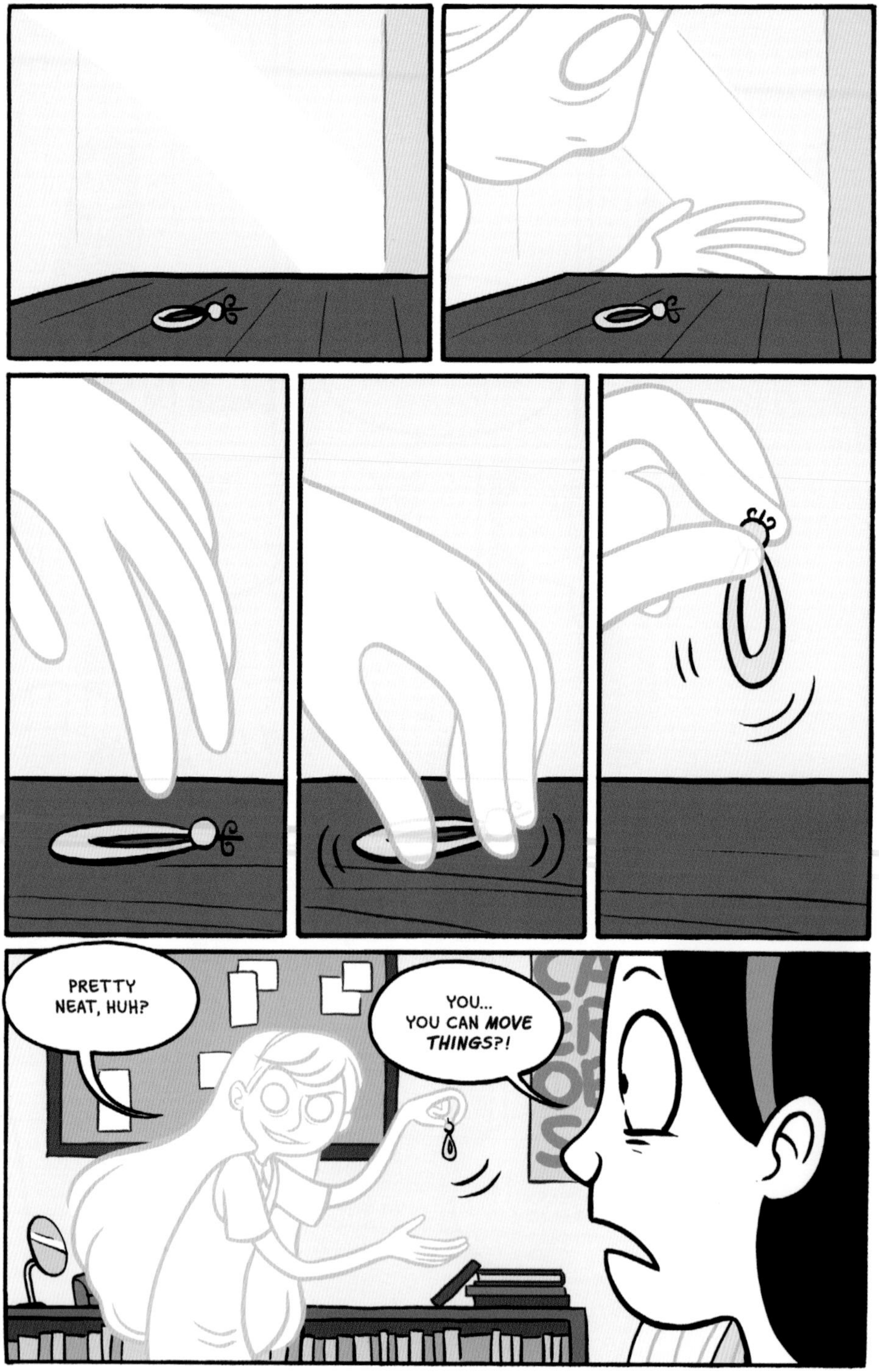
PRETTY NEAT, HUH?
YOU... YOU CAN *MOVE THINGS*?!

174

177

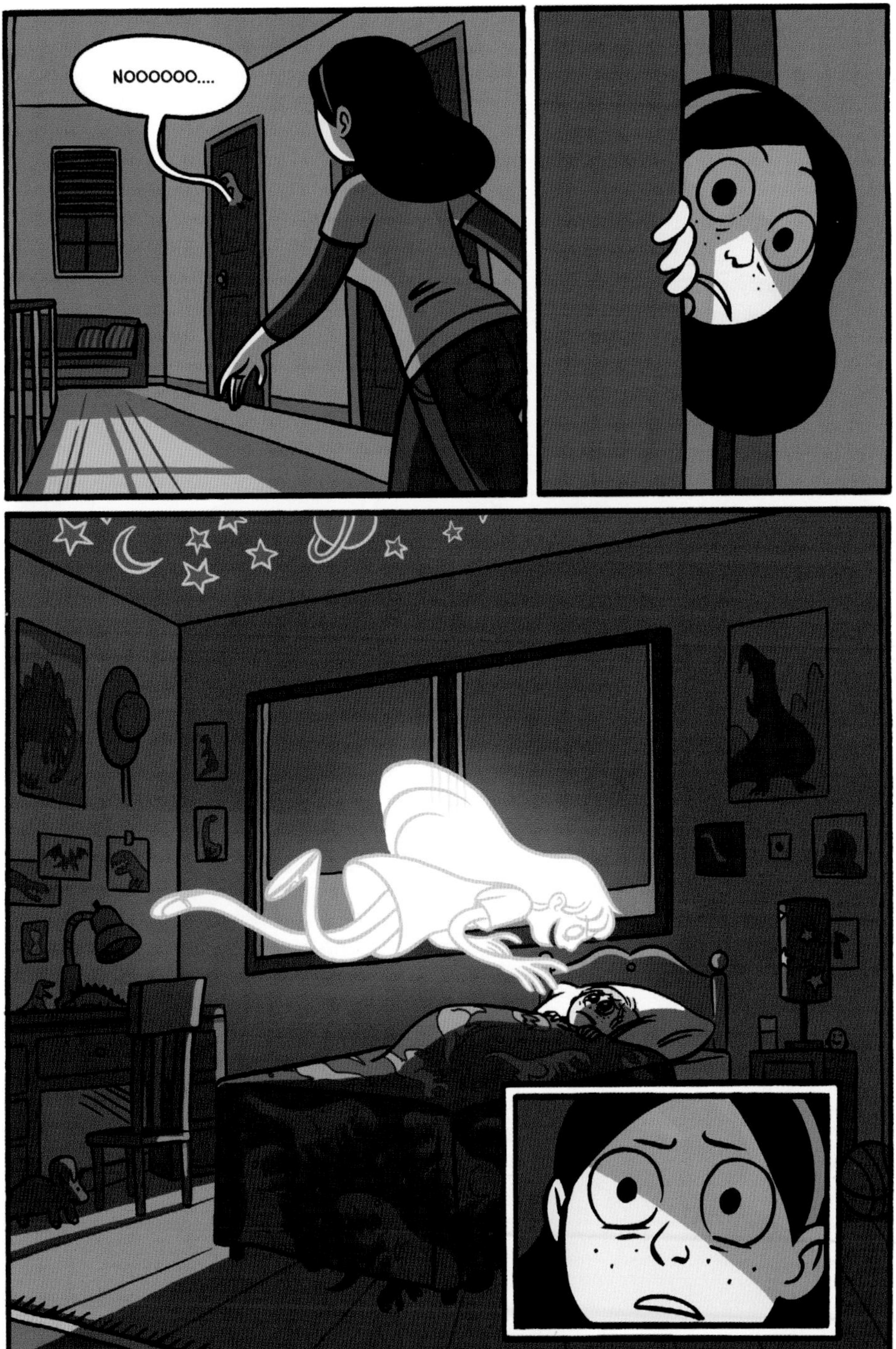
NOOOOOO....

181

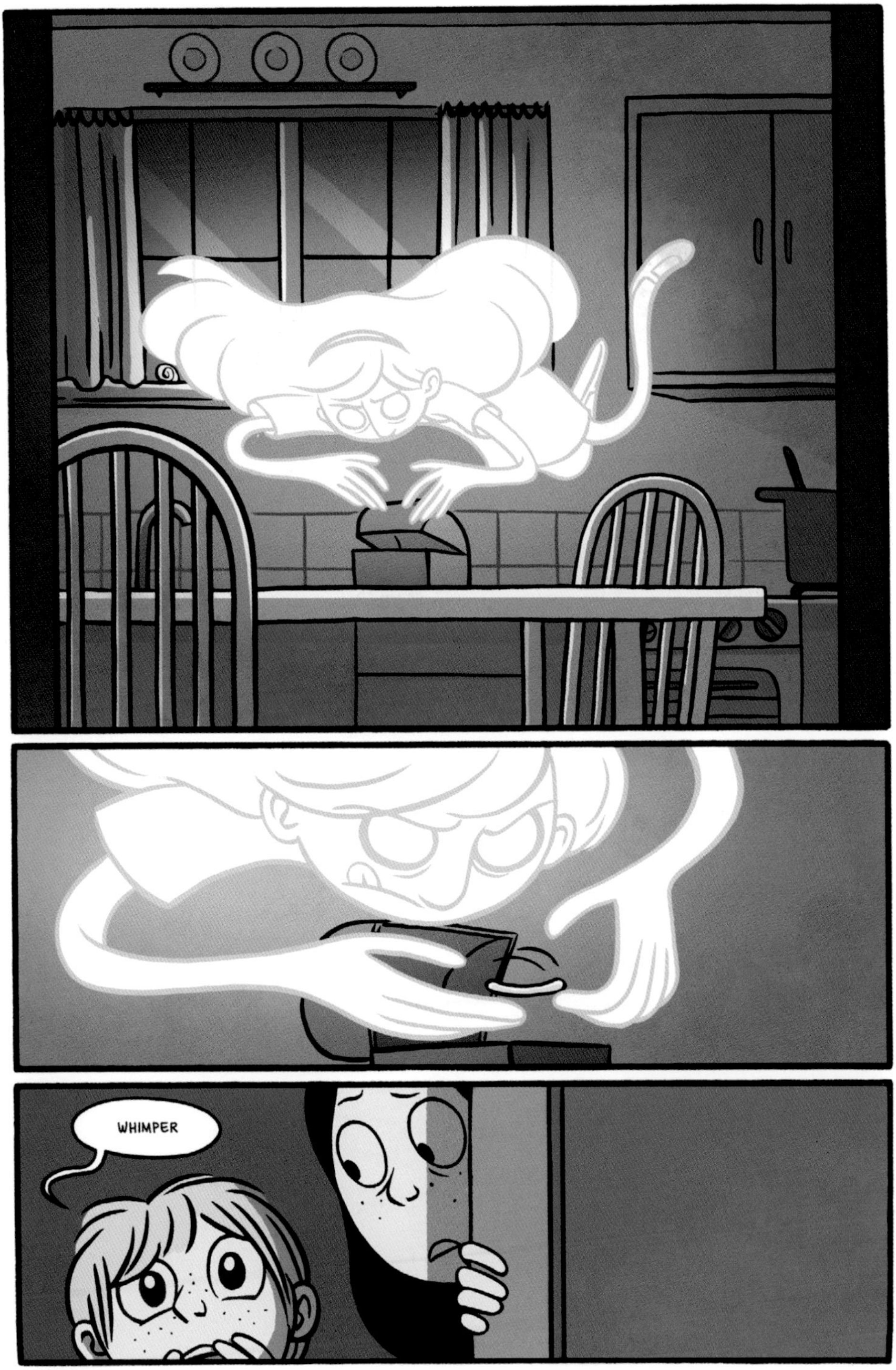
WHIMPER

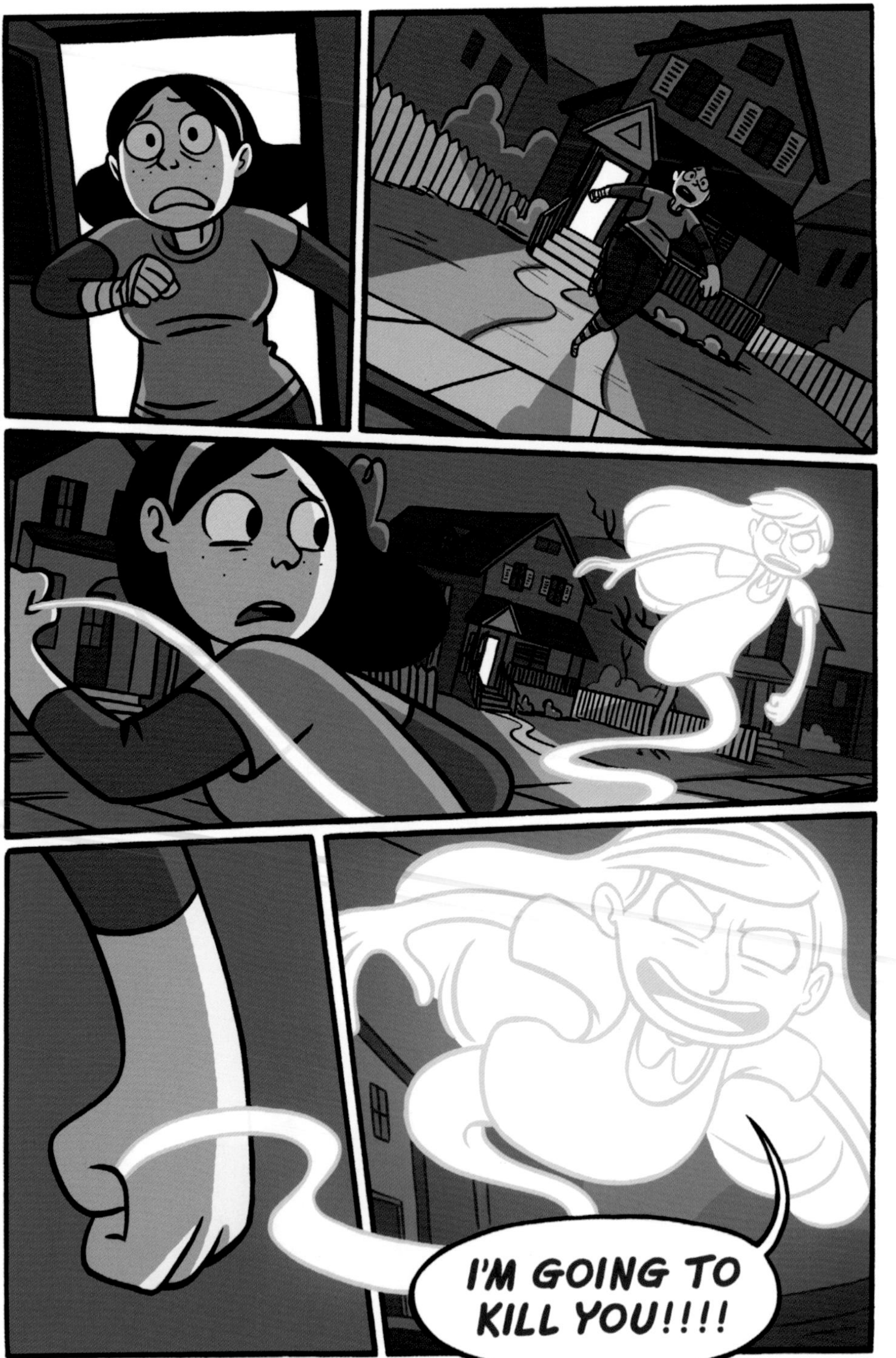
I'M GOING TO
KILL YOU!!!!

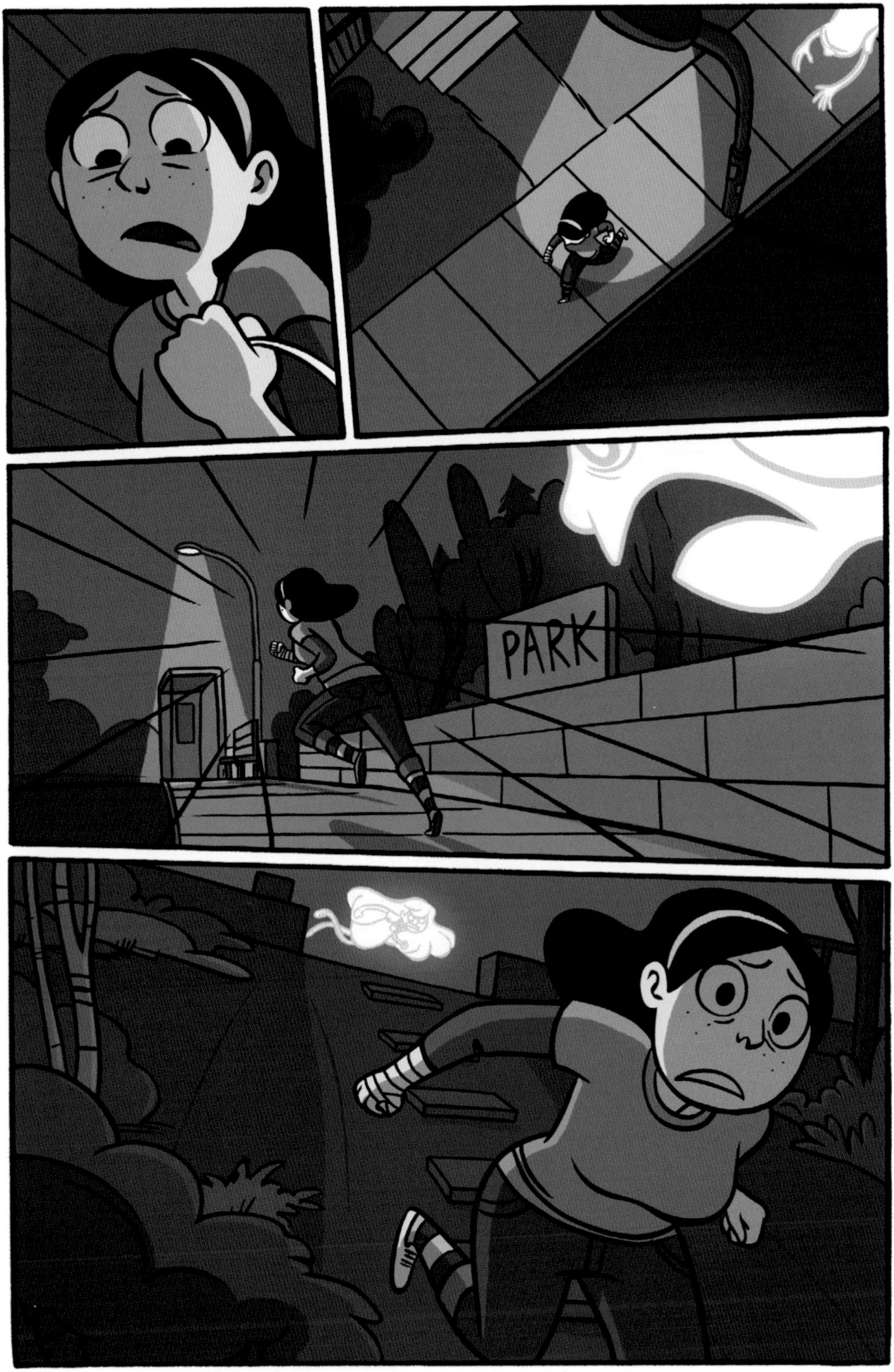
PARK

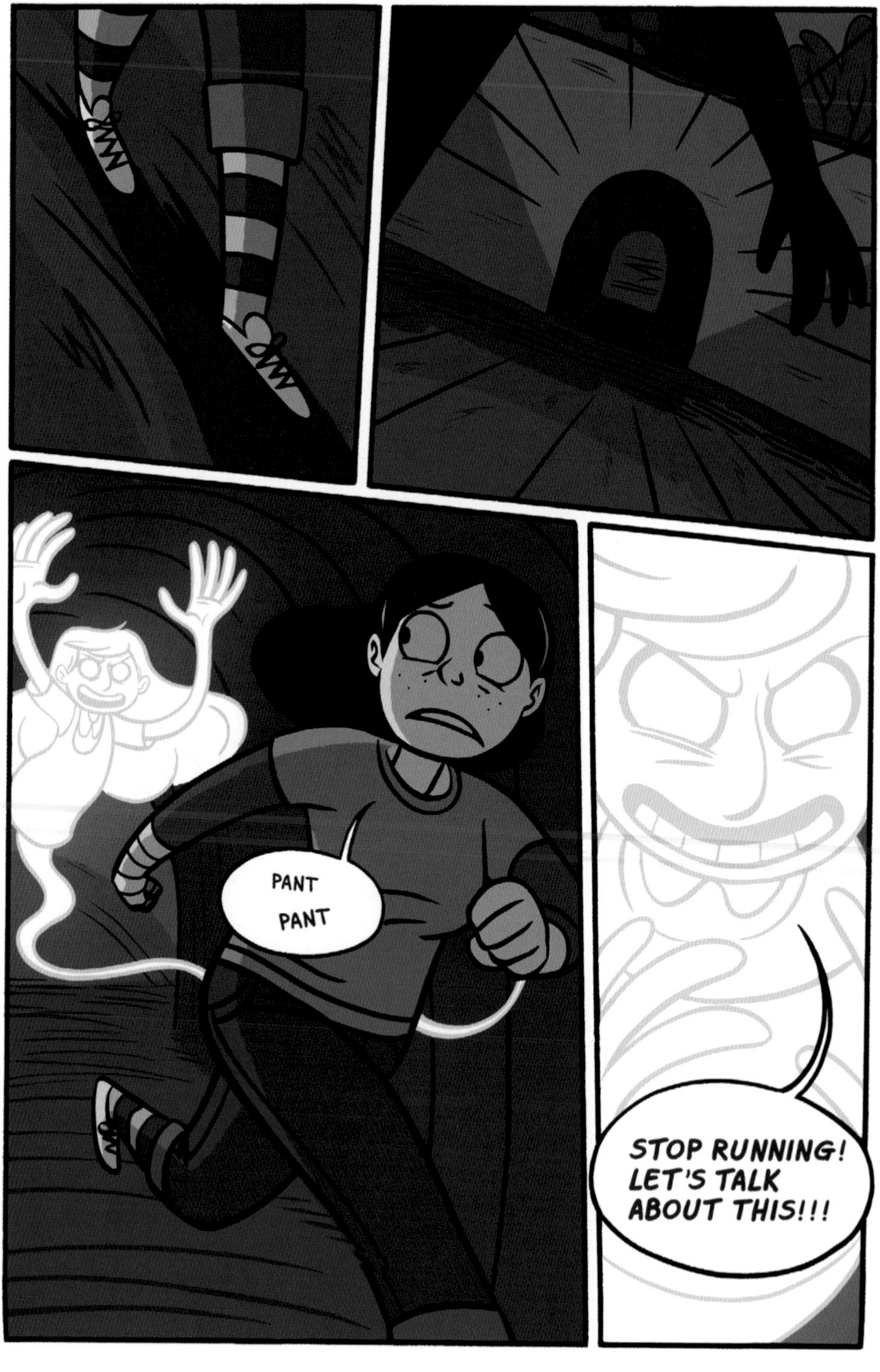
PANT
PANT
STOP RUNNING! LET'S TALK ABOUT THIS!!!

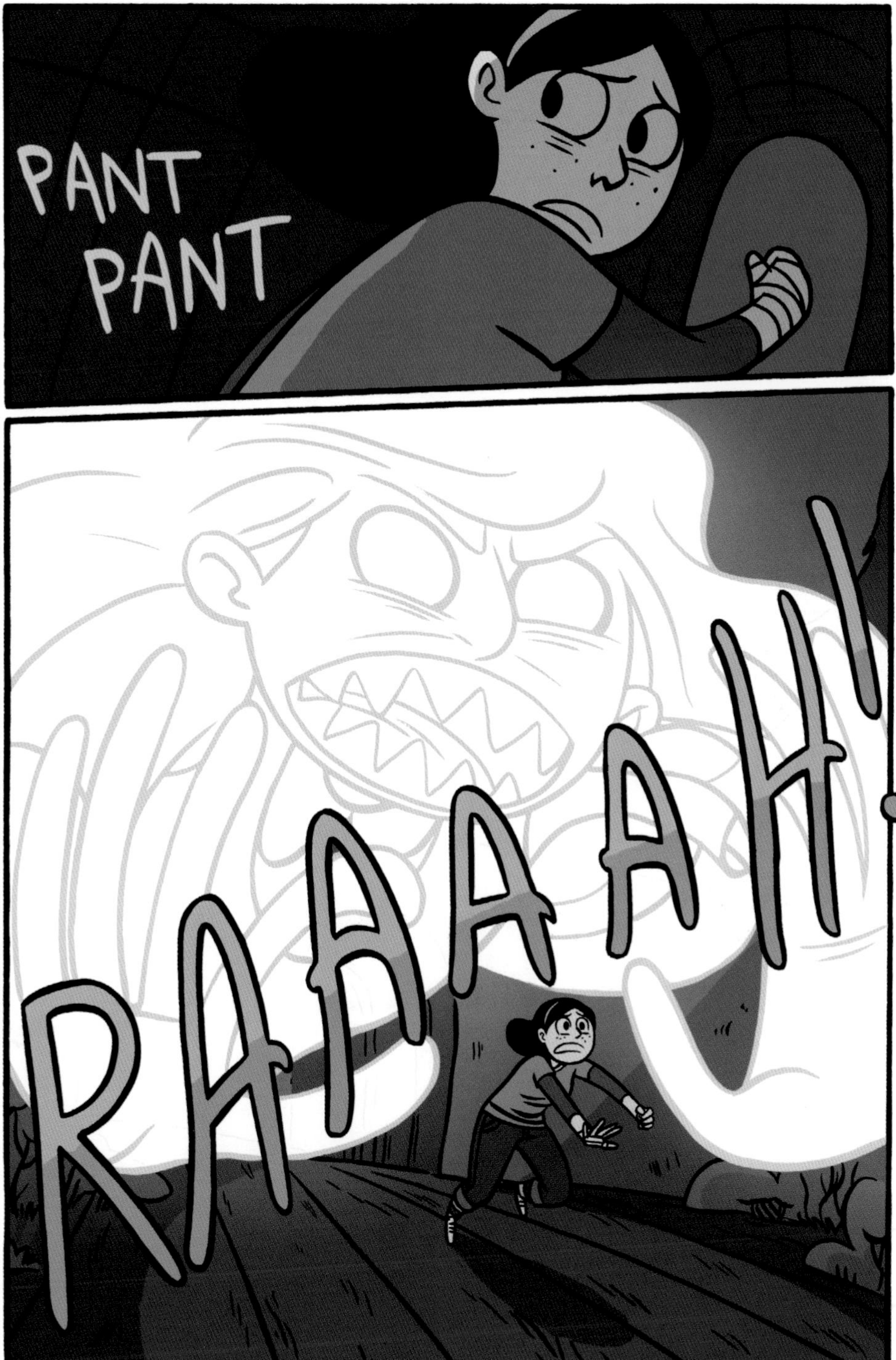
PANT
PANT
RAAAAAH!

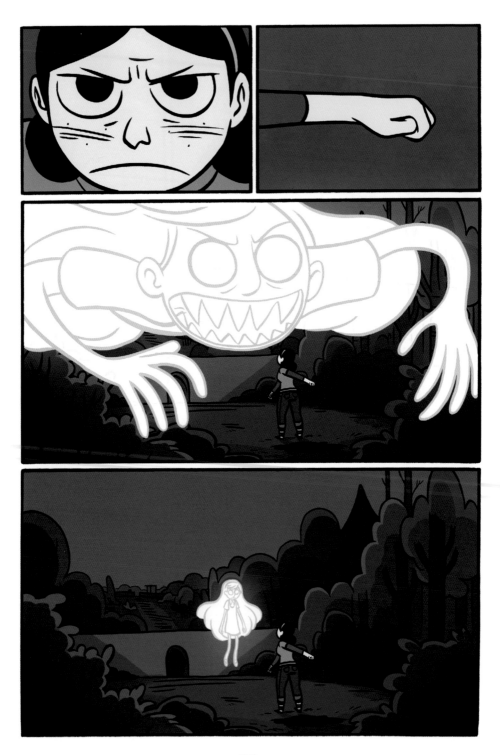

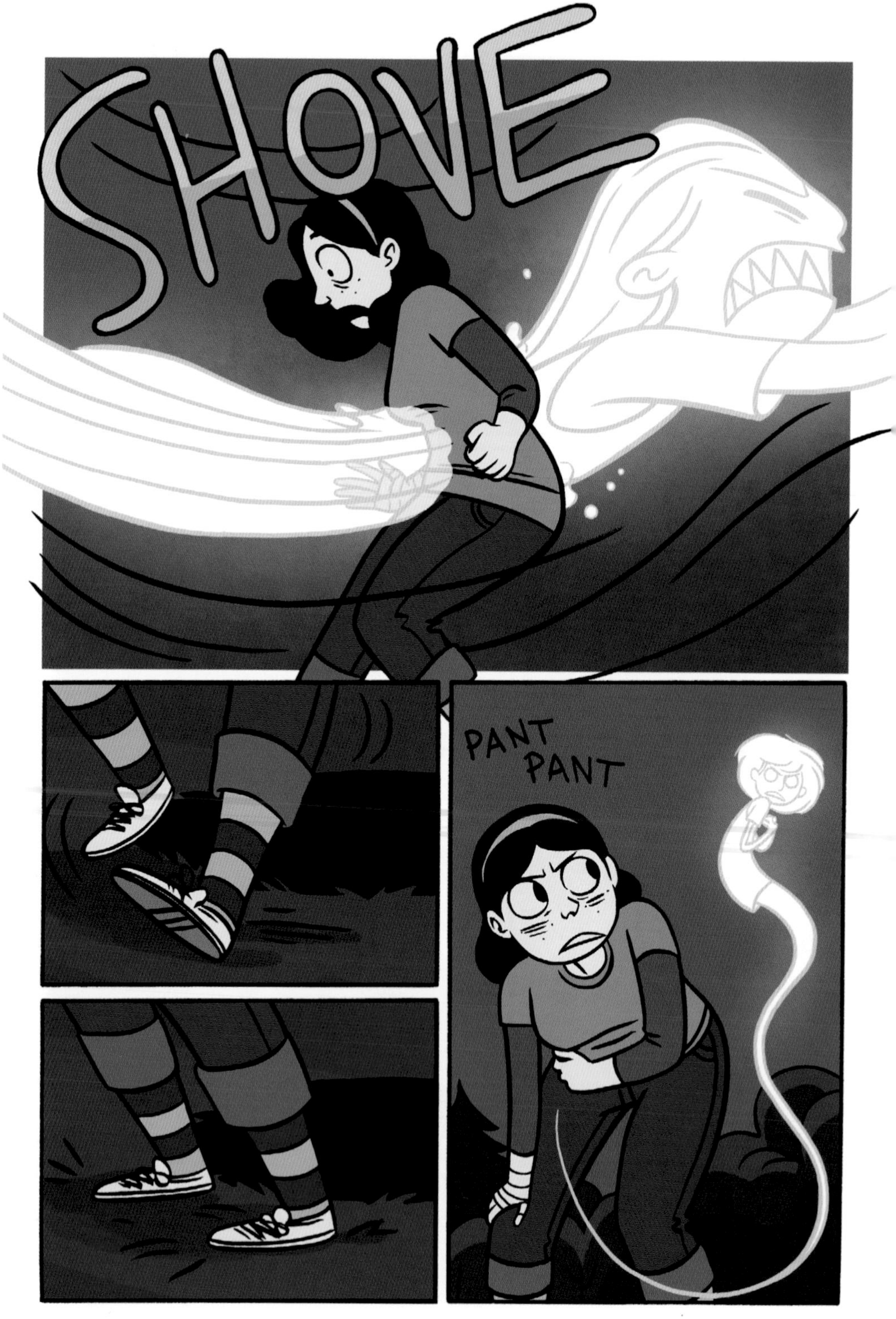
SHOVE
PANT
PANT

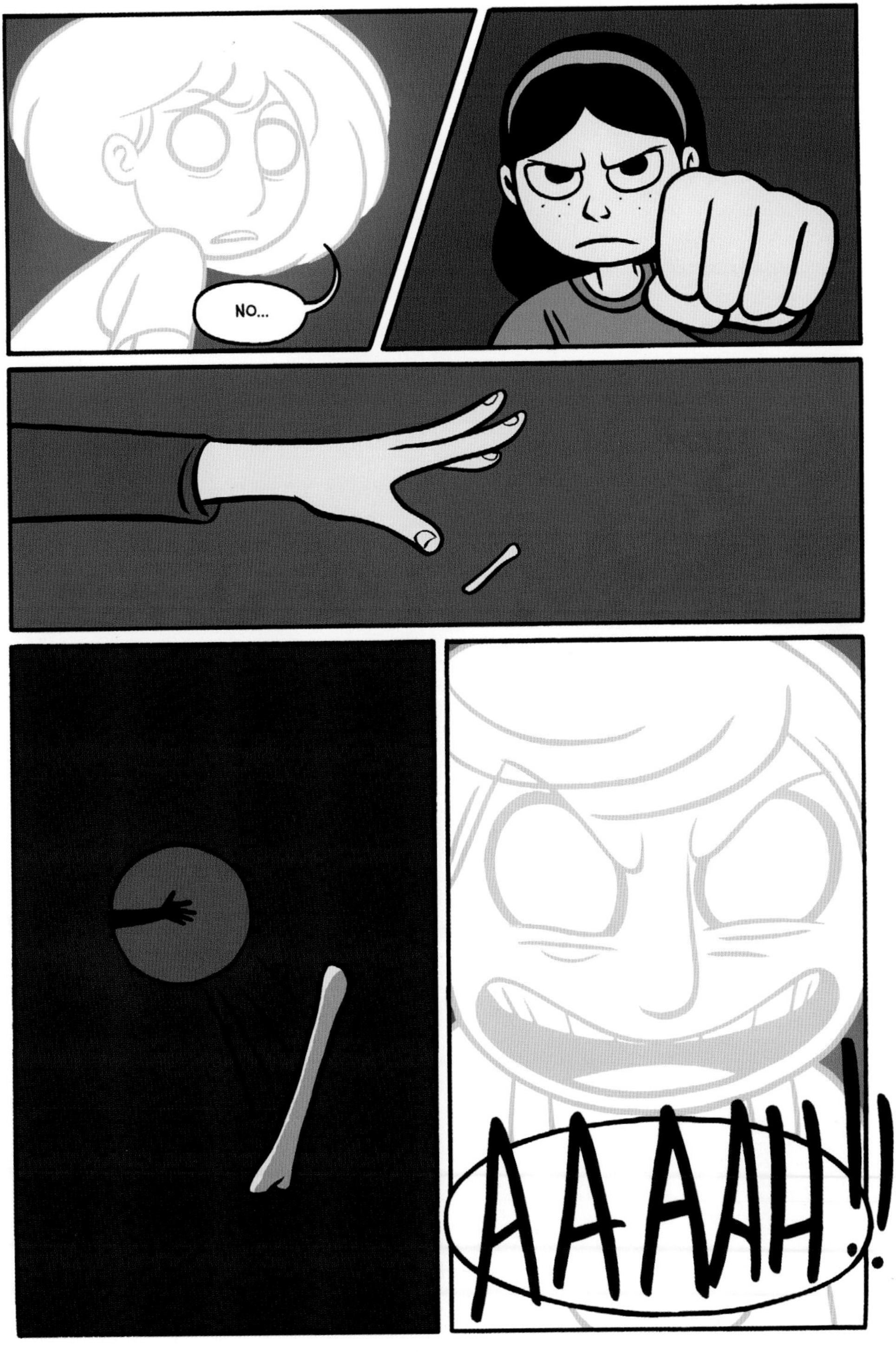
NO...
AAAAH!!

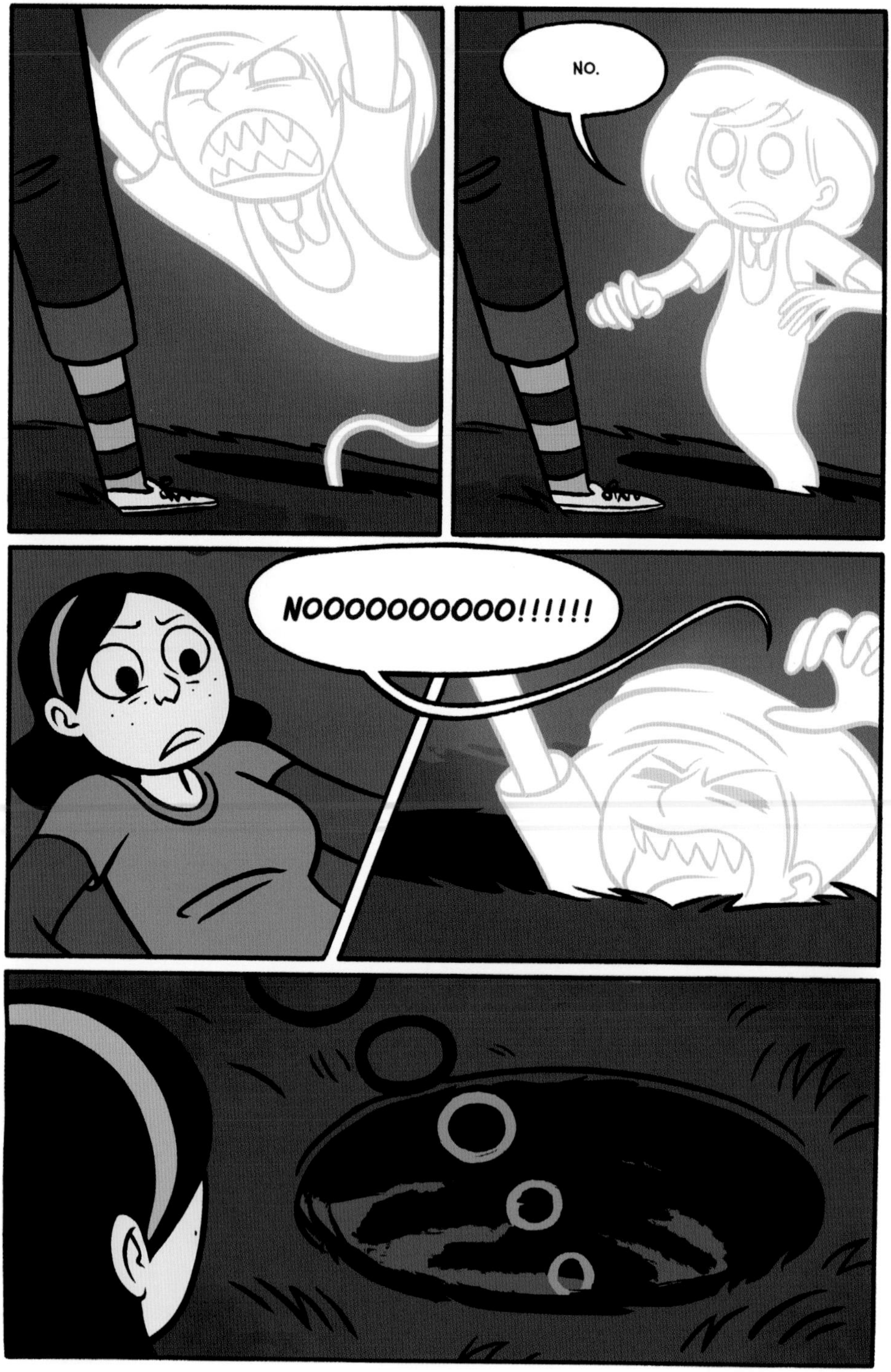
NO.
NOOOOOOOOOO!!!!!!

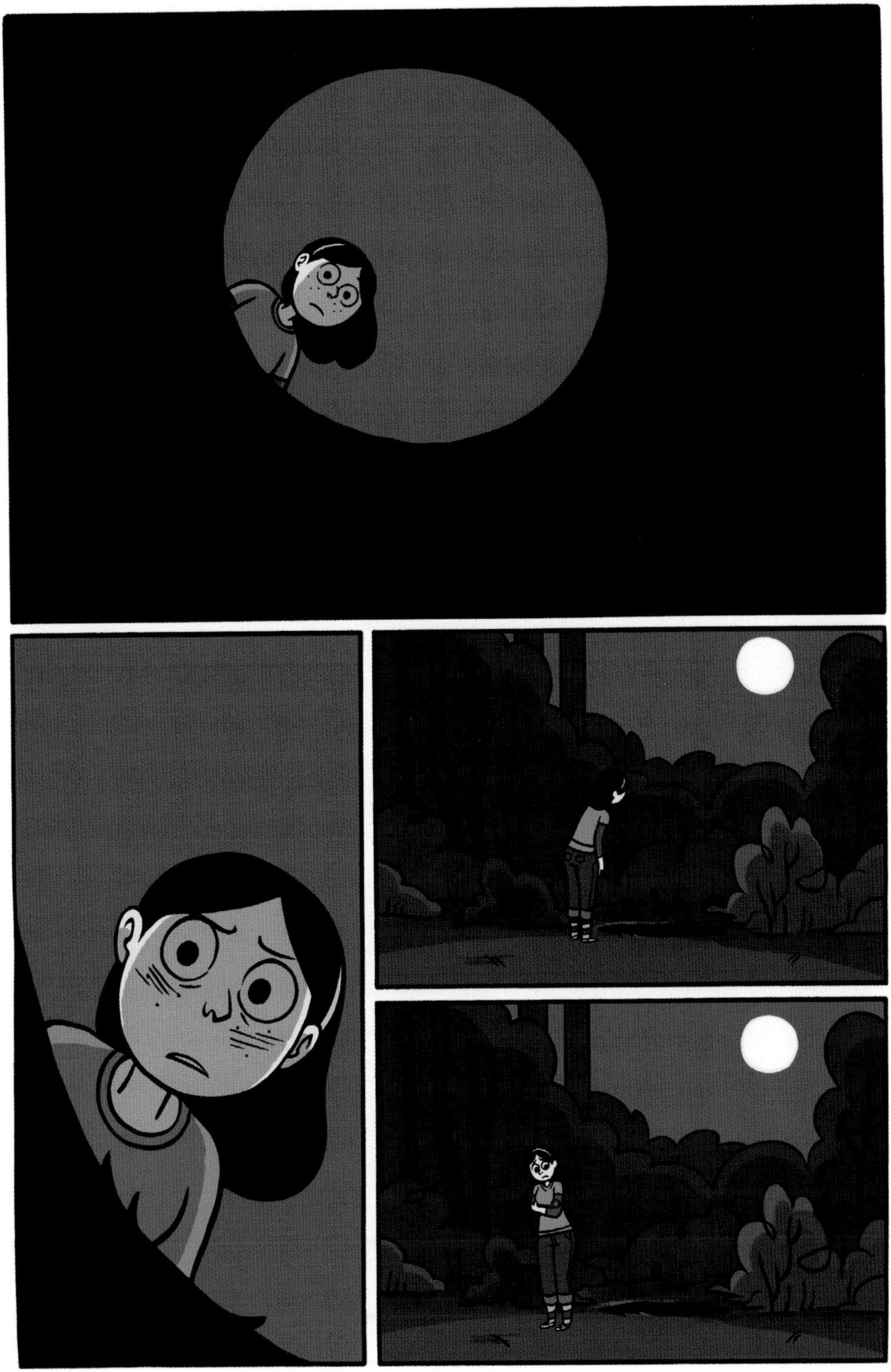

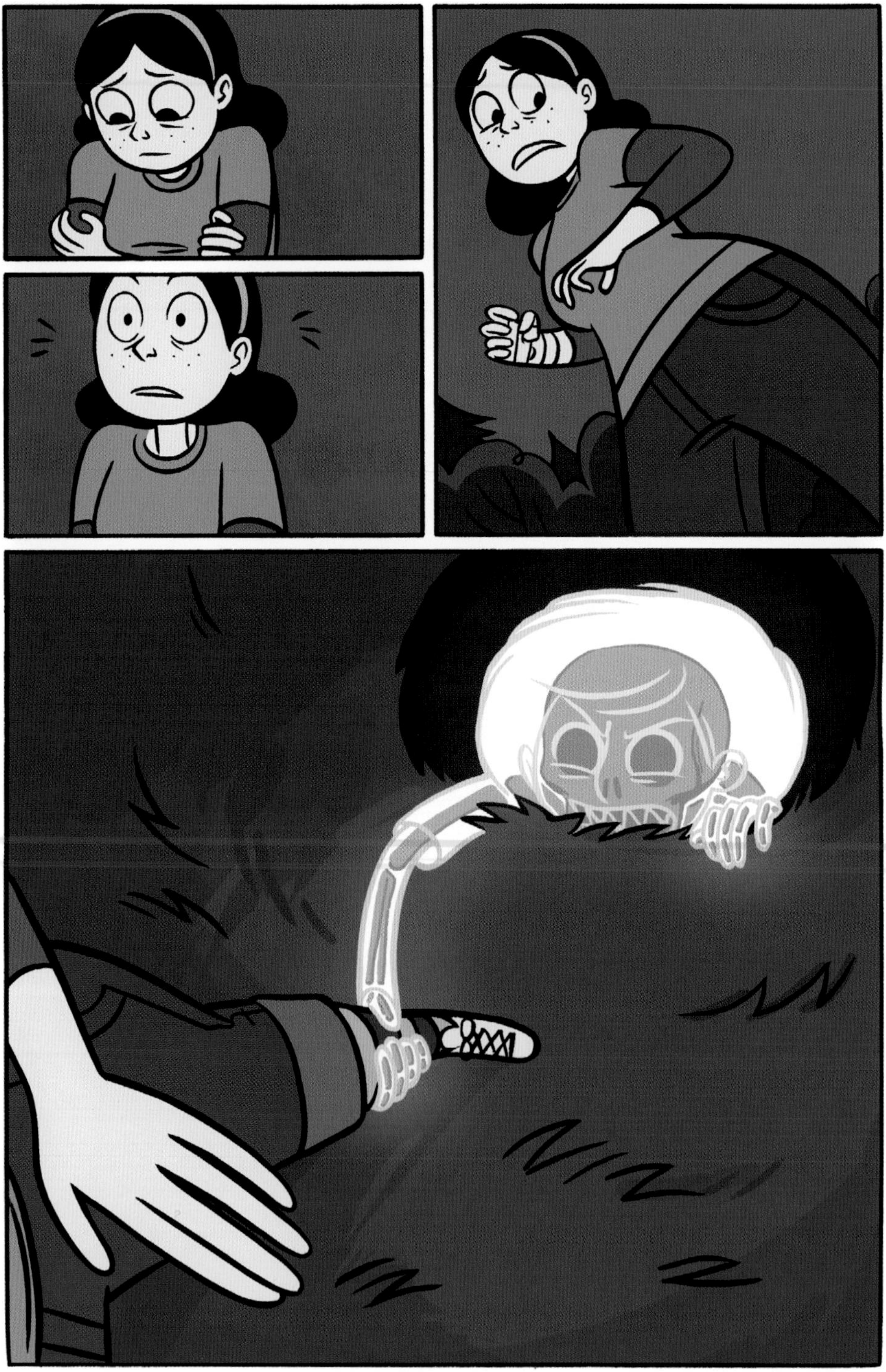

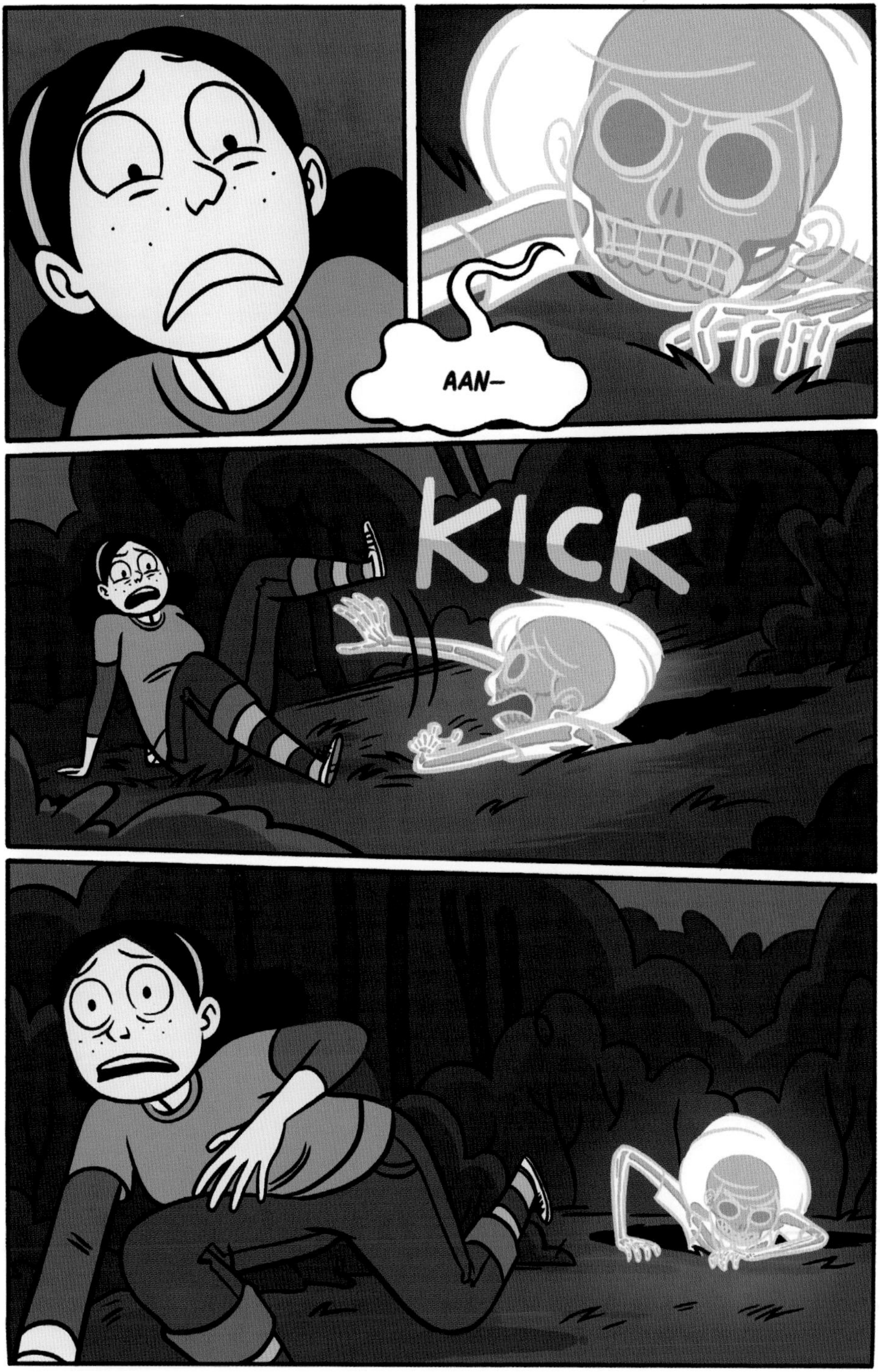
AAN-
KICK

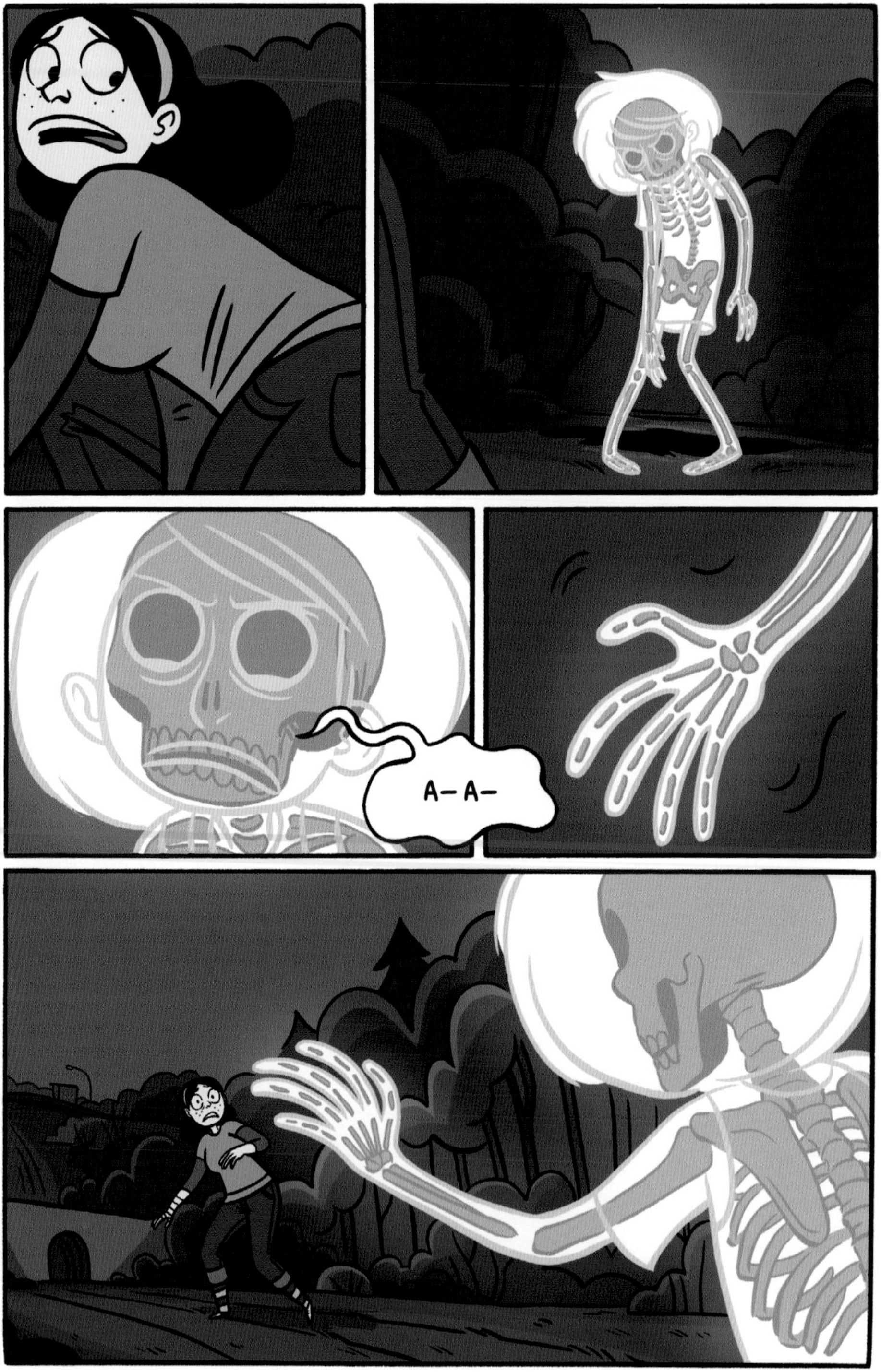
A— A—

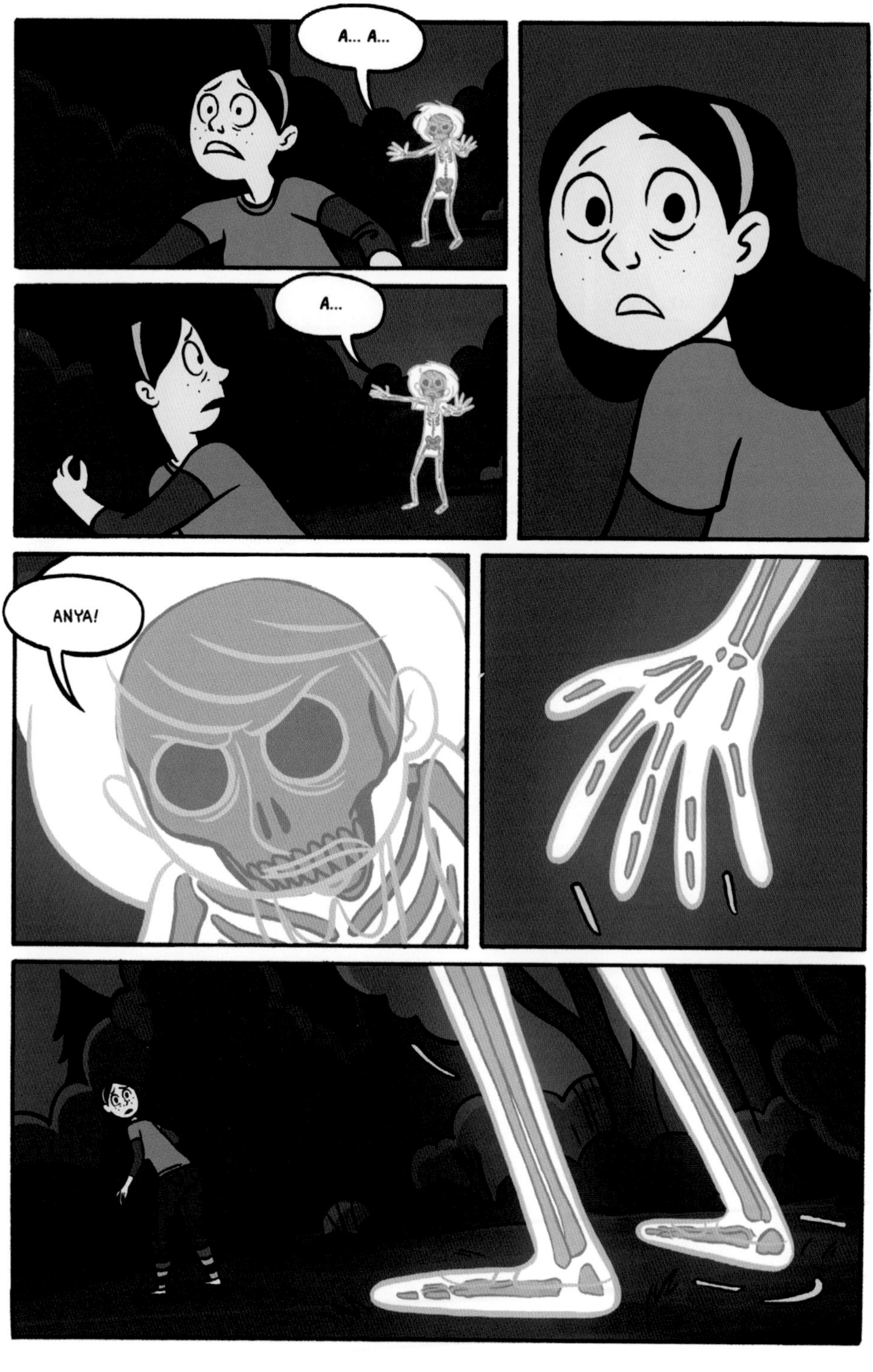
A... A...
A...
ANYA!

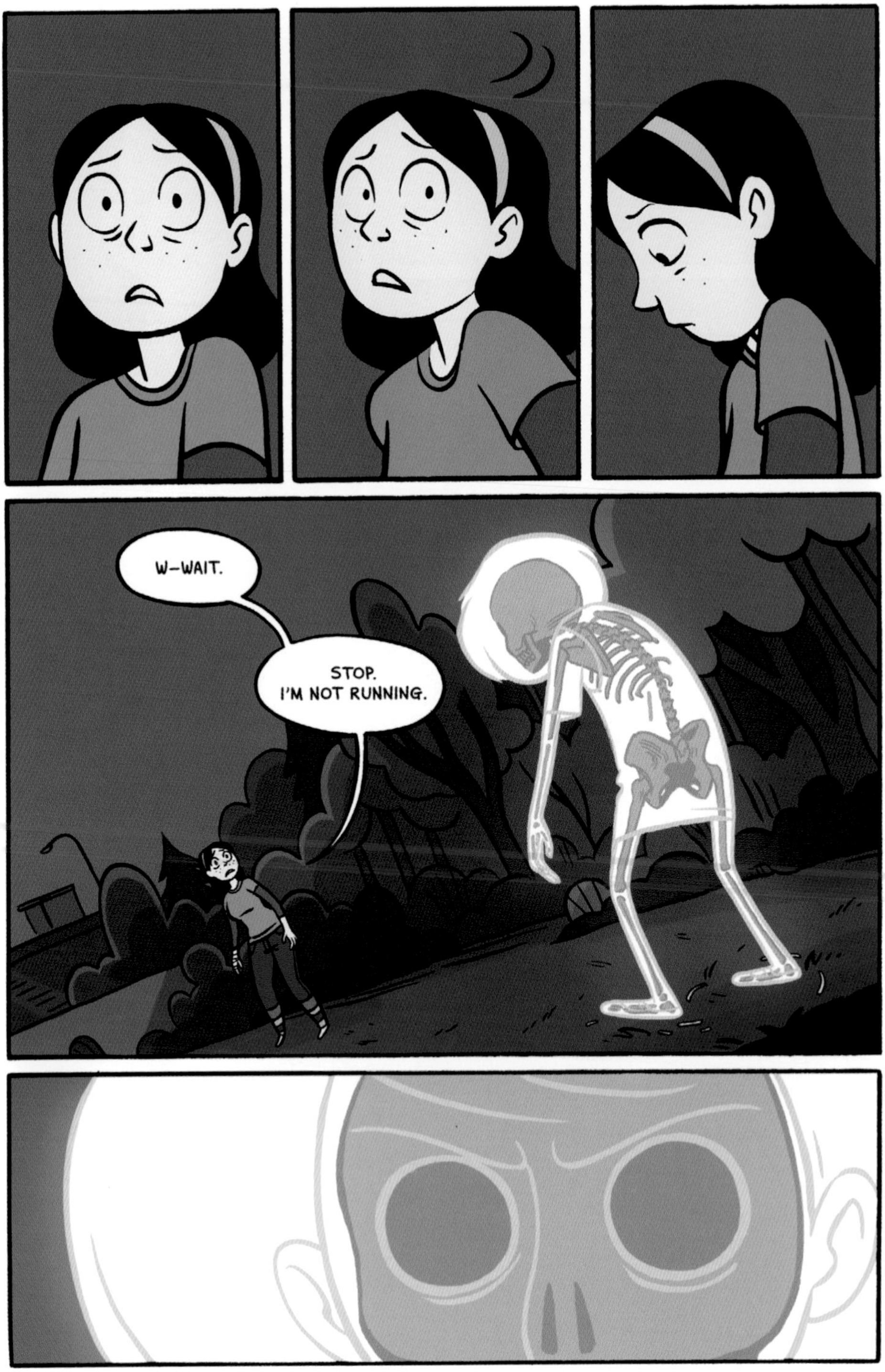
W-WAIT.
STOP.
I'M NOT RUNNING.

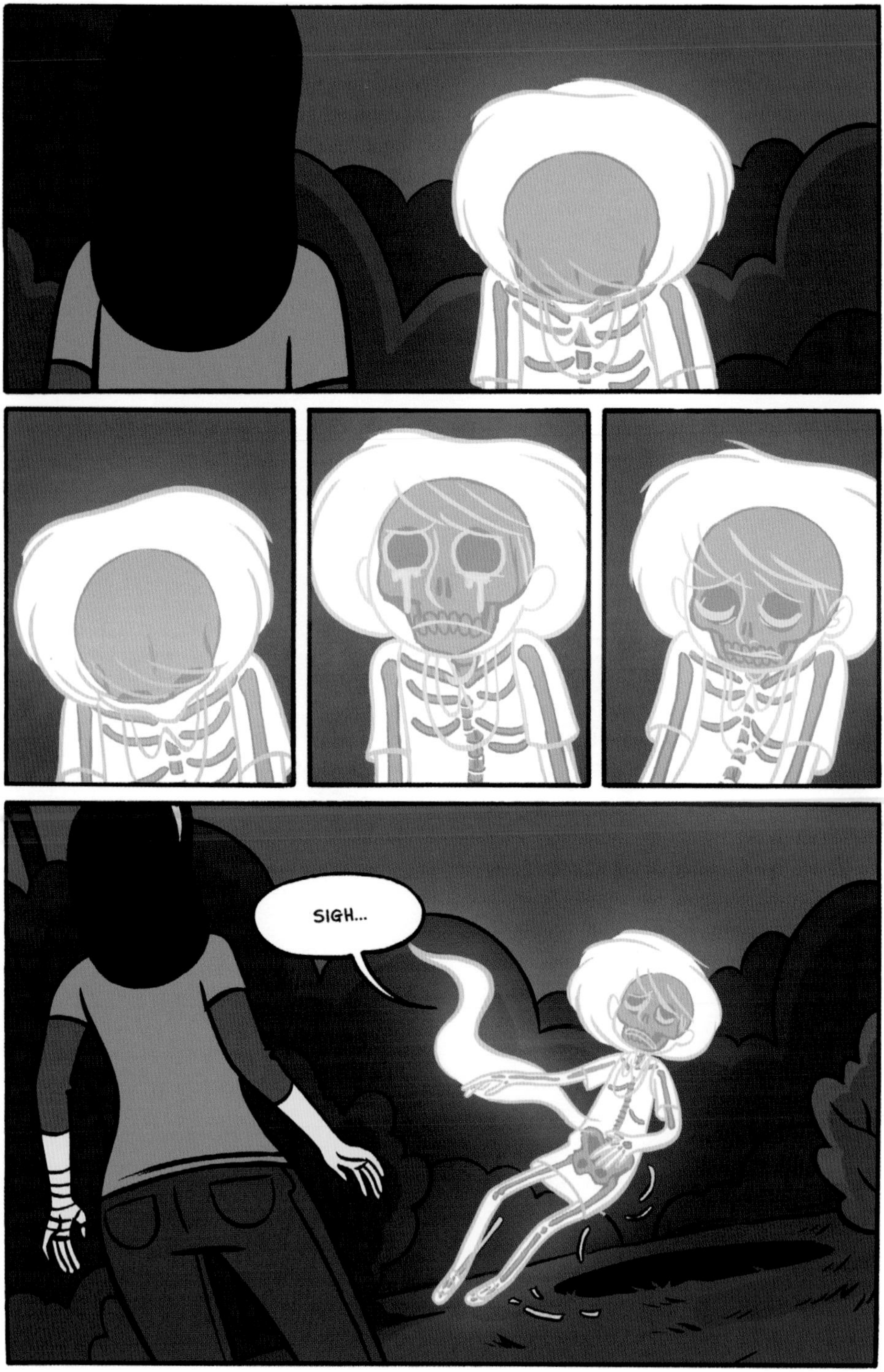
SIGH...

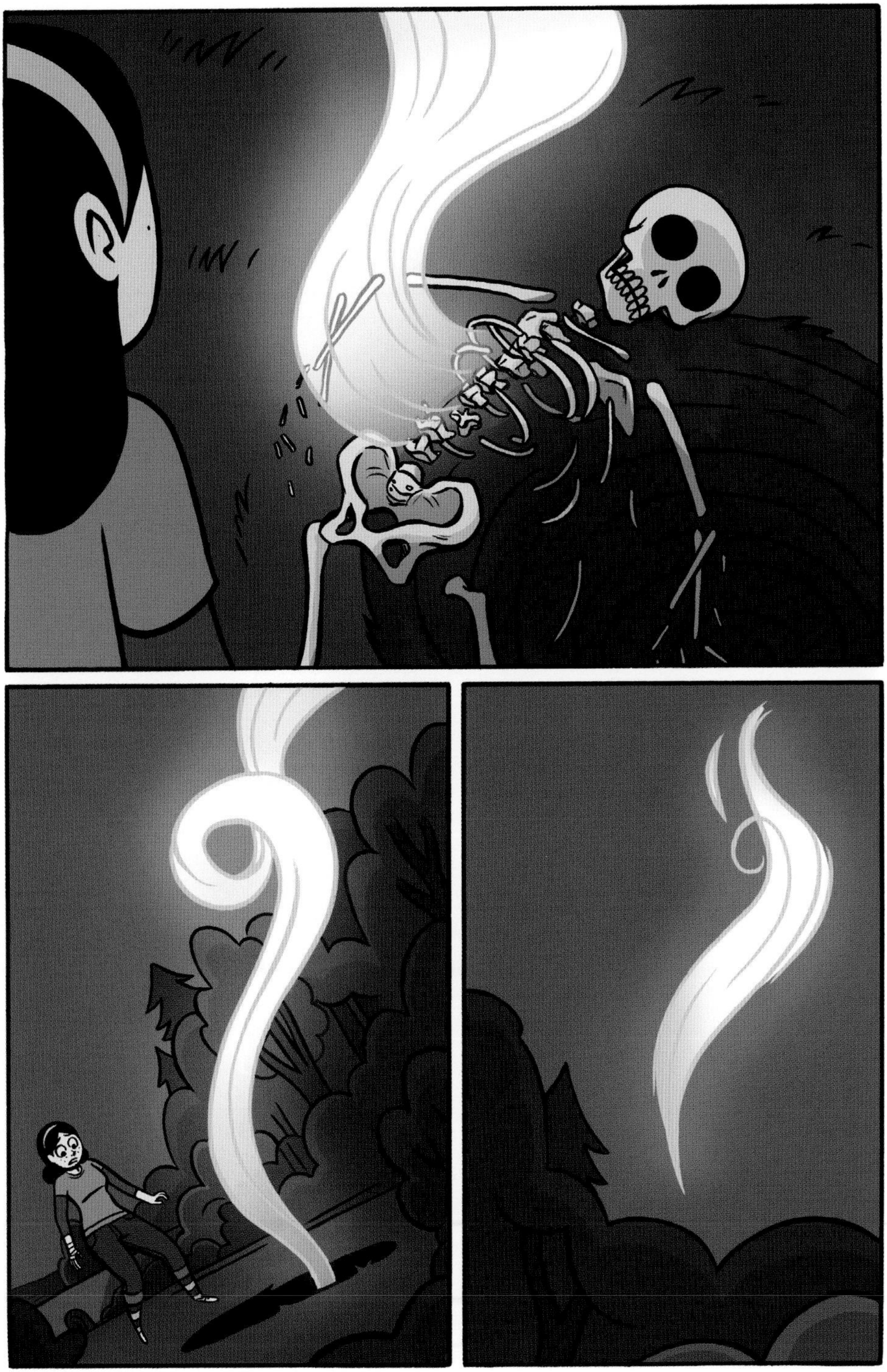

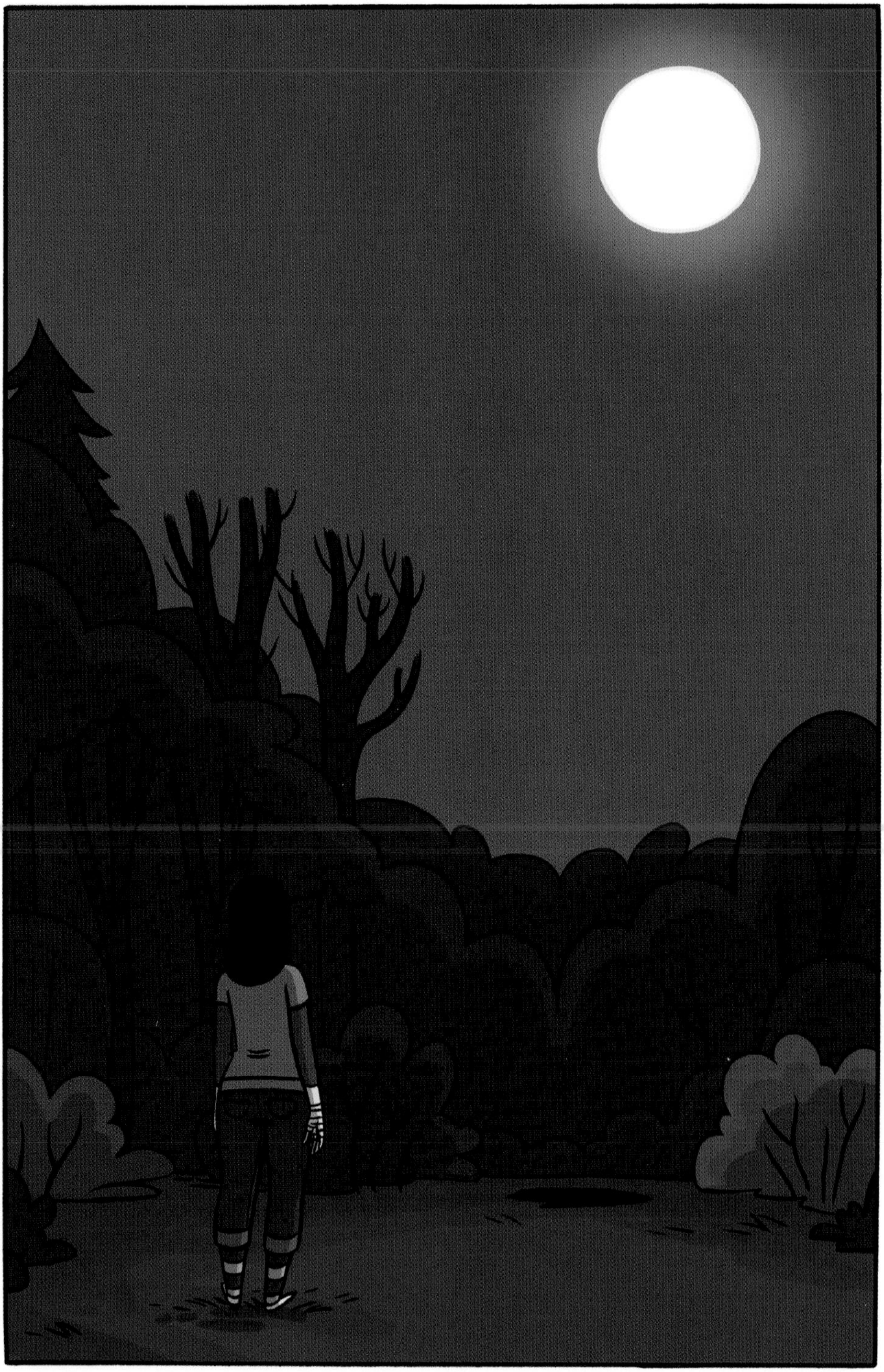

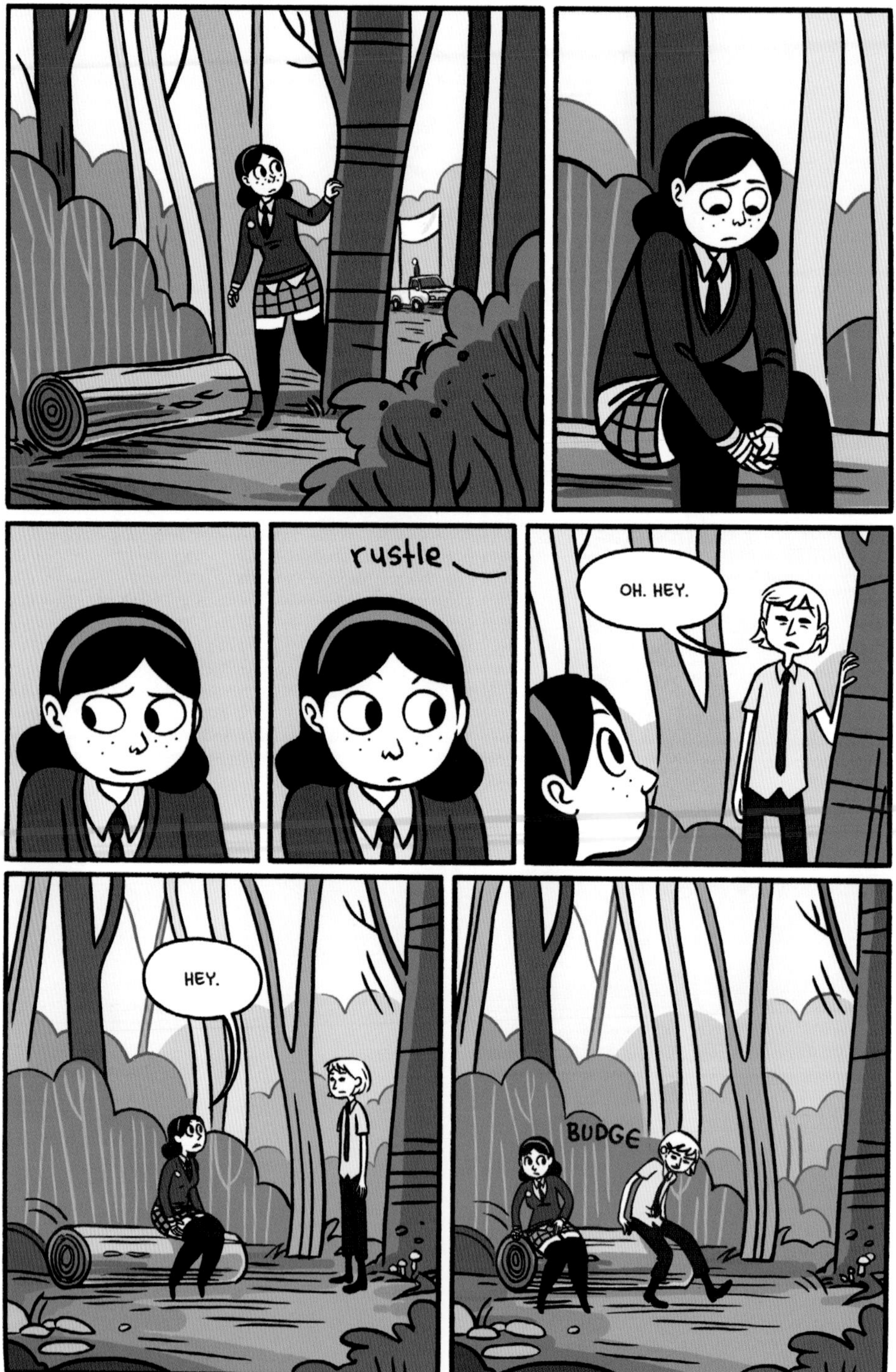
rustle
OH. HEY.
HEY.
BUDGE

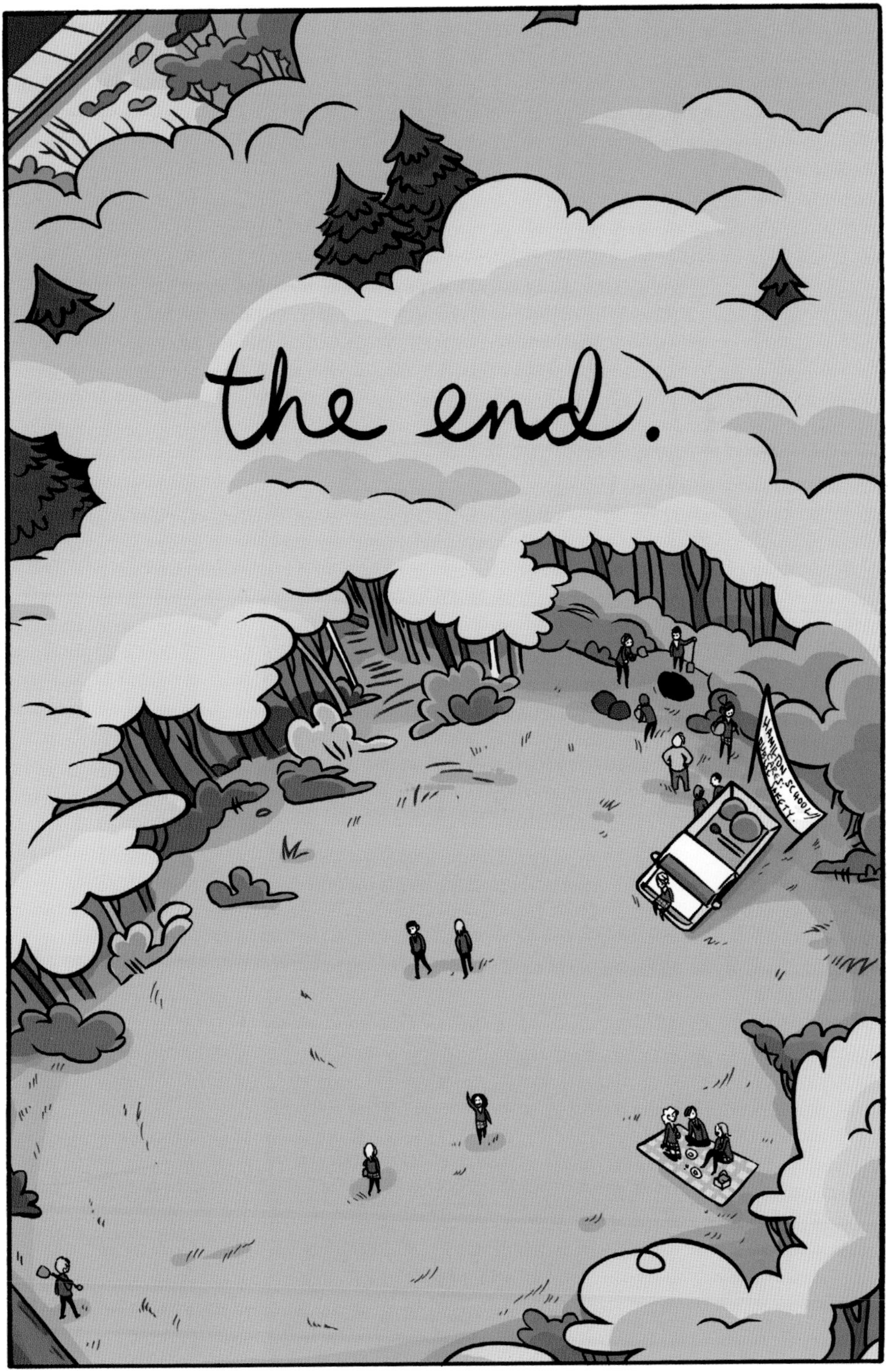
the end.
HAMILTON SCHOOL

First Second

NEW YORK & LONDON

THANKS TO: JUDY HANSEN, JEN WANG, GRAHAM ANNABLE,
RAINA TELGEMEIER, HOPE LARSON, AMY KIM AND KAZU
KIBUISHI, NEIL BABRA, SCOTT MCCLOUD, JEREMY SPAKE,
THE LOVELY FOLKS AT :01, AND MY MOM.

COPYRIGHT © 2011 BY VERA BROSGOL
PUBLISHED BY FIRST SECOND
FIRST SECOND IS AN IMPRINT OF ROARING BROOK PRESS,
A DIVISION OF HOLTZBRINCK PUBLISHING HOLDINGS LIMITED PARTNERSHIP,
120 BROADWAY, NEW YORK, NY 10271

ALL RIGHTS RESERVED

DISTRIBUTED IN THE UNITED KINGDOM BY MACMILLAN CHILDREN'S BOOKS,
A DIVISION OF PAN MACMILLAN.

DESIGN BY COLLEEN AF VENABLE

TYPE SET IN "HELVERICA," DESIGNED BY JOHN MARTZ.

CATALOGING-IN-PUBLICATION DATA IS ON FILE AT THE LIBRARY OF CONGRESS.

PAPERBACK ISBN: 978-1-59643-552-0
HARDCOVER ISBN: 978-1-59643-713-5

FIRST SECOND BOOKS ARE AVAILABLE FOR SPECIAL PROMOTIONS AND PREMIUMS.
FOR DETAILS, CONTACT: DIRECTOR OF SPECIAL MARKETS, HOLTZBRINCK PUBLISHERS.

FIRST EDITION 2011
PRINTED IN CHINA BY RR DONNELLEY ASIA PRINTING SOLUTIONS LTD.,
DONGGUAN CITY, GUANGDONG PROVINCE

HARDCOVER: 13 15 14 12
PAPERBACK: 20